THE HOLY WOMAN

Qaisra Shahraz

BlackAmber Books

Arcadia Books Ltd
15–16 Nassau Street
London W1W 7AB

www.arcadiabooks.co.uk

First published by BlackAmber
an imprint of Arcadia Books, 2001
This B format edition first published in 2007

A catalogue for this book is available from the British Library.

ISBN 1–905147–63–5

Typeset in Garamond Three by RefineCatch Limited, Bungay, Suffolk
Printed and bound in Finland by WS Bookwell

Arcadia Books gratefully acknowledges the financial support of the
Arts Council England.

Arcadia Books supports PEN, the fellowship of writers who work
together to promote literature and its understanding. English PEN
upholds writers' freedoms in Britain and around the world,
challenging political and cultural limits on free expression.
To find out more, visit www.englishpen.org or contact
English PEN, 6–8 Amwell Street, London EC1R 1UQ

Arcadia Books distributors are as follows:

in the UK and elsewhere in Europe:
Turnaround Publishers Services
Unit 3, Olympia Trading Estate
Coburg Road, London N22 6TZ

in the USA and Canada:
Independent Publishers Group
814 N. Franklin Street, Chicago, IL 60610

in Australia:
Tower Books
PO Box 213, Brookvale, NSW 2100

in New Zealand:
Addemda
PO Box 78224, Grey Lynn, Auckland

in South Africa:
Quartet Sales and Marketing
PO Box 1218, Northcliffe, Johannesburg 2115

Arcadia Books in the *Sunday Times* Small Publisher of the Year

Acknowledgements

Many, many thanks to Joan Deitch and John Shaw for their hard work.

My gratitude goes to my friends and colleagues: Professor Akbar S. Ahmed; Sajida Ahmed; Maulana Qamaruzzaman Azmi; Amanda Challis; Lizbeth Cheatle; Ann Gibson; Dr Afshan Khawaja; Shahed Saduallah; Jamil Dehlavi; Julie Northey; Maulana Habib Ur Rahman; Lynda Robinson; Richard Seidel and Masarat Shafi.

I would also like to thank Ken Ashberry; John O'Brien; Andrew Brown; Glenda Cox; Bel Crompton; Carl Delaney; George Hastings; Patricia Kushnick; Samima Ahmed; Marie Froggatt; Nita Patel; Cari Ryan; Jane Sladen; Habidah Usman; Ann Vause; Madeleine Bedford and Merillie Vaughan Huxley.

Thanks also go to: Colin Muir; Lavinia Murray; Peter Ridsdale Scott; Susie Smith; Lucy Scher; Sherry Ashworth; Elizabeth Baines; Cathy Bolton; Beverly Hughesdan; Pete Kalu; Jennifer Whitelaw; Cllr Qassim Afzal (ppc); Huma; Ali Azeem; Neil Broady; Khalid Hussain; Vice-Consul Jamil Ahmad Khan; Raza Khan; Keelin Watson; Bridgette O' Connor; Asad Zaman and Angharad Jackson.

Special thanks to Lord Nazir Ahmed of Rotherham; Iftikhar Qaiser; Zahoor Niazi; Elizabeth Wright; Dr Musharaf Hussain; Faisal Munir Khan; Saba and Aamer Naeem; Asad; Mohsan and Sherry Qureshi; Maqsood Ellahie Sheikh; Dr Sidra Hasan; Bashir Mann; Mohamed Sarwar MP; Habib Ullah; Ghulam Rabbani MBE; Tahir Inam Sheikh; Yacub Nizami; Naveed Aziz; Bailie Cllr

Muhammad Shoaib JP; Nisar Naqvi; Baldev Mavi; Rafaqat Hussain and Nazia Khalid.

In Pakistan my gratitude to my Uncle Mohamed Ashraf and his son Ejaz Ashraf; Muhammad Iqbal and Khalid Mahmood.

My deepest gratitude goes to my husband, Saeed Ahmad; my parents Mohamed Aslam and Amina Akhtar; my brothers and their wives – Dr Suhail Abbas; Dr Zulfiqar Babar; Dr Waqar Aslam; Sajida Parveen and Dr Naushene Sara and my sister Farah Shahnaz for their lasting support.

*For my sons Farakh Shuyab, Gulraiz Sarfaraz,
Shahrukh Raees and my beloved nephew
Raees Hamza*

Part One

How from my garden I chanced to stray,
And how I was whirlwind trapped, I cannot say.

Sir Mohammed Iqbal (1873–1938)
Translated from Urdu by K.C. Kanda
From *Masterpieces of Urdu Ghazal 17th–20th Century*
(Sterling Publishers, New Delhi, 1998)

Prologue

IN THE PROVINCE of Sind, on the outskirts of a small town, a *mela* was in full swing. Held in an open dusty field, the annual fair drew men from the surrounding villages to eat hot and cold snacks, to enjoy themselves and watch the antics of the clowns, jugglers and the other entertainers.

Travelling from the four provinces of Pakistan, the performers had come to show off their special skills and artistry to the rural people of Sind. Brusque clapping of hands, hoots of laughter and loud whistling by the young men lent an air of gaiety and expectation to the hot summer afternoon. Forming an ever-enlarging circle, they cheered one of the jugglers – a dextrous fellow who kept three balls simultaneously in the air.

Next into the dusty circle stepped a wiry old man, with a mirror beaded hat on his head, trailing a spider monkey by a lead. The spectators roared with laughter as the animal, dressed in a small frilly skirt and a red fez, started to dance and wriggle its tiny body on a jute mat. The owner turned a gap-toothed smile on his audience, then began to play a *tabla* drum with two slender sticks, prompting the animal to do a succession of comic somersaults around the circle. The cheering crowd of young men hastily stepped back to allow the monkey more space.

From a distance, a black Shogun Jeep carrying two men wound its way along the dusty road. It came to a halt close to the *mela*. The driver, a tall man in his early thirties, climbed out of the vehicle and, closing the

door behind him, leaned against the Jeep and stretched his long legs.

Removing his sunglasses, he scanned the scene in front of him with amused interest. A smile touched his face as he, too, followed the antics of the spider monkey in the open circle. After a while, bored with the act, his gaze strayed past the crowd to a horse tied to a minar tree. Near the horse, under the large green canopy of the tree, stood a young woman. The stranger's eyes halted in their track.

Dressed in an elegant black *shalwar kameze*, a matching black chiffon *dupatta* was casually draped around her shoulders and over her hair, forming a very becoming frame for her strikingly beautiful face.

The spider monkey was now in full motion, dancing vigorously to the beat of the drum. The woman's hands too now rose to join in the clapping. The warm summer breeze moulded the flimsy material of her *kameze* against her slim frame and blew the *dupatta* off her head, letting it fall in graceful folds around her shoulders. The woman made no move to put it back, ignoring the convention of covering her head in a public place amidst a group of men.

There were no other women present at the *mela*, apart from three elderly ladies, for it was not common or socially acceptable for young women to join openly in an all-male set of activities.

The stranger was both intrigued and amused at the woman's open show of defiance. His mouth curved into a full smile as he noted that she still hadn't made any effort to cover her hair.

As he watched, a young man came to stand next to her and untied the horse from the tree. The stranger's grey eyes widened; he was suddenly very alert.

A strange stillness entered his body as he studied the young man's face – which was, he discovered, almost a direct replica of the woman's.

The smile now shot to his eyes. He stood up straight.

Under the tree Zarri Bano's young brother, Jafar, stood in front of her and whispered in her ear. He turned to the assembled crowd, immediately catching sight of the man staring across at them. Jafar's face lit up. Smiling, he waved.

'The guests we were expecting from Karachi have arrived!' Jafar told his sister excitedly, then his expression sobered. 'Dearest sister, I wish you would make sure that your scarf manages to stay in place on your head when you are outside in a public place,' he nagged her gently. 'Look at your hair! Don't you ever tie it up? It is everywhere! It is not good for a woman to be seen like this. Men, especially *Badmash* men, give women looks when they are as beautiful as you. You look so wanton! It creates a very bad impression. Not only of you, but of us and our father. Only naughty women do that sort of thing.' He was very much conscious of the stranger's presence and roaming eyes.

'Have you quite finished, dearest Jafar?' Zarri Bano smarted from his patronising tone. Her cheeks coloured, 'I am not going to be lectured at by my baby brother. So what if my *dupatta* fell down for a few seconds? Have you never seen hair before?'

'I don't want to argue here, *Baji Jan*. You had better get home quickly. He has already seen you and it doesn't seem right. It is not good for our *izzat*.' The urge to usher his sister out of sight was very strong.

Jafar turned back to the man and waved his hand again in acknowledgement, aware of his bareheaded sister standing by his side. The stranger inclined his

head towards them in greeting. The thick dark waves of his hair fell over his forehead, glinting in the sun. He lifted his hand in return, a smile still hovering on his lips, his eyes now very much on Zarri Bano.

Zarri Bano felt the pressure of the stranger's gaze and swayed with it. She watched the exchange between the two men with alarm – her eyes widening.

'Oh no! Surely it cannot be him?' she whispered in dismay. She was in the wrong place, at the wrong time, seen by the wrong people. Her heart thumped away in painful anticipation. Drinking in his appearance at one go, she beckoned to her chauffeur.

'I am ready to go home, Nalu. Can you bring the car round to this side. There are too many men over there.' The words tripped for no reason.

'Yes, young Sahiba.'

She waited for the car to draw near, keeping her back to the stranger as she climbed in. She only looked out of the window when her car passed his Jeep. Unfortunately, her eyes immediately met his. Embarrassed, she hastily lowered hers as the car sped by.

After he had given directions to the two guests to follow behind him, Jafar fetched his horse. Riding in front of the Shogun, he led the way through the town bazaar to the outskirts and his family's villa in Tanda Adam.

The older man, Raja Din, sitting next to his son in the passenger seat, looked at the back of the young man ahead of them on the white horse.

'Well, if that is the brother, Sikander, then we can assume that the sister will be very attractive too,' he said.

'Father, she *is* very attractive,' Sikander stated quietly. He recalled the woman's face very clearly.

'What do you mean? Have you seen her?' Raja Din turned a sharp glance on him.

'No, I am simply guessing,' Sikander lied smoothly.

'Well, don't forget, my son, they have two daughters – and it is the elder one we are interested in. We don't want to end up with the wrong girl! It has sometimes happened, you know. People go for one match, and end up with the other.'

Sikander glanced at his father, the smile moment-arily slipping from his face. 'Of course,' he responded. Was she the elder or the younger? he wondered, frown-ing a little. She had been very pretty – a most pleasant surprise. The irony was, did she now know who he was?

Her suitor.

She *had* to be the one! 'One way or other, I am going to have this woman,' Sikander vowed silently, tapping his hand on the steering wheel.

As he watched the car in front of them disappear in a cloud of dust, Sikander Din had a strange feeling that, in the last few minutes, his life had suddenly and forever become entwined with the beautiful woman dressed in black.

Chapter 1

THERE WAS A flurry of activity at the villa. After alert-ing everyone that their expected guests from Karachi were well on their way, Zarri Bano dashed straight up-stairs to her bedroom, two steps at a time, and quickly changed into another designer outfit, this time in a pale shade of pink. Her younger sister Ruby came into the room and teasingly assessed Zarri from head to foot.

'You have changed! You are actually going to go down and face the guests! I don't believe it,' she said, pretending to be astonished. 'Normally you don't even deign to meet either your suitors or their parents. This man must therefore be very special if my *malika*, my queen of a sister, makes an effort to change.' Ruby's eyes moved appreciatively over her sister's slim figure.

'Oh, come on, Ruby. I have been to the *mela* with Jafar. I felt hot and sweaty and decided to change. Who says that I am actually going down to meet him? He has a cheek in coming personally, and not even bothering to send a photograph of himself in advance.' Zarri Bano chastised her sister in the mirror, while fixing a curl in place as she pinned her hair up in an attractive chignon on top of her head, letting some wispy tendrils escape around her ears. She was piqued that the stranger had seen her and probably knew who she was. He had caught her at a disadvantage.

'So that you could have a preview?' Ruby read her sister's thoughts accurately.

'No,' Zarri Bano lied.

They had both had a preview. Remembering his searing glance she felt herself go hot with embarrassment and indignation. When her car had passed his Jeep, he had again looked at her closely – almost as if he had dived deeply into her soul. Shuddering in front of the mirror she glimpsed a look of uncertainty in her eyes, and something else.

Finished, she went to stand near the window overlooking the large, beautifully landscaped central courtyard of their villa. It was then that the black Jeep entered through the open gates and came to a halt next to the Banos' grey car.

Sikander helped his father out, then both men stood and looked round the courtyard with interest. There was a central rose bed in full bloom, and on all sides, profusely flowering oleanders and perfumed bougain-villaea climbed to the top of the six foot walls. A long veranda, with alabaster pillars and a mosaic tiled floor, led into the house. As the young man's eyes swept up to the bedroom windows, Zarri Bano hastily stepped back behind the curtains, afraid that he might have seen her.

Noting her sister's actions, Ruby moved to the window and peered down. Jafar had now joined their two guests.

'Gosh, *Ma'shallah*, he is very attractive. No wonder you have changed.' Ruby chuckled at the tide of colour sinking into her sister's cheeks.

Irked by this teasing, Zarri Bano said crossly, 'Who says he is attractive? Do you remember Ali? Could any man compete with his looks!'

'Yes, Ali was very, very good-looking. But there is something about this man – some kind of charisma. I think he may have the bait to draw you into his net, his web – even if it is not his looks.'

'Don't talk to me about nets and webs!' Zarri Bano snapped, moving away from the window. 'I am not a fish to be angled at, caught and trapped, Ruby.'

'I am sorry, *Baji Jan*. That was unforgivable of me, especially knowing how you feel about such analogies and with you being a feminist too.'

'Yes, so you should be. I am a free woman. I will decide if I want this or any other man. This is why ten years have elapsed and I have still not married. You'll probably marry before me, and I will be an old maid,' she joked.

'You'll never be an old maid, Zarri Bano. You are too

beautiful and glamorous to be left on the shelf. Some-
one will snap you up some day, if not this man. Do you
know, I *will* probably end up marrying before you, the
way you are turning people down. I shall probably land
up with one of your jilted suitors. Do you know how
many times Chaudharani Kaniz has been to visit us,
even after you declined to marry Khawar? I think she
has got her eye on me now. If you won't marry him, she
thinks I'll do instead.'

'Neither of us will be marrying Khawar. He is more
like a brother to us. Anyway can you imagine you or me
as the next snobbish Chaudharani Kaniz in the village?
No thanks. I'd be bored out of my wits.'

This little exchange had done Zarri Bano the world
of good. It had helped her to recover her normal poise.
Just because I have caught him staring at me from a
crowd of people, and I have stared back, she told herself
resolutely, it doesn't mean anything. I am not going to
fall under his spell, as Ruby seems to think.

She did, however, wonder why, contrary to her nor-
mal practice, she was prepared to go and meet these
guests and spend time in their presence. Normally she
found these meetings with would-be suitors nauseous
and demeaning, particularly when she knew she would
be declining their proposals of marriage.

To hell with all the analysis, she thought emphatic-
ally as she descended the ornate circular staircase lead-
ing into the central hallway, and walked with a firm
step towards the guest drawing room. She was a mature
woman of twenty-seven years of age, not a simpering
teenager, whose hand had been asked for. She was going
to treat this man as a normal guest. Holding herself tall
and erect, Zarri Bano stood outside the door, ready to
make her formal entrance.

Sikander and his father Raja Din were sitting and talking to Zarri Bano's parents. Tea had been served by Fatima, their housekeeper. It was the first time that they had all met. Jafar and Sikander had got to know each other in Karachi on business. On one occasion Sikander had invited Jafar to his home.

A friendship had quickly blossomed between the two men. On one such occasion Sikander's mother mentioned to Jafar the subject of finding a suitable bride for her son. At that time all Jafar could think of was his own two sisters. The elder one, he had informed them, had declined so many suitors that they had lost count and were embarrassed on behalf of the people who had come to ask for her hand. 'You are welcome to try, however,' he had informed Sikander. 'If not, there is always my younger sister, Ruby,' he chuckled.

After meeting Sikander and getting to know him better, Jafar knew instinctively that his eldest sister, Zarri Bano, was the woman for his friend. In age, education, looks and temperament, they were well matched on all accounts.

On his return, Jafar had informed his parents and Zarri Bano about Sikander. She, for her part, had dismissed the matter from her mind straight away – she wasn't interested! Although for a moment or two it did occur to her that it would be handy to be married to someone settled in Karachi, when she set up her publishing company. Jafar's father, Habib, and mother, Shahzada were, however, very interested. They asked Jafar to invite his friend and his parents to their home.

Yet in their hearts they despaired. It had almost become routine, turning suitors away. It wasn't only

Zarri Bano who rejected the men who came to see her and ask for her hand; her father, too, was every bit as fastidious. Somehow, none of the callers ever seemed to measure up to his very intelligent and very beautiful eldest daughter. He always ended up by declaring arrogantly: 'The man has to be the best.' When Zarri Bano declined, Habib secretly applauded and was grateful for her decision.

His wife, on the other hand, saw things from a mother's point of view. She was on the point of sheer desperation. Zarri Bano was in her late twenties and still there was no marriage in sight. 'When will she settle down and raise a family?' she kept asking her husband, and Habib was wont to reply flippantly that there was plenty of time.

'Do you want to saddle our beautiful daughter to any *nathu pethu?*'he asked her. 'I'll only let her marry a man of the highest pedigree from a land-owning family at that, with a good name and social standing.'

His wife was then duty-bound to scold him. 'Don't say that, Habib Sahib. All children are precious in their parents' eyes, including those suitors. It is not good to keep dismissing them. You and your daughter will gain a bad reputation. They will think that she is too grand, proud and opinionated, when in fact, she's just been unable to make her choice. You haven't helped either. You have been colluding with her in rejecting the suitors, haven't you?'

'Don't be silly! I am just very possessive of my daughter and want the best for her.'

'That is just it – you are *too* possessive! That's the problem. It is not healthy, Habib Sahib.' Shahzada's gaze had pinned his accusingly.

'Now you are being melodramatic.' Habib turned

away from his wife, laughing, bringing the conversation to an end.

Here were the guests, come to meet and get to know their daughter. If all went well there would be a follow-up meeting two weeks later. If it came to some sort of rapport developing between Sikander and Zarri Bano, as well as between their two sets of parents, then Zarri Bano could visit them in Sikander's home in Karachi.

On seeing Sikander and exchanging a few pleasantries, Shahzada was highly pleased, her heart warming immediately to him. Her eyes often strayed to his handsome face. Habib, however, held himself in reserve. In looks and manner Sikander was most appealing – he couldn't fault him, but he was going to wait and see his daughter's reaction and then decide.

A knock at the door made them all look up.

Zarri Bano entered. She stood before them: tall, majestic in bearing and stunning in her smart pink outfit. Sikander swiftly took in her appearance, satisfied himself that it was the same woman of the *mela*, then bent forward, seemingly preoccupied in the act of breaking a biscuit on a plate. It was at that moment that Habib glanced across at him, to assess his reaction to his beloved daughter. His mouth tightened as he saw the time Sikander took in looking up.

His father, on the other hand, setting eyes on Zarri Bano for the first time, was totally captivated. A wide grin on his face, he followed her every movement as she walked towards them.

She bade them *Salam*. Sikander heard her and still didn't bother to look up. The voice was pleasing, he noted. It matched her looks.

Zarri Bano allowed her gaze to pass over everybody, catching their eyes individually and smiling.

Coming further into the room, she sat down next to her mother, on a sofa opposite Sikander and his father. Now she willed him to look up, piqued that he had not met her gaze, but had been more concerned with his stupid biscuit than with her!

She didn't know where the impulse came from but it was totally in character, in her case, to go against normal etiquette. She decided to address him personally, so that he would *have* to turn to her and look up. She wasn't going to be ignored by this arrogant, handsome stranger who had stolen into her peaceful world and had dared to violate her earlier with his gaze – suitor or otherwise!

'Sikander Sahib,' she began sweetly. She had learnt his name from Ruby on the stairs. 'Did you have a pleasant journey? Was our *mela* to your liking? We are a bit gauche in the country compared to the sophisticated world of Karachi, you see.'

He looked up then!

His eyebrows shot up; he was surprised at her audacity in speaking directly to him in the very presence of their parents, and without any formal introduction as such. Then, for her to remind him of that scene at the *mela*! It was most improper. A disapproving expression entered his eyes. She is too unconventional for my liking! darted the thought at the back of his mind.

Now he gave her the benefit of his full gaze. Smoky grey in colour, his eyes seemed to have plunged directly into her open soul again. Yet they remained cool and there was no answering smile on his lips.

'Yes, Sahiba, we had a lovely journey,' he said politely. 'And yes, too, your *mela* was a nice interlude on our way. It was a pleasant surprise – a preview of what to expect here in your home.'

Zarri Bano's cheeks delicately coloured. Only he noticed it, because he knew the cause of it. He had reminded her of their earlier encounter and was pleased to note that there was a dent in her poise after all.

Zarri Bano turned to Raja Din, dismissing Sikander neatly, and began to talk animatedly about Karachi and the university course she had studied there. Raja Din beamed at her, her incredible beauty swimming before his eyes. He envisaged beautiful grandchildren with the face of this woman. It was those eyes verging between blue and green, sparkling at him: to have a grandson with those eyes! He responded to her questions enthusiastically.

While they talked, Sikander covertly watched and listened, amused that his father was so smitten with her. Hadn't the same thing happened to him, Sikander, at the *mela*? One glance had him hooked!

After half an hour Zarri Bano left them. That was how far it reached with this first meeting.

Sikander and his father stayed for dinner. This time Ruby joined them, while Zarri Bano remained in her room. 'Even if I was interested, which I am not,' she said haughtily, 'Why should I go back to that room? I have never done so before, so why should I start now? Especially to please a man who has not even bothered to smile at me.'

She couldn't, however, stop herself from listening to the sounds downstairs and waiting to see when they would leave. At the end, she saw them go while hovering behind the curtain. 'You will return for me, Sikander, you conceited fellow,' she murmered. 'It will then give me great pleasure – to turn you down!' And Zarri Bano whisked away from the window, dismissing him totally from her mind.

When Ruby came up later and told her that they wanted to come again, Zarri Bano made no comment. Downstairs, she passed their housekeeper, Fatima, in the hall. A smile lit the older woman's face.

'This one is good-looking, isn't he?' Fatima teased. Very fond of Zarri Bano, Fatima was prone to talk honestly with her.

'Oh, he is all right, I suppose. We will see what happens,' Zarri Bano replied, her cheek dimpling playfully.

'But you do like him, don't you?' Fatima persisted, wanting to make sure.

Zarri Bano merely laughed aloud, as she turned to go into the dining room. Fatima stared after her young mistress. She wished for nothing more than to have their Zarri Bano, and her own daughter, Firdaus, married off happily. She prayed for their health and their futures. Above all, for her to have Khawar for a son-in-law – that was Fatima's own true dream.

Later, alone with her husband in their bedroom, Shahzada scanned Habib's face with trepidation. He sat on the sofa, a business account ledger spread out on his lap.

'I am not happy with the *munshi*'s land account. There is something not quite right here.' Habib glanced up briefly at his wife from across the room.

'But are you happy with Sikander?' Shahzada softly ventured.

Habib's head jerked up, but he looked quickly down again and crisply turned the page of the ledger, marking it in one corner with his gold pen.

'I think that our daughter has, at last, found her match,' Shahzada tried again. She experienced the urgent need to pursue the subject, for she had glimpsed

a strange look in her husband's eyes. She knew that he was hiding his thoughts behind the business ledger.

'You think so?' Habib queried, turning to his wife and throwing the gold pen on to the table in front of him.

'Yes,' Shahzada answered bravely. 'Did you not see, Habib Sahib, the look in your daughter's eyes when she returned from the *mela*, and her reaction as she met him? She has never looked like that before.' Disregarding the chilled look in her husband's eyes – they were as cold as the Kashmiri Mountains – Shahzada boldly persisted, 'I think this handsome tycoon will be our daughter's destiny . . .'

She abruptly stopped as her husband knocked the heavy wooden coffee table aside with his foot and stood up, a towering figure glaring down at her, letting the ledger fall to the marble floor with a loud clatter.

'I haven't decided yet.' He spoke implacably. 'It is obvious that you are besotted with him. That conceited bastard was more concerned with biscuits than giving my daughter the respect and attention she deserves. He barely glanced at my Zarri Bano, Shahzada! Men have been falling in love with my daughter since she was a teenager, whereas he could not even be bothered to look at her properly. That I find very offensive!'

'But what about your daughter? Didn't you see the look in her eyes?' Shahzada begged.

'Yes, I did,' he ground out. 'All the more reason for me to be cautious. I am the head of the family and *I* will decide what is good for my Zarri Bano. I don't like this man, Shahzada.'

'Habib, you are being too protective. I tell you, our Zarri Bano is keen on him. You must have seen how she reacted in his presence? Did you not see how she—'

'This man has the power to hurt my beloved daughter. I feel it in my very bones!' Habib replied angrily, cutting his wife short. 'I will not let anyone do anything to cause her any pain or insult her in any way. You forget, Shahzada, in our clan, destinies are made and dictated by us. *I* will decide if this man is to be my daughter's destiny or not.'

'No, Habib, no!' Shahzada appealed, her words echoing in the empty room, as Habib strode out of it banging the heavy walnut door behind him.

Shahzada stared at the intricate carvings on the back of the door with a sense of foreboding.

Chapter 2

CHAUDHARANI KANIZ WAS being driven back from a two-week holiday in the resort of Murri on the Kashmir border. She had also, on her way, visited two of her sisters, who were married and settled in Lahore, in the province of Punjab.

Despite the stifling summer heat of Sind she was glad to be nearly home. She hoped that her son, Khawar, was well and that everything was running smoothly in her household, left in the capable hands of her servant, Neesa.

In Chaudharani Kaniz's mind, the *rishta* or eligible bride to whom her youngest sister Sabra had introduced her in Lahore, would be an excellent wife for Khawar. The young woman was attractive and well-educated, but more to the point she came from a wealthy family of good repute and background.

The only snag, however, was whether the young

woman and her family would find their proposal acceptable. The thought was firmly lodged in Kaniz's mind like a thorn: would a middle-class, educated and citified Lahori woman relish coming to the quiet backwaters of a rural village in scorching Sind?

That was the problem and a big problem at that! For it was an understood fact boasted by Lahori women that very few of them favoured the rural life, no matter what facilities they were offered. Even electricity, video recorders and air conditioning were no compensation for the teeming nightlife, entertainment and shopping facilities offered by the old capital of Pakistan.

Born and bred in the rural world, Kaniz herself didn't care a *paisa* for city ways. When she had been given the option of either marrying into an 'ordinary' but very much an urban family, or staying on in the village and marrying a very wealthy landlord, Kaniz without a moment's hesitation had plummeted for the honour of becoming a *zemindar*'s wife. Blessed with a generous store of commonsense and shrewdness from an early age, coupled with an innate avarice, Kaniz thought she would have to be deranged to turn down an offer like that!

Becoming a *chaudharani* and reigning supreme as the headwoman in a close-knit village hierarchy was an opportunity which didn't walk up to one's doorstep every day. She had offered seventy thanksgiving *nafl* prayers to Allah for bringing such good *kismet* her way. Kaniz thus had no qualms at all about settling permanently in the village.

The shallow allure and glitter of the city life failed to beckon to her. 'With acres of land to his name and plenty of revenue coming from it, you and your husband Sarwar will never be short of anything,' her

mother had drummed into her excitedly. She didn't have to be told that her wildest materialistic dreams would be realised – and so they were.

The only thing that had spoilt it all, and continued to rankle unto this day, was the fact that her husband had been jilted by another village woman before Kaniz came on the scene. She had been his second choice. This was the thorn, the serpent in her rose garden, whose cancerous effect on her life she could neither dig out nor dislodge.

In the early years, too, she had chafed miserably from being labelled as the '*Second Chaudharani*'. For everyone knew and it was an undisputed fact that Shahzada was the first and most important local landowner. When Habib Khan and his Chaudharani Shahzada had moved to the nearest town, Tanda Adam, ten years ago, Kaniz had simply been elated. Only the old man, Siraj Din, remained in his large *hawaili*, in the village. Up till then Shahzada, as Siraj Din's eldest daughter-in-law, had unwittingly and innocently robbed all the lime-light from poor Kaniz.

Now she, Kaniz, was the only *chaudharani* in the village and she never let a single soul forget it! With her snooty manner and imperious ways, she kept most of the villagers at arm's length. For she had imbibed very early on the ancient wisdom that says it never pays to be too familiar with one's servants and neighbours. How else was she to maintain her special position and authority over everybody, Kaniz thought, if she rubbed shoulders with every Tom, Dick and Harry? Without her authority, she was nothing!

Kaniz winced as the car slid off the main road onto the bumpy track leading towards Chiragpur. She happily speculated as to how many people would note her

arrival. By tonight the whole village would know that Chaudharani Kaniz was back, for there were only four cars in the village: theirs, Siraj Din's and the two belonging to the *nouveaux riche* families who had recently begun to accumulate wealth thanks to their sons going abroad to work in the Middle East. First it was a giant fridge, then a VCR and finally they had ostentatiously progressed to brand new Jeeps!

Kaniz turned her head with a sniff, a sneer twisting her beautiful mouth. Jeeps and VCRs didn't change the lineage. She and her family had both background *and* wealth. Rows of shiny cars could not put their *shan* in the shade!

The dusty road wound through green vegetable fields for a mile. Kaniz peered out of the window, sniffing the fresh country air with pleasure. It was good to be back!

Squinting, her eyes latched on to the figure of a man on a white horse. Was that her Khawar? He was the only one with a white horse in the district. Without her glasses, she couldn't quite make him out at such a distance. Frowning, she tried to identify the other figure with him. It was a young woman, walking a few yards ahead of Khawar. Kaniz saw the woman trip and then fall to the ground, into the cauliflower field.

Her son jumped off his horse and helped the woman up. Khawar was now speaking to her and she was replying before turning to walk away. Taking hold of the horse's bridal, Khawar began to walk back with the woman, towards the village.

Who is that silly chit? Kaniz wondered waspishly. Why did her son have to behave so idiotically? It wasn't right for a young single man to be alone in the fields having a cosy *tête-á-tête* with a young woman, even if it

was by accident. It was a most *improper* thing to do, compromising both his and, more particularly, the woman's reputation. Kaniz must remind him about village proprieties and social etiquette when she got home. Chiragpur was a small place, and a woman's *izzat*, her honour, was the most treasured commodity of all.

Kaniz continued to watch as she saw the woman hasten her step. Then she turned round to say something to him. 'The hussy!' Kaniz hissed under her breath.

Khawar stopped following her. Climbing back onto his horse he cantered off in the other direction. Much to Kaniz's annoyance, her son still hadn't spotted his mother's car on the lane.

The young woman had now come onto the lane and was walking in the same direction as the car – towards the village. She turned her head to look at the car at the very same moment Kaniz herself looked out of the passenger window, her body swelling with curiosity as to the identity of the girl. As the car sped by, Kaniz fell back from the window, her face flushed with sudden heat.

Firdaus! The washerwoman's daughter! Daughter of her enemy! *How could her son do this to her?*

'How demeaning. That vixen! I bet she has got her claws in my son,' Kaniz spat, choking with outrage. 'We will see about this. I will nip this affair in the bud, if my name is not Kaniz!' she vowed, swiping her hand clean over her face from her forehead down to her chin, in a village gesture of personal challenge. 'Meeting my son stealthily alone in the fields! *Gushty!* The slut!'

*

Kaniz's son didn't return home until the evening. By that time she had managed to work herself up into quite a frenzy. The furnace of hate for that young woman sent her lashing out at her housekeeper, Neesa, as soon as she stepped inside her front door.

'Where has my son been spending his time, Neesa?' she demanded. 'It looks as if he has been making the most of my absence. As the old saying goes: "When the cat is away the house becomes overrun by mice". In this case, when the mother is away . . .'

'He has been in and out all the time, mistress. Getting on with his business, I presume,' Neesa hastily replied. 'You must be tired. Would you like to lie down? I will wake you when the young master comes home.'

'No, Neesa, I cannot rest until I have seen my Khawar. I am a widow and I shoulder all the responsibilities alone. I, therefore, need to be kept abreast with everything. If you have noticed anything untoward in my son's behaviour it is your duty to tell me, Neesa. He is my only son. I need to be made aware of every minute detail to do with his welfare.'

'What is the matter, mistress?' Neesa timidly enquired, curious to know the source of her *chaudharani*'s ill temper. 'Has something happened?'

'No, nothing has happened. Off you go now. Send Khawar to me when he comes in.' Kaniz dismissed her housekeeper.

Neesa stared at her mistress's broad, back-turned figure for a few seconds, then quietly turned and left the room. Kaniz wasn't an easy woman to work for. Both proud and cruel, she rarely praised, but expected everything to be done to the highest of standards. She kept all of her servants at a distance, including Neesa — her housekeeper for twenty-nine long years. As her

subordinate, she didn't think it was right to 'honour' Neesa with her confidence.

Sighing to herself, Neesa returned to her cleaning. She must go and check again every room, every pillar, for dust and cobwebs, in case she had the misfortune to have missed any odd crevice. A very tidy person and obsessively proud of her home, Mistress Kaniz would definitely be ritually fingering and inspecting all the windows, and all the surfaces for dust before she went to sleep. It was a task she always meticulously performed whenever she returned from a journey away from home – no matter how achingly tired she was.

Her employer was already in a foul mood. Neesa didn't want to give her another excuse to vent her temper, and this time on her. Resignedly, she picked up her dusting cloth and *boker* stick again.

Khawar, the twenty-six-year-old son and heir to all of his mother's worldly wealth, found Kaniz reclining on a small mountain of cushions on the sofa in front of the television, watching a video film – a new release from Bollywood, India.

'*Assalam-Alaikum*, Mother. I didn't expect you back yet. I thought you were returning next week,' Khawar informed her, bending down and kissing her warmly on the forehead.

'Apparently so. I have been waiting hours for you to come home, my son. Where have you been? Gadding about the fields on your horse, I suppose, or holding important *rendezvous?*' she insinuated hotly.

'I went to settle the account with our *chaprassi* for next week, Mother, and to sort out the flour-grinding machine,' he answered good-humouredly, choosing to ignore her petulant mood.

'I saw you earlier,' Kaniz snapped, her voice low, her dark, almond-shaped eyes now glittering menacingly in her fair face.

'Where?' Khawar slid down on the sofa beside his mother. She turned to give him the full benefit of a slow, detailed facial examination, evidently seeking any telltale sign of guilt.

'In the fields – with that young woman!' Kaniz spat, her eyes screwed into tiny slits.

'What do you mean by *that young woman?*' Undaunted, Khawar stared squarely back into his mother's eyes.

'Well, apparently you were so engrossed in that washerwoman's daughter that you didn't even notice your mother's car when it passed you by.'

'I was not engrossed, Mother – don't be silly! Firdaus fell down and I helped her up. That is all.'

'No, you didn't just help her up! I was watching you. You walked with her and were having a cosy chat with her.'

'What is this, Mother?' Khawar shifted irritably on the sofa. 'An inquisition? So what if I was talking to her! She is a fellow villager and, after all, I have played with her as a child. It is not a crime to talk to her, is it? I was only asking her about the school. Remember, I am one of the school's management committee members.'

Kaniz patiently heard him out, before addressing him in a measured tone. She couldn't afford him to make the mistake of taking her words lightly, or mis-understanding them. She was thus forced to spell it out for him. 'I want you to keep away from that woman,' she told him. 'I will not let you have anything to do with her, nor her family. It is too degrading for

a wealthy, well-born landlord to go chasing after a washerwoman's daughter.'

Unable to bear his mother's insults and taunts any longer, Khawar stood up and threw caution to the winds.

'Firdaus is a Deputy Headmistress of the school, Mother! Why is it that you always so conveniently forget that fact? You delight in insulting her by labelling her as the "washerwoman's daughter!" What sort of a kick do you get from verbally abusing her? She is *not* a washerwoman's daughter!'

'Well, I think she is. And I don't get kicks, you rascal! I am telling you, my son, not to dishonour our name by linking it with theirs. Anyway, I have a great match in mind for you, in Lahore, with a very beautiful and educated woman. Your Auntie Sabra has been so busy on your behalf.'

'Really.' Khawar whistled softly, releasing the tight rein of his temper. Proud, like his mother, he was unable to bear her imperious, tyrannical manner. 'You and Auntie Sabra can do what you like with that "Lahori" woman,' he said icily. 'If I want to, I can marry that *chit* – that *washerwoman's daughter* and there is nothing you can do to stop me, Mother.' He glared down at her, in no mood to humour her further.

Her beautiful mouth dropping open, Kaniz watched her son stride angrily out of the room. She was only prevented from going into hysterics by the realisation that Khawar was simply goading her. He has said that in anger to get back at me, she thought. He knows his duty and would never do anything so unforgivable as that!

With that calming thought, Kaniz managed to close her mouth. Propping the cushions beneath her, she

stretched out her big frame and long legs on the sofa to enjoy the film once more. Now where was she? Oh yes. The hero, Shahrukh, had just fallen in love with the heroine's sister . . . Her hand reached for the plate of sweetmeats.

Just as she was really getting into the plot of the film, Kaniz was interrupted by Neesa's timid entrance, informing her that Mansur, the village melon man, was at her gate, waiting for their order. 'No, Neesa! Tell him from me to chuck his rotten pock-marked fruit into the village well. I am in no mood for his out-of-season melons.'

Her evening now definitely ruined, Kaniz asked Neesa to have Kulsoom, the village matchmaker, summoned to the house. Having failed in her numerous attempts to bring her beloved son and Zarri Bano together, she was now ready and resigned to start afresh. That proud young madam had categorically stated that she did not want to live in the village, and also pretended that Khawar was a sort of a brother to her.

'Just as well.' Kaniz sniffed disdainfully. That woman was too glamorous, too educated and opinionated for her liking. Now shy Ruby was another matter . . . Thus, she now wanted Kulsoom to find out from Habib Khan if he would be willing to allow her to ask for his younger daughter, Ruby, as a bride for Khawar.

As Kaniz reached over to pluck another *ludoo* from the plate and pop it into her mouth, she had a sudden vision of Firdaus with her son and nearly choked. 'Never!' she screamed silently in her mind. 'Over my dead body!'

Chapter 3

BABA SIRAJ DIN, accompanied by his faithful companion and driver, Waris, ceremoniously decided to call at his son Habib's home, to discuss the matter of his granddaughter Zarri Bano's *rishta*. Once parked on the marble-tiled driveway of Habib's luxurious villa, Siraj Din waited patiently for his driver to help him out of the Jeep. Holding his ivory walking stick in one hand, he accepted Waris's hand to step down from his high seat. He straightened his long black tweed overcoat, and adjusted his turban at the right angle on his head. He always visited his son very formally dressed. 'Impressions matter a lot,' he forever preached to his sons and grandchildren.

His ivory stick tapping a distinct sound on the creamy white marble ground, Siraj Din climbed up the three steps of the veranda leading to the two sliding doors. Pressing the buzzer on the wall he waited impatiently.

Fatima came out of the kitchen. Wiping her wet hands on the end of her shawl she walked nonchalantly into the hall to see who had the audacity to have kept their finger on the buzzer for such a long time. On catching a glimpse of the stately old man standing outside the clear glass patio door, his head held imperiously at an angle surveying her coldly, Fatima rushed to the door. Over her shoulder she shouted to her mistress Shahzada, 'Sahiba Jee, Baba Siraj Din is here!'

'Bismillah! Bismillah, Baba Jee!' Fatima gushed, sliding the door fully open. Quickly stepping aside, she

obligingly bowed her head in front of him for the ritual patting. Dutifully, Siraj Din lightly swiped his hand over her shawled head before walking straight ahead into the hall.

Shahzada, his eldest daughter-in-law, had heard Fatima's shout. Siraj Din saw her dash out of the lounge, holding her *chador* firmly in place on her head, while she urgently tugged and draped the other half discreetly around her shoulders and over in front of her chest. With her gaze respectfully fixed on his coat and with smarting cheeks, Shahzada stepped before her superior-looking father-in-law. Dutifully, she inclined her head towards his raised hand. Siraj Din let his hand rest heavily for a moment on her head, at peace with himself. This was the head he never tired of patting. It belonged to his favourite daughter-in-law, the joy in his life after his wife Zulaikha's death.

'*Assalam-Alaikum, Aba Jan,*' Shahzada nervously greeted her father-in-law, fearful of her silk *chador* disgracefully slipping from its precarious position on her head and thus scandalously baring her head to his gaze. 'We didn't expect you, Baba Jee,' she stammered to explain.

'*Wa Laikum-Salam,*' Siraj Din returned the greeting before walking ahead into the drawing room, asking carelessly over his shoulder, 'Is Habib at home?'

Shahzada hovered two steps behind her father-in-law as he entered their large drawing room. Fatima had already scurried ahead into the room to set in place the *takkia*, the thick bolster, on the sofa. Siraj Din flashed a smile of appreciation at Fatima as he stretched his tall, wiry frame on the creamy brocade upholstery. Thoroughly disliking modern sofas, his heart still hankered after the *palangs*, the traditional luxury beds

that graced living rooms in days gone by. The *palangs*, however, didn't go well with the rest of the modern drawing-room furnishings. They were being relegated to rooms labelled ostentatiously as 'bedrooms'.

His eyes moved over the tall lamp in the corner, the long drapes with their matching brocade swags and tails drawn across the wall-to-wall patio window. They then rested on the three heavy marble tables placed between the two large luxurious sofa suites. There were enough seats around the room to cater for up to twenty-five people, Siraj Din counted at the back of his mind. Knowing his father's particular preference, Habib had especially purchased an elegant chaise longue from a quality department store in Karachi, which also matched beautifully with the rest of the plush furnishings, including the silk carpet completely covering the marble floor.

Shahzada left her father-in-law alone for a few moments while she went into the kitchen to inform her second cook to prepare a special meal for Siraj Din Sahib, and to use fewer red chillies in the curry dishes. Fatima was also in the kitchen preparing a hookah for Siraj Din, with freshly ground tobacco neatly placed amongst small pieces of coal in the *topee*. When Shahzada returned, Habib was with his father discussing business negotiations to do with their land. Siraj Din was asking his son whether it was worthwhile selling some land in his home village, Chiragpur, to another landlord, Master Khawar.

'It is hard for me to manage at this time in my life,' the old man told him, 'and you and Jafar have enough to do already with the land around here. Yes, I think that I'll let young Khawar buy those acres. He is a

clever chap and will look after the land well. I wouldn't want to sell them to anyone else.'

'I agree with you, Father. Zarri Bano is thinking of opening a publishing company in Karachi, with Jafar's help. Therefore, with my son involved in that business, I don't think I'll have time to oversee both the land here in Tanda Adam and in Chiragpur.'

'Where is Zarri Bano?' Siraj Din asked of his daughter-in-law as she sat beside her husband. He had already greeted Jafar and his youngest granddaughter Ruby.

Habib cast a hostile glare at his wife. Siraj Din merely fixed his green eyes, so similar to his son's, on his daughter-in-law's face. Shahzada's gaze faltered before them both. Fidgeting with the crocheted lace edge of the *chador*, she waited nervously for Habib to explain.

Seconds passed. Habib didn't explain.

His thick triangular-shaped brown eyebrows raised over his aquiline nose, Siraj Din was now intrigued by the pair's silence.

Having by now realised that Habib's silence was deliberate, Shahzada was miserably compelled to explain. She understood: this was Habib's revenge for her action in letting Zarri Bano go to Karachi to Sikander's home.

'She is in Karachi,' Shahzada stated with quiet dignity.

'What is she doing there?' Siraj Din asked sharply, suddenly realising that as the rest of the family was at home, his eldest granddaughter must have gone there alone.

An awkward silence ensued. Siraj Din's speculative glance moved from his son to his daughter-in-law. The undercurrents of tension in the room spelt to him that

something was definitely wrong. The pair sitting in front of him were apparently bent on playing games with one another, each shunting the responsibility of explaining Zarri Bano's whereabouts onto the other.

Shahzada first peeped up at her father-in-law and then at her husband, her heart sinking at the look of pure malice in her beloved Habib's eyes. Bitterly she accepted that Habib was in a cruel, uncompromising mood.

'Zarri Bano is visiting Sikander's home.' She slipped the information in while moving the glasses of drinks onto the tray. 'His family wanted her to come and visit their home.' Shahzada's voice trailed off into the silence of the room. All of a sudden she experienced a strong urge to rush out and into the fresh air of the rear courtyard.

'Are you telling me, Shahzada, that my young, unmarried granddaughter has gone to stay, all alone, in a strange family's home and is in the company of a single young man?' Siraj Din's words cut Shahzada's ears like a whiplash. She turned to look at the stately old man, dismayed at the harsh words. Her father-in-law had never spoken to her in such a disparaging tone or manner before.

'I have done nothing wrong!' Shahzada rebelled, trembling inside with rage. Remembering her beloved eldest daughter's wistful eyes, Shahzada found the courage to look her father-in-law straight in the eye: she also had the presumption to speak boldly in front of the most revered elders of their clan.

'*Aba Jan*,' she said quietly; she always called him 'Father': 'Zarri Bano has lived alone in Karachi in a hostel, as you well know, while she was studying at

University. She will be moving to Karachi anyway, because of her new editorial post and the company she is hoping to set up. She is a mature woman of twenty-seven years of age. Also, she *didn't* go alone – Jafar went with her. Sikander's parents asked her to stay a few more days. I think it is good for her to get to know Sikander and his family before she marries him.' Shahzada mentally excused her new spirit of rebellion by telling herself that she was doing it for her daughter's sake.

'I see,' the old man commented in a dangerously calm voice. 'And that means staying in the same house, does it? Spending time with a young man – two people with no blood or any other legitimate ties between them? Since when did we become so immoral?' Siraj Din's voice lashed.

Taken aback by her father-in-law's verbal assault and the chilly vehemence of the words, colour flooded Shahzada's cheeks.

Tapping a rhythm with his stick on the silk carpet, Siraj Din waited for his daughter-in-law to say something, to apologise for her temerity in both speaking and answering him herself instead of letting her husband do it. And to top it all, she then had the audacity to justify her action to him! Siraj Din was now very, very angry with his most favourite daughter-in-law. Truly dismayed, he shook his head in disbelief. This was not the Shahzada he knew and loved.

Shahzada cast another helpless look at her husband, desperate for his support, hoping that he would say something in her defence. However, Habib, his eyes as cold as his father's, remained self-righteously silent by her side.

All of a sudden Shahzada again experienced the urge

to escape from that oppressive atmosphere. She rose, but Siraj Din's words rooted her to the sofa again.

'Shahzada, I know that I am an old man and am fast becoming obsolete in this rapidly changing world. Day by day we are being invaded by Western values, via the satellite dishes and television programmes. But I must be allowed to say that my clan hasn't yet had the misfortune to become so outrageously "advanced", so morally corrupt that we let our beautiful young un-married daughters stay in strange people's houses unchaperoned. Alongside our land, our wives and daughters, our *izzat* – our honour – is the most precious thing in our lives. We never *ever* compromise on the issue of our women and our *izzat*! No matter what age we live in; no matter what the world outside dictates; no matter what evil lies outside our door. Even if you sacrifice, forget, or part with all the other etiquettes of our land-owning class of feudal landlords, we will never let you sully our *izzat* or our women's honour, Shahzada.'

Chastised thus, Shahzada didn't dare to raise her eyes, let alone speak. She sank into a stupor of humilia-tion as her father-in-law, in a calculated gesture of insult and a demonstration of his displeasure, neatly dismissed her by turning his back on her and lying down on the chaise longue.

Biting her quivering lower lip, Shahzada shot a look of pained betrayal at her husband. With an awkward movement and making sure her *chador* hadn't by chance slipped off her head, she quietly walked out of the room, leaving behind the two males.

Chapter 4

SIKANDER AND ZARRI BANO were taking a walk alone around the orange orchard of Sikander's home, in a leafy suburb of Karachi. The afternoon sun was shining brightly above them.

As they walked side by side, an air of expectancy and excitement hung about them. Making small talk, both were happy to skirt around the main topic on their minds by indulging and humouring the other.

This was their third meeting. Zarri Bano, especially invited to visit Sikander's home, had accepted graciously. Sikander did in fact, as predicted by Zarri Bano, return to Tanda Adam for a second visit. This time they had an opportunity to spend a whole day in each other's company. And she didn't turn him down, as Ruby learned later.

After dinner, Sikander had volunteered to show Zarri Bano around his family orchard. This time there were no parents to chaperone them. There was no need. They were two mature adults, needing and wanting to communicate and explore with each other their feelings for one another, before sealing their fate together.

They had walked away from the large house. Strolling amongst the orange trees, Zarri Bano had reached forward to pluck a ripe satsuma from the branch.

'Here, let me help you, Zarri Bano.'

It was the first time he had used her full name instead of the polite term of 'Sahiba'. The name rippled like music to Zarri Bano's ears.

Sikander reached forward and pulled the satsuma off

the branch, touching Zarri Bano's hand accidentally in the process. She went still, a strange, potent awareness entering her body. She waited for him to remove his hand.

He didn't.

It was Zarri Bano who eventually jerked her hand away, deeply offended. Confronting Sikander directly, her hand still smarting from the touch of his fingers, she said in a low, passionate voice: 'Sikander Sahib, we are all alone in this orchard and talking together. However, let me make it clear to you that I never allow anyone the liberty of being too familiar with me. No man has ever touched me or dared to do so, no matter how innocently.'

Sikander steadily held her gaze. A humorous glint dancing in his eyes, he looked pointedly down at her hand again. He understood her perfectly!

'What liberty have I taken, Zarri Bano?' he asked softly. 'If an unfortunate and accidental contact of my hand has deserved this harsh rebuke from you, then perhaps we have both misunderstood the nature of this situation, of why we are here in the first place – walking alone, as you say, a man and a woman with no ties between us. I had hoped that there was a purpose in this walk of ours – a purpose to your stay in my home, in fact. That is why your mother and brother left you here, isn't it?'

Colour rushed to Zarri Bano's cheeks. She had come to the orchard to give him her answer personally that she would marry him, but now, perverse delight overtook her in wanting to hold it back, to teach him a lesson – to punish him for his audacity.

'You presume wrong, Sikander Sahib. There is no purpose in our walk together. I am just a guest in your

house and I wanted a stroll around your gardens. You volunteered to accompany me, that's all.' She smiled politely back at him.

'Well, if you think that I am too familiar, Sahiba, and there is no purpose to our walk together, I will leave you in peace. I, for my part, do not make a habit of taking unmarried women around our orchard. I'll see you later in the house,' he threw back at her before striding away, leaving a stunned Zarri Bano behind.

'Sikander Sahib!' she called after him, collecting her wits about her, deflated by his action. He had neatly turned the tables on her. 'You do treat your guests shabbily. I thought there was a *handani*, a Sindi code of chivalry and etiquette.'

He swept round to look back at her. She was standing next to the orange tree, her arms held behind as if she were embracing it – almost moulded against it. The warm breeze played with her clothes and the long wavy strands of her hair as it fell around her face and shoulders.

Sikander caught his breath. She was looking at him with the same wistful expression of innocent abandonment that she had worn under the tree at the *mela*. This time she was dressed in dark green and looked exquisite. As if drawn by a magnet, Sikander retraced his steps and came to stand in front of her.

Zarri Bano watched and waited, a wave of sudden excitement coursing through her veins. Unable to make sense of her feelings when Sikander had angrily marched away from her, she had panicked. With a thud, the realisation dawned on her that she cared deeply for him, and that his opinion of her mattered to her.

Her eyes, unbeknown to her, thus spelt out and

whispered to him what her heart and mind had refused to recognise and to signal.

She was a tall woman, but he was still a few inches taller. She looked up at his face, her eyes lingering on the deep cleft in his chin. Then they lifted – locked with his.

Unable to help himself, Sikander reached forward and took her hand in his own. This time she didn't draw it back. Sikander marvelled at its shape, suppleness and its colouring, with its well-manicured nails. He let his fingers tentatively trail over the soft skin.

'Such a beautiful hand,' he murmured, his eyes challenging her to remove it from his grasp. Then before her shocked gaze, he turned her hand over and his fingers began to move over her palm.

Zarri Bano watched in stunned surprise, her heart beating fast, before snatching her hand back, horrified both at his action and her own reaction to it. She had liked the feel of his fingers against her palm. Commonsense and female etiquette demanded that she remove her hand from his.

She went into further shock when he drew forward her other hand and did the same. She tried to draw it back, but he wouldn't let go. Her colour heightened, she looked away in embarrassment, seeing the raw passion in his eyes. She floundered. He was invading the very perimeters of her intimate world.

By his action, both recognised that they were being drawn into a new bond. There was to be no retreat for either of them. They knew too much about each other.

Sikander was satisfied. Horrified she had been, but she hadn't removed her hand, the second time, from his grasp. Her eyes had eloquently betrayed her as nothing

else could have done and whispered volumes for her heart.

'I am afraid I have now committed a further crime in your book. It appears I am destined to sink fast in your estimation,' his seductive tone teased. He smiled gently down at her. 'I have been even more familiar. Is Shahzadi Zarri Bano now lost for words?'

Zarri Bano's face spread into a smile, revealing an attractive dimple in her left cheek.

'I wouldn't have allowed you to become so familiar if I had not wanted you to,' she answered softly.

'Then I am honoured.'

'So you should be. It is the first time that I have let a strange man touch my hand.'

'But I wouldn't be touching and holding these beautiful hands of yours in mine if I didn't think that I had some right to do so. I, too, know the parameters of social proprieties.'

'And what right is that, may I ask?' she prompted, now ready to play with fire. 'You are too presumptuous, Sikander Sahib.'

'The right of your future husband, have I not, Zarri Bano?' he coaxed, his eyes still caressing her with their dark warm glow.

There it was – the proposal in plain words. No more fencing around the subject. He now waited tensely for a response from her.

This was the moment that Zarri Bano had both dreaded and anticipated with delight. Instead, she was overcome by the utter solemnity of the occasion. The smile and dimple receded and she stared at him in awe, unable to look away.

Sikander watched and waited. Was she or was she not going to accept his proposal? Gently he dropped her

hand. Not wishing to swamp her with his physical presence he moved to stand at a decent distance from her.

Zarri Bano watched his retreat with a sense of loss. She had, by now, long recognised the charismatic power of attraction this man held over her. Totally lost to him she gloried in that realisation. There was to be no regret.

He was the first man who had managed to arouse anything in her. In fact, she was beginning to be terribly afraid of the feelings he *was* arousing in her. She wanted to share her life with him. Be with him, touch him and to feel his touch. Without him life loomed like a void – empty, colourless and without meaning. She allowed herself to be swept into his magnetic field, knowing instinctively that he was her ultimate fulfilment in life.

On impulse, she walked up to him; reaching forward, she placed her hand in his. He grasped it tightly, his shoulders relaxed. It was a most pleasant surprise, but he still sought a verbal response from her. He turned to look at her, his eyes again coaxing hers, endeavouring to demolish any relics of female reserve she still harboured.

She immediately responded. First with a smile and then she leaned forward, so that her shoulder was almost touching his.

'You have every right, Sikander Sahib. I wouldn't allow my hands to be touched if I didn't think it was right.' Honesty of thought and feeling were of paramount importance at this moment in time. 'I am most honoured by your proposal and I hope you are in turn honoured by my acceptance.'

Sikander's eyes closed. *She had accepted.*

'Zarri Bano, I'll never let you regret this. I'll make

you the happiest woman on earth,' he proclaimed both to himself and to her in a voice rich with promise.

'I hope so, for you see, I have turned down many, many suitors. I was almost tempted to turn you down too.' She dimpled at him. 'But you are the only one who has finally caught me, as my sister would say. However, I do cherish my freedom. Above all, I will not be moulded in any way. You must understand and remember that always, Sikander Sahib.'

'I will be honest with you too. You are the first woman who has "caught me in her net". I want you as you are. That is what I most like about you – your unconventional behaviour, your wit and sparkle. Let's now go inside and tell my family the good news. They will be delighted, particularly my father, who dreams of grandchildren with your eyes. You can phone your parents.' His eyes again roamed over her face, noting the blush that had spread over her cheeks, before he pulled her along with him.

They walked a few yards together, side by side, in silence. Both were lost in thought and the magic spell that their walk had woven. As they approached the villa, Zarri Bano stepped away from him.

'It's going to be hard keeping my distance from you, especially when you are in the same building,' Sikander whispered in her ear, an impish smile playing tenderly on his lips.

Shahzada entered the guest room unobtrusively, holding the hookah smoke pipe and base in her hand. She placed it down gently next to her father-in-law and then sat on the sofa. Habib and his father had finished their meal and were now enjoying drinking their pink *shabz* tea. They were engrossed in a keen discussion on

the subject of the brick factory, the *bhatta* that had opened near their village, and didn't pay any attention to Shahzada.

'We have always prided ourselves on the beautiful green landscape of our estate. Now with the brick-making business leaving huge ugly craters in the ground, the land is unbecomingly scarred. Habib, we will need to do something about it soon. I will not allow another of these smoke-belching kilns to be built in the vicinity of our village, never mind the heat from them. In the countryside we take pride in the fresh air.'

Siraj Din cast a look at his daughter-in-law as she stood up and picked up the hookah again. She, thinking that a change of position might be more convenient for him, placed it near his legs. Leaning over, he pulled the pipe towards him and took a long powerful puff, making the water in the shiny round aluminium base gurgle.

As he puffed he glanced up at Shahzada, seeing the smile etched on her face and the radiant glow beaming from her cheeks. Unable to help himself, he smiled back at her, his own eyes softening with fatherly love and fondness. Shahzada would always remain his favourite daughter-in-law, even if she had had the misfortune of displeasing him. The truth of the matter was that he had a soft spot for Shahzada. He just wished that all his other daughters-in-law were like her. Magnanimously, Siraj Din decided that he was going to forgive her. 'She is a human being, after all, and all human beings make mistakes sometimes.'

Siraj Din's green eyes narrowed in thought as he noted the stern lines on his son's face. Siraj Din was unable to fathom Habib's mood and the present tempo of his relationship with his wife. Earlier in the

afternoon there had been a distinct coldness between them, almost as if they were two strangers. No words or look of warmth had passed between them. On the contrary, Habib had been almost malicious towards his wife denying her any support. 'What is going on between them?' Siraj Din wondered, intrigued yet disquieted by the chasm that had opened up between his two loved ones.

Siraj Din swept a questioning look at his daughter-in-law.

Blushing red under his gaze, Shahzada announced with quiet confidence: '*Aba Jan*, Zarri Bano has just phoned from Karachi. She tells me that she has decided to marry Sikander and that she is very happy.' Shahzada scanned both their faces expectantly.

She waited, switching from one face to the other, but only total silence greeted her words. Confronted with the grim look on her father-in-law's face, Shahzada faltered nervously, her two fingers kept tapping on the gold rim of her china cup. When she turned to her husband, a steely glare greeted her. 'Why are they treating me so coldly?' Shahzada asked herself in pained bewilderment. 'Aren't they happy at the news?'

From the natural well of her maternal instinct, both outrage and defiance reared their ugly heads. She decided to address her *Aba Jan* directly.

'Aren't you both happy that at last we've succeeded in arranging a match for our Zarri Bano, and to our satisfaction?' she asked, and was unable to mask either the accusing tone, or the look of resentment in her eyes.

Shocked by the audacity of his 'beloved' daughter-in-law, Siraj Din ruthlessly turned on her.

'Arranging, Shahzada? We have done no arranging. You and your daughter have had the impudence to

arrange it all. You didn't even have the courtesy to tell us that Zarri Bano was going to Karachi or indeed consult us on whether she ought to be allowed to go, without your presence as chaperone. It appears, my Shahzada, we have no say in this matter. Amazingly, you have by-passed both Habib and myself. I hadn't realised what an industrious daughter-in-law I had. In fact, I am beginning to wonder who actually rules this home. Who is master in this house? You or my son, Habib . . . ?' Siraj Din stopped as he watched his son stiffly get up and leave the room.

Shahzada watched with hurt bewilderment. Habib hadn't said a word. Was he not happy for his daughter? What *was* the matter with him? Her mouth now very dry, she turned to her father-in-law's equally hostile stare. He pulled his legs up on the sofa and took another puff on his long smoke pipe.

'*Aba Jan*, you knew those people were interested in our Zarri Bano,' Shahzada felt obliged to explain. 'Jafar introduced us to them. Habib Sahib has kept you informed of everything. You know we never do anything without your authority or your blessing. Please forgive me if we gave you any other impression. Habib Sahib is the master of this household, how could you ever doubt that? And how could I, a mere woman, take such a step as arranging my daughter's marriage without involving you two? You insult both me and yourself by such a preposterous assumption. I am not guilty of any crime, *Aba Jan*. I have not done anything wrong. If love for my eldest daughter and concern for her future happiness in marriage to the right person are crimes in your book, then I am guilty indeed,' Shahzada ended quietly, holding herself with dignity.

'Then tell me, Shahzada, why is my son behaving so

oddly towards you?' Siraj Din rasped, leaving aside the smoke pipe. 'I have not lived for over seventy years to remain blind to the signals that my son has been shooting forth at you all this afternoon. He offers no blessing to this match to this rich tycoon, that you and your daughter appear to be so keen on. Tell me, Shahzada, why is this so?' Siraj Din's eyes bored accusingly into hers. He had never, ever stared at her with such disapproval before.

'I don't know,' Shahzada said miserably, her head bowed, unable to make sense of either her husband's antagonism towards Sikander or her father-in-law's disapproval.

Tears pricking the corners of her eyes, Shahzada got up, keeping her face averted. 'I will see if Jafar is back from his horse riding,' she mumbled and left the room.

But instead of Jafar, she went to look for her husband.

Shahzada found Habib in their bedroom. He was standing with his back to her, looking out at their fields of wheat and corn. He heard his wife enter and instinctively knew it was Shahzada. Stopping in the middle of the large bedroom, she waited for him to turn and look at her. He didn't.

She aimlessly moved around the room, picking up the large fleecy towel from Habib's bed. Folding it she placed it on the chair. Next, she straightened the books and Habib's business ledgers on the coffee table in front of the sofa. Propping up the cushions she placed them at neat angles on the leather sofa. Shahzada stood and surveyed the room – there was nothing further for her to do.

Habib's back was still turned to her. Resigning

herself to the fact that her husband was neither going to speak to her or acknowledge her presence, Shahzada swallowed her pride.

'Habib Sahib,' she whispered gently, walking to stand behind him and touching his arm. 'Isn't it wonderful that Zarri Bano has agreed to marry Sikander? I am so happy.' She felt his muscles tense under her hand. 'Aren't you happy, Habib Sahib?' she repeated.

'*Happy*, Shahzada?' Habib violently swept round, fuming down at her from his towering height. 'I told you that I can't stand that man! Do you think I am going to let him marry my beloved daughter? He is unworthy of her.' He ignored the look of utter horror on her face.

'Habib, Zarri Bano has just told us that she wants to marry Sikander. Our daughter is in love with him!' She desperately appealed for his understanding.

'Love!' Habib spat out the word. 'Since when did our women start falling in love before marriage?' he snarled, his eyes now twin green beams of fury.

Her heart pounding loudly Shahzada raised her distraught face to her husband. 'You can't fight something as natural as love, Habib,' she replied. 'What disease is eating you up?' she demanded, her eyes wildly scanning her husband's face.

'I will tell you what disease is eating me up!' Habib hissed into her face. 'If you encourage my daughter to marry this man against my wishes, I will divorce you on the spot, Shahzada – not once, not twice but *thrice*! You will receive three divorces, three *thalaks*! And all at one go!' he ground out cruelly, his eyes boring vindictively into hers.

Shahzada stepped back in shock, her mouth half open, a look of utter outrage and betrayal in her eyes.

Her gentle, kind husband had turned into a warped stranger, threatening her with the cruellest of all punishments a woman could receive from her husband, the three *thalaks*.

'You! You . . .' she stammered in a trembling voice, holding her hand hard against her heaving chest, 'you would do that to me? You would divorce me? Me, Habib, your wife?' Her warm brown eyes stared up in wounded amazement. 'What evil force has possessed you, my beloved husband? What form of madness is this?' Choking on her words, she stumbled away from him and careered straight into the arms of her housekeeper, Fatima, as she hurriedly entered the room without knocking.

The two women stared at each other, unable to understand the look on the other's face. Both wore masks of pain and horror.

'Mistress! It is Jafar,' Fatima gulped, her face deathly pale. She looked at her master. 'He – He . . .' She stopped, unable to go on. Instead she buried her head on her mistress's shoulder.

'Jafar?' Shahzada uttered, her brain reeling, as she saw her husband run out of the room.

Chapter 5

THE SMARTLY DRESSED waiter hovered around the table where Sikander and Zarri Bano were dining in a semi-secluded alcove in a prestigious Karachi restaurant. Once he had moved away with the plates, Sikander looked tenderly across at Zarri Bano. Too shy to fathom the look in his eyes, she watched the other people

dining in the air-conditioned lounge, beautifully dec-
orated with a Mughal theme.

'You are a very beautiful woman, Zarri Bano,'
Sikander whispered. 'That waiter couldn't bear to take
his eyes off you.'

'I am finding it very embarrassing, Sikander Sahib,'
Zarri Bano felt compelled to state, knowing for sure
that a tide of colour had suffused her cheeks. 'I have
never eaten out alone with a bachelor before.'

'Am I still like a single man, Zarri Bano? Surely not!'
She heard both the indignation and the hurt behind the
words.

'You are, Sikander, that is until I step into your
home as your wife.' Her eyes on a seventeenth century
Mughal painting of a Maharani taking a walk in
her garden, Zarri Bano felt the urge to clarify the
situation to him. 'At the moment, there is nothing
between us.'

'I dispute that, Zarri Bano.' He leaned forward on
the tablecloth, his soft gaze warming her face. 'There is
everything between us, and you know it! It was love at
first sight, from the moment we saw each other at the
mela!'

She gently contradicted him. 'There is no blood tie
between us, Sikander, you are not my relative or
brother.'

'God forbid, Zarri Bano. I could never be your
brother! What sort of talk is this? Let's change the
subject. Tell me more about the publishing company
you were talking about yesterday and which you plan to
set up here in Karachi.'

Zarri Bano ignored his request and instead found
herself asking, 'Do you often bring women here to
dine with you?' For some reason it had become very

important for her to know how many other women had sat across the table from him. Surprised by the question he paused, and then looked down at the napkin in his hand.

'Not very often, but I bring my male friends and colleagues to this place. Why do you ask?'

'I just wondered.' Blushing, she explained, 'Because the Karachites are supposed to be, let's say, more "advanced" than us in the countryside. For all I know, you bring a new woman here every evening. They do things here that are not so morally acceptable to us in the countryside, especially the free interaction between men and women.'

'And you, Zarri Bano? Where do you fit into all that?' Sikander asked, more and more intrigued by the woman sitting in front of him.

'Nowhere, Sikander.' A serious look entered her eyes. 'Don't be fooled by the modern image that confronts you. I may look the part, but on the inside I am very much a product of my clan. Never, ever forget that. I think and behave in a manner consistent with my clan's traditions. I respect and follow our centuries-old traditions. The essence of my life lies with the well-being of my family.

'Luckily for me I have a loving, indulgent father and grandfather – both of them dote on me and have let me do what I wanted to do. For instance, it was unheard of ten years ago for a woman from my clan to live away from home. I did so. I lived here in Karachi for three years, while I was studying at university for my Master's degree. Now my father, who I am ashamed to say, according to my sister's teasing "would sell the world" for me, is helping me to set up a large publishing house. Did you know, by the way, Sikander, that

you'll be marrying a very wealthy woman?' Zarri Bano said playfully.

Sikander's grey eyes glittered. 'It is not your wealth I care for. I have enough of my own to be able to comfortably compete with your father.' Leaning across the table he whispered, 'It is you I want!'

Colour flooded Zarri Bano's cheeks, prompting Sikander to sit back in his chair and suggest kindly, 'Shall we leave?'

'Please!' Zarri Bano said gratefully. Her mouth very dry, she got out of her chair.

They passed through the rows of round tables. Noting two men's appreciative glances at Zarri Bano's elegant frame dressed in Karachi's *haute couture*, the thick waves of her long hair swinging freely around her shoulders, Sikander moved protectively by her side, leading her out of the building.

Sitting in the car, he asked, 'Would you like to go for a walk in Clifton Park and along the beach, before we return home?'

'Yes, that would be nice,' Zarri Bano readily agreed.

The journey was a silent one, as she enjoyed the view of the busy nightlife of Karachi's teeming shopping promenades and plazas. Stopping at one of the plazas, Sikander told her softly, 'I want to buy you a gift, Zarri Bano.'

She shook her head vigorously. 'Sikander, no gifts, please. Not yet. It is only your ring I want and that at the proper time and via your parents.'

'I see.' Sikander tried not to show his disappointment by turning to look in the car mirror before moving off again into the traffic.

Wanting to humour him, Zarri Bano dimpled at him, somehow knowing the effect it would have on

him. 'I will make you stop at this plaza every weekend, Sikander,' she teased. 'Then you can buy me all the gifts in the world, including from Singapore while we are on our honeymoon over there.'

In a companionable silence, as if they had been living together for years, they wandered around the grounds and night funfair at Clifton Park, before climbing down to the beach.

Across the water of the Indian Ocean, a halo of dusky red light cast a golden glow over the shimmering waves. An old ship etched against the horizon stood abandoned a mile away from the harbour. The warm evening breeze blew Zarri Bano's hair around her face. Laughing she swept it back.

A camel with two children on its back trudged along at a leisurely pace, led by its owner. The man selling corncobs cooked over the charcoal fire like the other snack-sellers was still busy, with queues of people eager to buy even the semi-charred ones. Sikander led Zarri Bano away from the other night beach-strollers.

'I come to the beach often at night-time. I find it very relaxing,' he informed her, picking up a pebble and throwing it in the water.

'For me, because we don't have any sea or river near us, it is the fields of my grandfather's land in our village.'

Sikander squatted down on the beach and picked up three sea shells. She watched him shake off the sand and standing before her, he held up one for her to see. 'I have loved every minute of this evening, Zarri Bano. I know you have refused to accept gifts from me, but please keep these as a memento of this day,' he tenderly requested.

Touched by his words, Zarri Bano opened out her

palm and grasped the sea shells tight in her hand. 'I too have enjoyed myself very much, Sikander, but if my grandfather were to see me now, all alone with you in the night, he would have a fit.' They both chuckled guiltily.

'Then, my Zarri Bano, marry me very quickly,' he said hoarsely. 'Please don't make me wait for you.'

Zarri Bano looked beyond him at the shimmering golden waters of the Indian Ocean. Then turning her face to him, instead of words, she offered him her eyes. Simply letting him read the tender message they flashed back at him. '*I too want the same.*'

Chapter 6

RETURNING FROM A visit to Sikander's offices, their laughter ringing in the hallway, Zarri Bano and Sikander entered the drawing room with their faces flushed with happiness. Their laughter sank into the eerie silence of the room. Sikander's mother, Bilkis, hurriedly wiped tears from her eyes. His father looked away sheepishly from Zarri Bano's glance.

'What is the matter?' Zarri Bano asked in alarm. 'Why are you crying, Auntie Jee?' Quickly moving to stand by Bilkis's side she draped an arm around her shoulders.

'I am afraid we have some bad news for you. You must return home immediately, Zarri Bano, my daughter,' Bilkis gently informed her, mopping her face with her shawl.

'What has happened?' Zarri Bano asked, trying to stay calm.

Sikander was alarmed on her behalf. He looked at his parents questioningly.

'Sikander, please make arrangements for Zarri Bano to return home immediately. It . . . it is her brother. Jafar had an accident last night. He died this afternoon.'

'Oh *Allah pak*!' Zarri Bano whispered, shaking her head from side to side, as if trying to rid herself of the image conjured up in her mind by Bilkis's words. Then she stared into space, as shock overtook her.

Sikander watched in growing horror, sharing Zarri Bano's despair and the trauma she was undergoing. How was it possible for a young, handsome man to die, just out of the blue? It was so unfair.

'Father, I'll take Zarri Bano home myself. She is in no state to travel with her chauffeur. Both of you, I presume, are coming too. Did they telephone?'

'Yes, one of Habib Khan's servants rang. Jafar fell off his horse, hurting his head. Brain haemorrhage, they said.'

When they reached her home two hours later Zarri Bano still hadn't shed a tear. She continued to stare ahead, numbed to her very soul. Sikander kept glancing at her, wanting to comfort her, to put his arms around her and draw her to himself. Social etiquette, however, had kept his arms firmly down. At the moment, in the eyes of the world, they had no legitimate relationship between them. 'There is nothing between us,' she had said the other night, he recalled bitterly. Only her husband, father or brother had the honour of comforting her physically.

With a dread step, Zarri Bano entered her home. The happy house had turned into a mausoleum, a place of mourning. Relatives, friends, neighbours and servants

were everywhere – either weeping or chanting. As they caught sight of her, their chorus of chanting grew louder, and they rushed towards her to offer their condolences. Two women flung their arms ceremoniously around her and sobbed heartily on her shoulders. Standing woodenly in their arms, Zarri Bano was unable to either shed a tear or make sense of the scene around her. Sikander and his parents remained by her side.

Fatima led them into the large drawing room, where Jafar was laid out on a *palang* in the centre of the room. Fatima and her daughter Firdaus were delegated with the honour of receiving the guests and local mourners alike. They, themselves, had only arrived from the village that afternoon. Abandoning everything, mother and daughter had hurried to offer comfort and support to Shahzada and Habib.

Milling around the large bed with its walnut headboard, the stream of mourners peered over the body, paying their respects. While some women openly wept, others chanted traditional songs of mourning. Some women even gently beat their breasts in the village tradition. Others preferred to express their grief in more subtle ways: quietly weeping in their *chadors* and shawls and on the shoulders of their loved ones. Ritually they turned from shoulder to shoulder.

Still in shock, Zarri Bano walked to her brother's bier. On seeing her approach, a hushed group of mourners respectfully parted to let her pass. Dry-eyed, she stared down at her handsome young brother, lying there. Why are these stupid people gathered around him and weeping? she thought, gazing wildly around at the crowd of people assembled.

'Wake up, Jafar, my darling! It is past the afternoon!

Wake up, Jafar!' Bending over the bed, she began to tug urgently at her brother's cold hand.

At her words, and noticing the state she was in, the hall resounded with fresh chanting and wailing. Even those hitherto dry-eyed were now forced to cry, empathising with Zarri Bano's agony.

Shahzada, sitting next to her son's bed on the floor, got up and gently led Zarri Bano away, cradling her tall frame against her own body. Then she beckoned to Ruby, sitting on the other side of the bed, to take her sister away from the scene. In an emotionally bruised state of mind herself, Shahzada couldn't bear people watching and witnessing her eldest daughter coming to terms with her raw grief.

Ruby led Zarri Bano up to her room. The two sisters sat on the sofa, hand in hand. Ruby was talking, but Zarri Bano didn't respond – just continued to stare into space.

'Please, sister, snap out of it! Cry, because that is all we have left. Our Jafar is no more.'

'He held my hands, Ruby. I think I simply adore him. It has happened to me at last, Ruby. I think I am in . . .' Zarri Bano turned with a look of wonder on her face, breaking the strange silence between them.

'Who held your hands, *Baji Jan?*' Ruby asked, in surprise.

'Sikander Sahib.'

'Why?'

'Because I agreed to be his wife.'

'Oh, I am so pleased for you, sister,' Ruby replied, heartened to hear Zarri Bano talking once again.

'I must tell everyone that I have, at last, found the man I want to marry. Where is Mother? I must tell her!' A glazed look still in her eye, she stood up to leave.

'Sister, please wait!' Ruby pulled Zarri Bano back in
alarm. 'This is not the time to tell them or anyone else.
Please remember we have just lost Jafar.'

'Where have you lost him? He'll be in the stables. I'll
tell him first.'

'No, listen!' Ruby cried, with desperation. 'He is
dead! Please try to understand. He is not going to be
able to hear you. He has gone for ever. He won't be at
your wedding.' A cry of utter anguish rang around the
room, as Ruby broke down and wept.

Zarri Bano stared dumbfounded at her sister's bowed
head, trying to make sense of what she had said. Then,
the words 'he is dead' pounded in her head.

'No! No! No! My darling brother!' Her mouth
trembling, she let out a piercing scream. Running out
of the room she dashed along the corridor of bedrooms,
down the curved staircase, straight into the large draw-
ing room. She wasn't aware that she wore no *dupatta*,
nor shoes on her feet. Going up to her brother's bed, she
fell on the ground before it and wept. Touching her
brother's face lovingly, she stared in mute agony at the
faces around her. The sound of wailing and mournful
chanting arose again, punctuated by Zarri Bano's
anguished cries.

Sikander sat with the other men on one side of the
hall helplessly watching Zarri Bano. Angry with fate.
Why did life have to be so cruel? Just last night he
had been one of the happiest of men on earth – now
this! They had been planning their wedding in the
restaurant. Talking about the places he would show her
in Singapore on their honeymoon.

It wasn't a good omen. He was not a superstitious
man by any means but an uncanny feeling of dread
swept over him. Jafar's death would definitely mean

that their wedding would have to be postponed. Bitterly he cursed his *kismet*. They hadn't even had a chance to formally get engaged or exchange rings. With the loss of their precious and only son, Zarri Bano's parents would be in mourning for a long time. The wedding would probably have to wait a few months, if not a year.

'Zarri Bano, I can't wait that long. I simply can't!' he silently beseeched her. He got up to go to the bathroom. Before he left the room, he went and stood close to Zarri Bano for a short time, wanting to offer her moral support and words of comfort.

Sitting in the far corner of the room surrounded by other men from the village, Habib had noted Sikander's action. Even in his grief his sharp mind was working. How had Zarri Bano found Sikander's family, their home and customs? he wondered. Was she definitely going to marry him? Habib wanted to know what had passed between his daughter and that 'arrogant' man in Karachi.

The next three days were a nightmare, not only for Habib, his family and relatives, but for all the neighbouring families too, in the small town of Tanda Adam and his home village, Chiragpur. A shroud of doom hung over every household. Everybody unreservedly and respectfully paid homage to Habib's grief. A feudal landlord with great wealth, his family descended from the highest of castes, Habib Khan was also blessed with three beautiful children and acres of land to pass onto his heir. He was a much envied, yet liked and respected, figure in his town.

Thus, everybody mourned for Habib's son – and what a son Jafar had been! One of the handsomest!

Tragically so young; yet unwed and no children to pass on the male line. 'What a terrible way to go!' they agonised, keenly empathising with Habib's grief at having lost his only son and heir, their hearts going out to him. In a culture and land where sons were tradition-ally cherished, an only son was the most precious com-modity of all worldly goods for any father. Hence, to lose your only son was like losing life itself – the worst calamity one's worst enemy could face.

How did one come to terms with a grief and loss of this kind? they wondered bleakly amongst themselves. Would Habib and his family ever recover from this calamity? Moreover, they secretly speculated about the future. Would Habib follow his centuries-old tradition of making one of his daughters his heir?

All of Zarri Bano's relatives, including her paternal grandfather, Siraj Din, and a maternal grandmother came to mourn and attend the funeral. All the rooms were occupied. Bedding was changed daily. The large kitchen had three full-time cooks, as well as Naimat Bibi from the village, preparing meals throughout the day and serving the guests. There was a constant stream of movement with men, women and children moving around the villa. They sat inside the rooms, as well as outside in the courtyard, in groups. This time of gathering, although meant to be a time for mourning, also provided a great opportunity for guests to share and exchange news, social gossip and matchmaking.

Zarri Bano and Ruby shut themselves in their rooms, only allowing their housekeeper, Fatima, in with the food. It was only there that they had something akin to personal privacy. With over a hundred people swelling their home, they couldn't get away from prying eyes

and ears. They let their father, grandfather and mother see to the guests and the funeral arrangements.

Jafar was laid to rest in his family's splendid plot of land in the local cemetery, annexed to the mosque in Chiragpur. His body was ceremoniously taken there by a truck on the second day. This was the most unbearable day for all, particularly for Jafar's parents, his two sisters and for his old friend from the village, Khawar. Khawar had wept openly on Siraj Din and Habib's shoulders a number of times, overtaken by the horror of his personal loss. The two sisters also wept in each other's arms all day, thinking of their beloved brother lying beneath the soil.

On the third day, Sikander and Zarri Bano happened to pass each other. He and his parents had stayed on like the other guests after the funeral.

They stopped and looked at each other sadly. Wanting to say so much, Sikander managed very little, social niceties restraining him. Until they were formally engaged, in the eyes of everyone they had no right to liaise or to seek out each other's company.

Zarri Bano, for her part, now displayed no recognition of their special relationship. The days spent together in Karachi appeared to have happened eons ago. 'It is almost as if, with the death of her brother, she has wiped me and those tender moments in the Karachi orchard and on the beach out from her mind,' Sikander noted with despair. Only a ghost of a smile signalled to him that she knew who he was.

'How are you, Zarri Bano?' Sikander tenderly enquired, pained by her grief-stricken appearance. The dimple in her left cheek appeared to have been ruthlessly erased. She was still very beautiful, in her

subdued coloured outfit and white chiffon headscarf, but the sparkle in her green eyes was no longer there. The gaiety of youth had been snuffed out – the laughter in the eyes all gone!

'As well as one can expect, in the circumstances, Sikander Sahib. Thank you for being here and for all your support. I am sure that my father appreciates it,' she answered politely, not quite able to look him in the eye, ready to move away.

'Not at all,' he answered, managing to muster a similar tone.

Seeing that they were in a public place, out in the courtyard, with men and women watching and listening to them with interest, Zarri Bano felt awkward in Sikander's company.

'I must go, Sikander Sahib.' Excusing herself, she walked away from him.

Reluctantly he let her go. Stared after her with despair. He had long since recognised that he had fallen deeply in love with her, from the day of the *mela*. He now ached to protect and shield her from all this pain and suffering. If only they had been married before Jafar had died! He could then, have taken her away from this sad place and comforted her with all his loving heart. Now he was helpless to do anything. Almost as if he had no part to play in her life.

The mourners weren't the only ones watching the short exchange between Habib's beautiful eldest daughter and the tall, handsome businessman. Fatima had darted a conspiratorial smile at Shahzada in the courtyard as she saw them.

It was only as Fatima passed Kaniz and saw her face turn livid that she glanced in the direction of the woman's furious glare. Over in the far corner of the

courtyard, Firdaus was sitting with Ruby, but Khawar was standing behind her, bending over her shoulder, whispering something in her ear. Firdaus had looked up at Khawar and laughed.

Kaniz had throughout kept a careful watch over her son. She looked up, just as Fatima moved away, but not before she caught the triumphant look on her rival's face. The plate of food in Kaniz's hand shook and fell with a crash on the concrete floor. Turning back, Fatima quickly and neatly whisked away the debris from around Kaniz's feet.

'Chaudharani Kaniz, would you like me to fill your plate again?' she asked politely, while still squatting on the ground.

'No, thank you. I want nothing at all from *you*!' Still livid, Kaniz whispered her insult loudly enough for all the other guests and village women to hear.

Her face going a shade paler, Fatima managed to hold onto her temper by refusing to rise to Kaniz's bait. Instead she judiciously moved away.

Kaniz can say whatever she likes, but she cannot do anything about damming her son's affection for my daughter! thought Fatima happily. With a smirk playing prominently on her face, she moved on to attend to the other mourners and passed trays of fruit around. She didn't offer Kaniz anything else.

Habib Khan, too, had watched the short exchange between Sikander and his daughter. Shahzada glimpsed different emotions chase over her husband's face. She tried to interpret them as best she could, after years of having lived with him. Catching her looking at him, Habib gave his wife the benefit of a pointed stare.

'Tell our Zarri Bano that she mustn't converse with

strange men,' he ordered sharply, 'especially in this gathering, with all and sundry eavesdropping and waiting around for a titbit of gossip. It is not good for my daughter's reputation.'

'But Habib Sahib, Sikander is *not* a stranger! He is our special guest, somebody who will soon become a member of our family – our son-in-law, in fact,' Shahzada replied, her voice raised slightly for some reason she didn't yet understand.

'Perhaps it is *kismet*. Perhaps Sikander was never destined to become a member of our family. Not as Zarri Bano's husband anyway.' Habib turned away, speaking quietly almost as if to himself.

'What? What do you mean?' Shahzada croaked, jerking her head towards him. A cold fist of fear clutched at her heart. Her eyes stood large in her grief-ravaged face.

'Nothing. Forget what I said,' Habib hissed back at her, before rising and crossing the courtyard to speak to his father, Siraj Din.

Shahzada, however, couldn't forget. Stumbling up from her seat she left the courtyard in a daze, wanting to seek the privacy of her own room. He had threatened her with divorce if she encouraged Zarri Bano to marry Sikander – but this! Her husband's chilling, cryptic words shook her nearly as much as the death of her only son. 'It cannot be!' Alarm bells rang loudly in her head. Surely he couldn't be planning that fate! Not for her beautiful daughter! They couldn't be so cruel. They couldn't! she thought feverishly, her head assaulted by different distressing visions.

Still agitated, she sought her daughter. Zarri Bano was in her room. The appearance of her daughter reading the Holy Quran, with a shawled head, gave her mother's runaway imagination a horrid reality.

'Zarri, darling. Please place the Holy Quran on the mantelpiece and let's talk,' Shahzada appealed in a trembling voice, sitting down on the sofa. She tried hard to smile at her daughter, but failed miserably.

'Yes, Mother.' Kissing the Quran's cover reverently, Zarri Bano placed it on the mantelpiece and then flicked the shawl off her head, shaking out her glossy waves, letting them tumble around her shoulders and face, cascading down to her lower back.

'Tell me, Zarri Bano, you do want to marry Sikander, don't you?' Shahzada began, not daring to look her daughter in the eye.

Her pale cheeks colouring a delicate shade of pink, Zarri Bano nodded. 'Yes, Mother. Two days before I learnt of Jafar's death, Sikander Sahib proposed to me and I accepted. That is when I phoned to let you know. But how can I even think about marriage, having lost my dearest, beloved brother?'

'You must, my love. You must get married quickly.'

'But it is the wrong time, Mother. How can you advise me to do this? We have only buried our Jafar yesterday. It would be so insensitive. What will Father say?'

'You must tell him immediately, because I think that he may have other plans in mind for you, now that he has lost Jafar.' Shahzada's voice had sunk to a whisper. She waited for the significance of her comment to register in her daughter's mind, hoping she understood, but as Zarri Bano continued to stare blankly, Shahzada was compelled to explain.

'Your father . . .' Shahzada swallowed, finding it hard to say the words, '. . . wants you to become his heiress, and our *Shahzadi Ibadat*, our "Holy Woman", in the traditional way.'

Zarri Bano stared, stupefied, as the meaning of what her mother had just said sank in. Her mouth opened, but no sound came out.

In fear Shahzada looked up and Zarri Bano saw her own horror mirrored in her mother's warm brown eyes. The eyes of a hunted, wounded animal. The world turned on its axis for Zarri Bano.

'No, Mother! *No!*'

The cry arose from the very depths of her soul.

Chapter 7

SURELY MOTHER HAS misunderstood! Zarri Bano thought wildly in her room after Shahzada had dropped the bombshell and then rushed out, her long white *chador* trailing behind her.

'It cannot be! – they couldn't do that to me!' Zarri Bano implored the walls of her room. 'I must talk to my father and rid this bizarre idea from my mind.' She shook her head to see if that would do the trick, but she only felt more dizzy and confused than before.

Pacing up and down in her room, Zarri Bano wondered who she could confide in. If she told Ruby, her sister would be just as horrified and shocked as herself. Why burden her further in her grief?

Later in the day, she tried to talk to her father, but all to no avail. Wearing a mask of mourning, Habib was surrounded by other men and she couldn't reach him. Zarri Bano couldn't rest, however, until she confronted him with it. 'I must talk to him tonight!' she fretted.

At about half past eleven, when she knew her parents would be in their bedroom, Zarri Bano knocked on

their door and entered. The large room with its tall ceiling was in semi-darkness, but the walnut furniture gave it a warm glow. Her mother was praying in one corner on her prayer mat. Habib sat on the sofa near the bed, flicking through the *Jang* newspaper. He put it aside when he saw his daughter enter.

'How are you, my princess?' he began indulgently, his face splitting into a smile. 'With all these guests everywhere, I haven't been able to talk to you or to comfort you, my dear daughter.'

When Zarri Bano sat down next to him, Habib gave his full attention to his favourite child, his beautiful gem. Even his only son hadn't been able to compete with the affection he felt for Zarri Bano. Taking hold of his hand, she kissed it and held it against her cheek.

'Father, I miss our brother. How will we ever survive without him?' she cried, leaning her head against his shoulder. Putting his arm around her, he squeezed her tight. Then, remembering why she had come, Zarri Bano pulled her head away.

'Father, I didn't have a chance to tell you about my visit to Karachi,' she said.

Habib lowered his gaze to the newspaper. 'Huh-umm!' He made a noncommittal sound in his throat. Zarri Bano watched as the kindly smile was replaced with a blank look.

'Sikander Sahib proposed to me,' she continued softly, waiting for him to look up so that she could see his reaction. Instead she saw his shoulders and neck go rigid. 'Did you hear me, Father?' Zarri Bano prompted nervously.

'Yes, I heard you, Zarri Bano.' Habib turned towards her. 'I knew about it. Your mother told me. What did you say to him?' His voice was hard.

Stooped on the mat, Shahzada forgot the prayer sequence she was reciting as she waited, with a thumping heart, for her daughter's reply.

'I accepted. I know that it is the wrong time, but I thought that I ought to tell you first, before Sikander's parents approach you.' Zarri Bano found herself rushing the words in one breath. Her cheeks burnt with embarrassment when no reaction was forthcoming. 'Aren't you pleased, Father? For years you have waited for me to choose a man to marry and now that I have done so at last, you are silent. It is almost as if you didn't wish me to marry!'

Habib flinched at the anger in her voice. 'You are too highly strung, my daughter. This is not exactly the time to discuss your marriage. We only buried your brother yesterday.'

'I am sorry, Father. Forgive me – you are right, this is not the right time. It is very insensitive of me.' Zarri Bano forced herself to apologise through gritted teeth. For the first time in her life she felt a flicker of hatred for her father – a totally novel experience.

'What *is* the matter with him?' she wondered. Why was he making everything so difficult?

Standing up tall she crossed the room, and caught the troubled look in her mother's eyes. Fear gripped her once again as she re-entered her bedroom. Something was amiss – terribly amiss, in fact. Her father always had time for her, no matter what mood he was in or at what time. And that coldness in his eyes! She shuddered.

Later in bed, Zarri Bano stared at the white ceiling above and wondered whether she and her mother had imagined it all. After all, Habib was right: it *was* insensitive of her to have mentioned her marriage so

soon after her brother's death. Anyway, her father couldn't do *that* to her . . . not to his beloved child, the daughter he would reputedly 'sell the world for'.

Feeling happier now, she turned on her side and was soon fast asleep.

Shahzada found finishing her *isha* prayers an ordeal. With trembling fingers she folded the velour-trimmed prayer-mat and placed it on her dressing table. From the corner of her eye, she covertly watched the stiff figure of her husband. He was still sitting in the same position.

Shahzada frantically debated in her mind: what should she do? Should she talk to him about it or not? If she was wrong, she might actually place the seed of the idea in his mind, and she couldn't risk that. Sighing, she climbed into her own bed.

Ten minutes elapsed. His eyes were still. 'He isn't reading, I know that for sure,' Shahzada told herself. 'What are you thinking about, Habib Sahib?' she said aloud. 'You have not moved since Zarri Bano left the room. Is anything the matter?'

'No,' he replied, his back to her.

'I couldn't help hearing what Zarri Bano said. I am so glad she has accepted Sikander. At last our daughter has found somebody she wants to marry. Sikander is just ideal for her,' Shahzada said bravely, very much aware of her husband's earlier antagonism towards the suitor and knowing that she was playing with fire.

'Please don't talk about her marriage! We have only just buried our son, and already you seem to be planning Zarri Bano's wedding.'

'You misunderstand me. I am planning no such thing. Like you, I have been robbed of my loved one –

my baby. As a mother, I'll never recover from the loss, Habib,' Shahzada stammered defensively.

'Let's not bandy childish words as to whose loss was greater, Shahzada.' His voice breaking, Habib finally turned towards her, his expression haunted. 'He was our angel, and we have lost him. Now I have fallen at the greatest hurdle of my life. What is to become of us and our inheritance?'

An iron fist of fear clutched around Shahzada's heart. Mesmerised, like a hare in the clutches of a python, she stared into his eyes. 'What do you mean?' she whispered.

'Well, now that I have no son, who is going to be my heir, Shahzada? To whom am I going to bequeath all this land? I am not going to hand it over to some stranger who just happens to marry my daughter. This is *our* land, accumulated and paid for by the sweat and toil of my forefathers, down the centuries by different generations. Tell me what would you do in my position?' He paused for what seemed to his wife to be a moment of doom. Then: 'There is only one choice that is facing us.'

'*No!*' Shahzada's deafening cry shook every corner of the dark room. Her breathing ragged, she leapt out of her bed and stood in front of him. 'No, Habib! Say it is not what I think you mean.' His ominous silence terrifying her, she beat her fists against his chest. Alarmed, he pushed her away from him.

'Stop it! Control yourself, woman!' Shahzada's face paled. Glaring down at hers, his eyes were colder than the peaks of the Himalayas. At that moment something died in Shahzada. She was staring at a total stranger – the ruthless feudal landlord, not her husband.

'No, not until you tell me what is on your mind.

Don't hold me in suspense, I beg of you, Habib!' she pleaded, reaching up to beat at him again. Alarmed by the primitive violence that had erupted in her body, Shahzada surprised both herself and him in the process.

Habib again grasped her arms tightly and held her away from him. 'All right, I will tell you. I am going to talk with my father about Zarri Bano becoming a *Shahzadi Ibadat*, a Holy Woman. Are you satisfied now?' he snarled down into her face.

'*Shahzadi Ibadat*,' his wife echoed dully, her voice sunk to a whisper, moving away from him – his touch now scorching her. 'So you are going to sacrifice your beloved daughter?'

'Sacrifice?' he ejaculated, caught on the raw. 'How dare you say such a thing! My daughter will become a Holy Woman – the most pure, devout, scholarly, and revered by all.' As the words left his mouth, the better he felt.

'You are mad, Habib Sahib! How can you do this to your own daughter? I won't permit it! This is not the Emperor Akhbar's time. It is the twentieth century – it cannot happen.'

'It can and will happen! Do you think that you, a female, can prevent it? The scales are weighted against you, woman.'

'Habib, listen to me,' Shahzada appealed desperately. 'She is going to marry Sikander. She has just told you.' Shahzada felt as if she was walking in quicksand and the ground was fast disappearing beneath her feet.

'Oh no, she is not. I have decided! You had better tell her. I have lost a son, and I am not going to lose my inheritance to a complete stranger. I want you to support me in this. That is your duty as a wife. If you

don't do it, our ancient traditions will outweigh your opposition, so you had better get used to the idea. Remember what I said: I will divorce you on the spot if you rebel against us.'

Habib fixed his wife with a cruel stare. 'And stop talking nonsense about sacrifice. My beautiful Zarri Bano was destined for this fate. Her brother's death sealed her future as a *Shahzadi Ibadat*. This is what has always happened when only sons died in people of our class: the inheritance then was passed on to the next female member – you know that.'

'So you are going to wed your daughter to your fields and to her faith.' Tears of anguish rolled down Shahzada's face. 'It is *zulm*, cruelty of the worst kind. If you go through with it, I will never, never forgive you, Habib – never! You can divorce me! There will be nothing left between us. Remember this, you'll have made your daughter a Holy Woman, but you will have buried a wife too, at the same time.'

'I will not listen to any more of your foolish prattling. I am going to sleep in another room,' he blustered, storming out with heavy strides and banging the door behind him. His wife's words had upset him. He knew what she felt, for he had felt the same pain. Unlike her, however, he had no choice. He was alarmed by what Shahzada had said about not forgiving him but, 'she will change with time,' he told himself emphatically.

In his mind he recalled the vision of another *Shahzadi Ibadat* from his childhood. How fascinated he had been by that woman and the fame and reverence she had elicited from everyone. Wherever she went, '*Bibi, Bibi*,' had echoed reverently around her.

His Zarri Bano and her personal charisma would

surpass every *Shahzadi Ibadat* of all time. She was both beautiful and educated. She even had a post-graduate university degree. The more he thought about his daughter becoming a Holy Woman, the more convinced he became that it was the right decision. His wife was of a weaker sex, and was thus bound to see it in a shortsighted way.

'Does she not wish glory and honour for our daughter?' he addressed the stars above as he took a stroll around his estate. The light from the starlit sky beamed down on the acres of cultivated land. Habib's broad chest swelled with pride, as his eyes happily scanned the moonlit meadows of sugar cane and rape as they disappeared far beyond the horizon.

A sigh of utter self-satisfaction escaped his lips. Wealthiest of all land owners, nobody could rival his fortune or his influence. 'Yes! All this will be my Zarri Bano's, hers to inherit. She will be the sole mistress of all this after my death. As my beloved child, my princess, she deserves it all.'

His spirits soaring, he strolled back to his villa. His agile mind, however, was running ahead and rapidly making decisions. Tomorrow he would consult his father about Zarri Bano. On second thoughts, he wanted to talk to him straight away.

Siraj Din was still awake, unable to sleep. He missed both his village home and bed. He puffed heavily at the hookah pipe, making the water gurgle in its steel base – disgusted. Even the tobacco didn't taste the same here in town!

Habib found his father on a *charpoy*, on the rear veranda, watching the stars dance in the sky above. Siraj Din greeted his son and patted a place on the chair next to his portable bed.

'Father, I need to talk to you. It's about Zarri Bano and our inheritance,' he said quietly. Siraj Din forgot the tobacco and sat up straight in his bed to listen. There was a lot to be discussed.

Shahzada lay curled up on top of her bed, staring dejectedly into space. This was the darkest hour of her life. Horror at what her husband was about to do engulfed her for the hundredth time. 'How can they do that to my beloved child?' she cried. 'It is cruel and inhuman. Zarri Bano is made for love, for life, for bearing children. How can they seal her fate to a barren life, with only *ibadat*, worship – for comfort?'

The dark, suffocating silence of her room mocked her. It taunted her, revealed her impotence as a woman, as a mother and as a wife. Shackled to the centuries-old traditions and customs of her husband's clan, she could do nothing. Zarri Bano's fate was indeed sealed. There was to be no escape for her daughter.

By the time her husband returned to their room, Shahzada was still wide awake. He didn't come near her bed and she made no move to acknowledge his presence – a new phenomenon for them both. It was as if a thick wall had suddenly descended between them, sealing them away from each other like enemies. She didn't fear him any more. In fact, she feared nothing and no one. Not even her father-in-law. All she feared was the ordeal that awaited her daughter.

In the darkness, Shahzada's eyes shone with bitterness and hatred. She knew, with chilling precision, what she had to do. She would stand by her husband and endorse his decisions. She would, however, never forgive him or the barbaric traditions that made men like him enslave their women and force them into alien

roles. Men like him who forgot their humanity and bargained with the lives of their loved ones, for the sake of their precious parcels of land.

She wanted to rush out of her home and put a torch to the fields, reduce them all to ashes. She wept: 'Land represents fertility. For my family and daughter, it spells doom and sterility. To keep the land in the family, my daughter is destined to remain forever barren and childless, denied the joys of motherhood; her arms never to know the aching joys of holding a newborn child to her breast.'

Shahzada wondered sadly what her daughter was dreaming about at that moment. Did Sikander feature in those dreams? Did she sleep peacefully, unaware of the sentence which had just been passed on her and the noose waiting to be tied around her neck?

'I am a mother, but a traitor,' Shahzada sobbed into her pillow.

When she awoke early in the morning to the sound of the muezzin's call to prayer from the nearby mosque, Shahzada wept again. Her daughter who had led such a carefree, secular life would soon have her whole life pivoted around the prayer-mat. Totally devoted to *ibadat*.

Rising with slow, measured movements Shahzada went into the bathroom. After her ablutions, she offered her *fajr* prayers.

Habib had woken up, and watched her from his bed. He noted the length of time she had spent in saying her personal prayers – her *du'ah* to Allah. What had she prayed for? Was it for their daughter?

When Shahzada stood up, he was confronted with her vanquished, bereft face. Dark rings lined her eyes.

In one night she had aged. There was no condemnation, but no forgiveness either in those warm brown eyes.

'Have you been praying for us, Shahzada?' Habib asked, a hesitant timidity entering his voice for the first time in his life.

'I have prayed for all my family. For my dead son, may he rest in peace in *Jennat*. For you, and may Allah forgive you and us, for what we are about to do,' Shahzada replied with quiet dignity.

'Shahzada, there is nothing to forgive. Why do you persist in such talk?'

'I will not argue with you, Habib.'

He noted her deliberate omission of the respectful *Sahib* after his name. It saddened him, but he let it pass.

'What I'll say is this,' Shahzada continued. 'I will never forgive you, but I'll do my best to support you in everything, as it is my duty.'

'Thank you,' he responded with a sigh of relief, grateful for her support.

'Don't thank me,' Shahzada spat bitterly. 'I am just a puppet, a mere worthless woman to do your bidding. You and your father are the puppeteers, Habib. You hold my daughter's fate in your hands. What choice do I have? I can only swing and dangle along in whichever direction you pull and manoeuvre my strings. What can *I* do to save my daughter from the fate you have destined for her? People say it is their *kismet*, but it is bullies like you who carve other people's *kismet* for them and dictate their destiny – as you told me so gloatingly the other day. I am shackled to the chains of your male domination, your *ressmeh*, your traditions.'

'Don't talk nonsense!' He turned on her angrily, sitting up in his bed.

'There you go again. That is all you believe I do –

talk nonsense. As far as you are concerned, Allah has only blessed *you* with any commonsense.' She turned away from him and left the room. Habib remained sitting on his bed, bemused by her words.

'Oh Jafar, why did you have to die?' he cried out. 'It is because of your death that I am forced into doing this. I feel that the rift in our family will never heal. Your mother will never forgive me, and that will be so hard to bear.' He put his head in his hands and wept whole-heartedly.

Chapter 8

SHAHZADA WENT DOWN to the kitchen quarters of the house, to check if everything was in order for their guests' breakfasts. She prayed that Zarri Bano wasn't awake, for she could not face her yet. The task that loomed ahead of her was a mammoth one: to prepare her beloved daughter for her role as the Holy Woman.

Standing forlornly in the middle of her large, well-equipped modern kitchen, Shahzada tried to supervise the work of her three women cooks as they prepared *halwa puri*, *chana* curry, tea, pastries and *parathas*. Her mind in a total whirl, she hid her face a number of times in the folds of her head shawl, as tears kept gushing silently down her cheeks. Her housekeeper, Fatima, was the first to notice her crying.

'Shahzada Sahiba, please, you mustn't cry. We all loved our handsome Jafar. We have the rest of our lives to cry and mourn for him, so please stop,' Fatima urged, also now unable to stop herself from weeping. 'Please go and sit down in the other room, we can manage

here.' Brushing her eyes with the corner of her *chador*, Fatima led her mistress out of the kitchen.

They went into an adjoining room, and sat on the comfortable sofa together. Treating all her servants and subordinates as equals, and with innate kindness, Shahzada had built a special rapport with Fatima: she had been with them for over twenty years, and was therefore almost like another member of the family.

Although commonsense dictated that she mustn't do so, the urge to confide in and to share her anguish with Fatima wouldn't be denied. Otherwise, Shahzada felt she would go mad, hugging such a lethal bomb to her chest.

'Oh Fatima, Fatima!' Shahzada began in a broken voice. 'I thought I was the happiest woman alive. I have a beautiful home, a wonderful lifestyle and was, until my Jafar died, blessed with the most beautiful children that I could ever have imagined or dreamt of. I know all mothers are proud of their children. I tried not to be, but I was. How can I forget my handsome son? My lovely Ruby, and as for Zarri Bano . . . ' She choked on her tears.

'Please, Sahiba, you still have your Ruby and your Zarri Bano. Don't cry. You have every right to be a very proud mother. No one can compare with the beauty of our Zarri Bano, and she is still alive.'

'Do not talk about her beauty – for what use is it when it is hidden away, for no living man to admire, to love and to reproduce it?'

'What are you saying, Sahiba? What is the matter with Zarri Bano?' Fatima squeaked.

'She is doomed.' Shahzada looked directly at her friend and helper, her eyes shimmering with tears.

'I don't understand.' Fatima stared back at Shahzada

with fear etched across her plump face. 'Tell me, why is she doomed?' A believer in black magic, *Kala Jadoo*, Fatima was now very alarmed indeed. Had somebody used a *tweez*, an evil amulet, to ruin her pet's health? Fatima's mind became ablaze with all sorts of ideas and superstitions. 'It used to happen in the village, but surely not here in the town,' she whispered to her mistress.

'It is not black magic, Fatima. It is worse. She is going to become a *Shahzadi Ibadat*, a Holy Woman!'

Fatima stared back in horror at her mistress. 'Shahzada Sahiba, no!' she groaned, her voice low – almost a hiss. 'It cannot be true. Who said so?'

Shahzada watched Fatima's distress reliving her own reaction yesterday when Habib had first mentioned it to her. Hadn't she herself beaten her husband on his chest with her fists? And this, from an obedient, submissive wife who had never raised her voice at him before, let alone her fists! The unreality of it all washed over her. 'None of this is really happening! It has to be a nightmare,' she found herself gasping out the words.

She felt so old. The double loss of Jafar and now Zarri Bano had melted into her very bones.

She was the *chaudharani*, the queen of this clan. Yet in one single stroke, her husband had reduced her to the status of the lowest of the low. Even the fishmonger's wife had more autonomy and would have been able to battle against her husband's aggression for her children's sake. She, on the contrary, was tied to a gilded cage.

Even if her husband had weakened under her pleas, she couldn't fight single-handedly against the pressure of his male elders, especially his father. For who had ever heard of a daughter-in-law taking the law into her

own hands and defying their wishes? As a woman, she was of no consequence – her opinion counted for nothing. A law unto themselves, men's words were commands, and they were born to be obeyed. They possessed a successful knack of reasoning, and making everything sound so plausible. In the face of their thinly disguised tyranny one could never hope to win or to challenge them. They were always steps ahead of you and very adept at that.

Zarri Bano had no chance, crushed against this wall of patriarchal tyranny. Even with her youth, feminism, and a university education, and with an outgoing and assertive personality on her side, she was still fated to be the loser in this game of male power-play.

Like her mother, it had been drilled into her from infancy to both respect and pay homage to her father's wishes and those of the male elders. To veto any of their decisions was seen as the height of insolence and a sign of moral and social disorder, a form of rebellion which the elders deemed it imperative to crush immediately and in such a manner that it would never rear its ugly head again.

On the other hand, for Shahzada to help her daughter escape from her *destined* role was also unthinkable. For where and what would Zarri Bano escape *to*? The strength of her clan, like any other's, depended on their *izzat* – their family honour. For Zarri Bano to abandon her home would bring their *izzat* crumbling down on everyone's head. Nobody would be able to recover from the shock, the *baesti*, the loss of face.

For her daughter to marry before the Holy Woman ceremony was also out of the question. The marriage would give rise to a great scandal, especially if it wasn't sanctioned by her father and grandfather, and in the

light of her brother's recent death. They were to be mourning Jafar for three months.

In short there was no escape for her beloved daughter! Zarri Bano too, was going to be tied to a gilded cage, but she would be inside it. For unlike her mother, she could never marry, have children, enjoy the company of a husband, or lead a carefree normal life like any other woman. Her only role and duty was that of *Ibadat*, religious worship.

'Fatima, I wish I was a fishmonger's wife.' Now she spoke her thoughts aloud. 'For then I could protect my daughter's interests. Here I am a *chaudharani*, but I don't even have enough power in my little finger, to save my daughter from the fate that is awaiting her.'

'Please, Sahiba, don't cry. Of course it will not come to that. It cannot happen to our Zarri Bano. It is both insane and cruel. How can a beautiful woman, ripe for marriage and children, be denied the role for which we, like all women all over the world, are destined? That is what Allah created us for.'

'It can be, and it is going to be, Fatima. I tell you that I am powerless to prevent the tide of events which will likely take place in the next few days.' Shahzada looked at Fatima with eyes full of misery. 'You people of the lower caste envy us our wealth, but at this moment I would give anything to swap lives with you, or a woman living in a mud-baked hut. Fatima, my daughter's hands will never be painted with red henna wedding patterns.' She sobbed as if her heart would break.

Fatima's mouth remained open as the full implication of what her *chaudharani* had said sunk into her mind. It couldn't be! Her hands began to rub against each other of their own accord, signalling her inner distress.

Squatting on the floor, she laid her head against her mistress's lap and began to weep. Having brought her up since she was seven years old, she loved Zarri Bano like a mother would. She had fed her, bathed her and dressed her. Over the years, she had loved listening to her chatter, her sarcastic remarks, and had peeped at all of her suitors for her benefit and described them to her, prior to her meeting them. In her heart, like Zarri Bano's father, Fatima was never satisfied with any of them. She always thought her Zarri Bano was too good for those men. It was only Sikander who had passed the test. And only because she had glimpsed a light and a wistful expression in Zarri Bano's eyes that Fatima had never seen there for any other man. The housekeeper's heart had swelled with pride and joy, knowing that, at last, Zarri Bano had met her match. A man she could both respect and love.

Now this. 'It just cannot be!' She wanted to run and beat her head against the wall in Chaudhury Habib's presence, bring him to his senses!

They remained huddled together, locked in their personal grief for long silent minutes. It was only when the cook, Naimat Bibi, came to ask whether they should set the dining tables for breakfast, that Shahzada stood up with a heavy heart. Life had to go on. Personal crises had to be swept aside in deference to daily routines and appearances.

An hour later, most of the guests, dressed and washed, had come down to the large dining room. They sat in groups and while they ate, they talked and passed the food round the tables. When Habib came in, he sat alone on a sofa, not at any of the four large dining tables, and chewed a cake rusk with his tea. He was

deep in thought as Shahzada looked at him, while hovering around the tables, making sure that all their guests were well served. Even with her personal grief tucked deep inside her heart, she kept a keen eye on everything, checking that the china was spotlessly clean, and that napkins were widely available.

Ruby and Zarri Bano entered the dining room. Looking round and smiling warmly at everybody, they sat down together at a table with two vacant seats. Everybody stopped eating, feeling sorry for them – poor sisters who had lost a beloved brother.

Habib and Shahzada exchanged a nervous glance across the room as their eyes rested on Zarri Bano's bare head. In the presence of her relatives, Zarri Bano had never made any effort at covering her head.

Ten minutes later Sikander and his mother Bilkis came into the dining room. Zarri Bano had her back to him, but she happened to look up from her cup at her father at that moment, and the wary look on his face alerted Zarri Bano to Sikander's presence. On seeing him, her mouth curved into a warm smile – her eyes shone with pleasure. Sikander smiled back, his eyes caressing her face; he did not care who witnessed it.

The dried rusk in Habib's hand snapped loudly, shattering the moment. Sikander politely moved away, leading his mother to the other end of the room to another dining table. Zarri Bano followed his movement with wistful eyes. She turned to her father and noticed his tense expression and the nervous movements he was making with his hands. A dread feeling tugged at her mind, as she recalled once again her mother's words.

As if testing, her eyes sought Sikander's. Again she

found her father's gaze intercepting theirs. She felt guilty, as if she had been caught doing something wrong. 'It isn't a crime to make eye-contact with the man I am going to marry!' she wanted to shout at Habib. She looked at her mother for an explanation, but Shahzada avoided her in a pretence of handing a napkin to one of the guests.

Reluctantly, Zarri Bano raised the muslin shawl over her head and then deliberately stared at her father. She didn't smile at him this time, he noted. There was something else in her eyes and expression now.

Has the penny dropped? Has she realised? he thought wildly. He quailed at the thought of what the future held for them, wondering if his precious Zarri Bano would ever smile at him again. Already he could sense her antagonism seeping out of every pore of her being, from across the room.

Chapter 9

'YOU ARE TO become a Holy Woman, Zarri Bano!' Habib imperiously informed his daughter.

It was now two weeks since the incident in the dining room. In all that time, father and daughter had said very little to each other, systematically avoiding the other's company.

Sikander and his mother had left to return home. He was due to go to Singapore on business. Sikander and Zarri Bano didn't have a chance to speak privately, nor for that matter had his mother been able to say anything to Zarri Bano's mother. Shahzada was never quite available to have a private *tête- á-tête*. Thus both mother

and son had left without sorting out anything about Sikander's engagement to Zarri Bano.

Zarri Bano had noted her father's almost antagonistic attitude towards Sikander. It just didn't make sense: once her father had begged her to marry someone, but now he appeared to be giving his future son-in-law the cold shoulder treatment.

Most of the guests and visitors had departed. Only very close members of the clan remained behind, for the fortieth-day special prayer ceremony *chaleesema*, for Jafar.

Like cowards, Shahzada and Fatima had opted for silence, and kept away from Zarri Bano. Guiltily, they guarded the evil secret, waiting fearfully for Habib to break it to her. And then for the world to explode around them.

In the end, it had taken Habib two weeks to summon his daughter to see him. Now, standing in front of him, he could tell that her tall body was like a coiled spring. She had refused to sit down. Standing up, Habib cleared his dry throat. Never before had he found it so hard to speak to his beloved 'star'. Once they had never stopped talking to one another. Since Jafar's death, an ocean seemed to have sprung up between them.

'I think Zarri Bano, my daughter, it is time we had a talk about your future,' he said heavily, and began to pace around the room.

'You mean my marriage,' she ventured boldly, causing her father to flinch. She wasn't going to make it easy for him.

'No,' he said coldly, then decided to grasp the nettle. This was no time for dilly-dallying. 'Not your marriage. Your *future*, Zarri Bano.' He paused. Then: 'There will be no marriage for you, my daughter. Instead, there will be a ceremony of a different kind. We have

decided that you should become a Holy Woman, a *Shahzadi Ibadat*.'

Zarri Bano stared blankly at her father. What was he saying? Surely he couldn't mean it!

'Why?' she whispered. 'I don't want to be a Holy Woman, Father. But you don't mean it, do you? It is a joke – and a terrible joke at that.' She looked at him reproachfully.

'No, my dear daughter, it is no joke. I have never been so serious in my life.' The ruthless, clinical voice speared through her. 'You know very well about our tradition, about the male heir dying and the eldest daughter becoming a *Shahzadi Ibadat*. I have no choice. You must try to understand.'

'No choice? I don't believe you. There is no way I will become a Holy Woman, Father,' she warned him. 'I know what it entails and I am not cut out for that role. As you know I have hardly ever covered my head properly. I know very little about religion. I am very much a worldly woman. I *cannot* become a nun!'

'You will grow into the role soon enough,' Habib said implacably.

'This is madness. Father, you cannot be serious,' she said steadily. 'I have accepted Sikander Sahib's marriage proposal. You yourself blessed and encouraged the match. I have decided to marry him. I *want* to marry him!' She was ashamed of the appeal in her voice and the colour that she knew had rushed into her cheeks.

'The situation has now changed,' came that same implacable voice. 'We have lost your brother. There will be no marriage ceremony for you. I will not grant permission for you to marry this man or any other man, Zarri Bano. *Ever*.'

'Father, no!' Zarri Bano stepped away from her father as if he was the devil.

Habib watched the fleeting expressions of disbelief, horror and anger chase over his daughter's face. He saw her struggle with herself, trying to make sense of his words. Then as the reality of the situation hit her, her face turned deathly white and she stumbled out of the room.

Once in the corridor, she didn't know which way to turn. A continuous ringing noise roared in her ears and her eyes were blurred with tears. Somehow, she found her bedroom door and, fumbling with the handle, she thrust it open and staggered inside. Her legs gave way and she slid onto the floor in a heap.

This weakness was followed by a merciful blackness. Blissfully unconscious, Zarri Bano lost all sense of time and space. On the wall clock, the seconds and minutes ticked away, while Zarri Bano lay on the cold marble floor and her father paced up and down in his room.

Chapter 10

AN HOUR LATER Shahzada joined her husband. She found him standing near their bedroom window, as usual gazing down into the courtyard at the flowers in full bloom. She noticed the dejected angle of his head. Without further ado, he obeyed the urge to tell her what he had done. 'I have spoken to her, Shahzada.'

The tray of food in his wife's hands shook and she placed it on the dressing table.

'Wh-Where is she?' she stammered, her eyes swelling with tears.

'I don't know.' He turned to stare out of the window again. 'She left some time ago,' he said flatly.

Shahzada walked quietly out of their room. Blindly, she made her way across to Zarri Bano's room. The door wouldn't open: something was blocking it. Pushing it further ajar, Shahzada squeezed her head in.

In the semi-darkness of the room Shahzada saw her daughter lying in a heap on the floor, her eyes open but staring blankly into space. Choking back a scream, Shahzada stepped inside the room. At the back of her mind she still remembered that there were a lot of guests in her home and most were prone to eavesdrop.

Squatting down on the marble floor, Shahzada raised her daughter's head in her arms. Cradling it, she began to rock her gently to and fro. Rivulets of tears trickled down her cheeks.

'Zarri Bano, speak to me, my child. Are you hurt? Why are you lying on the floor?'

Heaving her daughter up by the shoulders, Shahzada dragged her across the cold floor and managed to lift her onto the bed in the centre of the room. 'Ruby! Ruby!' she called out to her younger daughter, down the corridor.

'What's wrong?' Ruby asked, as she came running out of her room. Shahzada didn't answer but gestured her into Zarri Bano's room and switched on the bedside lamp.

'What's the matter with Zarri Bano, Mother? Why is she staring like that?' Ruby asked in concern.

'Go and fetch a glass of water for your sister, she is not well,' Shahzada told her. 'I think she has fainted.'

There was no reaction from Zarri Bano as her mother moved around the bed and cradled her head in her lap once again. The girl's eyes remained open but they

didn't focus on her mother's face. She drank the water held up to her lips by a solicitous Ruby, but said nothing.

'Shall I call Father?' Ruby asked, panicking. She had never seen her sister like this. It was too frightening, on top of her brother's death.

'No, Ruby,' said Shahzada slowly. 'It is your father who has done this.'

'What do you mean?' Ruby didn't understand.

'Your father has just told Zarri Bano that she is to become a *Shahzadi Ibadat*,' Shahzada whispered. A quiet stillness cloaked the room.

'Oh my God!' Ruby gasped. 'Mother, it cannot be true. Zarri Bano is engaged to be married.'

'No. There will be no marriage for my beautiful daughter,' Shahzada said tiredly.

Her faraway voice frightened Ruby more than hysterics would have done. 'But Mother, listen to me! Who says that she has to become a *Shahzadi Ibadat*?' she asked, pulling sharply at her mother's arm.

'It has been decided by your father and grandfather.' Shahzada recalled the occasion when she was summoned to see Siraj Din, and was informed that Zarri Bano was to become a *Bibi* – the Holy Woman. And that she, as her mother, was expected to prepare her for that role. 'Don't turn against us in this, Shahzada,' Siraj Din had warned her in his quiet, semi-menacing tone.

'I will not let this happen!' Ruby shuddered. 'Mother, this is insane. How can Father do this – hide my gorgeous sister behind a black veil?' She recoiled at the images in her mind. 'Oh my God. To have my sister enveloped in a *burqa*, covering her from head to toe. Surely it cannot be? I will see my father! He cannot do

this or let it happen.' She turned to leave but her mother caught hold of her arm and pulled her back.

'No, stop, Ruby! I have tried to persuade him, but it is no use. How can you succeed where I have failed? From this fate our Zarri Bano can never escape.' Ruby watched her mother with horror dawning on her face by the second. 'He has his traditions, his father and all his male relatives to support him,' Shahzada continued fiercely.

'But Mother, why are they doing this?' Ruby was now trembling with fear and rage.

'Don't you understand?' Shahzada's voice dripped with sarcasm. 'Don't you yet know that your sister is to be tied to these rotten fields of sugar cane around our property?' At this Shahzada broke down.

'Are you saying that my sister is to be wedded to our *zemin* – she is not allowed to get married, *ever*?' Ruby gasped. 'But Zarri Bano doesn't need our wealth. Sikander can provide well for her.'

'Ruby, my darling Ruby, listen to me. Zarri Bano is your father's heiress. She cannot escape from that role, or from her inheritance. The two are forever entwined. It is only by taking on the role of Holy Woman that she can become the legitimate heiress . . .' Shahzada stopped, staring wide-eyed at the open door, as Habib's shadow fell across the floor.

He read the scene in one glance. Ruby's accusing glare; her mouth half open ready to shout at him, his wife's restraining pinch on her arm from behind, stopping her. Ruby then turned and glared at her mother, Shahzada signalling with her eyes to calm down. 'So Ruby knows as well.' Habib came heavily into the room. A tall, stiff figure, he stood by the bed and looked down at his eldest daughter, lying motionless

before him. He felt low. A novel experience, for him to be so estranged from his family.

'Please, Shahzada and Ruby, will you leave? I wish to be alone with Zarri Bano,' he requested. Shahzada made no move to leave.

'Please do as I say!' he ordered. 'I am her father. I love her too. Don't treat me like a leper. Do not usurp or undermine my authority.'

The iron timbre of his voice immediately prompted Shahzada into laying her daughter's head back on the pillow and pulling an angry Ruby out of the room behind her. Only years of filial duty and respect for parents and elders had prevented Ruby from shouting back at her father and venting her rage openly on him.

Habib watched them leave. Sighing, he turned to look down at his daughter. Zarri Bano was still staring into space. Bending down, he lifted her head and cradled it in the crook of his arm. Almost squatting on the cold marble floor, Habib gently turned Zarri Bano's face towards him. Smoothing away the curly wisps of hair from behind her ears, he whispered, 'Look at me, my beloved daughter. Do not shut me out!'

At his firm, quiet tone Zarri Bano's eyes lifted to his face.

'Thank you, my beautiful princess.' He caressed her cheek the way he used to when she was a little girl, and used to fall asleep in his lap. Once she was grown up, propriety dictated that they just talked, or at the most he kissed the top of her head. What he had always wanted to do was to caress her beautiful dimpled cheek, especially when she laughed and smiled teasingly at him. Today he wanted to communicate with her pain, on a level which did away with propriety.

Zarri Bano continued to look at him. All of a sudden

everything came jolting back like a black cloud and she hid her face from him.

Habib stood up, letting his arms fall to his side. No matter how he tried to pretend to himself, the rejection hurt.

'Forgive me, Zarri Bano, but it won't be that bad,' he told her. 'I have no choice . . .'

Zarri Bano stared at her father in horror. Habib saw the look of a trapped animal in her eyes.

'Of course you have a choice!' she told him. 'Every human being has a choice! There is nothing in the world that is bound for ever. What you really mean is that you don't have the choice of whether to give your daughter acres of land or nothing at all. I don't want your fields, Father! And I don't want to be your Holy Woman, your *Shahzadi Ibadat*.' She paused, scanning his face closely for signs of having penetrated his core of human decency.

The implacable expression, the cold, distant eyes only spelt one message to Zarri Bano. She was merely clutching at straws. Her voice sinking in appeal, she burst out anew, 'I want to be a normal woman, Father, and live a normal life! I want to get married. I am not a very religious person, as you know. I am a twentieth-century, modern, educated woman. I am not living in the Mughal period – a pawn in a game of male chess. Don't you see, Father, I have hardly ever prayed in my life, nor opened the Holy Quran on a regular basis. How can I thus become a Holy Woman? I am not suited to that role. Father, I want—'

'What you are trying to say is that you want a man in your life,' he sneered, cutting her short.

Her cheeks crimson with shame and shock, Zarri Bano stared mutely at her father. Then her gaze fell as

embarrassment and a torrent of boiling rage assaulted her body. For the first time in her life, she hated her father as she never thought possible. The sexual connotations to his words had shaken her to the core.

'I didn't say that I wanted a man!' She spoke so quietly now that he almost couldn't hear her. 'I just want to be normal and lead a normal life, like any other woman.'

'If you don't want . . .' Habib stopped. One didn't talk to one's daughter in this vein or manner. 'If you don't want the company of a man,' he amended, 'or desire it, then why are you so against becoming a *Shahzadi Ibadat*? As a normal woman, as a wife, you will be tied to one man. That life in no way can compare to the *izzat*, the honour and the fame that your new role will bring to you and your family.'

'The glory? The *izzat*? The fame? I don't want any of those, Father. Don't you understand? Please leave me alone!' Zarri Bano shouted. 'Am I banging my head against a brick wall?'

Habib stood up and crossed to the door. There he stopped and turned, and with a sinking heart, Zarri Bano read the cold, determined glint in his eyes.

'You can shout as much as you like, my proud, beloved daughter, but you will do as I say – I know you will. We are two of a kind. You will never let me down, I know, nor our traditions, nor your grandfather. If you cannot abide by my decision, at least think of your grandfather.' He saw her eyes, shimmering with tears like huge emeralds in her face, but today they had no impact.

Zarri Bano was hit by the first panic attack of her life. Sheer terror engulfed her: her mouth was dry, her breathing laboured.

Her father had set a trap and had captured her neatly, using sexuality as ammunition. The words thundered through her head: *'what you want is a man.'* Zarri Bano physically recoiled, holding her arms against her chest as she recalled her own feelings for Sikander. Yes, she desired him, but her father had cheapened and degraded marriage and what it stood for, insulting both her and the essence of her womanhood, by his underlying insinuation that what she *really* craved was a man's presence in her life.

Still wrestling with the terrifying sensation of being at the bottom of a dark pit, Zarri Bano recognised bitterly that her father had won. For she could never let him or the world know that she wanted and desired Sikander. It was an impossible situation. And there was no way out for her.

Minutes lapsed into hours. The clock remorselessly ticked away in the night. Nobody came to her room. Thoughts fled and dashed through her mind as she gazed up at the high whitewashed ceiling.

'I cannot let him or my family down,' she sobbed. 'He has won! He has psychologically managed to blackmail me.'

She definitely couldn't look at Sikander ever again. Her father had spoiled it all, tarnishing something so natural, so beautiful, and making it into something sordid. Even mothers didn't allude to such matters with their daughters, let alone a father. Again Zarri Bano's cheeks smarted with the heat of shame. Hate for her father burst out anew and inflamed her whole body.

She got off the bed and went to stand in front of the mirror. She stared bleakly at herself. She knew what she had to do.

*

When Shahzada entered a little later, Zarri Bano was in full control of herself. Her hair, combed and swept away from her face, was tied into a simple knot at the back of her neck. There was a certain calmness in her expression that Shahzada hadn't glimpsed for days. Shahzada smiled tentatively.

'Are you all right, my daughter?' Zarri Bano was sitting on the sofa with a book in her hand. Then she stood up. Shahzada's sad eyes took in her daughter's tall, proud figure.

'Yes, Mother. Today I have grown up. I am not only your daughter or my father's daughter, I am me! But you and Father have brutally stripped me of my identity as a normal woman and instead reduced me to a role of a puppet. I am, he said, to do his bidding. And so I shall.' The bitterness pierced her mother's heart. 'I never knew my father could do this to me. I used to feel sorry for other women, whose menfolk were tyrants. Little did I guess that I was being brought up in the lap of male tyrants myself. My father made me believe that he would "sell the world for me" when in fact he eventually decided to "sell" me to his male whim and ancient traditions. What can I do alone, Mother? You have all jailed and numbed me into a commitment, which I will have to go along with – but not willingly, Mother. Never willingly. At this moment in time, I feel nothing but burning hatred for Father. Only time will tell whether he will ever have his old Zarri Bano back.'

Zarri Bano held Shahzada's gaze steadfastly, noting her surprised expression. 'Here I stand before you, Mother, my father's *Shahzadi Ibadat*.' She spread her hands in a flourish. 'The Holy Woman. The woman he created by killing me. Did you not know that men are the true creators in our culture, Mother? They mould

our lives and destinies according to their whims and desires. The irony of all ironies, for which I can never forgive myself, is that it has happened to me – a feminist, a defender of women's rights. I have been living in a glass house of make-believe, Mother. Your Sleeping Beauty has been rudely awakened to taste the true world of patriarchal tyranny. Don't look so sad, I absolve you of any guilt. I know you can't help me. I do not hold you responsible for anything.'

Shahzada had listened, her hand held up to her mouth, wanting to say so much but unable to offer anything – only tears and guilt-ridden silence. Zarri Bano stepped forward and pulled her mother gently into her arms.

Dry-eyed, she remained thus for a long time. Nothing mattered any more. Despondency had numbed both her mind and her body. Quietly and with a dignity that only Zarri Bano possessed and could summon to her aid, she whispered in her mother's ear: 'Tell Father he can start the preparation for my wedding to the Holy Quran.'

Chapter 11

THE VILLAGE OF Chiragpur was larger than most other neighbouring villages, but it had the same features: a mosque and two schools, one for the boys and one for the girls. With its conspicuous mosaiced green dome and a tall white minaret, the mosque was strategically built at the centre of the village, fronted by a baker, a butcher, a potter's and other shops. The schools, by contrast, were built on the outskirts of the

village, amidst fertile green fields of vegetables, wheat and sugar cane. The entire village was neatly criss-crossed into eight lanes, with rows of houses of all shapes, sizes and façades.

The *hawaili*, the large house belonging to Habib Khan's father, Siraj Din, the feudal landlord, was located near the mosque and thus enjoyed the most central position in the village. With its ample grounds and a very large square-shaped courtyard, it took up one quarter of the land occupied by the whole village. Siraj Din's family had ruled over Chiragpur for decades, even before the influx of Muslim refugees from India after Partition.

On this particular day, the sun shone brightly in the clear, blue summer sky and over the fields; an air of tranquillity blanketed the entire village. Farmer Faisal was ploughing the land with his new tractor. The twenty-four hour 'chug-chug' sound of the flour mill as it tirelessly ground wheat into flour could be heard distinctly all day and well into the night – a sound that the villagers would be lost without. The women were busy in their homes or out in the fields, and most of the children were at school.

Fatima's eldest daughter, Firdaus, was taking her morning break on the veranda outside her office, when the school clerk came and gave her a message: Fatima had phoned to let her daughter know that she was returning to the village later that afternoon.

After a few minutes, Madam Sadaf, the headmistress of the girls' school, joined Firdaus on the veranda. They had an urgent matter to discuss. 'So your mother is coming back for good, my dear?' The headmistress looked enquiringly at her twenty-six-year-old deputy and protégée.

'I don't know, madam, probably just for a few days. The family she is supporting is quite dependent on her, especially now that their son Jafar was killed in a riding accident and their eldest daughter, Zarri Bano, is likely to get married. Madam Sadaf, you must have seen her!' Firdaus said enthusiastically. 'She came to spend *Eid* with her grandfather here in the village. She is simply gorgeous. So tall, so slender, her skin is like ripe peaches, her hair is all glossy curls and her eyes like emeralds – *and* she's so well educated. My mother never tires talking about her. When we were young we used to be jealous of her and accused our mother of loving her more than us, her own daughters.' Firdaus chuckled at the memory. 'That was a long time ago. These days, when Zarri Bano comes to visit her grandfather Siraj Din, we cannot wait to call on her. She would make a wonderful principal of a college. I can just see her students spellbound by her personality and looks. Mother is delighted that, at last, she has met someone whom she is really interested in marrying.'

'So you'll probably be going to the wedding?' Madam asked before she was interrupted by the ringing of the telephone in her office. She stood up to answer it. 'Excuse me, Firdaus, I'll be back.'

Firdaus looked down at the document in her hand. Her eyes quickly skimmed over the paper, which was giving them notice of an impending government inspection. At the sound of a horse's hooves, she raised her head and looked in the direction of the concrete wall surrounding the school's large courtyard. Above it appeared the upper torso of a man, apparently sitting on a horse.

It was Khawar, looking directly at her. As he caught her eye, he smiled, giving his handsome features a

rakish look. Firdaus quickly glanced back down at the papers, embarrassed both by his look and his presence. When she next glanced up, he was moving on, but his eyes remained on her face. Suddenly he lifted his hand and saluted her.

Firdaus was alarmed by this brazen act of flirtation. Since that incident in the village cauliflower field a few weeks ago, Khawar had become overtly familiar in his manner towards her. Anger swept over her. Just because he had helped her up, it didn't mean that her reputation had to be compromised. What if somebody had seen him salute her just now? Tongues could begin to wag! A hot little titbit of village gossip could escalate to a volcano. She was soon to become headmistress, when Madam retired in the summer, therefore really couldn't afford any hint of scandal to tarnish her reputation.

What would happen when she took over here? Firdaus mused. Would she stay on in the village, or would she eventually move to the city and carve herself a career there? Of course, it all depended on who she married. Firdaus sighed to herself.

Marriage was, at the moment, a major issue for Firdaus and for her family. Her mother had lost no time in enlisting the aid of three matchmakers to find a suitable partner for Firdaus. 'As my daughter is so well-qualified and educated, as well as being quite attractive, only the best will do for her. I am not going to saddle her with any run-of-the-mill fellow,' Fatima had smugly boasted. The trouble was, as she delighted in lamenting to everyone: 'There are hardly *any* suitable eligible men in the village, who are near enough compatible with my daughter's qualifications and status in life.'

At the end of the day, as the future Headmistress of a

large secondary school for girls, her Firdaus couldn't marry just *anybody*. The only man who Fatima thought was suitable was Khawar – and he was suitable in every way – well-educated, good-looking and from a rich land-owning family. An added bonus would be that, married to Khawar, Firdaus would remain forever firmly ensconced in the village and she could be the Headmistress for life.

Now that, in Fatima's mind, was truly an ideal match!

The problem was: Khawar's mother. For Kaniz had let the whole world know that she would never *ever* contemplate such a match for her son – 'a match with a washerwoman's daughter!' It was a blemish that even Firdaus's status as a Deputy Headmistress couldn't delete at any cost.

Firdaus wished, with all her heart, that her mother would give up her demeaning, menial job. She had no need to work. Why did she do it? It was a disgrace for a Deputy Headmistress's mother to work as a servant in someone else's household. If she returned home on a permanent basis they could all live like an ordinary family. Her mother could look after her bedridden husband, rather than leave him in the care of her daughters, who had their own lives to lead anyway.

Today she was definitely going to have a serious talk with her mother, Firdaus promised herself. Fatima kept paying out good money to matchmakers for suitable *rishtas*, yet she persisted in creating an obvious obstacle to a good match by remaining in her present job. Khawar's mother would continue to look down her long arrogant nose at them, while her mother still worked 'washing dishes', as Chaudharani Kaniz so offensively termed it.

Firdaus had known for the past three years that Khawar had eyes only for her and was interested in pursuing a relationship that surpassed that of the sisterly feelings all men in the village were supposed and expected to harbour as a decent act towards the women. The elder women were *aunties*, and the younger women were supposed to be *sisters*.

Firdaus and Khawar hadn't had a chance to explore each other's feelings, or even to make them known to one another. They only met in the company of other people – or sometimes, by chance, in the village lanes. On these occasions, as befitted social decorum, they maintained their silent distance. She always, nevertheless, felt his eyes on her whenever she passed. In the last few days he had begun to ride his horse on the path going in the direction of the school, and passed the high wall, just at the time when Firdaus had her break and drank her tea on the veranda.

Firdaus wasn't sure exactly why he singled her out. His mother was apparently still chasing after Habib Khan's daughters. Also, there were other fairly attractive village women. One or two of these young women would be well tolerated by his mother, if not applauded.

Khawar's family ranked second in the village hierarchy after Siraj Din's. They had some land to their name, a large house and two comfortable places of residence in the nearest town. As the only son and heir, Khawar had taken over the responsibility of running the family business, which consisted of leasing out acres of fertile land to the village tenants.

Like Baba Siraj Din, in whose footsteps Khawar was eagerly following and liked to follow, he had in the last year or so begun to play a prominent role in the village

management committee, overseeing and governing the school. Firdaus normally kept away from the meetings, letting the elder Headmistress chair them. Khawar had specifically requested for Madam's replacement to be recruited from the village.

'If we have a woman from the village,' he had asserted at one meeting, 'she will be more likely to be committed to both the school and the pupils; she will have a similar commitment to try to instil in them the ethos of village life and etiquette, because she will be like us. Therefore we can safely leave our children in her capable hands, for she will share our fears and interests. Also, she could be consulted at any time by the parents because she would be residing in the village.

'In short, I believe we will gain greater dividend by having somebody from the village, rather than from town. You can never retain urban people for long here. They have a different lifestyle and way of going about things, and they always seem to hanker after that. They have no sense of allegiance to us or village life at large; nor can we expect them to. Also, I have learnt from my experience that they tend to have a condescending attitude towards us anyway. As if we people who live in the country are nothing but bumpkins.'

He finally ended, letting his eyes move over the other six male members of the committee and Madam Sadaf. He had spoken passionately and he thus wanted the right response from them.

'I see,' said Siraj Din. 'How many candidates will be applying from the village for this job?' As a founding member of the school he too, like Khawar, took a keen interest in the issue of Madam's replacement. He had originally helped to set up the school, with the assistance of his two sons. Sharing some of Khawar's ideas he

too, wanted to keep the village ethos as pure and rural as possible. He wanted no 'flighty' miss from the city to corrupt impressionable young girls in her care. The influence of the Headteacher was a very strong one. The matter thus merited a great deal of thought. Ideally, he would have wanted his granddaughter, Zarri Bano, to head the school – but he knew that she loved city life too much to come and stay here. She would be smothered by the tranquillity of village life.

'Apart from Firdaus, there is no one else, is there?' Siraj Din continued. 'She is a very young woman and, as yet, unmarried. Then we are back at square one . . . '

'Why is that, Uncle Siraj Din?' Khawar asked quickly. 'Women can still work after they are married.'

'Of course they can. I didn't mean that. I only meant that she is bound to leave the village soon,' Siraj Din explained. 'Her mother has been on the lookout for a good *rishta* for Firdaus for the past three years. There is no one in the village who appeals to Fatima's taste. Unless, of course . . . ' He raised his eyes meaningfully towards Khawar but then quickly dismissed the thought, knowing full well that Kaniz wouldn't even stoop to listen to the suggestion, let alone allow it to happen. She had been badgering him to act as a go-between for the last three years for Zarri Bano's hand in marriage.

Khawar knew what Siraj Din had alluded to.

Firdaus also knew as she listened sitting behind the curtain at her desk; the window was open and she had heard everything. She flushed indignantly. Did the old man mean that Khawar should marry her so that she could remain in the village? What a cheek! Did her opinion not matter at all? She had no desire to link herself with Khawar or have anything to do with his

snobbish and bitchy mother. She would marry some-
body suitable, but would also remain in the village.
Her husband would definitely not be Khawar! *She* was
the good catch, not that conceited fellow!

Chapter 12

FATIMA RETURNED TO the village, laden with boxes
of goods and with much pomp and ceremony, in Habib
Khan's black Audi car. There were groceries, clothes,
and other items that could only be purchased in the
town's boutiques, including presents for her three
daughters. Shahzada had personally helped Fatima to
pack everything and then later had waved her off.

'We will miss you, Fatima. But please stay at home
for at least a week – you owe it to your family. Try to
sort out Firdaus's *rishta* this time. If you need me I will
come and help you find an eligible young man for your
most eligible of daughters!'

Fatima had simply beamed with pleasure at her mis-
tress's words. She was a good, kind and generous
employer. 'Thank you, Chaudharani Sahiba!' she called
from the car window.

Driving through the open cobbled streets of her
home village, Fatima saw some of her friends and her
heart swelled with pride as she watched them staring
curiously at the shiny black car, and begin to follow it.

The car stopped first outside Baba Siraj Din's house.
Fatima always followed the ritual of greeting him
and calling on him first, whenever she returned to
the village. As the *buzurg*, the village elder, he also
enjoyed the position of the highest-ranking inhabitant.

Siraj Din, however, wasn't at home this morning. She was informed by his manservant that he was out in the fields, taking a walk.

Fatima dutifully climbed back into the car and headed for Kaniz's territory, the other section of the village. Delighting in driving past Khawar's family home, she prayed that the almighty Chaudharani Kaniz would be looking out from her high chamber balcony of her room on the second floor.

Peering out of the car window, Fatima stealthily glanced up at the shuttered window of Kaniz's room. When she saw a woman's face appear Fatima decided to get out. She imperiously ordered Ali to stop. Her loud voice was intended to be heard, not only by those people in the street, but also by those listening from behind the scenes. 'Ali! Please take all of my parcels to my home,' she said grandly. There are ten of them. I will just visit my friend Rani, before I go home. Afterwards, my daughters will not let me step out of the house,' she ended with a laugh.

Swishing her new black cashmere *chador* over her shoulders, Fatima entered the house directly opposite Kaniz's home, her cheeks plumped out with laughter. Fatima was enjoying herself immensely. She was ninety-nine per cent sure that Kaniz was still watching her, for she could almost feel her sharp, eagle eyes boring warm holes into her back.

The lady in question swept away from the window and banged it shut, causing the wooden shutters to rattle on their hinges. She knew full well she had played directly into Fatima's hands by looking out. 'What is the world coming to?' Kaniz snorted in disgust. 'A washerwoman barking orders to another servant, and riding in an Audi car! How vulgar she sounded.

"Ten parcels",' she mimicked. As if it mattered to any-
one here how many bars of Lux soap and Colgate tooth-
paste she had brought from the city for her daughters.
'The parcels probably contain cast-off clothes from
Chaudharani Shahzada's daughters anyway,' Kaniz
sniffed bitchily to herself.

'Mother and daughter are different in personality,
yet they share one distinct trait: they are both proud
beyond their status,' Kaniz decided. Firdaus, however,
was a lot worse than her mother. Just because she had
managed to get herself educated and taught in a school,
there now appeared to be no end to her airs and graces –
the self-important young madam! She expected the
whole village to pay homage to her as if she, and not
Kaniz, was a *chaudharani*!

Kaniz's worst secret fear and ultimate nightmare,
which sent cold shudders crawling through her body,
was that Firdaus would somehow end up trapping her
beloved son into marriage. She had distinctly heard
through the village grapevine that Firdaus had said
there was no one suitable for her here – the sly, double-
dealing little witch! In Kaniz's opinion, Firdaus had
had her eyes on Khawar ever since she was a twelve-year
old, peering down doe-eyed at him from the rooftop of
her home.

'What do they take me for? Do they really think I
am stupid enough to allow a washerwoman's daughter
to be foisted onto my only son, the heir to acres of land?
Never!'

Fatima could gather all the parcels in the world, ride
in rows of shiny cars into the village; her daughter
could become a university professor, for all she cared,
but it *still* wouldn't remove the stigma of Fatima's
menial job. Some things never change! No money or

achievements could alter certain realities, or purchase an unblemished lineage and background.

Kaniz laughed in the mirror, examining her rows of neat white teeth, before brushing and chiselling them with the *muswak* stick, and later with *sak* which stained her lips red. As she peered closer in the mirror, she saw to her horror a small *chaiei* – a brown mark forming just under her left eye on her very fair cheek.

Kaniz's eyes widened. This was a bigger problem than Firdaus and her scheming mother. For no blemishes were ever allowed to mark her face – she had always made sure of that. The mirror was probably playing tricks on her. She picked up the small hand mirror from the wooden dresser, and decided to go up on to the top balcony, to have a better look in the open sunlight.

Chapter 13

FIRDAUS AND HER two sisters saw their mother some two hours later, long after Ali had deposited her parcels and headed back for the town. Highly indignant and with their tempers frayed, they waited impatiently.

'She should put her family first, instead of gadding about visiting her friends.' They all agreed with Salma on this issue. But then, that was their mother – a law unto herself, accountable to nobody!

Their father, too, was waiting patiently on his bed in the *pasar*. He hadn't seen Fatima for nearly two months. His daughters had changed his clothes and bedding, and performed a last-minute rush of tidying up the whole house for their mother's arrival. She always

looked around critically. Salma, the second daughter, had already fried some fresh fish – a favourite dish, she knew, of her mother's. Accompanying that was the dessert – *karai halwa*.

At last the wooden gate of their home creaked open and Fatima's bulky figure burst forth, her arms outstretched to her daughters in joy. Immediately Salma ran into her mother's arms, followed closely by Fazeelet, the youngest daughter and finally Firdaus.

'You should have taken your time, Mother dear. We could have waited another month,' Firdaus teased, laughing in her mother's sheepish face as she embraced her warmly.

'Come on, girls. You know that I just had to say "hello" to my friends on the way. Well, here I am, and you have got me for two full weeks. How are you all?'

They led her into the *pasar*, to their father. With the window shutters open Fiaz had avidly drunk in the picture of his daughters' welcome, in delight. His gaunt face creased into a smile, the lines of age pre-maturely criss-crossing his face. It was good to have Fatima home. The next few days would indeed be excit-ing. 'It is a strange world,' he mused sadly to himself, 'for a husband to wait patiently for his wife to come home from work. Normally it would be the husband coming back from the fields, or the city or from abroad.'

Fiaz harboured no bitterness in his heart towards his wife. On the contrary, he had learnt to accept his lot philosophically. If it wasn't for Fatima's work in Habib Khan's family home, how would he and his young family have survived when he had lost one of his legs?

Fiaz could still recall vividly to this day the raw pain and the terrifying shock of waking up in hospital to

discover that his right leg had been amputated. His eyes closed, automatically blocking out the memory of an event which had played havoc with their *kismet* and his destiny.

After ploughing in his field he was taking his two bullocks back to the farmyard, when one of them suddenly turned round, making Fiaz lose his grip on the harness, stumble and fall. In those few seconds, his worst nightmare was enacted as he felt the weight of the bullock's hooves trample on his legs. Then everything had blissfully blacked out for him.

During the following month, having lost the use of his other leg, too, Fiaz was faced with the heart-rending need to sell his bullocks and his portion of land, and to borrow money from his neighbours to pay for the medical bills. Neither his family nor Fatima's were in a position to help them.

Out of sheer desperation, and faced with the dire need of feeding her four small children, Fatima had swallowed her pride and approached the big house for work. Employed immediately, she helped Siraj Din's eldest daughter-in-law, Shahzada, to bring up her three young children, as well as lending a hand in running the large family home. To do this, however, Fatima had to abandon her own children at home with her husband, appealing to her neighbour Naimat Bibi, the village cook, to keep an eye on them for her. Dry-eyed on the outside, inside she wept for her young children left alone without their mother. 'I have no choice. It is either that or no food in their mouths,' she cried to herself as she hugged them to her chest at night-time.

When Habib moved his family to the city, Fatima moved with them, albeit reluctantly. Acutely aware of what it entailed for Fatima and her family, Habib and

Shahzada had asked her to bring them with her, but
Fiaz wouldn't hear of it. They in turn showed their
appreciation by their generosity. They paid for her
children's school fees and their books, and her hus-
band's medicine, as well as giving her a generous salary,
a large portion of which she stacked away in the bank.

When their mother moved to the city with the Khan
family, twelve-year-old Firdaus took on her small
shoulders the full responsibility of running the house-
hold, looking after her sick father and her two younger
sisters and brother Sarfaraz. Habib's home in the city
was too far for Fatima to return on a daily basis. Even-
tually her visits had dwindled to twice a week.

As the years sped by, Fatima's children got used to
living without her. It was her money, however, that had
sent Sarfaraz to Dubai and Firdaus to an illustrious
teaching college, and Salma to study for two years at a
sewing college in the city. Now Fatima's goal in life
was to amass thousands of *lakhs* of rupees for her three
daughters' dowries. It was a hard pill for Fiaz's male
pride to swallow. He, the traditional male breadwinner,
had been forced by fate to become a dependent and
simultaneously had lost his wife too.

Over the years he noticed a change in her. She had
become very attached to Habib Khan's children, espe-
cially Zarri Bano, almost as if they were her own. Her
tastes too had moved very much 'upmarket'. Living in
the lap of luxury in the Khans' palatial dwelling,
Fatima found everything in her own home in the
village both gauche and shabby and very much on the
small side. Although she didn't make an issue of it, her
family knew how she felt from the way she spoke and
looked around at everything.

In the first few years, she found the transition

between the lifestyle of her employers and that of her own home in the village unsettling. For instance, she was now used to the constant air conditioning in every room of Habib's home, including in the kitchen. Fatima thus, on return, felt hot and bothered in her own small kitchen. Apart from the fact that there were no modern units gracing the wall and she had to squat on the floor to do her cooking, there was only one ceiling fan. 'That fan is useless,' Fatima told her daughters exasperatedly, while fanning her flushed face vigorously with a piece of hard cardboard. 'All it does is throw more hot air in our faces!'

'You have become spoilt, Mother dear, with all that air conditioning in the town,' Salma replied tartly.

'You are right, girls. The life in Shahzada's house has sadly rubbed itself off on me. I am indeed spoilt. Fancy a mother becoming more spoilt than her own educated daughters,' she chuckled, banging another buttered *chapatti* on the flat frying pan.

'How are you, my dear?' Fiaz asked, when Fatima greeted him and sat down in the chair next to his bed. Feeling as if she was a stranger – an errant wife, to be precise, who had abandoned her home and family – she just hoped that he understood and forgave her. Somehow, she always felt guilt-ridden whenever she returned home.

'I am fine. How are you?' The words came in a rush from her mouth. 'I am so sorry for taking so long to return this time. I have been phoning Firdaus regularly at the school to make sure that you were all right. I am a terrible wife, Fiaz Sahib, I know. Forgive me, but you do understand, don't you?'

'Yes, I do, my dear. You are not a terrible wife – you

know that. We have missed you, of course, but we
know that you were needed there. Never feel guilty,
Fatima. If it wasn't for you, where would we all be? *I*
sometimes feel guilty. You should have married Sarwar,
then you would never have been in such a situation.'

'Shush, Fiaz Sahib! Don't be silly. I married you, not
Sarwar. This was my *kismet*. You are a good husband and
so understanding. I have only worked, Fiaz Sahib,
because I want to give Firdaus a grand dowry. I do not
want her to pay from her own pocket – my pride will
not let me do that! She can help towards her younger
sisters', but I insist on preparing for hers. Here, let me
massage your leg for you.'

She sat down at the foot of the bed and began to
knead the wasted muscles of her husband's calf. Fiaz lay
back on the bolster and closed his eyes, savouring the
feel of her hands. He looked forward to this daily ritual
for the next few days.

Chapter 14

HALF AN HOUR later, the couple were interrupted by
the sound of Kulsoom's rich booming voice and the
jangling sound of over two dozen multi-coloured glass
bangles on her bony arms. The village matchmaker had
arrived, apparently having lost very little time upon
hearing that 'Fatima Jee' was back in the village, for
Fatima's four extremely eligible children represented
an excellent business proposition for Kulsoom.

The initial greetings and exchanges of social niceties
quickly dispensed with, Kulsoom and Fatima neatly
switched to the subject uppermost in both their minds.

'Now — have you found a suitable *rishta* for my Firdaus, Kulsoom Jee?' Fatima began eagerly.

'I have.' Leaning forward, Kulsoom cast a gleeful glance at Fatima. 'Two, in fact.'

'Oh, that is good!' Fatima was now all eyes and ears. Sitting up in her chair she too leaned forward. 'Tell me about them,' she prompted.

'One *rishta* is in the neighbouring village. The boy is good-looking and a graduate — B. Com or something. His family are well off. They have a two-storey house with six bedrooms, built on fourteen *merlas* of land. And guess what? They only have two other children. They are elder daughters, both of whom are married and settled far away.'

'I see.' Fatima let the information sink into her brain. So, the boy was an only son — excellent! Her daughter would have no other sister-in-laws, and the house would become theirs eventually. And her Firdaus would become the reigning queen in that household.

'What about his parents?' she asked sharply.

'The father is dead. There is only a mother, and she is such a sweet, gentle soul. I don't think you could ask for a better mother-in-law than this woman for your daughter, Fatima Jee. I know of some vipers . . . you can guess who I mean, don't you?' Kulsoom winked at Fatima, aware of Firdaus's presence in the courtyard outside. She could both hear and see them from the open window. Leaning forward, Fatima closed one of the window's wooden shutters.

'I see,' Fatima uttered, lost in thought once more. This family appealed to her; she wouldn't let them slip through her fingers. It was a very attractive package and she wanted to get cracking on it before it was too late. God knew how many other mothers had their

eagle eyes on this boy and his family. He lived in the neighbouring village, so her daughter wouldn't be travelling too far either. That was a mighty big plus in their favour.

Coming to a quick decision, Fatima put her hand in her tunic and, from the neckline, fished out her small purse. Unzipping it, she took out a 500-rupee note and handed it ceremoniously to Kulsoom.

'Here, Sister Kulsoom, I think we might be interested in this boy and his family. I am giving you this as a reward for your research and to ask a favour that you keep this *rishta* a secret and not barter it at a higher price to any of our neighbours or other clients of yours. If I find you have whispered a word about it to anyone else, I will wipe my hands of you and enlist the help of another matchmaker. I will not let you anywhere near my children or those of any of my friends again. Is that understood, Kulsoom Jee?' Fatima gave the matchmaker the benefit of a hard stare.

'Oh, come on, Fatima Jee, you can trust me. I will not breathe a word of this to anybody until everything has been finalised to your satisfaction. You should know me better.' All affronted, Kulsoom hastened to reassure her favourite client.

'Now tell me about the second *rishta*.' Her mind now totally at ease, Fatima relaxed back in her seat again. With three daughters to marry off, she had to explore as many avenues as possible.

'The second one is in the town. You know my popularity,' Kulsoom boasted, her large round face split into a self-satisfied smile. 'I have good connections with other matchmakers, you see, in other towns and villages. The only trouble with this *rishta*, I am afraid, is that the boy comes from a large family. He is the

eldest son, and there are five daughters – all unmarried, all of them younger than him as well as the other two brothers.'

'Stop right there! Don't say any more, Kulsoom Jee. I don't think we'll be interested in this family.' The vision of her daughter embroiled and ensconced in a large household with so many sister-in-laws and brother-in-laws and with so many dowries to arrange, had Fatima creasing her forehead in distaste. Having given away precious years of her life working in someone else's home in order to raise and educate her daughters, Fatima wasn't going to waste it all by planting any of her daughters in the household of a large family. Her girls were cut out for much better things.

'Kulsoom, what about *her*? You know who I mean!' Fatima hissed, raising her eyebrows in a conspiratorial fashion, hoping that the matchmaker understood. She didn't want Firdaus to hear what they were discussing. 'Has she found a *rishta* for her son? I know you are working for her too. Do not cross me on that one, Kulsoom. You must keep me abreast with what is going on there. If I find that you have kept something from me ... ' Fatima's voice trailed off, her stare hardening again.

'No, of course not, Sister Fatima, I will not cross you. But I can tell you brutally that she has no intention of making your Firdaus her daughter-in-law, ever! Now that Zarri Bano has refused to marry Khawar, she has switched her attention to Ruby. Therefore, dear sister, if you were to pay heed to me, do not either raise your hopes or cast your eyes in the direction of the *hawaili*. It is a dead course. I know you have set your heart on Khawar and have liked him for a long time, and regard him as a desirable match for your daughter, but his

mother is another story entirely. You are truly out of your depths there, my dear. That woman, as you well know, is a viper, I tell you she hates you and your family, and would eat your daughter alive with her taunts.'

'OK, OK, Kulsoom, please don't rub it in!' Fatima agitatedly interrupted. 'One day she'll regret it. Tell me how many young women in the village are Head-mistresses or so well-educated. I tell you, my Firdaus will go – just like that!' As if to emphasise the point, Fatima snapped her fingers at Kulsoom. 'It is just that I wanted her to stay in the village. Firdaus wants to stay here, too, and the only person who is compatible with her education and personality is Khawar . . . '

'But not his family, Fatima. You must be realistic! Your background is different from theirs. I don't want to be offensive, but that woman is very proud and a snob. She will not contemplate such a *rishta*. The only family she thinks is on a par with her is that of Habib Khan. You know what I mean: she claims that your daughters are beneath her.'

'Yes, I know precisely what you mean,' Fatima answered, her face flushing in indignation. 'Does she begrudge me for working to support my family? If a similar thing had happened to her husband, what would she have done? Let her children starve? Is my family to be forever penalised and condemned because I have worked to support them? You know my job wasn't inherited, nor one of our trades. We are farming people like most of the other villagers – just like *her* family. I am very cross at the injustice of it all.' There were tears in her eyes.

'I am not going to give up though,' she ranted on. 'I have known for years that Khawar wants to marry my

daughter. It is his mother who is like a thorn in everyone's back. I am going to have a word with our *buzurg*, Siraj Din. As the village elder, and the man to whose family I have devoted the most precious years of my life, perhaps he can intervene and put in a good word for us and sway that woman's opinion . . . '

'Stop! Mother, stop!' Firdaus dashed into the room to stand beside Fatima, her cheeks fiery red. 'I have heard enough. My ears are burning from the sheer shame of it all. I tell you now, Mother: even if that proud woman were to come begging on her knees. I would not step one foot into that household. Don't we have any pride, or aren't we entitled to any, Mother? Who do they think they are? Out of which soil have they sprung? Have they lost their bearing on humanity, by their self-importance and acres of land? Mother, how dare you demean us all by throwing yourself at them? It is as if God had created Khawar and no one else. Are there no other men or families in the world?' She paused to take a deep breath.

'If you are bent on marrying me off to Khawar, then listen to me, Mother, carefully – I will remain a spinster! I will not marry to please you, nor the school committee, so that they can keep me here in the village. If you want me to marry any man, I am willing to consider the one Kulsoom Jee mentioned earlier, from the neighbouring village. I could commute to my school from there. I am personally interested in him, Kulsoom Jee.' Firdaus addressed the matchmaker. 'Please let me know about him and his family and then you can arrange a meeting between our two families.'

'Yes, little Sahiba,' Kulsoom offered with alacrity, her small eyes dancing from daughter to mother. Truly gagged by her daughter's outburst Fatima didn't have

anything further to add for the next few minutes while they sipped tea and ate biscuits. Apart from telling Kulsoom the sad news of Zarri Bano becoming a Holy Woman.

It was an hour later that Kulsoom left Fatima's home, a most contented woman. Waited upon by Fatima's three daughters, she had first dined in style and then been given a special gift of a suit from Fatima, as well as a pot of moisturising cream for her dry, pigmented skin. Kulsoom knew for sure that she would be amply rewarded, once she managed to match Fatima's daughters to good worthy *rishtas*.

As she made her way to her friend Naimat Bibi's house in the village lane, Kulsoom spotted Khawar on his white horse in the field. Purposely she hastened her pace towards him.

'*Assalam-Alaikum*, how are you, my son?' she greeted him, while keeping discreetly well away from the horse's legs. She wasn't an animal lover by any means. Her bony legs had only just come out of plaster last month.

'*Wa Laikum-Salam*, I am fine, Auntie Kulsoom. What brings you to this side of the village?' he humoured the reputable village matchmaker.

'I went to visit Fatima.' Kulsoom eagerly took up her cue, looking up at the handsome young man. 'She has just returned to the village. I have been telling her about some suitable *rishtas* for her three very lovely daughters.'

'Including one for Firdaus?' Khawar asked quietly, bending down to pat his horse on his flanks, while keeping his expression neutral.

'Oh, of course, especially Firdaus. She is the eldest

and the most eligible of Fatima's three daughters,'
Kulsoom replied, letting a secretive smile deliberately
play on her lips.

'Where are these *rishtas*?'

'One is in the city. The man is a general,' she lied
glibly, looking up from the ground and staring back at
him. 'The other one is in the next village. He is the only
son and a graduate. He has a very nice mother and a
huge *hawaili*. He works as a manager in the city.' She
added the last bit herself as an afterthought. She had a
knack for exaggeration, when it suited her or the
situation.

'I see. Well, our Firdaus is going to be lost for choice.
Such good matches!' he bit out sarcastically, his nostrils
flaring, his hands tight on the horse's reins.

'Oh, I definitely think so,' Kulsoom slyly dug in,
noting both his look and action with interest. 'There is
nobody suitable in the village for our Firdaus. She her-
self was adamant that she doesn't want to marry anyone
here, even if they begged her to, or even if the school
committee threw her out of the school. You should have
heard her, Khawar. She was spitting fire and daggers at
me and her mother.'

'Why?'

'Well . . . ' Sobering, Kulsoom decided to play with
destiny and tell him the truth. 'You know, Khawar,
Fatima has always nurtured the idea that you and
Firdaus make a nice pair. But of course your mother
will not hear of it, and now Firdaus definitely does not
want to have anything to do with you. Do you know
what she said, Khawar dear? She said that even if your
mother came on her knees, begging for her hand, she
wouldn't step into your home. Can you ever imagine
your mother on her knees begging, Khawar? Firdaus

seems bent on pursuing this match with the man from a neighbouring village. I thought it important to let you know, my son. For I am aware that you have always had a soft spot for our Firdaus and I wouldn't want you to blame me when it was too late.' The woman sighed.

'She'll be "snapped up", as her mother says, from right under your very nose, Khawar. I won't say any more – I have already said enough. And your mother will not thank me. I have probably made an enemy of her already and lost her business too – but I care, you see, Khawar! I care for you both. You are the children I never had. Yet, I don't want to cause a rift in your family. Good evening, my son, and may Allah fulfil all your dreams,' she ended solemnly and entered the village lane.

She left Khawar on his horse, having given him much food for thought. He knew what game Kulsoom was playing. His male ego was wounded, nevertheless, by Kulsoom's suggestion that Firdaus wouldn't marry him, nor set foot in his home. It seemed that he had two proud women to contend with. A woman he wanted to marry and a mother who wouldn't let him marry her.

It was time for action! This matter had to be resolved, one way or another. He didn't relish it, but it looked as if a confrontation with his mother was imminent. As Kulsoom had said, Firdaus would most certainly be snapped up by these so-called 'generals' and 'managers'. Where would that leave him or their school? He had a double interest at heart and both, at the moment, were at stake.

When he reached home, his mother's furnace of hate for Fatima and her brood was now well ablaze.

She therefore failed to notice the cold determined glint in her son's eyes.

'That washerwoman was parading her parcels she had brought from the city!' Kaniz began, flying at her son with her tongue. 'I bet that they only contained cast-offs from that family,' she sneered. He was tight-lipped, she saw, but paid no heed. In fact, he was smarting from his mother's abusive term of 'washerwoman', in describing Fatima. Khawar's long curly eyelashes swept down and hid his expression from his mother's gaze.

'Mother, she wasn't always a washerwoman!' he broke in. 'She has worked hard to raise her family. Pampered women like yourself don't even know how to feed their children, let alone raise two families and also support a disabled husband. I admire that woman, if you would like to know.'

Her lips parting in surprise, Kaniz snorted in disgust. 'I know why you admire that woman,' she said, her voice dipping dangerously low. 'It is because of that chit of hers! That upstart, with her high and mighty airs.'

'That chit is the woman I would like to marry, Mother. But like you, she is very proud. She has raved that she will not step foot in this house, not even if you came begging on your knees.' He stopped, laughing inwardly at the sight of his mother. Kaniz's mouth had gaped fully open in shock, as she struggled to form and roll the words out of her mouth.

'I . . . I . . .' The breath was choked out of her. '*I beg her* to marry you?' Kaniz's fair cheeks had flamed red, her almond-shaped eyes were flashing. 'Never! If you want to marry that woman then you'll do it without my permission and outside this home! And . . . and I would

never ever let her set foot inside this house!' she finished, her bosom heaving.

'Listen to me carefully, Mother,' Khawar rasped, for once not caring if his mother was on the verge of hysterics. 'Firdaus is the woman I want to marry.' He had not wanted to say this, but his mother had goaded him into blurting it out.

'Then you will have to choose between me and that chit. I will cast you out and renounce you as my son!' Kaniz shrieked, now having lost total control, her hand pressed to her heaving chest.

'So be it, Mother! I will not put up with your tyranny any longer. I am nearly twenty-seven years old and I can make my own decisions. If you are so small-minded and petty, then I will be forced to act alone and do what is right. I don't want you to chase other *rishtas* for me. I'll not lose Firdaus to some city slicker. She belongs here in the village, with me, and in my home. Either come to your senses, Mother, or I'll walk out of this house.' He gave her the ultimatum, his eyes totally hostile.

'Never, never, *never!*' Kaniz shouted at him, going hoarse and almost stamping her foot on the floor. 'You can walk out, you ungrateful, love-sick brat! Couldn't you have chosen to fall in love with a better girl than a washerwoman's daughter, the daughter of my worst enemy? You have betrayed me, Khawar. I will never forgive you if you marry that *chit!*' Kaniz was now livid, her cheeks red flags of colour.

'I *will* marry that chit! That chit will soon be the Headmistress of the school and will be able to hold her head higher than you ever could from your original family status. People from all walks of life will show her respect. She is worth twenty of you any day, Mother!' Khawar threw back cruelly at her.

Then, angry with himself and his outburst he strode out of the room, knowing full well that he had been very wounding and offensive to his mother, but so be it. Today he had expended his last ounce of his patience in humouring her.

Kaniz sank down heavily on her seat – thunderstruck, her mind reeling. The sky had just fallen and shattered around her shoulders. Her only son, to whom she had devoted twenty-seven years of life, had given her an ultimatum. 'How could he betray me like this?' Kaniz asked herself in a daze, her eyes filling with tears.

Never! She would rather die than welcome that young woman into her home. Her son had gone truly mad. *Majnoon*! He had probably been drinking *tweez* prepared by that witch. That was how she had wormed herself into Khawar's heart. 'How Fatima must now be gloating!' she moaned.

Her heart thudded wildly against her chest. 'I will die first than accept that woman as my daughter-in-law.' Kaniz shuddered in loathing. Her worst nightmare was staring her in the face. To lose her son to that woman, and have her mother, that fat washerwoman, parading around her beautiful home.

'Not in a thousand years!' she shrieked alone in her room.

Chapter 15

AS A FAITHFUL good friend, Kulsoom Bibi the matchmaker decided to call on her best friend, Naimat Bibi, to 'honour' her with the exciting news about Baba

Siraj Din's eldest granddaughter becoming the Holy Woman.

Making sure she didn't break her glass bangles against the heavy wooden door of Naimat Bibi's humble three-roomed house, Kulsoom pushed it wide open. While Naimat Bibi was at home, the door was always left open. Stepping carefully into the dark narrow hallway, leading into the smallest of the courtyards in the entire village, Kulsoom's nose crinkled up in distaste. She held up her new white chiffon *dupatta* to her nose, in an effort to block out the strong smell.

The main feature of the courtyard was the large guava tree. With its heavy branches swollen with pear-shaped fruit, it cloaked almost the entire yard, robbing it of any meagre rays of sunshine that happened to slant on the rooftop of Naimat Bibi's home.

'Naimat Bibi!' Kulsoom merrily chirped, carefully stepping off the worn concrete step into the courtyard. She had many a time twisted her ankles on this step. Her eyes wandered over the peeling plaster of the walls, which showed the cracked brickwork underneath. Her friend was crouched over a large wok-like pan of boiling water on a pedestal gas stove on the veranda, which she used as her kitchen. With a large wooden spoon she was busy stirring in heapfuls of flour into the water.

When she caught sight of her friend, Naimat Bibi hurriedly got up, almost tripping over her footstool. With a broad smile creasing her amply *chaie*-pigmented face, she greeted Kulsoom with '*Bismillah! Bismillah*, Kulsoom Jee.'

'What are you doing with that water?' Kulsoom asked, mystified.

'Making soap,' Naimat Bibi cheerfully piped, giving her a full customary hug of greeting. Kulsoom held

herself stiffly in her friend's arms, wondering irritably whether Naimat Bibi's hands were clean. She feared for her new white chiffon *dupatta*.

Naimat Bibi returned to the large pot of soap mixture. Before Kulsoom's interested gaze she began to stir in some portions of animal fat she had picked up from the butcher, along with some mustard oil.

'Mind your hand, Naimat Bibi. Remember what happened to you last time you added soda,' Kulsoom dutifully warned as she saw her friend spoon in a generous amount of caustic soda.

'I know, but,' ashamedly, Naimat Bibi lifted the corner of the threadbare shawl she wore especially on such occasions, 'I am afraid I have already burned another hole in it.'

Kulsoom laughed in a patronising tone, wondering cynically why her friend worked so hard. 'Why do you bother with all this, Naimat Bibi? Don't tell me you have made two lots of soap already.' Kulsoom walked up to the two large earthenware brick-red basins, painted and glazed with a geometric pattern on their rims, left to set in the sun in a corner of the courtyard. She poked the creamy yellow mixture with her thumb.

'They have hardened nicely, Kulsoom Jee. It's OK, you can touch it. As to why I make it, it's because I can't afford the Surf powder. They come in such small boxes and are quite expensive. They barely last a day anyway, especially when there is the bedlinen to wash. The small household bars of soap are no good for me. They keep slipping out of my large clumsy hands. I am used to the easy task of slopping over a wet article of clothing and giving it a good quick swipe in the soap.

'Here, I have made one extra soap basin for you,

although I know you hardly ever wash any clothes yourself. Do you know, Kulsoom Jee, I actually *like* making soap. I must be the only woman making home-made soap these days. The younger girls laugh in my face when they see me grinding grains of wheat myself to make flour. Everyone has fallen for the modern life of luxury and idleness these days. They just don't know how to be self-sufficient any more.'

Amused at her friend's lofty tone, Kulsoom Bibi could not help retorting, 'Listen, Naimat Jee, some people have better things to do with their time than grind wheat at home and make endless basins of soap. I, for one, have no free time at all. If I sat at home grinding wheat every morning and setting basins of soap, how would I run my matchmaking business? I have to be out all the time, visiting different households, culti-vating relationships with everyone. Why do you like to make your life so difficult? Don't you have enough to do as a village cook? Your services are always in demand whenever unexpected guests arrive at any household in the village, and of course your *chapatti* oven is burning twice a day, baking for almost half the village.'

'Well, my business is not so profitable as yours!' Naimat Bibi defensively threw at her friend. 'I don't get presents of clothes and gold earrings as well as money, you know. From the *chapattis* I only get coins, *paisas* or food for my work. What I want to do is some sort of work which will not be so menial, but would bring in hard currency. Any ideas, Kulsoom Jee?'

'No, I haven't!' Kulsoom answered waspishly, now quite annoyed with the direction the conversation had taken. 'And for your information, you probably make more in total in your *paisas* on a daily basis. I, on the other hand, have to wait for months to be rewarded for

my hard work. Anyway, I haven't come to talk about soaps and flour-grinding! I have come to tell you about our Zarri Bano. I have just heard from Fatima that she is to become a Holy Woman.' Kulsoom stopped, satisfied with the effect her words had on her friend.

Naimat Bibi's mouth with its thin pursed lips and a set of uneven teeth had virtually dropped open. She simply forgot about the hot mixture she was stirring. It bubbled away.

'What did you say?' Naimat Bibi asked in wonder, ignoring the wooden spoon she had just dropped to the bottom of the pan. 'Are you telling me that our glamorous, educated young madam is to become a *Bibi*? But I thought they only did that in the olden days – here in the village, not in town. How? Why?'

'Well, it is to do with the death of our young master, Jafar, and their inheritance.'

'Do you think they'll actually make her into a very religious woman? I can't believe it is possible. She dresses like a movie actress all the time. I just can't see her wrapped in a *chador*.'

'I have a terrible feeling that they will marry her off to the Holy Quran, to her faith. These *zemindars* are fierce men, like tigers and bulls. And very possessive about their womenfolk.'

'So that will mean the poor girl can never marry or ever have any children?' Naimat Bibi's wrinkled face now expressed both her horror and a kindly concern.

'She isn't the only one not to be blessed with children in our village,' Kulsoom said gruffly. 'I was widowed before I was able to have any. You, on the other hand, I am afraid had a womb that was never destined to be blessed with children.'

'But my husband stayed with me for ten years,'

Naimat Bibi hastened to remind her friend, offended by her patronising tone and the slur on her fertility.

Shaking her head, 'I know, my friend. I still believe you should have stayed with him, rather than divorcing him when you gave him consent to marry again. He would have looked after you and supported you, as was his duty. You wouldn't have to light your *tandoor* then.'

'No, my friend. I have no regret. I am a very independent, self-sufficient sort of person. I couldn't have lived with his second wife, and helped to look after her brood. I am happy that he has children now by another woman, but I have no maternal love for them nor do I begrudge them. Why do you talk about me? Think about Chaudharani Kaniz. She is still a beautiful, wealthy landlady, and only in her fifties. She never married again, did she? She sacrificed all her life for her son. The landlord, Younus Raees, from the neighbouring village, tried to woo her for nearly three years, but she never did marry him or any other man. Did you know he has just become a widower?'

'Oh, let's not talk about her, she is just a cold fish,' Kulsoom remarked bitchily. 'She is incapable of loving anyone – except herself. What husband could put up with her haughty ways? She is losing her son now through her stubbornness, because she won't let him marry Firdaus. I have just been talking to him. With regard to the Chaudharani, I am supposed to be going to visit her next, to tell her about Zarri Bano.'

Naimat Bibi laughed sarcastically. It was her turn to have a gentle dig at her friend.

'Those two families, Siraj Din's and Khawar's, are like twin families. The first person Siraj Din would have told would have been Khawar. Kaniz would not

now be waiting for *you* to come and tell her—' The old woman stopped as her friend looked up in shock.

'Ugh!' Kulsoom shouted as she felt a crow's dropping fall on top of the new white chiffon *dupatta* on her head.

In disgust Kulsoom stepped away from under the tree. Naimat Bibi's hollow cheeks filled with laughter, but she sensibly turned her face away from her friend.

'It always happens to you, doesn't it, Kulsoom Jee?' she mumbled, trying to keep her face straight.

'Yes, it does. And I am definitely not amused. Look at my new *dupatta*. It has come all the way from Barra! Every time I stand under your tree I get showered by those damn crows of yours. You must cut down this tree. Whenever you look at this brick-lined floor of yours there are droppings everywhere. It is disgusting to see and a health hazard.'

Flushing red, 'I wash my floor every day, Kulsoom Jee!' Naimat Bibi indignantly fumed.

Kulsoom threw down her *dupatta*, on the floor at Naimat Bibi's feet. 'You have got plenty of soap so now you can wash it for me!'

'Oh, I have lots of soap, don't worry about that. These crows have been crowing all day. I wonder if I am going to have any visitors?'

'It is probably your brood of stepchildren coming to visit their stepmama from the town.' It was now Kulsoom's turn to tease her friend.

'God forbid!' Laughing, and making a comical face at her friend, Naimat Bibi went inside her small storeroom to fetch another scarf for her friend to wear. After all, she couldn't go bareheaded in the street.

Taking Naimat Bibi's new silk *dupatta*, Kulsoom called over her shoulder 'I'll return it to you later!' and walked out of her friend's home.

Suddenly fancying a cool glass of skimmed milk, *lassi*, and knowing there would be plenty of it at Sardara's house, Kulsoom headed for the milkwoman's property. She would also, of course, be doing Sardara a big favour as she suffered from arthritis and was totally wheelchair-bound. Naturally she was now very dependent on kindly souls and faithful friends like herself to pass on any news, trivial or otherwise.

Now, the beautiful, glamorous daughter of their landlord becoming a Holy Woman was reckoned in the estimation of most people to be 'major' news indeed. If that wasn't, Kulsoom didn't know what was. On second thoughts, perhaps Queen Elizabeth of England visiting their village would create slightly more of a stir. In any event, all the households that Kulsoom would honour with her presence would, by the end of the day, know what was going to happen to their 'poor' Zarri Bano.

Chapter 16

'IT CANNOT BE!' Sikander banged his fist on the coffee table, his eyes spitting fire at his mother in their home in Karachi. He stood up tall, towering over her, sitting on the sofa. 'Zarri Bano a *Shahzadi Ibadat*! What nonsense is that? Tell me, Mother!'

Bilkis gazed at her son helplessly. Hadn't she herself gone into a deep state of shock when Habib had phoned and told her curtly, 'Zarri Bano has decided to become a *Shahzadi Ibadat*, a Holy Woman.' She felt the loss deeply, knowing that now there could be no marriage between her beloved son and that tall,

attractive woman who had captured Sikander's heart and mind.

Later she had phoned back and asked to speak to Shahzada. The first thing that Bilkis had noticed was the subtle change in the other woman's tone and manner. Her stilted speech lacked its habitual warmth. Even miles away, Bilkis knew that something was dreadfully wrong.

She had listened with a sinking heart, her mind grappling with the two images of Zarri Bano. The beautiful, elegant young woman with that of a veiled religious recluse, shut away from the ordinary gaiety of human life and fated never to marry nor to have any children.

Bilkis had tried to break it gently to her son, but in the end the effect was the same – a bombshell for Sikander.

'They can't do this! It is barbaric! What age, what country do they live in? In Islam there are no nuns, no such things as women married to the Holy Quran! What nonsense is this? No woman is to be denied her natural role as a wife and a mother. Who has invented these traditions? Have they studied the Holy Quran, where it categorically states that widows and divorcees should be encouraged to remarry at the first opportunity? So how can a beautiful, young maiden be deliberately denied marriage? That is the crux of the matter, isn't it? So that she doesn't marry anybody. Habib doesn't want her to marry me, I know it! Do they realise that they are committing a crime? Do they—.' His mother cut short his rage-filled outburst.

'Please stop, Sikander. It has happened for generations amongst a certain class of people in remote parts of Sind – and is very much a hushed affair.

Their traditions are very strong. Nobody can stand up to these people. They are very powerful and have great influence over the local community. Their women-folk, in particular, have little or no independence or autonomy.'

'No, Mother. I cannot believe that this is true of Zarri Bano. She defies all stereotypes. I don't believe that she'll go through with this preposterous idea. She enjoys life too much to want to take up austerity. Not Zarri Bano. I'll not let it happen!'

'Sikander, please relax. Come and sit down.' Bilkis patted the place on the sofa beside her. Sikander glared down at the spot she indicated, his body tall and tense.

'I am just as shocked as you are, Sikander,' Bilkis reasoned softly. 'I too liked Zarri Bano very much. If it will help you, you can talk to her, my handsome son, but I think that you'll be banging your head against a brick wall.' She sighed.

'It is strange to recall the incident now, but I remember hearing some women talking, after Jafar's death, about "Holy Women" of the past in this clan. They were gossiping, and I paid no attention to them at the time as I thought they were only legends, but I do remember being alarmed by what I heard. I also noted Habib's coldness towards us, especially towards you. It was almost as if he hated you. His eyes often followed you like a hawk. As though you were a personal threat to him. At the time, I just put it down to grief at the loss of his son Jafar, but in retrospect, I think I should have taken more notice of these hints. One doesn't treat one's future son-in-law in such an antagonistic manner or his mother with such bare civility. Didn't you notice anything?'

'No, Mother. Like you I just put it down to a sign of

Habib Sahib's mourning for his son. I cannot give her up, Mother! I am going to break these traditions of theirs. Even if I held no personal interest, it is still a cruel thing to do to another human being.'

He moved away from his mother and stood, deep in thought, in the middle of the drawing room.

'I will go to their home town,' Sikander decided. 'I will see Habib and Zarri Bano tomorrow.'

'All right, my son. Do as you wish. After all, you have every right. Although Zarri Bano is not officially engaged to you, she is still your fiancée.' Bilkis lovingly stroked his shoulder blades, trying to relax and ease his stiff shoulder muscles.

It was a warm sunny morning in May, exactly one month since Jafar's death. Zarri Bano sat in the court-yard in front of the dining table on the lawn, enjoying the morning sunshine before it grew hot. Her eyes closed, she basked in the smell from the rose bushes and the singing of the sparrows on the trees.

Ruby had joined her for breakfast in the patio area and then had gone to the bazaar with her mother to buy some fabrics. Habib had left to go on business in Hyderabad. By now all the guests had departed and only three servants remained in the house, busy clean-ing different parts of the building.

The serenity of her surroundings lulled Zarri Bano to sleep. Leaning on the cushioned back-rest of the cane chair she let the newspaper on her lap fall to the ground.

Zarri Bano woke with a prickly feeling of awareness that she was being watched. A tall shadow lay strewn across her body. Fully awake, her eyelids fluttered open and her gaze travelled over a pair of white linen trouser-clad, muscular legs, to a broad-shouldered chest in a

crisply starched shirt, and rested on the tanned handsome face in which a pair of cool grey eyes was steadily staring down at her.

'Am I dreaming?' Zarri Bano asked herself. When the full masculine lips curved into a lazy smile, Zarri Bano jerked upright, her heart skipping a beat. This wasn't a dream! Sikander stood in front of her with his charismatic presence. Sheer waves of pleasure lapped and coursed through her body, watering the rose garden of her heart, to burst into full bloom.

She became embarrassingly conscious of her dishevelled appearance. Her long, wavy hair was around her shoulders in wanton disarray and she felt bare without the *dupatta* draped across her chest. Holding one arm against her breast she put the other hand on her cheek, wanting to shield herself from his eyes. Yet, perversely, delighting in the attention they were giving her.

They were everywhere! Bent on a languorous trail over her face, moving down the creamy white column of her throat, her soft feminine curves, her half-bare arms and over her deliciously tousled hair.

Drowned in the sensuous spell his eyes had woven around her, Zarri Bano couldn't look away from them or his handsome face. Her heartbeat had accelerated of its own accord. A warm blush caused a pinkish mantle to rise from her throat to her cheeks.

All of a sudden, social etiquette and female modesty rudely asserted themselves. With an awkward movement of her arm she reached for her *dupatta* from the other chair. Before his searing gaze she draped it over her shoulders and in front, covering herself discreetly and fully.

Zarri Bano was now angry with herself for having been caught in such a manner. His gaze had stripped

her bare. The heat of shame racing through her body, she stood up clumsily, straightening her *dupatta* around her shoulders again.

'Sikander Sahib, how did you come here?' she asked. 'You surprised me.' She was unable to look him in the eye.

'I can see that, Zarri Bano Sahiba,' he returned softly, his tender eyes warm with laughter. 'I came the normal way. Fatima told me that apart from you, nobody else is in the house. This suits me beautifully. You see, it is you I have come to see.'

'Please, Sikander Sahib, sit down.' She gestured to the other chair. Sitting down, he waved his hand to her to do the same. She sat down, facing him, tense but unable to take her eyes away from his face as if memorising each and every minute detail.

'Do you know, Zarri Bano, I hope that after we are married we will have beautiful children like you.'

Her cheeks crimsoning at the mention of children, her eyes fell to her hands in her lap. A bolt of pain and longing shot through her body, leaving her face pale and sheer misery reflected in her eyes. She turned her gaze to the rose bed, looking at, but not quite seeing the pink and yellow roses in full bloom. Ruthlessly, she trod upon the rose garden of her love. Turning to Sikander she sat upright in her chair. Her eyes sunk into his; a poignant appeal flashing in them, that she hoped and prayed he would recognise and understand.

'Sikander Sahib,' she began in a low voice, coming from the depths of her heart, 'for you and I, there will be no marriage nor children – at least, not with me. You have probably heard by now that I am to become a *Shahzadi Ibadat*.'

'It is your parents who have put you up to this?' he accused, barely able to contain his rage.

'No, Sikander. I am doing this of my own free will. The tradition is ours, but in the end the decision is mine. The idea was put to me, requested of me by my father and I accepted.'

'But why, Zarri Bano?' he asked heatedly. Bending forward he took her hand in his own. Instinctively, he wanted to reach out to her, to communicate with her on a physical level, in case words failed him.

Zarri Bano watched the movement of his fingers in fascination, mesmerised by their touch. Again, as before in Karachi, she found herself enjoying the feel of his masculine fingers on her palm. All of a sudden she wanted them to reach up and caress her face. Then like lightning her father's words jolted through her with condemnation: 'You desire a man in your life.' Shaken and ashamed, she snatched her hand away, as if Sikander's touch had both soiled and burned her, and averted her face.

'From today, Sikander Sahib, we have no legitimate relationship of any sort. Therefore you must not touch me. You must maintain your distance. We mean nothing to each other.' She prayed that he didn't notice the agony behind each word.

'Zarri Bano, for Allah's sake! How can you say this? Doesn't our engagement mean anything to you?' Anger and condemnation vibrated in him.

'That was a long time ago,' she uttered in a faraway, bleak voice, recalling the night beach scene with painful clarity. 'So much has happened since then. Sikander Sahib, please forgive me.'

'I don't believe this!' He stood up; a towering, angry figure. 'Look at me, Zarri Bano. Let's cut out this

nonsense. You wanted to marry me and I want to marry you. It's what we both want — and wanted from the moment we laid eyes on each other at the *mela*. We have something special between us — we both know we have! Don't you feel it? On that afternoon, at the *mela*, it was as if our two souls met and melted together to become one. Don't let them part us, Zarri Bano, I beg you. We were destined to become lovers. This is what we are going to do: we are going to be married! I don't know about your barbaric customs—'

Zarri Bano's head shot up. The word 'barbaric' stung her out of her pain and brought the proud, arrogant Zarri Bano back to life. Her eyes sparkling with anger, she snapped: 'Who are you to judge our traditions as barbaric, Sikander Sahib?' She too was now standing up and looking directly into his face with disdain. 'You know nothing about them.'

'It's true that I know very little about your family's traditions, but I do know, however, that if you become a Holy Woman, they will have robbed you of your womanhood and individual freedom. Listen to me, Zarri Bano. You cannot sacrifice yourself for the sake of your family's customs and traditions.'

'Sacrifice?' Zarri Bano queried, for without realising it, Sikander had touched her on a very raw nerve. 'Who says I am going to be sacrificed? Do you know what a *Shahzadi Ibadat* is? What an important role it is?' Her voice sounded hollow to her ears.

'I don't know about the role, but I do know that you cannot become my wife or a mother to my children, or be allowed to live a natural human life with me as a woman. Don't you want to be a normal woman? Does that mean nothing to you? Don't *I* mean anything to you?' he asked in desperation, watching in fascination

as her eyes glimmered and flashed fire at him. Glittering like jewels, they were one of the things that had initially attracted him to her.

'I do not need a lecture from you, Sikander.' She turned on him, standing tall and proud in bearing. 'In your typical male manner you presume too much of what I want. Not all women want children or desire a man in their life. Do you think I cannot live my life without your lordly *male* presence in it? Do you think I want you so much that I would give up my family for you? What arrogance! Never! You are a very self-centred man. Why do you think I had never chosen a suitor before? It was mainly because I was never sure whether I wanted to get married in the first place. You are no different, Sikander Sahib! Marriage is as much an institution as any other aspect of life. In our patriarchal world, marriage can be a bigger sacrifice than the one that you imagine me going through with.

'In fact, in my role as a Holy Woman, I will have gained greater freedom and independence as a woman. I will not be tied to any man, nor any roles or commitments, only to my faith and what that entails like any other normal person. What can be better than commitment to our faith? I am not interested in the "meeting of the souls", or "your" soul, that you delight in referring to. I have no intention of becoming your lover! Do not insult me by such shameful talk. You are talking to a different woman now, Sikander Sahib,' she finished, looking squarely at him.

A feeling of hopelessness assailed him. If she herself wanted it, what could he do? The fight suddenly went out of him as he desperately tried to reconcile the woman standing in front of him with the one he had fallen in love with at the *mela*, and later in the orchard.

Disillusioned, and feeling betrayed he moved away from her, and let his eyes linger on the heavily swollen grape tree in the corner of the courtyard. The seconds ticked away. Zarri Bano remained standing, watching him, her eyes now green orbs of misery. As if in a daze, Sikander turned to her once more.

'Listen to me!' he began again. 'Forget about marriage, men, me, children and souls, but think of your individuality, you as a person. Your personal freedom is at stake here. Do you not see, Zarri Bano, that you are going to be made into another person? Where have your feminist beliefs and idealism disappeared to? How can a woman of your calibre, with a university degree, a former editor of a magazine, at the end of the twentieth century, be so blinded? I just cannot visualise it, Zarri Bano. This is the age of women prime ministers – Benazir Bhuttos.'

'Sikander Sahib, please do not try to pigeonhole me into any role. You do not know me at all, or what calibre of woman I am. Just because I have a university degree, does it make me so radically different from other women who do not?'

'You are educated. You can think for yourself, Zarri Bano. Do you know how ironic it is that the subject of your study was psychology? Has your research and fieldwork not taught you anything about human behaviour? You are falling prey to your family's traditions and to your father in particular!' The earnestness in his voice wasn't lost on her.

'Sikander Sahib, again you presume too much. I know a great deal about human behaviour, and I have studied it, as you say. I know what I am doing. Please do not insult my intelligence. Education I may have in abundance, a member of the women's APWA

movement I may be, and I have debated on and sup-
ported women's issues – but what you seem to forget is
what I told you in the restaurant in Karachi: I am still a
microcosm of my clan, a daughter of a wealthy and a
very powerful *zemindar*. Our family, behaviour, social
etiquette is dictated by a code of ethics and customs
peculiar to my clan – that you, as an outsider from
another social group, cannot begin to understand. I am
a part of that whole, and that is where I belong. I
cannot cut myself off for you from that whole, it is not
that simple!'

'So your individuality is to be sacrificed for the sake
of your clan's "customs", for that "whole". If you have
been brainwashed into doing something that normal
people loathe, then what can I, an ordinary *gher* man, do
to prevent you from being sacrificed?' He laid a bitter
stress on the word *gher*. She still regarded and treated
him as a virtual stranger. He would never forgive her
for that betrayal. He noted the tightness around her
lips, knew that she was made indignant by his words.

On impulse, born out of a desperate desire to com-
municate with her, once again, on a physical plane,
Sikander took her hand in his and held it between his
palms.

Her heart was beating powerfully, but she made no
attempt to draw her hand back. When he raised it to
his lips, she felt a warm glow light up inside her, fan-
ning the rose garden of her heart to bloom again. She
closed her eyes. His continued to journey over her face.

Both were startled by what happened next. Zarri
Bano's fingers had taken on a life and will of their own.
They began to move against his lips, touching and
caressing the area around his mouth and jawline. With
his eyes still on hers, watching, he moved his face to

accommodate her fingers' sensuous, tentative journey, until they lay against his lips once more, responding to the pressure of his mouth.

Horrified, her eyes fluttered open. Her cheeks on fire, she jerked her burning hand away from his lips. 'What have you done to me?' she accused in a hiss, stepping away from him and glancing down in bewilderment at her fingers – ashamed.

The spell was broken!

'We mean nothing to each other, you say, Zarri Bano?' Sikander mocked bitterly. 'Well, you have just betrayed yourself. We will always be lovers!' Looking at her lowered eyes for a long time, he said hoarsely, 'Goodbye, Zarri Bano. Don't expect me to come to your veiling ceremony, but I will invite you to my wedding ceremony. You will die for me on that day. I can vow that you will never get me out of your mind and heart till the day you die. I promise you this revenge, Zarri Bano. You'll wish that you had never heard of my name or set eyes on me.' He turned and walked away from her, without another backward glance. Out of the courtyard, into the house and out of the front entrance.

From where Zarri Bano was standing, she heard the roar of the Jeep as it sped away. She remained rooted to the spot, her hand still smarting from his touch, his words piercing her in the deepest recesses of her heart. Slowly she came to herself and collected her scattered wits about her. Had anybody seen her touching his face? She had forgotten the world around her. Thankfully, nobody was in sight. Sitting down on the cane chair, she closed her eyes, her fingertips rubbed themselves of their own accord against her thumb, vividly recalling the feel of his warm mouth against them.

She recoiled in horror at what she had done.

Sikander's last bitter words drummed through her head again. He said that he would invite her to his wedding and she would remember him till the day she died. Her body was wracked by a sudden pain. 'I will bleed for him on that day!' she whispered in a moan, her eyes remaining tightly shut.

Her father would never know what it had cost her to let Sikander walk out of her life. Giving up Sikander was a far greater sacrifice than her own womanhood. She had bartered her love for family tradition. 'It is too high a price to pay!' she muttered in agony, wrapping her arms around her chest.

Chapter 17

ZARRI BANO STAYED out in the courtyard well into the afternoon. There was no inclination to get up and do anything; only a dark void inside her to contend with. Sikander was gone. She had given him up. It was the end of a sweet, shortlived episode in her life – her passionate awakening as a woman and her discovery of love.

Her brain was suddenly attacked by the image of herself enveloped in a long black cloak. 'How can I wear a *burqa*?' she moaned to herself. 'I will never get used to it, not me. I, who have a natural instinct for glamour and fashion, I will be smothered alive behind it.'

At that moment, Habib Khan came out into the courtyard and strode straight up to his daughter, fixing her with his stern gaze. 'I hear that rascal from Karachi came here today. Is that true, daughter?'

Zarri Bano raised dull eyes to her father.

'Yes, he was here,' she stated flatly, omitting the tag 'Father', experiencing a peculiar reluctance to use the word, born out of hate. Habib sat down; a stiff, tall figure pulsing with nervous energy, in the chair opposite her.

'Yes?' he prompted sharply, his eyes intent on her face.

Zarri Bano didn't respond, but kept her face averted, staring at the green lawn around them.

'Zarri Bano—'

'No!' she cut in quickly, sweeping round to glare at him. 'Zarri Bano is dead from this minute onwards. Do not call me that!'

Startled, a spate of nervousness overtook Habib. She had said that Zarri Bano was dead. Did that mean she had turned Sikander away? He opened his mouth to get the truth out of her.

Then he closed it, seeing the mutinous line of her mouth. He knew that his daughter was, at this moment in time, shutting him out deliberately in an effort to physically and emotionally distance herself from him.

'Zarri Bano, my daughter, is very much alive and well,' he coaxed, summoning a lighter note to his tone. 'She is sitting before me – so how can she be dead?'

Zarri Bano swivelled her head round and looked at him, defeated.

'Father, let's get this farce over and done with. You have left me with no choice, have you? Make the arrangement for the veiling ceremony as soon as you can.'

Habib was scarcely able to bear the misery and defeat he beheld in his princess's eyes. He reached for her, but she backed away from him and escaped to her room.

Habib watched his daughter go with mixed feelings.

He was glad that she was going to become the Holy Woman, yet he couldn't come to terms with the misery and unhappiness that suddenly assailed him.

Apparently he had won and lost at the same time. In a way Zarri Bano was right – she had indeed died, for she wasn't the same person any more. The twinkle in her emerald-green eyes, the love bursting out for him, they were quenched for life. His heart trembled, recalling the look of naked hate he had glimpsed in them.

'Oh *Allah pak*!' He spoke out loud to himself. 'What must I do in these circumstances? I love my daughter. This is what I think is right for her, my family, our traditions and inheritance. Above all she will gain fame, respect and homage. With all this, why do I still thus feel the pain? It is as if something is terribly wrong, and I am walking in the land of the dead.'

His migraine was now back with a vengeance. Since his son's death, he had been plagued by headaches. He stood up tired, but not defeated. There was now a distinct purpose in his life.

Only one course of action faced his family. Much had to be done for the ceremony. It wasn't a traditional wedding, but by God, he was going to make his beautiful daughter's veiling ceremony into a celebration, an event to remember for decades. He was going to give away his princess to her new role, with all the pomp and ceremony that any grand wedding boasted.

As his mind began to entertain images of a grand ceremony, Habib felt his energy rekindle. 'I am the master, the head of the household, the ultimate authority, which I was born to enjoy,' he told himself with relish, straightening into shape his bushy auburn moustache.

Chapter 18

SIKANDER SAT IN his Jeep, on the same spot as on the day of the *mela*, over two months ago. Raising his head he looked at the tall minar tree with its canopy of green leafy branches, swaying in the afternoon breeze.

Closing his eyes, he allowed himself the luxury of recalling and revelling in the picture of Zarri Bano standing tall and thoroughly ravishing under the tree in her black outfit. He saw the beckoning smile playing on her lips, and the curtain of hair framing her beautiful face.

He relived the moment of her grand entrance into the guest room of her home, looking so exquisite in pink. It was then he had heard her voice for the first time. His mind next hopped to the scene of both of them walking together, chaperoned by their parents, around the fields of Zarri Bano's home. He smiled wryly, remembering the surreptitious glances he had cast her way during that long walk. He had thought that she was too arrogant and too confident for his liking. Yet these very qualities, combined with her compelling beauty, had drawn him to her like a reluctant moth to a lit candle, in the end.

Finally, a sigh escaped him as there flashed before him the poignant tender scene in the orchard of his home in Karachi. So much had happened at that time. He had touched her hand, and managed to reach out to her on an emotional and spiritual plane and finally won her over with his proposal. The evening in the

restaurant together was full of laughter, with him being dazzled by her wit and intelligence.

The feel of her soft, exquisitely shaped fingers still burned his lips. Next his mind darted back to the moment of them returning home from their evening out and finding that their lives had been turned upside down.

And now, at this present moment, he had lost all control over his life and over his fate. The woman he had passionately fallen in love with was being snatched from him, from his very grasp.

A thriving business tycoon in Karachi, the world, until a week ago, had been Sikander's oyster. People ran to do his bidding. Financial success, popularity and good looks had made him a very eligible bachelor. Since his early twenties, parents from the upper strata of Karachi society were forever parading their daughters in front of him. Yet here, in connection with Zarri Bano, he felt both belittled and inadequate. It was a new phenomenon in his life and he didn't relish it one iota.

Sheer disbelief empowered him once more. How was it possible that at the end of the twentieth century, something like this could happen? If it was against her will, he could call on the law and authorities. He could get the court to intervene. He was a man of influence. He knew he could do it, but it was she, herself, *she* had turned him away! She had turned her back on him and marriage.

A rush of warmth spread through his body as he remembered the feel of her fingertips tracing and caressing his lips, her touch soft and hesitant. Surely she had to feel something for him! For why else would a proud and respectable woman allow a man to take such

liberties with her hand, and she, in turn, to reach out and touch his lips . . .

From the very beginning, Sikander's instinct had signalled to him that Zarri Bano was a very passionate woman. The irony was, he doubted whether she knew that fact herself. He was also sure that he was the only one to have kindled the flame of passion in her, and for the first time. Did she honestly know what she was renouncing? Giving up human love, passion and all its pleasures!

For what? To embrace the sterile life of a religious hermit – totally alien to her nature. How could they do this to her?

Sikander banged his head on the steering wheel in frustration. Her father and mother had apparently led a fulfilled life and shared all its pleasures, so why were they denying the same for their daughter?

In the culture of the local community, it was the custom to marry daughters off at an early age – quite often soon after puberty, for their *izzat*'s sake. Here, then, was the case of parents deliberately preventing their fully-fledged daughter from marrying. Why? So that they could hold onto their fields and inheritance!

'Damn it! I will tell them that I don't want their inheritance,' he decided. 'They can pass it all on to Ruby. I have enough wealth of my own to keep Zarri Bano for life and in the style to which she is accustomed,' Sikander shouted aloud – the words echoing in the Jeep.

It was no use! He swept the lock of hair angrily from his forehead. His gaze lingered on the tree facing him. He knew in his very soul that she would never marry him in the present circumstances. She would never

injure her own or her family's pride or status. And her pride was her Achilles heel – a weakness her father had discovered and exploited.

He raised his head to look through the windscreen as he heard another vehicle approach. It was a car with two men inside, and it came to a halt in front of his Jeep. Sikander's body stiffened as he recognised Habib sitting next to his chauffeur. Rage gushed through his body; his hands gripped the steering wheel tightly. Sikander returned Habib's cold gaze steadily, allowing his hatred to show and be communicated. His eyes still fixed on Habib's face, he switched on the engine and drove past the car.

Habib watched the departing Jeep. With his thumb and forefinger, he started to smooth and curl his hennaed-brown moustache, deep in thought. If anybody can thwart our plan of making my daughter a Holy Woman, that man can, the alarming realisation darted in his head. Then: has he been to the house? Has he seen my daughter? Remembering with dismay that apart from the two servants and Zarri Bano, there was no one else at home, Habib was now very anxious to get home. A great deal was at stake here.

At home he had sought Zarri Bano and had questioned her in the courtyard. Prior to that he had come across Fatima and had quizzed her harshly as to whether Sikander had visited and what had transpired. Then he probed further to find out whether he had spoken to Zarri Bano.

'Yes,' Fatima had responded defiantly. She had witnessed that intimate tender scene from behind the curtains of one of the bedrooms, which overlooked the rear courtyard and lawn. Personally, poor Fatima still

cherished the idea of Sikander eloping with Zarri Bano and herself helping them.

'Where were you, Fatima, when he was here? Is there nobody here to chaperone my daughter?' Habib thundered down at her. 'As a longstanding member of my household and my housekeeper,' he continued, 'I would have thought that you would take it upon yourself to safeguard our *izzat*, our honour, rather than allow an unmarried man to violate our code of behaviour, and gain social access to my daughter.'

Fatima's cheeks burned in silent rage. 'I was around, Sahib Jee, but Sikander Sahib is, after all, Zarri Bano's betrothed.' She bravely plunged forth. 'He has a right, therefore, to gain social access to see his fiancée.' She daren't look at him now.

Angered by her semi-caustic remark, Habib's cold green eyes let her know exactly what he thought of her and of what she had said. His mouth a thin forbidding line, he barked at her. 'You forget yourself and your place, Fatima! I will, however, allow your impudence to pass this time for I know that you love Zarri Bano very dearly as a daughter and would do anything for her. But remember that in the future, Zarri Bano *has* no fiancé. She is going to be the pure one, the holy one! A prerogative of that role is her seclusion from the opposite sex, apart from close family members.

'Now would it look good, Fatima, for our future Holy Woman, representing the pinnacle of purity and respect, to have her name associated with any man? And Sikander is a bachelor! As she is not to marry, it would therefore be wrong to link her name with any man, apart from me, her uncles and grandfather. No young men, not even her cousins, have a right to socially interact with her. For her *izzat*'s sake she is to

be chaperoned at all times. Her reputation has to be impeccable. Is that clear, Fatima?' he asked, his voice lowered to a hiss, his ruthless gaze flickering over the servant's pale face, before dismissing her.

Through numbed teeth, Fatima mumbled a quiet 'yes.' Her eyes had long since dropped under the weight of oppression of Habib's stare, helpless to retaliate or say anything further.

As he strode off out into the courtyard to look for his daughter, the vision of their Zarri Bano eloping with her fiancé seemed totally ludicrous now, in Fatima's mind. Habib had indeed neatly caged his daughter. With a heavy heart, she realised that Zarri Bano, a woman of principle, could never elope with any man. Another woman, in another place, of a weaker sort, could do that – but not Zarri Bano! She would rather enter a lion's cage than seek safety and a haven.

The sunny day had lost all its sunshine for Fatima. She didn't need to ask Zarri Bano what she was going to do. Fatima already knew.

Again she recalled the image of Sikander and the young woman in the courtyard, standing together, Zarri Bano's hand held to his mouth. Fatima's heart lurched for them both. Why was life so unfair? What a handsome couple they had made. Any blind person could see that they both desired each other. Oh, *Allah pak*, why couldn't they let her be? Why couldn't they marry and Zarri Bano still become a *Shahzadi Ibadat*?

Hysterical laughter rumbled in Fatima's throat. Why bother fooling herself? For the chief attraction of the Holy Woman's role was that she never married. Who had ever heard of a sexually active *Shahzadi Ibadat,* with a husband and children! To become the

Holy Woman, Zarri Bano was destined to remain forever alone and pure of mind and body.

With a heavy heart and step Fatima returned to the kitchen and gave instructions to her assistant for the afternoon dinner. She had wished so much for Zarri Bano and her own daughter Firdaus. It seemed that both had their future paths strewn with thorns.

That evening, in the Karachi villa that was Sikander's home, his mother Bilkis tentatively asked as soon as he came into the lounge: 'How was your trip, my son? Did you talk to Zarri Bano? What did she say?' She looked at his face anxiously for any expression or tell-tale signs. The grim line of his mouth didn't bode well. Sikander gave his mother the benefit of a hard stare and then answered all her questions.

'She is going ahead with the *Shahzadi Ibadat* rubbish. Marrying herself to the Holy Quran. I mean nothing to her! Only her traditions seem to matter. Don't expect me to attend the ceremony. I am going up for a shower, Mother,' he ended bitterly.

He left a bemused Bilkis standing in the large cool hallway. She watched her son go up, taking in the tense lines of his shoulders, her heart aching for him. How unfair life proved sometimes. How unfortunate for her son, to fall in love with a woman who was out of his reach.

Bilkis shook her head mentally. So what if her son couldn't marry Zarri Bano? There were thousands of other eligible women for him to choose from. Sikander was one of the most eligible bachelors in the upper strata of Karachi society. If Zarri Bano wasn't available, that didn't mean that other women were out of his reach too. They weren't all becoming *Holy Women*.

As Bilkis walked around the orange orchard next to their villa, her thoughts dwelt on her son's anguish, and she wondered just how long it would take him to get over Zarri Bano . . .

Chapter 19

ON THE DAY of Zarri Bano's veiling ceremony, the *kothi* was garlanded with thousands of small colourful light bulbs flickering away, like a merry beacon in the evening light.

Most of the surrounding neighbourhood and some villagers from Chiragpur had been invited to Habib Khan's daughter's ceremony. Relatives from all corners of Pakistan had descended on the family residence two days earlier.

A hive of activity, the villa heaved and resounded with the guests' laughter and chatter. The seven guest rooms, each furnished with four beds, were fully occupied. Luggage was strewn and littered in every available inch of space.

The wedding guests, as was the custom and befitted human nature, had naturally formed themselves into discreet small groups, depending on their age, sex, background and, of course, how well they knew one another or not. A sense of excitement ran through everyone, as the subject on most guests' lips centred on Zarri Bano and her veiling ceremony. Some had heard about the *Shahzadi Ibadats* of the past and thus knew what it entailed. For others it was a new phenomenon, intriguing and repelling them simultaneously.

'You don't mean it!' exclaimed one woman, her

eyebrows raised to meet the upper crease on her fore-
head.

'Yes I do!' came the prompt reply from a guest called
Nilofer, attracting the attention of a group of women. 'I
tell you, sisters, it's a bizarre ceremony. They use the
Holy Quran,' she ended on a whisper, ducking her head
down and slyly looking from right to left. 'There is no
groom, yet it is very much like a wedding, with all the
wedding trappings. Now tell me, sisters, who in their
right mind would do this to their own daughter? Espe-
cially to an independent type like Zarri Bano? I mean,
have you ever seen a *dupatta* stay on that girl's head for
more than five minutes?' Nilofer scanned the women's
bemused expressions with relish. 'Well it is going to be
more than a *dupatta* she'll be wearing now, I can assure
you!'

They had just finished dinner. Huddled together on
the sofas or squatting on the carpeted floor in comrade-
ship, the time was beautifully ripe for the women to
have a really good gossip. Commanding their full
attention by leaning forward, Nilofer intended to turn
the situation to her advantage. She had a score to settle
with her Cousin Shahzada from a long way back. Her
heart thus leapt at this glorious opportunity, graciously
landing her way, to rubbish this high and mighty
family!

'Who would spend millions of rupees on a ceremony
that isn't even a wedding? Would you, my sisters?' Her
glittering eyes defied them to disagree with her. 'All
that expense, and for what purpose? You have seen her
trousseau, her *jihaz*, haven't you?' she enquired, a mis-
chievous expression on her face. When one woman
shook her head, Nilofer stood up, readily offering to
take them on a tour.

'You don't know what a surprise you are in for, my sisters. I'll take you round into the marquee in the courtyard. There is so much to see; so much to marvel at. Do you know how many outfits Zarri Bano has got? I tell you – hundreds! I am not exaggerating, my friends, because I have been here for two weeks already, and helped to collect and prepare Zarri Bano's trousseau. Ruby and I chose most of the things. Zarri Bano had nothing to do with it. Poor thing! She has kept herself away from all this. I bet even Benazir Bhutto didn't have a trousseau like this at her wedding. It is just like a grand bride's.' She sighed dramatically, and turned to look each one in the face.

'But it is a macabre experience, truly, I tell you,' she said in hushed tones, 'for when will Zarri Bano wear all of these clothes, if she is going to be cloaked in a long black veil, the *burqa*? We had that especially designed for her, you know, from a master tailor in Karachi. Which husband is she going to tantalise with her glamorous outfits? What social function is she going to grace? Where will she show off her wedding finery? As I envisage it her life is going to rotate more or less around the *madrasa* and the prayer-mat. A life of total religious devotion and simplicity.' Nilofer stopped to catch her breath. A triumphant glow brushed her face, as she took in their discomfited expressions. A shiver of delight ran down her spine.

She wanted to cap her triumph further, by taking some of them on a tour to show the display in the *jahaiz* marquee. The group of eager women cantered dutifully behind her, out through the courtyard and into the large green marquee erected on the adjacent field, brimming with Zarri Bano's trousseau and gifts.

For the village women in particular it was like an

Aladdin's cave. As they trailed behind Nilofer, their eyes grew wide in wonder at all the gold and silver jewellery lovingly displayed in red and green velvet boxes. There were so many sequinned *shalwar kameze* suits, each vying for attention.

'What is the purpose of all this? Nobody will see her wear it,' one woman muttered loud enough to be heard by her friend.

'Our Habib Sahib wanted to lavish everything on Zarri Bano,' another woman told her in clear, soft tones, happening to overhear the disparaging comment. A close member of Habib's clan, she had been left to supervise the trousseau display.

'Although there will be no groom at this ceremony,' she continued, 'you may regard it as a sort of wedding ceremony and all that goes with it. Habib Sahib didn't want his daughter deprived of her trousseau. She will wear all these.' The woman swept her arm around the marquee, pointing to all the boxes of clothes on display in rows, and the jewellery cases. 'Of course she can't be vain now like the rest of us, and show off all her finery at functions like weddings,' she said pointedly. Open incredulity was painted on one or two of the women's faces; a distinct sneer on Nilofer's.

They all wondered what Zarri Bano thought of all this. The thing was, hardly anybody had seen her. She had ignored the presence of the guests in her home, and nobody had the temerity to approach her – let alone have a heart-to-heart chat with her as they so ardently wished.

The only person honoured to have that right was a *Shahzadi Ibadat* from another clan in the town. Invited personally by Habib to the ceremony, she had been

delegated with the task of supporting and inducting Zarri Bano into the ceremony and the code of etiquette that the role demanded.

Sakina, a *Shahzadi Ibadat* and heiress of her father's home and land, was ceremoniously taken upstairs to Zarri Bano's room by Fatima. She walked with measured steps through the house, looking round her with detached interest at the preparations for Zarri Bano's veiling ceremony. Her mind buzzed with a feeling of *déjà vu*, recalling poignantly her own ceremony, some twenty years earlier.

Fatima left her at Zarri Bano's door and Sakina reverted to the present. She knocked gently and the door was opened by a young woman. Sakina noted detachedly the glamorous outfit that the woman wore and her immaculately made-up face.

Zarri Bano sat in front of the dressing table in a sequinned red chiffon bridal outfit. Her long, wavy hair was being braided by Ruby, to shape it into a knot on top of her head. An intricately designed gold filigree necklace hugged her neck. Its long matching earrings dangled becomingly from her ears, while her rounded white arms shone with dozens of beautifully designed gold bangles.

'Is that me?' Zarri Bano asked in bemusement, staring at the mocking bridal image in front of her. 'I look like any bride in Pakistan.' Even her hands had been ritually painted by her sister with henna patterns the previous night. She grimaced at the sight of her reddish-orange stained palms.

The mockery of her finery and jewellery was too much. 'All this pretence!' she sighed. 'What is it for?'

She blinked – looking up. A black shadow stood ominously behind her stool.

Her heart skipping a beat, Zarri Bano visibly recoiled at the sight of Sakina's black cloaked head, allowing only two thirds of her face to be seen. There was no forehead. Only half a chin was visible.

'This is what I am going to look like,' her mind screamed in horror. 'This paintwork on my face, my jewellery and the elaborate hair-do – all of this is going to be hidden behind a heavy black veil.'

'*Assalam-Alaikum*, Zarri Bano.' The dark forbidding image addressed her in the mirror, alarming Zarri Bano out of her reverie. 'May I sit here on this stool?'

Zarri Bano desperately tried to collect her wits about her. '*Wa Laikum-Salam*. Of course!' she assented.

'My name is Sakina. You have probably heard of me – my father was Murad Chaudhury.'

'Yes, yes, of course, *Baji Jan*. Father spoke about you.' Zarri Bano rose to greet her guest, quickly recovering her customary poise.

Sakina caught Zarri Bano's profile in the tall dressing-table mirror; watching it in wonder. It was just as exquisite as her front.

'You are a very beautiful woman, Zarri Bano,' she uttered on impulse. 'I had already heard about you, but today, seeing you in this finery, I must admit that the person did justice to you in her praises.'

Zarri Bano stared ruefully at Sakina. 'I am just an ordinary young woman in the prime of my life. Please, there is no need to praise.' The subject of her beauty had long since lost its appeal to Zarri Bano.

She stared down at her fair hands with their intricate henna patterns, at her long tapering fingers, with their immaculately shaped nails. They were graced by rings of all shapes and sizes, studded with a multitude of different gems. Rubies, emeralds and diamonds.

'Tell me, Sister Sakina, what use are these?' she asked quietly, a hint of sarcasm seeping through, raising her hands to Sakina. 'Why are my hands bedecked in this ridiculous fashion? Normally I never wear more than two rings at a time. Here, look, I have eight rings on my fingers! They couldn't find one for the thumb! Who am I going to impress? Which in-laws? Which husband is going to admire their design and count them? You don't wear anything on your hands. Did you go through this macabre drama, of being dressed up as a bride before you became a Holy Woman?' At this Zarri Bano stopped, pinning Sakina with her intense green gaze.

Sakina looked around awkwardly, aware that they had an interested audience, Ruby and two other women. It wasn't fair to Zarri Bano to have others witness the agony she was undergoing. Only she, Sakina, as a Holy Woman herself, could identify with Zarri Bano's traumatic experience. For she, too, had lived through this pantomime of a ceremony, propelled helplessly on by a tide of events over which she had had no control.

Like Zarri Bano too, she had been blackmailed into it by her male elders. The only difference, and the most poignant difference of all, Sakina sadly noted, was that Zarri Bano was exquisite, whereas she herself had been quite plain. It seemed a crime against nature. Not to marry. Not to have children. Not to lead a normal life. Sakina stared at Zarri Bano, feeling very sad all of a sudden.

'Zarri Bano, is it all right if we can have a chat on our own?' Sakina ventured to ask.

'Yes, of course. Ruby . . . ' Zarri Bano swivelled an apologetic gaze at her sister.

'Of course, sister. Come on, girls.' Ruby beckoned

her Cousin Gulshan and her two friends out of the room. Zarri Bano and Sakina watched them go and turned back to look at one another.

'Please, Sister Sakina, come and sit on this armchair.'

'Thank you.' Sakina went over to the armchair and sat down.

Neither knew how to begin. Zarri Bano stood awkwardly in the middle of her bedroom, wanting to say so much, yet not trusting herself to say anything to a total stranger. Her eyes drawn hypnotically to the bed, Zarri Bano shivered at the sight of the *burqa*. Sakina's face softened in understanding.

'Yes, Sister Zarri Bano, that is all that is left for you to wear, before you are ready for the ceremony in the hall. Shall I help you into it?' she coaxed softly.

Was it her imagination or did she actually see Zarri Bano shrink back a step? The expression in her eyes was that of a wild, wounded animal – trapped!

Sakina came to a quick decision. Her responsibility entailed not letting anybody down, neither Habib Khan nor Zarri Bano. With a firm step, she strode up to the bed and gently lifted the *burqa* in her arms. A gentle look on her face, she turned to Zarri Bano.

'My sister, it will seem very strange to wear this veil at first, but you'll soon get used to it. Female modesty, and the general veiling of women is part of our faith and culture, as you know. Therefore, this is no different garment than that worn by any other Muslim women, say in Iran, for example. They have been wearing these since the revolution – ordinary women, who wear it outside for their modesty. Here in Pakistan we have always had the *burqa*. It's just that you have never worn it before and it has gone out of fashion somewhat, lately. The *chador* has replaced it. Therefore you're

bound to find it a little strange at first. Shall we try it on?'

Zarri Bano nodded mutely, staring at the black cloak in Sakina's arms. The *burqa* slithered over her head, her shoulders and down to her feet. Sakina then fixed the hood over Zarri Bano's hair, planting it firmly in place so that it only showed a small triangle of the bride's face.

Zarri Bano stood frozen in the *burqa*, dehumanised.

Like a large black tent, it hid her red ceremonial suit totally. Only her slippered feet were visible. The sleeves of the *burqa* reached below her wristline. The countless number of gold bangles she wore jangled awkwardly inside. The seam of the face triangle chaffed her delicate cheeks and she felt hot.

'You look lovely,' Sakina smiled. 'Would you like to have a look in the mirror?'

Zarri Bano's eyes widened in surprise at Sakina's words. Hysteria spiralled wildly inside her. Shaking her head she closed her eyes, suffocated behind the black cloak.

Unable to contain herself any longer, she burst forth: 'Look *lovely* – in this? Can any woman look lovely in this garment? I loathe this cloth, Sister Sakina. It burns my body! I have never even worn a shawl, a *chador*, let alone a *burqa* in my entire life. This thing – I cannot bear it! It is smothering the life out of me. Do you know that black was my favourite colour, two months ago? But this!' Her body began to shudder uncontrollably behind the cold soft fabric.

'I know, my sister, but you will have to bear it. You will get used to it soon.'

'Never! Never!' Zarri Bano's harsh voice tripped over a lump rising in her throat as she turned her face away from Sakina, hiding her vulnerability.

'You'll change, Zarri Bano, I can personally assure you. I went through this phase that you are going through. It is a moment in time only, my friend. Like all phases of time, it brings with it emotions, pains and heartaches. For you, life will never be the same,' she promised. 'You'll have the most exciting time you can imagine. You'll become knowledgeable about Islam – a scholar. You'll have followers – respect, dignity, honour and fame. I have all that. I could never have had it, if I had just married like an ordinary woman, and had a family.'

'Sister Sakina, I don't want respect, honour or fame! I want to be my normal self – an ordinary woman,' said Zarri Bano, her voice quivering with emotion.

'Once I said the same, Sister Zarri Bano. Later I changed my tune. I have never regretted it and you'll not regret it either, my sister. Of course, occasionally there will be pangs of nostalgia, that is quite normal. You'll feel those when you see women surrounded by their children, or when they are having an intimate *tête-à-tête* with their husbands. But those losses are just a drop in the ocean, compared with what you will gain. You'll have freedom and independence. I have travelled all over the world. I have studied at university. I have been to international conferences. Could I have done all this if I was tied to a husband and a family? I tell you this to make you feel better, to convey to you that the gains of becoming a *Shahzadi Ibadat* surpass by miles the losses you make.'

Listening politely to Sakina and letting her words wash over her, Zarri Bano couldn't hold back her agonised cry. 'All I know is that,' she pinched a fold of the *burqa* in front of Sakina, 'with this cloth, Zarri Bano is dead. The woman who lived in this room for the past

twenty-seven years, is gone. I have been stripped of my identity and a stranger is taking my place. I am, at this moment in time, wrestling with the death and mourning of one woman, while preparing in fear for the birth and rise of another. I don't want Zarri Bano to die! But I cannot keep her alive. I have to part with the woman in love, Sister Sakina, in order to fall in with my father's aspirations and wishes and our clan's customs. You know why this is so, because the same must have happened to you. This is in order to guard our inheritance, our precious land, which will be penned to my name, by the time this day ends. I don't want the fields or to become the heiress, Sister Sakina – but then, that is beside the point, isn't it? It has been willed by my father and grandfather that I will be *made* the heiress and the Holy Woman.' She took in a deep and shuddering breath.

'But I have my pride too, Sister Sakina!' she went on passionately. 'Nobody can take that away from me. I will not do *all* their bidding. There is a bit of Zarri Bano that I will retain for all time, even though I will kill and bury the rest. And that is my personal pride and integrity! If you'll excuse me, Sister Sakina, I have something to do before I go down. I will not go down as a bride-cum-nun – I can only be one, not both!' Her eyes sparkled in her flushed face.

Sakina stared back, dumbfounded. 'Yes of course. Will you be all right?' she asked meekly.

'Yes!' Flashing her most beguiling smile at Sakina, Zarri Bano's cheeks dimpled. Sakina immediately felt better.

Now fully in control of the situation once more. 'I will call you when I am ready,' Zarri Bano gently informed her visitor.

Sakina left the room and stood outside in the corridor, talking to Ruby.

Inside the room, Zarri Bano threw the *burqa* off onto the bed. With quick deft movements, she removed each piece of jewellery from her neck, ears, arms and fingers. Slipping out of the red bridal outfit, comprising of a long sequinned pleated skirt, with a short matching tunic, she stood tall in her ivory silk slip in front of the mirror and surveyed herself.

Next she unpinned the wavy coils of her hair piled high in a becoming regal style. Shaking her head, Zarri Bano let the heavy silky curtain fall around her shoulders. She gazed at herself for long poignant seconds in the mirror, etching forever the picture of her face onto her mind.

Then, taking a large pair of scissors from the dressing-table drawer and holding her hair in a heavy bunch at the top of her head, Zarri Bano sheared it across with a strong steady movement. Eight inches of glossy hair fluttered in feathery bunches on to the marble floor. Zarri Bano glanced again at the image in the mirror. Like a newly hatched chicken, her hair stuck out in an unbecoming style around her face.

Not recognising herself Zarri Bano stared, mesmerised by her appearance. Then, taking a tissue, she wiped her face clean of all traces of make-up.

Satisfied with her work, she slipped the *burqa* back over her head, feeling much lighter now. There were no pins digging into her scalp, no necklace painfully bruising her neck, no heavy bangles weighing down her arms, and no heavily embroidered outfit being crushed by her cloak.

The cloak hid the shape of her body totally. 'I could be fifteen stones in weight and obese, but nobody

would know the difference,' Zarri Bano mused. In effect nobody would ever guess that apart from a silky slip and other pieces of lingerie, she wore nothing else.

'Ruby,' Zarri Bano called. She wasn't ready to face Sakina yet.

Ruby came running in, then stopped – transfixed. She bravely battled with the image of her sister in the *burqa*, her lips quivering with distress.

Zarri Bano read and analysed the fleeting expressions chasing over her younger sister's face. First there was shock, then an urgent wrestling with her facial muscles as Ruby tried desperately to smile at her sister, and failed miserably.

Her heart sinking, Zarri Bano looked sadly at her sister's face.

'Ruby, you are my mirror,' she whispered. 'I think what you think. I feel what you feel, my darling.'

'Have you not seen yourself?' Ruby gulped.

'No,' came the sad reply, prompting Zarri Bano to move away from the tall mirror.

Suddenly, Ruby shrieked in horror as she spotted the hair on the floor. Squatting down, she picked up the soft waves and held them out to Zarri Bano. 'Why have you done this to your hair, *Baji Jan*?' she questioned in shock.

'What use is it, under this *burqa*?'

Shaking her head in disbelief, Ruby fingered the silky waves in her hand. Then her eyes fell on the jewellery scattered on the dressing table and the bridal outfit thrown on the armchair. She turned a look of sheer incredulity at her sister.

'I can either be a Holy Woman or a bride, Ruby. I cannot be dressed for both,' explained Zarri Bano. 'These things are yours to inherit – my trousseau as

well as my waves. You always envied me my hair. Now you can pin the waves to your head, for you will not have to hide *your* hair.'

With firm dignified steps, Zarri Bano went out into the corridor. Sakina was amazed at the transformation she saw there. The tension, the misery, the devastation had indeed been *killed* off! Zarri Bano's poignant words that 'Zarri Bano was dead' and that 'now a stranger had taken her place', darted back in Sakina's mind. A stranger did indeed stand in front of her! For who else could look as serene as this woman did, after the heart-breaking scene they had earlier shared in her bedroom?

'Are you ready to go down, Zarri Bano?' Sakina smiled at the young woman, offering her hand to her.

For one electric moment, Zarri Bano's heart skipped a beat. Then, in control once more, she inclined her head proudly.

'Yes, Sister Sakina. Thank you for coming to see me, and talking to me. We are two souls locked together by our special fate.' The wooden words didn't manage to mask the sorrow in her tone.

'There is no need to thank me, my beautiful sister.' Sakina saw with wonder that Zarri Bano's beauty would shine through like a beacon, in all its glory, even in a *burqa*.

Sakina called to Ruby. The girl came out of the bed-room, still reeling from the shock of knowing that her sister was almost half naked under her *burqa* and her hair was shorn. She stared bemused at the two head-to-toe black-clad women.

'Are you all right, *Baji Jan*?' she asked in a voice thick with tears, her eyes on Zarri Bano's face.

'I am fine.' Zarri Bano pressed her sister's hand. 'Be assured that I will not let you, our father, or the clan

down,' she whispered in Ruby's ear, pushing aside her earring. 'I will go through with it.'

'I know you will, my dear sister, but I don't *want* you to go through with it! I just wish to God that it was a bad dream and that I would wake up with a sigh of relief.'

'It is no dream, Ruby, my sister – I should know! Have I not wished a hundred times to wake up from this nightmare that has tormented me for the past two months? It *is* happening, Ruby. Wake up!' The bitter edge to her tone marred the smile she flashed for Sakina's benefit.

'Let's then go and get this farce over with,' Zarri Bano mumbled to no one in particular as she started to walk down the stairs.

Chapter 20

TOGETHER, ZARRI BANO, Sakina and Ruby descended the wide circular staircase. An eager entourage of women and children awaited at the foot of the stairs, supposedly to catch their first glimpse of the Holy Woman in her ceremonial veil. Weddings were a common affair. This, however, was a very rare event and seeing Zarri Bano, the glamorous daughter of Habib Khan, become a Holy Woman and in a *burqa* was an event indeed.

Zarri Bano didn't disappoint them! Her eyes flickering cynically over their excited faces, she smiled becomingly, acutely aware of the spectacle that she and her sister made.

What a contrasting pair! the women thought.

Both sisters were beautiful, one looking her best in her special party outfit for the occasion, while the other was enveloped in a shapeless black cloak, with ninety per cent of her body totally hidden from sight.

Crowding together and leaning over each other's shoulders, the women guests perked their ears, trying to listen to the chink of Zarri Bano's gold bangles. They were sure that she was wearing gold jewellery under the *burqa*, because they had seen it displayed in the marquee. 'Pity she didn't come down in her finery and show herself off before she got into that black crow's outfit,' mumbled one woman to her friend in exasperation, feeling cheated.

In the large drawing room, Zarri Bano's arrival had already been announced prior to her entering it. As the sisters stood on the threshold, all eyes turned with a hypnotic stare in their direction.

Gazing steadily in front of her, Zarri Bano saw rather than heard the guests take an in-drawn breath, knowing she had indeed created a spectacle. Nobody had ever glimpsed Zarri Bano in a *burqa* before. Nor would they have expected it of her in a hundred years for, amongst Habib's clan, she had the reputation of being the elegant and fashionable one, on whose head the *dupatta* never stayed in place. Also, she was the one reputed to turn men's heads.

Now seeing her dressed in such severity, some of the guests, both men and women, felt ill at ease as the stark implication behind the ceremony suddenly came pressing heavily down on them. The ceremonial trappings in the room were reminiscent of a wedding. Yet it wasn't a wedding they were gracing with their presence. There was no groom to congratulate or happily garland with money. Nor a coy bride to admire in her splendid bridal

finery. Just a beautiful woman hidden from sight in a severe-looking black cloak, with a very unbecoming slit for her face. Today it was an upside down world.

Stunned, and with her mouth half open, Gulshan, Zarri Bano's cousin, sat next to her mother with the other guests. She had earlier helped to dress Zarri Bano, but now she found it difficult to come to terms with her cousin in a *burqa*. An envious admirer of Zarri Bano, she had spent much of her short life hating and admiring her cousin for her good looks, poise and finesse.

Her envy dated back to her childhood days. Gulshan had always felt overshadowed by Zarri Bano, to such an extent that she had found it almost painfully claustrophobic to be in the same room as her cousin. Sharing Zarri Bano's traits of arrogance and vanity, she, nevertheless lacked her wit, charisma and beauty.

When Gulshan had first heard of Zarri Bano becoming a Holy Woman, she had felt a jolt of perverse delight, followed by guilt. Like everyone else in the hall, she had waited with bated breath to see if Zarri Bano would actually do it, would actually come down in a *burqa* as a Holy Woman.

Now as she beheld her in the black sack-like cloak, a storm of feelings rent Gulshan apart. Instead of gloating, she was overcome by horror and compassion. It is an outrage! she thought shakily. The other woman is suited to the part, but not our Zarri Bano. Tears pricking her eyelids, she longed to shout out to the guests: 'Don't do this to our Zarri Bano, please!'

Her lips, however, remained sealed, bound by centuries old patriarchal customs and conventions of female silence and obedience. What could she do, anyway, if Zarri Bano's own mother and sister had been powerless to help? She cast a surreptitious glance at her

grandfather, her Uncle Habib and her father. An aggressive vehicle in full motion, well engineered and oiled, the ceremony was rapidly heading for its inevitable destination. Gulshan, as a mere young woman, was just a small pebble in the company of giant rocks, to be easily trodden upon and crushed if the need arose.

Gulshan noticed the broad-shouldered young man who sat with his mother in the same row of chairs as herself. He, too, was watching the proceedings with a hypnotic fascination. Gulshan admired his clean, good-looking profile. A flutter of attraction curling inside her, she marvelled: 'Does Zarri Bano feel nothing for this man?'

The man whose looks had attracted Gulshan was, however, receiving glances from a number of people. It seemed so strange, for if Jafar had not died, it would have been Sikander sitting next to Zarri Bano as a groom. This was *kismet* indeed!

Immune to all the interested glances cast his way, Sikander's eyes remained fixed on the black-cloaked woman. Could that be Zarri Bano? His mind wrestled with the image. This figure bore no resemblance to the woman he knew and had desired. He recalled her peach-like skin, her glossy curls, her feminine curves – where was everything? He clamped down on the insatiable urge to rush up to her and tear the ugly garment violently aside from her body. In vain he tried to reason with himself as to why he was reacting so strongly. Older women had worn the *burqa* for centuries. Most women, in certain sectors of Pakistani society, still wore them, but he could not bear to see his Zarri Bano dressed that way.

Sikander riveted his steel-grey gaze on Habib – the master puppeteer in this macabre theatre. Tasting gall

in his mouth, Sikander felt the heat of hate rush to his cheeks.

His eyes on his eldest daughter, Habib pretended to be oblivious of Sikander's stare and his animosity. Like everyone else in the hall he, too, was shaken by Zarri Bano's appearance in the *burqa*, but he managed to keep his face poker straight as he sat with his father, Siraj Din, his brother and another village elder.

Facing the four seated figures of the men on the stage was the group of women, comprising of Zarri Bano, Ruby, Shahzada, Sakina, an elder aunt of Zarri Bano's and Chaudharani Kaniz from the village. The latter, as the late landlord's wife, had been given the special honour of sitting on the stage.

The stage was set up at the top end of the hall. Like the rest of the room, it was elaborately festooned with balloons, colourful bulbs and streamers. A special red floral Persian silk carpet graced its floor. Near Habib and the other members of his family sat two village elders on a large velour-backed *chaise longue*. In the centre of the stage stood a mahogany coffee table with a large bouquet of fresh flowers in a vase. Next to it, on an elegantly carved walnut trellis, rested a large Holy Quran with an exquisitely hand-painted cover. Facing the stage, on rows of velvet-backed chairs, sat the guests.

Coughing to draw attention to himself, Habib stood up to face his audience. Zarri Bano sat with her dark head lowered, gazing down at the silk Persian carpet. Clearing his throat, her father began.

'Welcome everybody, my brothers and sisters, relatives and friends, to my daughter's ceremony. I am most honoured to have you here today. For those guests who arrived a few days ago, I hope you have enjoyed

your stay in my home. For those of you who have arrived today, I hope that you will be able to stay with us for a couple of days, at least, and accept our humble hospitality.'

'I have invited the most revered of all the *buzurgs* in our district to perform this ceremony. He has been connected with my family and clan for a long, long time. Of course, as you are probably aware, the ceremony that you are about to witness is not a typical wedding ceremony, or an engagement party. It is peculiar to our clan and we are very proud of it. It elevates, in a unique way, our women into a role far beyond the common lot of women. My beautiful eldest daughter . . . ' He glanced at Zarri Bano with love shining out of his eyes.

'My Zarri Bano is to be my heiress, our Holy Woman. She will become a scholar of Islam, a moral and religious tutor for hundreds of younger women in our town and province: a female symbol of purity and *Ibadat* in its purest form. Eventually, we hope, she will have her own school of thought, her own *madrasa* or college. She will return to university and study Islam at a higher degree level. To these ends I am thinking of sending her to Misr, Cairo University, which is the oldest Islamic university in the Muslim world. As part of her new life, she will attend Islamic conferences around the world – whenever or wherever they are offered. She will be under the wing of another Holy Woman – Sakina, who is a good friend of our family. Mohtarama Sakina is going to initiate my daughter into her new role. For, you see, it is not an easy matter to become a Holy Woman, as there is so much to learn and many expectations to fulfil. In fact, it is a new life.'

'The only difference is that in order for my Zarri

Bano to do all of this, she will not have the time or the will for mundane things – the everyday things.'

Habib stopped to catch his breath, letting his gaze travel over the assembled guests. The large room was now blanketed in an eerie silence. Only the purring sound of the ceiling fans could be heard. A sigh of pure satisfaction escaped him. Now mightily pleased with his own eloquence, he continued.

'As I was saying, my daughter will be too busy to become involved in the trivial things that girls enjoy doing, like going to the bazaars for bangles. She will not have time for marriage, husband or family. Which husband, I ask you all, would tolerate a wife devoting herself totally to *ibadah*, to worship. To perform this role well, you must give yourself totally to it. My daughter has agreed to do all of this, and to commit herself to becoming our clan's Holy Woman in the traditional style of our family. She will also, from henceforth, become my sole heiress, to whom all this wealth and land of mine I bequeath, when I die. It will then be up to her how she disposes of her inheritance. Normally it is passed on to the first male heir of a sibling. So, for instance, if my Ruby were to have a son, he would become the heir.

'This is why we are all gathered here today, to initiate and hand over my daughter to her new role. Our *buzurg* will perform the ceremony. He will start by reciting some *surahs* from the Holy Quran and *surah Al-Yasin*.

'Please begin!' Habib turned to the elder *buzurg*, before returning to his seat.

Dressed in a long black coat and with a white, starched turban on his head, the *buzurg* stood up. Clearing his throat, he read from the Holy Quran.

Hearing his voice ringing out clear and loud in the hall, the women quickly hastened to cover their heads with their scarves in deference to the sacred words. Then the elder *buzurg*, lifting the Holy Quran from the wooden trellis stand, bent down in front of Zarri Bano; he held it up over her head first and read some more *surahs* and then put it close to her face.

Zarri Bano looked up at him, not knowing what was expected of her. Then when understanding dawned on her she took the Holy Quran into her hands and kissed it reverently on both sides. The *buzurg* prompted her to repeat some *surahs* from it. She obliged, while the guests watched and listened spellbound. The *buzurg* was not an Imam, but the ceremony had become very much like a *nikka*, a wedding ceremony. When Zarri Bano had finished reciting after him, the old man thanked her and then gently and respectfully placed the Holy Quran back in its place.

'Now you are wedded to your faith,' he told her in a voice that echoed around the room.

Going up to Habib, he offered his hand. Habib pulled the *buzurg* into a warm embrace. Then, turning to his father, Suraj Din, he did the same. The words of congratulation – *mubarak* – echoed eerily around the almost silent room.

For some of the male guests, this was a cue to get up and talk to their fellow men. The ceremony was over and the hall had become noisy, all of a sudden. The guests began to embrace one another in a manner reminiscent of wedding ceremonies. Zarri Bano remained sitting with her eyes fixed on the Holy Quran, not quite taking in the scene. When the noise level eventually penetrated her mind, she turned round to look at the guests.

Her gaze swung over the crowd, meeting eyes and then darting away, until they fell upon a pair of grey ones. Her befuddled brain came alive. Those eyes! She knew that man! An aching awareness raced through her body. 'He has come after all, even though he said that he wouldn't.' Both gratified and humbled by his presence, her eyes sought to communicate her apology, trying desperately to spell what her lips wouldn't say for her, and what her hands couldn't tell him. 'Please forgive me!' they begged of the man whose love she had sacrificed. 'Please forgive and forget me. It is all over!'

Sikander latched onto her eyes, both captivated and loath to let go of the accidental contact. They were the only tangible means of communication he had, by which he was able to relate to his old Zarri Bano. While hers expressed sorrow and apology, his eyes darted frustration and betrayal at her – flashing out his own particular message: 'I will never forgive you, Zarri Bano!'

Her father's hand on her shoulder ruthlessly broke the contact from across the room. Chilled, Zarri Bano dropped her gaze, withdrawing once again into the shell of numbness she had built around herself. When her father called her name, she raised empty eyes at him. Smiling, with love shining out of his eyes, he congratulated her and kissed her on the top of her cloaked head. Then her grandfather, Siraj Din, came to her and did the same. Turning to Ruby, Habib told her to take Zarri Bano into the other room as the ceremony was now over.

With a confident gait, Habib stepped off the stage, and went to accept his guests' congratulations and the placing of money garlands around his neck. Zarri Bano, flanked dutifully by Sakina and Ruby on either side, was quietly led away through the crowd of bemused

guests. Nobody dared approach Zarri Bano or had the temerity to come and congratulate her or place garlands around her neck. It was a noticeable omission. In the minds of many was the question: 'What is there to congratulate? A young woman caged into a barren life!'

On reaching the door of the hall, Zarri Bano discovered the exit was semi-barred by Sikander. First she shot him a look of surprise. Then a shuttered expression descended in her eyes as she looked over his shoulders and beyond into the other room.

It was then that Sikander painfully accepted his defeat. Impotent to do anything, he stepped awkwardly back into the hall and stared around at the guests. Had everyone in that room gone mad? What was the *mubarak* for? Were they celebrating the imprisonment of a woman? Had nobody the guts to have stopped it? Did that *buzurg* actually perform a ceremony? What sort of ceremony was that? Did he substitute the Holy Quran for a groom? Was Zarri Bano wedded to her faith, instead of a living man?

His mother, Bilkis, tugged at his arm and gently led him out of the room. She had watched him nervously, trying to follow the train of his thoughts. Bilkis feared both for him and Zarri Bano. Now in her new role, Zarri Bano was forbidden from mixing freely with the male sex. Before Sikander left the hall, he turned and caught Habib's eye. The two men stared steadily at one another. Habib's eyes were triumphant while Sikander's flashed sheer hatred and disbelief.

Glancing from one to the other, Bilkis pulled her son out of the hall and into the marquee on the lawn. The dinner was already being served by the turbaned chefs when Bilkis sat at the table. Sikander looked down at his mother as if she had gone mad. 'What is the matter,

my son? Sit down and eat. It is all over!' she whispered, looking up at him in concern.

'Sit down and eat!' he mimicked, shaking his head in disbelief at her. 'Mother, I am going out of my mind. I cannot eat! I don't know why I came. In my heart, I still foolishly believed that, somehow, Zarri Bano wouldn't go through with this farce, and that somebody, somewhere would put a stop to it. But we have all failed her and colluded with her father. I am going, Mother. This place is hell! Everybody's gone mad!'

He stormed out of the marquee, not caring that some of the guests had overheard each and every word, and were staring agog at him and his mother. Bilkis, in an embarrassed silence, stood up and, smiling awkwardly, followed her son out of the *kothi*, and out of Zarri Bano's life.

Fireworks and rockets were lit and shot into the sky, bursting into thousands of small speckled stars, much to the delight of the guests and small children from neighbouring families. Like a colourful garland of flowers, the lights were a merry beacon to neighbouring places and people, letting them know that jollity was still afoot in Habib's home.

To end the celebrations, Habib had arranged for a group of musicians to perform folk songs for the guests. The men, with their various musical instruments including the tabla drums, sat cross-legged on a raised cushioned platform in one of the marquees.

Soon they had everyone swaying to the sound and rhythm of their music. First they sang religious verses, focusing on the life of the prophet Mohammed, and then secular ones, celebrating love and human passion.

Sounds of sheer enjoyment were punctuated by the words, '*Wa wa!*' from every quarter. Some guests either jumped out of their seats to dance or fell in a delirious trance, their heads swaying from side to side and their feet tapping to the beat of the tabla drums and the clapping of hands.

Spellbound and in the throes of musical enjoyment himself, Habib tapped a beat with his fingers on the armrest of his chair, as he sat in front of his male guests. The music had washed away all the tensions of the day from his body. He looked around the marquee for his wife, wondering whether she was listening too – but Shahzada was nowhere to be seen!

His wife was in Zarri Bano's room, trying to coax her eldest daughter to eat something. Since the ceremony, Zarri Bano had said very little and had eaten nothing. She sat in her black veil on the edge of her bed, staring at her mother and sister as they perched on the sofa in front of her.

'Please, Zarri Bano, you must eat something,' Shahzada pleaded.

'I am not hungry, Mother,' Zarri Bano replied quietly, her eyes seeming to look right through her.

'You will become ill, my princess.' Shahzada got up and gathered her daughter into her arms. Standing passively in the embrace, Zarri Bano's arms stayed by her side.

'I cannot eat, Mother,' she said at last, pushing Shahzada gently away from her. 'Please go. You have guests to attend to. Ruby, you too must go, my darling. I know you love the musicians – I can hear them from here. I will be all right. After all, brides are normally left alone at the end.'

pared

Mother and younger daughter stared at one another. She had used the word bride!

Chapter 21

IT WAS PAST midnight. Most of Habib's guests had gone to sleep in their allocated rooms. A small group of them, however, remained sitting together in the marquee on the lawn and continued to discuss the day's events.

Shahzada, as the hostess, left them to it – she had had enough. Going to her daughter's room and peering inside, she found it in darkness. Thinking that Zarri Bano was asleep, Shahzada quietly closed the door. She then stood in the corridor, loath to enter her own room and be alone with her husband.

When she finally entered, in the semi-darkness, Shahzada's chest heaved in silent rage. How could her husband sleep peacefully? She glided silently around the room and didn't see Habib sit upright in his bed.

The moonlight from the window streaming into their room cast shadows on the wall. 'Have they all gone to sleep?' he asked quietly. Shahzada's hand froze in mid-air, in the sleeve of her night-shirt *kurta*. Her shoulders stiffening, she didn't reply nor turn round to face him. Instead, she walked into the bathroom adjoining their room.

Disappointed, Habib lay back on his pillow, his eyes staring at the ceiling. When Shahzada returned to the room and climbed quietly into her own bed, he waited for her to speak. She said nothing. He gasped in surprise. It was never like this before!

'It was a great ceremony. Shahzada, wasn't it?' His words sliced through her, stinging her into responding as nothing else would have done.

'Yes, it was a great ceremony – for *you*, Habib!' she spat bitterly.

'For me? What about you?' he asked, turning his face towards her. She was staring at him with her wide, eloquent eyes.

'For *me*, Habib?' She almost choked on the words. 'To sacrifice my daughter to such a fate – do you call that great?'

He struggled to keep hold of his temper. 'I wish you wouldn't go about spouting such nonsense. If you say that, as a mother, what will other people say?'

'I am not concerned about what other people say, Habib.'

He flinched at her impolite way of addressing him by his first name without her customary respectful term *jee*. It was a deliberate and insulting omission on her part.

'All I know is that you have won. You have finally achieved what you have always craved in your heart for your daughter. Your son's death gave you the ideal excuse,' Shahzada continued inexorably and unafraid.

'What are you saying, Shahzada! This is so unfair . . .'

'Unfair!' she screeched, sitting bolt upright. 'Don't talk to me about fairness! Is it fair to forcefully prevent your daughter from marrying? You never really meant to marry her off to any man, did you? Especially not to Sikander. Oh, no. You love her too much. She is your treasure, your possession, and you couldn't stomach the thought of another man—'

'*Silence*! You stupid, stupid woman.' Sitting up, he glared at her, his hand trembling on the quilt. 'You do

not know what you are saying.' He desperately tried to control his anger and the rapid beat of his heart.

'Yes, Habib, you are right. I *am* a stupid woman. For only a really *stupid* woman would have let her daughter go through that pantomime of a ceremony – just in order to please you. What I do know is that I hate you, Habib, so much for sacrificing our beautiful daughter.' She turned her back to him, her heart thumping against her ribs. Her mouth was parched. She had never spoken to her husband in such a vein before or with such venom.

Thoroughly shaken by his wife's unexpected outburst and her seething hatred, Habib fell back on his pillow. As he stared into the darkness around him, his mind tossed the question at him: *Do I really love my daughter too much? Did I really not want her to marry anybody? Am I such a possessive father?* 'No! No!' he screamed silently in denial. 'It was Jafar's death. We must never forget that!'

Zarri Bano lay in the dark with her eyes wide open, wrapped in the silky cocoon of the *burqa*. She hadn't taken it off, for there was no reason to. Life seemed to have lost all its meaning and momentum. Today had been the strangest day of her life. She couldn't yet begin to make sense of the physical and mental numbness that had seized her from the moment she had embraced the *burqa*. Her stomach had moaned with hunger, but her mouth refused to take anything in. The tray of food remained untouched on her dressing table.

She didn't know exactly when she fell asleep, but she must have done so for when she woke up, light was streaming through the gaps in the drawn curtains. Zarri Bano's eyes journeyed tentatively around the

room. Memories of the ceremony assaulting her, she tightly shut her eyes again, desperately, wishing that it had all been a dream.

Her hand crept to her cropped head; the spiky shards felt unfamiliar under her fingers. The rustle of the *burqa* reminded her that she was still wearing it. Feeling suffocated all of a sudden, she had the violent urge to tear it off.

Holding tightly onto her quilt, Zarri Bano told herself, 'I do not have to wear it, least of all in bed.' There were no rules about wearing it. It was, however, a striking symbol of her new role. How else would people recognise her as the Holy Woman? 'Hence I will always have to wear it,' she reminded herself bitterly.

In the shower room, in one swift movement she peeled off the black garment and threw it onto the marble tiled floor. Immediately she bent down to retrieve it, and then hung it carefully on one of the pegs on the wall, mentally reprimanding herself. 'This is to become my second skin. I must learn to like and respect it. To want to tear it away is tantamount to destroying a part of myself – my new identity.'

Stepping out of her under-garments, Zarri Bano stood under the showerhead, letting the warm water cascade down over her body as she began to lather herself with soap. Catching sight of herself in the mirror-like shine of the tiles, she let her gaze dwell on her body, moving over each contour. Then, closing her eyes tight, she blocked out the image on the tiles. She had always been pleased with what Allah had graced her with.

Her face held up to the shower spray, Zarri Bano let the water wash away the salty tears from her cheeks. 'This should have been my first wedding ritual bath

after a night spent not alone, but with somebody.'
Sikander's face loomed all of a sudden in front of her
eyes. She could still remember the shape and the
sensual texture of his lips.

'How am I going to come to terms with a longing
that has to be denied and to a life of total sterility?' her
heart cried.

What she wouldn't do was deny herself the luxury of
dwelling, for the last time, on her past life and the
people who featured in it. Later she would ruthlessly,
and for ever, shut the door on that compartment of her
mind labelled 'the past'. 'I will,' she vowed, 'but not
today.'

Today, she would allow her mind and heart to
luxuriate in the past and the lost life of Zarri Bano and
what would have been if Jafar hadn't died. 'He said that
I would remember him until the day I died. How can I
forget you? I want you, Sikander!' she wept.

Her hand held against her stomach muscles she
doubled over in pain, a cry of anguish mingling with
the sound of the water spray. How would she ever be
able to quell the ache of an empty, forgotten womb, the
longing to cradle a child against her breast. 'I want
children too, like other women, *Allah pak*!' she
beseeched.

It was the longest shower she had taken in her life.
Physically refreshed, the desolation, however, was
marked in her heart, bones and eyes. Drying herself she
changed into fresh underclothes. Going to her ward-
robe she looked for the simplest and most dowdy of
outfits. Glancing at all the elegant clothes hanging
there, chiffons, crêpes, cotton, lawns and velvets, her
hand lingered on the black chiffon outfit she had worn
on the day when she had first seen Sikander.

With a quick flourish she drew out all the outfits and dumped them onto the floor of her room, including the black one. 'They have no purpose in my life now,' she said. She would ask Fatima to take them away.

Eventually she decided to wear a plain linen suit. Much to her dismay, her eyes once again smarted with tears. Today she should have been bedecked in the most elaborate of bridal outfits in glorious colours. There would have been an air of excitement and gaiety around the place. But then, if it had been her wedding, she wouldn't have been in her own bedroom. She would have been in Karachi, in Sikander's home, and in his bedroom or in Singapore . . .

Zarri Bano strode to the dressing table and draped a towel over the tall mirror, blocking out the image of her short hair. With no face to make up no curls to twist and set elaborately in place, no angling in front of it to see how she looked, the mirror had lost its functional use.

She swiped the dressing-table top clear of bottles, creams, lotions, sachets and perfumes. Dropping everything into a large carrier bag, she knotted it tight. Now only a comb, a tube of hand cream, and a tub of moisturising cream stood on the stark, clean surface. From the drawers, she took out the velvet boxes of jewellery. Opening each one she gazed at its contents. Silver, gold, rubies, opals and emeralds sparkled in front of her face. Closing the boxes, one by one, she placed them in a pile on one corner of the dressing table. She would hand them over to her sister and Cousin Gulshan. 'My only ornament in life now is going to be the veil, the *burqa*,' she told the shrouded mirror.

Her wet hair combed, Zarri Bano slipped back into the *burqa*, assessing her reaction to it. Strangely, it

didn't feel too bad. With a serene expression schooled in her eyes and face, Zarri Bano left her room. The *burqa* swished with each step she took. As she passed her parents' room, the door opened and her father stepped out. Visibly disconcerted, his eyes swept nervously over her beveiled body. Zarri Bano painfully held on to her control. How can he look at me like this, with such horror? she thought. When it is he who has forced me into it!

Immediately pitying her father, she nodded pleasantly at him. The past was over. They had both to accept and reconcile themselves to the present. Dutifully she bade him, '*Assalam-Alaikum*, Father,' and walked on.

'*Wa Laikum-Salam*, my daughter,' he answered quietly, following closely behind, his mind somehow unable to reconcile the two images of her. This was what he had wanted, wasn't it? The *burqa* was an important part of that equation. He couldn't surely have his daughter as a figure of fashion as *Shahzadi Ibadat*. Religious piety and glamour had never gone hand-in-hand.

Watching her descend the stairs, the loathing he felt for that black *thing* signalled to him forcefully that he would never get used to it. Did the head part have to be shaped at such an ugly angle? he fretted. Couldn't it have been a loose wrap that she could casually drape around her head and shoulders, rather than this severe, unbecoming sack of a garment? She was like a black ghost. His daughter had epitomised style and fashion. Surely she didn't have to wear this shapeless sack at home? He would have to talk to her about it.

Unaware of her father's thoughts, Zarri Bano had by now reached the dining room. On seeing her, some

guests stopped talking. They watched her move around the room, intrigued and uneasy at the same time.

Gulshan was the first to recover and stepped forward to greet her cousin with a smile. 'Zarri Bano, come and sit down with me. I wasn't sure whether you were awake, otherwise I would have come upstairs and helped you to dress.'

'Why? To help me to choose one of my trousseau outfits, perhaps?' Zarri Bano replied dryly, lifting the hem of the *burqa* to reveal the shabby suit she wore underneath. Gulshan's eyes widened.

'What did you expect – my bright orange *lengha* that you and my mother ordered from the best tailors in Lahore? I am not a bride to be decked up; after all, I am supposed now to be a devout woman – a woman of simple taste,' retorted Zarri Bano. 'It matters to me very little now what I look like, Gulshan. For you see, vanity is one thing that I have managed to exorcise from the old Zarri Bano. Do you know, I thought that would be the hardest thing to do, but I have managed it quite easily.'

'But you will not be wearing this all the time, surely?' Gulshan stuttered. 'It is only a symbolic covering. Even women in purdah do not wear it all the time, only when they go out. At home they dress like queens.'

'Gulshan, please remember that I am not in *purdah*, to be hidden behind four walls. I can do whatever and go wherever I like, within the parameters of my role and the different demands that it makes on me as a person and as a Holy Woman. I must now live up to that name and learn to adapt to a life of simplicity and humility and, wherever possible, avoid any contact with men.' As she spoke, Zarri Bano looked at her

father. He had heard everything, she knew, for he had
dropped his gaze.

Ruby, standing behind Zarri Bano, found these
words painful, having noticed the signs of grief on her
sister's drawn face. She, herself, had wept half the night.

Zarri Bano's smile faltered a little as she beheld the
tears shining in Ruby's brown eyes.

'Ruby, darling. You and Gulshan can look at my
jewellery and split it up between you, for I have no use
for ornaments any longer.'

Ruby couldn't bear it. Her chest heaving, she fled
from the room. It was as if Zarri Bano was dying before
her eyes and bidding them farewell.

Once she reached her room, Ruby wept bitterly. For
the rest of the day, she kept away from her sister, unable
to bear the sight of the hideous black garment draping
that shapely body. *Burqa* and Zarri Bano just simply
did not go together! If only Jafar had still been alive
today, Zarri Bano would have been returning from her
in-laws' by now, and instead of the black garment, she
would have been dressed in all her wedding finery. A
marvellous gem glittering amongst other gems, with a
strikingly good-looking groom by her side. Now,
wherever Zarri Bano went she would stand out as a dark
forbidding figure – disconcerting all who came in con-
tact with her.

Ruby maintained her distance from Zarri Bano for the
next few days. It was made easier for her by the number
of guests present and the so-called 'religious women'
who came to visit her sister, all eager to impart their
knowledge of Islam.

Sakina remained like a dark shadow by Zarri Bano's
side, making Ruby jealous at times. Zarri Bano now

appeared to be forever praying, rolling beads from her rosary bead chain and reciting verses from the Holy Quran, visiting local religious schools and holding sisterhood seminars with groups of women.

As far as religion was concerned, Zarri Bano acknowledged to herself that she was very ignorant indeed. However, blessed with an agile mind and an academic brain, within two weeks she had not only imbibed the basic knowledge of her faith, but had also progressed to reading scholarly works. Books on Islam now littered every corner of her room.

By the third week a chasm had naturally opened between the two sisters, and both were experiencing a reluctance to have a heart-to-heart talk. Zarri Bano was succeeding in deliberately suppressing memories relating to her past, and Ruby, her beloved sister, was a direct link with her old self. By the time a month had elapsed, Ruby sadly accepted that she had indeed lost her sister to her faith.

It was true. Zarri Bano had now become a fully-fledged Holy Woman. She never did anything half-heartedly.

Chapter 22

PROFESSOR NIGHAT SULTANA thankfully left her room on the campus at Karachi University. With aching legs and her briefcase bulging with assignments to mark, she wasn't looking forward to the Friday holiday.

The telephone rang in her study just as she reached her bungalow.

'It's for you, Mother. It is Aunty Zeenat,' her daughter shouted from the study.

'Thank you, dear. I'll take it,' Nighat told her daughter. 'See if the table is set. I am starving. I also have a splitting headache. The tutorials never seemed to end today.' She sat down on the leather-backed chair at her desk. Taking the receiver in her hand she began to talk to her best friend.

Rucksana left her mother alone and went to the dining room, where she saw that the table had been set for their meal by their woman helper.

Five minutes later, Nighat came into the dining room. Rucksana stood up and, out of respect, held the chair for her mother to sit down. The worry lines were very prominent on Nighat's forehead. Since she had been widowed, seven years ago, they had become a permanent fixture.

'Is everything all right?' Rucksana asked, leaning over the table to fill her mother's plate first.

'Yes, dear. You eat, I am not so hungry,' she replied and went into the drawing room to sit down on the sofa.

'You said you were starving, a moment ago!' her daughter called out to her.

Nighat began to massage the tension away from her forehead. It was like a weight of lead.

'Mother, what is wrong?' Rucksana asked in concern, following her into the drawing room.

'Nothing. You go and eat. I'll join you later.'

'Not until you eat as well. I know that you are extremely tired and hungry.'

'I have lost my appetite, my darling. I am just so angry!'

'Why?'

'Something has happened to one of our APWA

women members – one of my old students, called Zarri
Bano. She has written a number of articles on our behalf
in the magazine she founded. According to Zeenat, she
has become some sort of a Holy Woman. Rucksana, I
cannot believe it of her. What has happened? Is it a
sensational rumour, has it really taken place? Zeenat
says that it is something to do with her family's ancient
traditions and her only brother's recent death in a
horse-riding accident.'

'Mother, what is a Holy Woman?' Rucksana felt
confused. She had never heard the term before.

'I'm not sure, my dear. Zeenat says that she has
become sort of a recluse, and lives in isolation, away
from menfolk. She goes around everywhere in a black
burqa. And the most scandalous part of all this is that
she can never marry anyone – ever! Zarri Bano was one
of my most brilliant students,' Nighat said wistfully.
'She had everything going for her – intelligence, per-
sonality, beauty, and a wealthy family behind her. Most
importantly, she has campaigned strongly for women's
rights. If this has happened to such a strong member,
then we are all lost. Our cause, our aspirations, our
wishes – everything, Rucksana!'

'Don't fret, Mother. Why don't you talk to this Zarri
Bano, or visit her? It might not even be true,' her
daughter suggested helpfully, holding her mother's
hands in hers to give her comfort.

'I definitely intend to talk to her,' Nighat replied,
the preoccupied look still in her eyes.

'Good! Now let's eat. I am ravenous,' said Rucksana,
pulling her mother with her into the dining room.

Sitting in her seat, Nighat toyed with her food. Her
thoughts remained firmly with Zarri Bano all that
evening, the assignments to be marked now totally

forgotten. At night-time, she lay awake, her mind ablaze with strange images, molten anger racing through her body. Anger at Zarri Bano, at what she had done, at her family and above all at the Pakistani women's ineffectuality in the face of overwhelming patriarchal power.

On Friday afternoon, a week later, Nighat left her home in Karachi and went to visit Zarri Bano at Tanda Adam. As she drove along the dry, dust-covered Sindi roads, her mind dwelt on what she was going to say.

When she reached the family residence it appeared to be alive with people. A group of men with thick dark moustaches and long black jackets were coming out of the courtyard when Nighat parked her car in the drive. She could hear the laughter of adults and children from the rear courtyard.

An old male helper led her into the drawing room, informing her that Zarri Bano had gone out on a visit with her special friend and spiritual guide, Sakina. Nighat waited patiently, helping herself to refreshments served by Fatima. On learning that Nighat was a university professor, Fatima couldn't help talking proudly about her own daughter Firdaus, 'the Deputy Headmistress'.

A few minutes later, when Zarri Bano entered the drawing room, Nighat blinked in shock. The dark-cloaked vision assaulted her senses; a feeling of outrage sped up her spine. The urge to rip the garment from Zarri Bano's body gripped her. Her eyes crying disbelief, her lips moved to greet her ex-pupil but the words had simply fled.

Painfully aware of the reaction she had aroused in her old Professor, Zarri Bano read the negative expressions

on Nighat's face. They gave her an insight into what people like Nighat, in her station of life, thought of her becoming a Holy Woman.

'*Assalam-Alaikum*, Professor Nighat. What a pleasure to have you here,' Zarri Bano greeted her tutor warmly.

'*Wa Laikum-Salam*, Zarri Bano. How are you? I heard about you from my friend Zeenat.' Nighat at last found her voice, but the smile still eluded her.

'Thank you for coming to visit me. As you can see, I am fine. How is your daughter Rucksana?'

'She is well, Zarri Bano.' Nighat's eyes dropped awkwardly from her former student's. *It is all true*, her mind thundered. *Zarri Bano has gone through with it.*

The young woman waited with resignation for Professor Nighat to explode. She was, therefore, taken aback by her one, softly spoken word.

'Why?'

Zarri Bano didn't know how to begin. She appealed in her quiet, dignified voice. 'I had to, Sister Nighat. Believe me.'

'You *had* to?' Nighat's voice rasped with raw emotion. 'Of anybody else I would have expected that reply, but not from you. You said that women held their destinies in their hands. What a travesty! You have betrayed and let down a whole generation of us Pakistani women. If it has happened to a mature university-educated woman – a feminist at that, an extrovert, a modern woman – then Allah help a young, uneducated woman in the backwoods of rural Pakistan, who is at the beck and call, and at the mercy and whims of her menfolk. Zarri Bano, I feel so angry, so impotent. All our years of work down the drain. Why, Zarri Bano? *Why?*'

Zarri Bano had listened silently to her friend's outburst.

'You ask why, Sister Nighat. I will tell you. I owe you an explanation for you are my friend, my tutor and my role model. I woke up one morning, Sister Nighat, to find my identity stripped off me and learned that somebody else, my father, held it in his hands and that *he* was going to shape it for me. I woke up to find that books, feminism, campaigns and education are all *utterly useless* against the patriarchal tyranny of our feudal landlords. Stupidly I had convinced myself that as an educated, urban, upperclass woman, I was different from those "poor" women, lower down the strata of our society, who had to do as they were told.

'I found out, however, that in the end we are all in the same *pingra* – a birdcage to which our fathers and elders hold the key. My heart continues to ache for the quivering seventeen-year-old whose fate is decided and she is told to marry such and such a man. Our faith explicitly says that a woman must decide for herself. Moral and psychological pressure, however, is placed on her to accept male family members' decisions. Well, I wasn't even offered that choice, my friend. Marriage was forcefully denied me by my father. He said that I could never marry anybody!' Zarri Bano took in a heaving emotional breath.

'What?' Nighat looked disbelievingly at Zarri Bano.

'Yes, my father stopped me – psychologically blackmailed me – from marrying the man I fell in love with and so wanted to marry.'

'Oh my God!'

Zarri Bano sadly accepted her friend's expression of horror. She had laid her soul bare to this woman, and to nobody else. She owed it to her.

'You have probably heard about our tradition of a Holy Woman and heiress of a clan. Well, when the only male heir dies, in our clan, the inheritance, and especially the land, goes to the next female heir. The condition is that she stays and never leaves her paternal home. In effect, she can never marry. To make this more legitimate, our forefathers concocted the notion of a Holy Woman, a *Shahzadi Ibadat*. It is a measure for men like my father of ensuring that the land stays in the family.' There was a world of bitterness in her voice.

'You could have refused to become the heiress, and turned down the inheritance if you wanted to marry,' Nighat persisted.

'Whether I like it or not, Sister Nighat, I became the heiress. I had to! The land is now like a millstone, a hated talisman around my neck. I have gazed at the acres of our land so many times over this past week, unable to take in the fact that my freedom, identity and womanhood has been bartered for acres of soil. The land that God has generously bestowed on to us, which my family has protected like gold dust over the centuries, means more to them than humanity itself.' Zarri Bano suddenly stopped short, fearing that she had said and revealed too much. Family loyalty and filial duty were steadfast traits of her character.

'If you had told me about this Holy Woman farce, I would have helped you,' Nighat said passionately. 'This is against our Islam. Our *shariah*, our courts, both secular and Muslim, would have made a case for you against your family.'

'No, Sister Nighat, you do not understand. Yes, I could have refused. I could have turned to hundreds of people for help, if I had wanted to. It is the important "if" Professor Nighat. This is what you have to

understand. I could have married my fiancé, *if* I had
wanted to. He said and accused me of the same things
as you have done. He too offered me support and
refuge, and when I didn't take him up on it, was
astonished and outraged like yourself.

'Yes, I could have refused my father, *if* I had wanted
to. But I didn't at the end, for the same reason as
thousands of other young women in our patriarchal
society end up saying "yes". For our *izzat*'s sake, and
our family's honour, like other women, I became a
coward and a victim rolled into one, by suppressing and
sacrificing my own needs for the sake of my family. I
just couldn't be the cause of turning my family and
tradition upside down.'

'So you became this.' Nighat swept a dismissive
hand at the black garb Zarri Bano wore.

'Yes, Sister Nighat, you are right. There is more to
say, but I cannot talk about it. It is very personal and
painful. All I can say is that women in our society also
become prisoners of female modesty. If a father refuses
to grant permission for his daughter to marry, how can
she actively pursue marriage? She'll be labelled *besharm*,
a wanton.'

'I am all confused now, Zarri Bano. You are an adult,
a mature woman. You do not need your father's permis-
sion and you wouldn't have been labelled as *besharm*,
if you had wanted to get married. Our faith, our
society, encourages marriage. You wouldn't have been
criticised.'

'Yes, what you say is true. But in the end, female
modesty and my pride imprisoned me into a role of
obedience and going along with my father's wishes. He
said something that spoiled it all for me. After that I
could never think of marriage again. He achieved his

goal and I can never forgive him for that. I am learning, however, to come to terms with my new self and with my new identity.'

Zarri Bano suddenly stopped and a humourless laugh escaped her lips. 'Professor Nighat, you can devise a new title for your research and fieldwork for your post-graduate students – based on me ... "A feminist turned Holy Woman".'

'You will be in seclusion, won't you – almost like a semi-*purdah*. These are the things we have campaigned against, Zarri Bano. We are still recovering from Zia AlHaq's policies and their negative influence on women's lives. We have worked to get women out of their homes and to stand on their own two feet and have careers. And what have you done? Gone into seclusion yourself.'

Zarri Bano listened patiently to Nighat. 'No, Sister Nighat, you are mistaken. There will be no seclusion for me in that sense. It is true I won't have much to do with men, but I will be very much a public figure. I will be out there and everywhere. In fact I am hoping that I will have gained greater freedom than I had hitherto.'

'In this garb?' Nighat's stare was incredulous.

'Yes, in this garb, Sister.'

'Zarri Bano, I couldn't wear a *burqa* or cover myself like that. I would be suffocated.'

'Yes, Sister Nighat. I too have been suffocated by it. It's like a black shroud around my body. I had wanted to tear it into shreds, and to burn it on the first day. I learnt to respect it by the third day. I got used to it by the fifth day. Today I am just about comfortable in it. This is not an ordinary veil or *burqa*, but a symbol of my role. As I am getting used to the role, little by little I

am getting used to the *burqa* too. I cannot, however, look at myself in a mirror yet. Nor am I used to the speculative glances I receive from people wherever I go. I have learnt one thing, Sister Nighat. People physically and psychologically distance themselves from me now, whenever they see me. Especially the ones I know. My father . . .' Her voice died away.

'My father, the one who was so proud of me becoming the *Shahzadi Ibadat* has not been able to look me directly in the eye for the last week. My sister and mother both find my appearance painful and have taken to avoiding me. I have not even had a chat with either of them on this subject. The only companion I have is Sakina, the other Holy Woman.'

'That woman who came in with you?'

'Yes, that is Sakina. I have kept my sanity, partly through her support. She is always taking me here and there. She has remained with me since the ceremony. Do you know, Sister Nighat, through her a new world is opening out to me. Today I went to a *darbar* and I loved every minute of it. How long is it since you have been to a local mosque or a *darbar*, Sister Nighat? I am reading and reciting the Holy Quran quite extensively. I have found that I was such an ignorant soul, when it came to our faith. So you see, I will not live shut away. I shall be a bird with wings that let her fly into a new world. In truth, I am flying next week to Cairo for a year, to study Islam at Cairo University.'

Nighat didn't respond immediately. It was all too much for her to take in. 'I see, Zarri Bano, you have been well and truly brainwashed,' she said heavily.

'No, not brainwashed, my friend.' Zarri Bano softly and sadly added. 'I remember someone else saying the same thing to me a few weeks ago. I am trying to make

the most out of my situation, learning to adapt to my new role and status in life and to forget my past life as well as coming to terms with my present life. You are a psychologist. I have, as you would say, become a person of circumstances, moulded by her environment.'

Nighat couldn't argue further. She had come, full of anger and self-righteousness, but now all the wind had gone out of her sails. Here she was, come all this way to support Zarri Bano and offer her refuge; instead she found a woman who didn't need any one's support or help. A woman, in short, who was bravely tackling her new life and not hiding from the world outside. Nighat admired her tenacity. She didn't know what to say next, or what to do. In the end Zarri Bano came to her aid once again.

'Sister Nighat, I respect you very much. Please do not worry on my account. I am sorry if I have let you down, and if I have betrayed our cause – please forgive me. One thing you can all learn from my scenario is, and I have cried for millions of other women, that in the end, we women are just small beads in the tapestries of our clans, cleverly woven by our fathers and other male members.'

'I suppose there is nothing further that I can say, Zarri Bano?'

'No. Just wish me luck and pray for me that I learn to forget the old life and adapt well to my new one. *Insha'allah!*'

'You want to forget us? A huge chunk of your life in exchange for a life of total religious devotion?'

'Yes. That is the only way for me to keep my sanity. At the moment I don't know who I am. I am hanging perilously by a fragile thread between the two worlds, almost like a fish out of water. Zarri Bano, the

university campus woman, the feminist, fighting with the recluse, the Holy Woman, who is seeking to immerse herself totally in religious devotion.'

'I wish you luck, my friend. You mustn't forget me – even if you forget everything else. You must visit me sometimes and write to me from Cairo.'

'Of course I won't forget you!' Zarri Bano laughed. 'Won't you stay for some dinner?' she asked as Nighat stood up, ready to leave.

'No. I must go. It is almost two hours' drive to my home. Goodbye, my dear.'

'*Khudah Hafiz*. May God be with you.'

'You too, my dear,' Nighat replied. She smiled uncertainly at Zarri Bano as she climbed into her car, and drove away from the house. 'May God be with you' were strange words on Zarri Bano's lips, and the sound of those words throbbed in the Professor's brain as she picked up speed for the long journey home.

Chapter 23

AT KARACHI AIRPORT it was a low-key affair, as Zarri Bano boarded the Egypt Air flight destined for Cairo. Ruby, Shahzada, Habib and the chauffeur had accompanied her to the airport. Her eyes filling with tears, Shahzada kept discreetly wiping them away. Habib managed to stay dry-eyed, concentrating more on seeing his daughter safely off, than letting his emotions get the better of him in a public place.

'Thank you, Sakina, for accompanying my daughter. I leave her in yours and Allah's capable hands. Please look after one another,' were his last words to Sakina as

they were ready to disappear into the departure lounge. After embracing Shahzada and Ruby, the two women in their long flowing *burqas* moved away and were gone.

In the departure lounge, Zarri Bano was acutely aware of eyes roaming over her body – her first experience of being at an airport in a *burqa*. She didn't flinch from the stares, however, even those from the men. Her body remained straight and her stance poised. Opening a novel by her favourite author, she settled down to read on the comfortable sofa in the lounge, waiting to board the plane.

For her family it was a silent journey home in the car. Once there, they all dispersed in different directions. Habib instructed his driver to take him to visit his father in their home village of Chiragpur. Ruby went up to her bedroom and switched on a cassette. Shahzada entered her kitchen area, looking for her housekeeper.

Fatima was busy making a *karaila ghost* dish, and frying the *karailas* on the stove. On seeing her mistress, she turned the burner off and looked expectantly at Shahzada.

'Did the plane leave on time, Chaudharani Sahiba?'

'Yes, Fatima, my daughter flew away,' Shahzada replied sadly, walking out of the kitchen. Fatima put the wooden spoon down on the work top and followed her mistress out into the rear courtyard, and onto the lawn. Shahzada sat down on one of the chairs and Fatima on the other, her eyes on her mistress's face.

'Can I get you something to eat or drink, Chaudharani Sahiba?' she asked gently.

'No, thank you, Fatima. All I need is my daughter. Here, against my chest. She has gone, Fatima. I still don't understand *why* she has gone. This heart of mine has been daily bruised since Jafar's death. It can't take

any more battering.' In anguish, her eyes filled with tears.

'I am sorry, mistress. It is all for the best.'

'Best for whom, Fatima? Why has my daughter gone to a strange country and all alone?'

'Well, mistress, you know she has gone to become a scholar, to learn about Islam. That is why!' Fatima offered brightly, attempting to cheer her up.

'I know, that's what Habib keeps saying. But think, my daughter is very well-educated. She is nearly twenty-eight years old. Why does she need to become a scholar again, Fatima? Women of her age . . . her friends . . . most of them are now married and have children. And what is my daughter doing? What has happened to us?' Shahzada turned an agonised stare at her woman helper.

'I cannot keep up with anything any more, Fatima. I am drowning in my sorrow and sinking further and further into oblivion, this nightmare seems to have no end. Have I done something wrong, Fatima? Am I a sinner, a *ghunagar*? Is this Allah's way of punishing me? I have lost a beloved only son, my baby. He lies six foot deep in the family graveyard. I have lost an older daughter – she, who has never entered a mosque and hardly ever stepped onto a prayer-mat, has become wedded to her faith. I have lost her and now she has literally disappeared out of our lives.'

'Oh, come on, mistress. She has only gone for a few months. Many people nowadays go abroad for education.'

'But it is all wrong, Fatima! We have done something terrible, in changing the course of Zarri Bano's life. What right had we? She wanted to marry Sikander, set up a publishing company and settle in Karachi.

She loved social life and fashion. We have thrust an alien lifestyle onto her. Allah doesn't expect such total religious devotion from us. He wants us to live our everyday lives as well as remembering him. Think, there are no nuns in our faith, Fatima.'

'But this is good, Chaudharani Sahiba, isn't it? She will be a better person and a good Muslim,' Fatima tried.

'I am going out of my mind with the thought that there will be no grandchildren from my Zarri Bano. I loathe that black thing she wears all the time. My beautiful daughter is buried inside it. Since the day of the ceremony she has changed, yet not a single word of reproach has left her mouth. I have lost her, Fatima!'

Noting the trace of panic in her mistress's voice Fatima stood up and squatted on the grass in front of Shahzada. Taking the other woman's hands in her own, she began to gently massage them.

'Dearie me, mistress, we have not lost Zarri Bano. She has only gone to do a course. Come on, if she had married, you would have lost her too.'

'No, no! It is not the same! I could have coped with that loss,' Shahzada grieved.

'I had a big heart once, Fatima, as big as this court-yard. Now I carry a small hard stone in its place. I have lost my family, my peace of mind and my sense of marital duty. I feel nothing but hatred for Habib Sahib, almost as if I have never loved him in all my life. Hot rage floods my body every time I see him. I shrink inside and my tongue just clamps up. I don't want to share his room, let alone his bed. He looks at me with condemnation. I have closed the doors to myself to him, for ever. I will never let him inside. He might as well have given me the three *thalaks* that he threatened me

with, for we live together as strangers. I think he only talks to his father and to his acres of land, that he rides up and down in the evenings.'

'He is the real loser, mistress, not you. And so he should be, as the perpetrator of everything.' Fatima's voice had hardened.

'Ruby is the only one left,' Shahzada continued drearily, 'but I have lost her too. She is so bereft without her sister and feels resentful that Zarri Bano was allowed to go and study in Cairo, and she wasn't. Can you imagine it, Fatima? Ruby has a degree. Why does she want more? In our day we only had the basic primary-school education. These days there is no end to education.'

'Don't I know it, mistress. I have been paying for it for the past fifteen years, for my four children. For us poor folks, it is a very useful commodity, especially in the marriage market. The more educated a woman is, the more eligible she becomes. Not everyone is always blessed with your daughters' beauty, wealth and land to bargain with. Education is a good bartering qualification for most people nowadays, as you well know, Shahzada Jee. Men want educated women. Women want education.' Fatima chuckled suddenly. 'The *karailas* will turn into rubber if I don't hurry inside and see to them.'

'I'll come and give you a hand.' Shahzada sighed. She was feeling a little better after her outburst. 'You are a good friend, Fatima. What would I do without you?'

'Nobody is indispensable, mistress,' Fatima said lightly as they went into the kitchen together. 'But I will have to leave you soon, when my Firdaus gets married.'

Chapter 24

DRIVEN BY HIS chauffeur, Habib Khan was on his way to Chiragpur. Just as they turned off the main road to Hyderabad, a milk buffalo ran across the lane, almost careering into the car. With its large head swinging heavily from side to side, and the bell and the chain around its neck ringing merrily, the buffalo panicked and sprang off the road straight into the vegetable field on the other side, trundling its heavy steel chain behind.

'God forbid!' Habib shouted as his car screeched to a halt. 'Where did that beast come from?' He peered through the front windscreen. 'Whose buffalo is it, Riaz? Did you recognise it? Is it one of ours from my father's farm?' Habib climbed out of the car.

'I don't know, Sahib Jee,' the forty-year-old driver answered, also glancing through the front window to have a good look at the black milk buffalo, with its hide still caked in mud.

Habib wondered where the cowherd was. Surely the animal couldn't be roaming around willy-nilly. He saw two women, some 200 yards away, washing clothes near the head pump of the tube well which distributed water into the man-made irrigation channels that wound their way through the fields.

It happened to be Naimat Bibi's wash day. She had managed to enlist the help of her best friend, Kulsoom. Busy with the rigorous task of washing linen and bedding, when Naimat Bibi looked up and saw Habib Khan walk towards them, her mouth fell open.

Her hand remained poised in the air holding the bat-like *danda*, to beat the clothes with. She quickly swung it around and slapped it with a bang on the soapy wet cotton quilt cover on the worn wooden washing slab. She turned to her friend in panic. Kulsoom was rinsing a sheet in the water, leaning over the water pump.

'Quick, Kulsoom Jee, where's my *dupatta*? Khan Sahib is coming this way,' Naimat Bibi twittered.

Kulsoom started in surprise and turned to gawp, holding on with a tight grip to the heavy wet quilt cover in her two small hands. Her fragile wrists were definitely not designed to handle heavy washing; they ached terribly. 'I don't know where your *dupatta* is,' she panted, 'but here, use this, it will do the job.' With one hand she threw a dry pillowcase cover over Naimat Bibi's head, while she struggled to hold onto the dripping wet article of clothing.

Naimat Bibi planted the pillow cover firmly on her head, just as Habib Khan came to stand only a few feet away. He looked at them both with mild amusement, Naimat Bibi looked comical with a pillowcase propped on her head and tiny Kulsoom holding on precariously to the dripping bedding in her two hands, trying to keep it away from her own clothes. He glanced at the mound of washing still to be got through. The rest, soaped and rinsed, was draped over the nearby bushes to dry. There was a large earthenware basin of soap placed close to the wooden slab, on which the clothes were beaten with the *danda* as an efficient method of getting rid of the dirt.

'Sahib Jee, *Assalam-Alaikum*,' Kulsoom greeted him respectfully, blushing nevertheless. The last thing she wanted was to be caught washing by someone like

Habib Khan. And the washing was not even her own! Her friend dutifully mimicked the same greeting.

'*Wa Laikum-Salam*, sisters. Is it your wash day, Kulsoom Jee and Naimat Jee? Don't you use the washing machine you bought last year, Naimat Jee?' Habib teased, wondering at the logic and the sense in these two women carting all that washing, nearly one mile away from the village and then, presumably, lugging it all back.

'Those machines are useless, Sahib Jee!' Naimat Bibi quickly answered. 'Mine went bust with the power cut one day. How many repair men will actually come to the village? And as I have no means of transporting it to the nearest town, it's just too expensive and too much bother. Here, on the other hand, we have gallons of clean fresh water, pumping away, and of course, plenty of open air and sunshine will do the rest.'

'Why didn't you tell my father? He would have had it repaired for you. Anyway, I will send one of our repairmen to have a look at yours. And of course you won't have to pay,' Habib reassured her.

Naimat Bibi blushed with pleasure. 'That is very generous of you, Sahib Jee. Here my friend is helping me.'

Kulsoom Bibi allowed herself the luxury of a polite nervous smile, as she maintained her aching grip on the sopping linen. Convinced that her bony wrists were going to snap any minute now, she vowed to herself that this was *definitely* the last time she was going to help Naimat with her washing.

She suddenly wondered why Naimat Bibi didn't do her laundry at home, like everyone else. And why, oh *why*, did she gather so much bedding to wash at one go? Did she have no sense? This matter perplexed

Kulsoom. Naimat Bibi lived all alone, but Kulsoom was sure she had gathered the linen of ten people's bedding. Did she not remember her friend's poor wrists and have mercy on her?

A sudden thought galloped through Kulsoom's tired head. Had Naimat Bibi secretly taken up a new business – that of washing other people's bedding? And she had got roped into it. She, Kulsoom Jee, the respectable village matchmaker who hadn't done any washing for a long time and now wouldn't stoop to it. For the past fifteen years she had delegated the horrid, backbreaking task to the *Doban*, the village washerwoman.

Yet here she was, wringing the dirt out of other people's dirty linen!

Kulsoom suddenly let go of the quilt cover in the irrigation channel and watched it float away from her. As Naimat Bibi saw Sardara the milkwoman's special quilt cover disappear, she screeched and leapt to her feet. Throwing the *danda* aside she stooped over the brick ledge and, in the process, accidentally dropped the pillow case on her head into the water. She gasped out loud as that too was disappearing before her horrified eyes.

'Here, sisters, don't panic,' Habib volunteered. 'I'll get them for you.' His eyes danced with laughter as he saw the wicked smile on Kulsoom's face. Habib leaned over the wall and managed to skilfully pull out the two linen articles with the *danda*.

Highly embarrassed and with her cheeks plum red, Naimat Bibi gratefully took the dripping-wet washing from their Sahib Jee.

'Well, you cannot complain that your linen hadn't a thorough rinse, Naimat Bibi,' Habib teased, his cheeks bulging with laughter.

'Thank you, Sahib Jee,' Naimat Bibi mumbled, as her eyes focused nervously on the wet marks on Habib's long black coat. The lower half was soaked.

Kulsoom decided to address their influential village landlord, son of Siraj Din, the village elder. She had learnt at an early age of the wisdom and worth of cultivating the *wadairas*, the big people's company, and had for some time enjoyed the material benefits of ingratiating herself in their favour and remaining under their patronage. So Kulsoom now boldly allowed herself the luxury of asking a very personal question.

'Sahib Jee, how is Zarri Bano?' She knew, like everyone in the village, that Habib Khan doted on his eldest daughter.

Seeing the laughter disappear and a shadow cross his face, Kulsoom chided herself, wondering if she had asked both the wrong question and at the wrong time.

'She has gone, Kulsoom. She is, at this very moment, in an aeroplane on her way to Misr, in Egypt.' Kulsoom knew intuitively, that the landlord was missing his daughter terribly.

'To become a scholar of Islam, Habib Sahib?' she cleverly ventured to ask. This much she knew, having heard it from one of Siraj Din's servants.

'Yes, Kulsoom,' he replied heavily, and then wanting to change the subject. 'Can you tell me exactly whose buffalo that was, running wild around the fields? It almost crashed into my car.' Habib was remembering the reason why he was there in the first place.

'I think it is Khawar Sahib's. He has got a new young man helping on his farm, and this naughty buffalo is leading him quite a dance, I am afraid. This is the second time it has jumped over the low wall and snapped its chain and escaped, running out of the village. Luckily it

didn't come this way, otherwise it wouldn't be our washing floating in the tube channel, but us poor old women. There he is!' Kulsoom pointed to the running figure of a young man chasing after the buffalo.

'Well, I hope this stops. Milk buffaloes are normally very gentle creatures, and quite tame. I wonder why this one is turning out to be so wild? If she runs around the fields like this, we'll have no crops left to harvest,' Habib said irritably, watching the man grasp the chain around the animal's neck, at last, and lead it back to the village.

'*Allah Hafiz*, Sahib Jee,' they both piped at once and stood up as a sign of respect. While Kulsoom had kept Habib Sahib busy with her talking, Naimat Bibi had found her shawl and wound it firmly on her head and around her shoulders. It was a most unseemly thing to do, to be seen bareheaded by such an important elder man.

Habib walked away, back to his car. Nostalgically Kulsoom watched the vehicle disappear towards the village, leaving a cloud of dust behind. She looked down at the washing in distaste. Wouldn't it have been just wonderful to have abandoned her friend and her washing and climbed into Habib's car for a lift? She'd have been home by now.

Sighing and resigned to spending at least another hour getting through the second mound of bedlinen, Kulsoom reluctantly got down to work. Squatting on her haunches beside the brick ledge of the tube well, she began to swipe the wet sheet in the soap, before passing it to her friend.

'Isn't Habib Sahib generous, Kulsoom Jee? Did you hear about him sending a man to look at my washing machine?'

'Yes I did, Naimat Jee. But then we shouldn't be surprised. You know all the three landlords, Siraj Din, his son Habib Khan and young Khawar Sahib, are all kind and gentle *zemindars*. There are, however, still a lot of feudal landlords in our province who suck everything out of their fellow villagers and have had their families bonded as labourers to work their land for generations. Nobody is bonded to any of them or even owes them money in our village. Khawar Sahib and Siraj Din really do care about the welfare of us humble poor people,' Kulsoom told her friend knowledgeably.

'Where is Misr, Kulsoom Jee?' Naimat Bibi asked as she began the beating of the sheet on the wooden slab again. 'Is it really *saat sumundar par*?'

'I don't know about seven oceans away, but at least I know this much: there is one sea at least between Pakistan and Egypt. It is supposed to be near Saudi Arabia and in the olden days, people went on pilgrimages by ships, so there must be some seas and oceans on the way. Having said all this, you know very well, Naimat Bibi, I am not the best person to answer your question. I haven't been through any school doors. I am just as illiterate as you are. It is so unfortunate that there were no girls' schools in the village in our childhood days. It is so unfair. If I could read and write it would help me enormously with names for my business. I wouldn't have to keep memorising things – especially the names of all the boys and girls I have to remember, and also of their families. But never mind, my friend, we are managing quite well even though we are barely numerate and totally illiterate.'

'Speak for yourself! You definitely are managing quite well, Kulsoom Jee, with your matchmaking

business!' Naimat Bibi replied tartly, unable to disguise the envy in her voice.

Taken aback by this sarcasm, Kulsoom suddenly remembered the mound of bedlinen they were washing and turned squarely on her friend, her eyes shining meaningfully in her face.

'Naimat Bibi, whose dirty linen *exactly* am I helping you to wash?' She asked just as tartly. 'This can't *all* be yours, surely? What do you do? Change your bedlinen every night?'

There was a long pause.

'Well, half of it is Sardara Jee's,' Naimat Bibi replied, looking sheepishly at her friend. 'You know that she is wheelchair-bound and I wanted to help her.'

'I see,' Kulsoom commented, nodding her head knowledgeably. 'I suppose she is paying you for this?'

'Not exactly, but she won't charge me for my milk, for one full week.' Naimat Bibi was now studiously looking down at the washing slab.

Her brown cheeks flushed red, Kulsoom asked, 'So all this washing, breaking my poor wrists, is to get you *three* jugs of milk.' She turned away in disgust. 'If you wanted milk, for heaven's sake, Naimat Bibi, I would have bought it for you myself, rather than have to do this gruelling work. Have you thought how we are going to carry it all back? It is now late afternoon. You are supposed to be cooking at this very moment at Siraj Din's house. His son has just arrived. There is no one to prepare the meal there. We aren't going to sit here and wait for it to dry, are we? And now that it is wet, it is going to be twice as heavy. If my wrists give way today, I'll know who to blame it on!'

'Oh don't worry, Kulsoom Jee,' Naimat said airily. 'You won't have to carry it. I am sure some boy or man

will pass by and they can't refuse our request to help us carry it back.'

'OK, whatever you say,' Kulsoom Bibi tiredly offered, dumping another sheet to rinse in the clean water gushing out from the pump. She wished with all her heart that she could dump the whole lot in the water and let it float away. And then she, herself, could go home and leave her friend to it.

She knew, however, that she couldn't be so mean. For it was Naimat Bibi who was always there to nurse her when she was sick. She was the one who stayed glued to her side, when she had malaria last year. Resignedly, Kulsoom, lugged the clean sheet up towards her and began to wring it out, soaking her *kameze* dress, and breaking two of her beloved green-glass bangles in the process.

Chapter 25

LEAVING NAIMAT BIBI and Kulsoom doing the washing, Habib headed towards his father's home. The car hooted a tractor and a bullock cart out of its way on the dusty journey down the narrow road, pulling up in the centre of the village where a large white-washed villa, with attractive white wrought-iron balconies on all four sides, and rows of potted plants cascading down the white-washed walls, stood imperiously amongst the more humble buildings.

Habib's father now lived here with his three men-servants and the estate manager who oversaw the business side and collected the revenue from the land. Siraj Din was a true countryman, a *zemindar* to his very

bones. Nothing would have induced him to depart from Chiragpur the 'village of light', to join his sons in the town. He tolerated their move with fortitude and sadness, but he wouldn't be persuaded to do so himself.

'How can a *zemindar* be a *zemindar* if he lives away from his fields? Land is my life. My eyes need to gaze over and to feast on the smell of fresh green vegetables growing in the fields, ready to be plucked and harvested. I'll never leave it!' Siraj Din had firmly remonstrated to his sons, when they had pressed him to move to their homes after their mother, Zulaikha, had died.

At the end they let him be. An independent and proud sort of a man, he didn't need any close members of his family seeing to his daily needs – his servants could do all that sufficiently well. Naimat Bibi was their regular cook. Siraj Din was still a healthy man at the sprightly age of eighty years. Daily walks in his fields had kept his heart and lungs in good condition. Unlike his sons, he had not piled on surplus fat but had kept a sharp eye on his trim waistline. His sons and grandchildren visited him on a rota basis two or three times a week.

Entering his old home, a familiar scene met Habib's eyes. There was a large central courtyard with rows of rooms flanked on all four sides. In the middle of the courtyard, with its four red rose beds and three trees, his father sat on a chaise-longue-style *palang*, half-reclining on a high bolster. One male servant sat nearby, ready to hand him a hookah. Another stood over him, massaging his shoulders gently but firmly.

Siraj Din didn't bother to get up, but inclined his head to acknowledge his son's arrival. A ghost of a smile was allowed to touch his face. Habib came up to his father and, after greeting him, bent down. With a

gesture inherited from his childhood days, Habib lifted his father's hand and kissed it. Accepting the greeting, Siraj Din signalled his son to sit down on the other *charpoy*.

'Bring food and drink for your master!' he ordered the young man massaging his shoulder-blades, and sent him scurrying inside, seeking out Naimat Bibi, unaware that she was out in the fields still doing her washing.

'So, she has gone,' Siraj Din began, bending over and drawing a powerful puff on his hookah pipe, letting the water gurgle in the steel base for a few seconds.

'Yes, Father. In about six hours' time she should have reached Misr.'

'I see,' Siraj Din commented, his eyes on his son while taking another long puff. 'But I don't know what the world is coming to, my son, for young, unmarried women to be sent off, all alone, to foreign countries to live on their own. I find it totally unacceptable. I sincerely hope that you know what you are doing. I would have thought twice about sending my young daughter alone to another city in Pakistan, let alone to another country.'

'Zarri Bano has lived alone in Karachi, while she was studying at university, Father. If it had been your daughter, she would have been living in another era. Things have changed in many ways. We have to learn to move with the times. You have benefited from modern machinery like tractors to work your land haven't you, instead of the bullock plough? Women are more independent, educated, assertive and freer to do things now. We cannot keep them locked inside our houses any more. This is not the age of *purdah*, Father.'

'But she is now a devout woman – a *Bibi*, Habib!'

Siraj Din snorted in disgust. 'In my days, a *Bibi* would barely have set foot outside her home, for that was part of her modesty and devoutness. Her inaccessibility and seclusion from men gave her the devout rank of a *Bibi*. Such a woman was hardly likely to have gone gadding halfway across the world alone, and Allah knows who she'll encounter there.'

'My daughter is not a *Bibi*, as you well know,' Habib retorted, his lips curling in distaste. 'You are talking about old, ignorant *Bibis*, Father! Zarri Bano is a university graduate, remember. She is going to be a scholar, who needs to learn in order to teach others about Islam. How can she do that at home, amidst such ignorance? How much knowledge is there about our faith here in Chiragpur in this village of yours? Very little, I tell you. Especially amongst the women, who are barely literate. The place Zarri Bano has gone to is the best place for her to study. She is a mature woman, Father, not a child. You must try to understand. She can look after herself. In any event, I have sent Sakina with her, to chaperone her and keep her company, until she settles in. I will visit her myself in a few months' time.'

'Where is she going to stay?' Siraj Din asked quietly. This was the subject that had lain on his mind all day, as he imagined his beautiful granddaughter in a foreign country, being ogled by strange Egyptian men. Even in her *burqa*, she was bound to draw attention to herself. Her beauty was their pride, but also posed a threat to them when it came to men.

'She is going to stay with an Egyptian family that I met on pilgrimage in Jeddah, five years ago. We have kept in touch, and I have visited them once. The man has a daughter who is studying at the university Zarri

Bano will be attending, and a son who teaches there. It is he who has also arranged the admission for her.'

Shaking his head, 'I don't know, my son,' Siraj Din replied, not satisfied. 'You have still not convinced me of the merit and wisdom of what you have done.'

'Father, I do know what I am doing. Just as I am beginning to learn and regret what it is going to cost me.' Habib did not bother disguising the note of sadness in his voice.

'What do you mean?' Siraj Din asked sharply – pushing the hookah away from him. The male servant politely moved it back.

'I thought I had done the right thing, but I am so unhappy. I have lost my family. I walk all alone in my home, a solitary figure, Father.' Habib's eyes focused on the grapevine in the far corner of the courtyard, now heavily swollen with branches hanging down and laden with ripe green grapes.

'Don't be silly, son,' Siraj Din grunted, his green eyes glittering with laughter. 'You are getting soft in the head.'

'No, Father, I am not getting soft in the head, as you say. I am plagued by guilt, wondering whether we've done the right thing.'

'Of course we have!' Siraj Din returned immediately, the laughter whipped away from his eyes, his body tense.

'Would Selim have done it to his Gulshan?' Habib stared squarely into his father's eyes, daring him to disagree.

'Of course.'

'No, he wouldn't.' Habib wryly shook his head looking away from his father's gaze. 'You see, his wife wouldn't have let her. I forced my daughter: she obeyed

me. Shahzada desperately appealed to me not to do it, but in the end, she gave in and stood by me like a strong pillar of support.'

'Well, so she should!' Siraj Din snorted indignantly. 'That's her duty.'

'Yes, she has done her duty. But the payment is going to be very dear, as I have learnt to my cost. She will never forgive me, Father. Nor has she spoken to me since the night when I told her about Zarri Bano's fate. I have lost her.' Habib's eyes again focused on the other tree he used to climb as a boy.

Siraj Din sat upright, drawing his legs and feet down onto the marble floor. Pushing the hookah away from him, he leaned forward to look straight at his son.

'Now listen to me carefully, my Habib, I don't like what I am hearing. Are you losing your masculine touch? Who is the master in your house? I am very disappointed in you.' Siraj Din's eyes, exactly like his son's and which Zarri Bano had inherited, flashed with disdain. 'If you give into your weakness, you will find yourself tied to your wife's *perandah*, her plait. She will rule you and not just your household. She sent Zarri Bano to Karachi to Sikander's home against your wish, didn't she? Well! You will be a woman in your house!' Siraj Din concluded, with a look of disgust on his face.

'There is no chance of that happening,' Habib replied bitterly. 'My marriage, my relationship with Shahzada, is not like yours was to our mother. We have shared harmony in our household. There was no power struggle between us. Shahzada knows her place and her duties, as she has always done. I have not dominated her in the way you taught us to do and the way you dominated our mother. I didn't break Shahzada's spirit – a thing you spent all your life endeavouring to do with

our mother, but never quite succeeded. Mother stood up to you even on her deathbed. Shahzada is not a high-spirited woman as Mother was. That is the problem! I wish she was, for then we could argue and fight, but she has shut me out.' He paused, then said almost inaudibly, 'I stupidly threatened her with divorce. I think I killed something inside her that day. Her eyes, like Ruby's, were always warm with love and laughter, now they stare at me with hatred. I have cruelly hurt her, Father. She has lost two children in one go!'

Siraj Din settled back comfortably on his bolster and thoughtfully twirled his hennaed moustache into shape. He stretched his legs out fully on the *palang*. Drawing the hookah pipe back to his mouth, and wanting privacy with his son, he waved the approaching servant away, ordering, 'Go and find Naimat Bibi, wherever she has drowned herself. My son is here and she needs to prepare the dinner.'

He couldn't believe what Habib was telling him. 'At your age, Habib! You are nearly sixty. Why do you care so much about your wife? You don't need a wife to live your life.'

'Father, I am not like you. I cannot live alone. I have led a different life from the one you shared with our mother. You kept her at arm's length, always afraid that she might dominate you. In the process you have never really known a woman's affection, or what it is to live in mutual harmony, have you? You were always chasing after your land, and bent on showing her who was master in your home. What love she ever harboured for you must have been quenched from the day she married you. I remember it all.'

'You remember my wedding day?' Siraj Din grunted, unable to prevent the sarcastic rejoinder.

'No, of course not. But I do have childhood memories.
I saw both of you well-matched, and yet ill-matched.
Your nature demanded obedience and subservience,
hers equality and respect. You never gave her that, did
you? And she in turn was never subservient to you. She
was a strong woman. That was what kept the whole
family going. She was our citadel.'

His eyes now flashing menacingly at his son, Siraj
Din made his displeasure apparent. 'I don't know what
has come over you today, Habib. My son is now abus-
ing me and defending his mother! I think the whole
world has gone raving mad. It seems that I have become
obsolete, at this stage in my life. I am living in a
country where a young chit of a woman was ruling over
us. In an Islamic country, too! Why don't you go and
put your head in Shahzada's lap and let her massage you
back in her favours, rather than coming here to insult
me about your mother and our marriage, Habib!' The
elderly man was looking seriously annoyed.

'We were a different breed of men, my son,' he went
on heatedly. 'We knew our parameters, just as we
expected our wives to dutifully know theirs. It is true
that your mother Zulaikha was a strong woman. Per-
haps that was why I married her in the first place –
knowing that she could stand up to me, match my
temper with hers. In my own way, I too loved your
mother, Habib. I wasn't dominating her all the time, as
you put it. A man still needs the affection of a woman
in his life. Although you may find it hard to believe, I
do miss her.'

'Father, there was no harmony in our childhood lives.
Our lives were turbulent. I vowed that when I married,
it would be different. I said so to Mother. I think that is
why she helped me to choose Shahzada, rather than

Gulshan's mother. She said that Shahzada was better suited to my temperament. Shahzada has been a good wife in every sense.'

'You, I am disgusted to learn, are the epitome of my elder brother! He used to walk behind his wife. He truly was tied to her *perandah*, obeying each and every command of hers and in the end, he became her shadow and a laughing stock with us. Consequently he didn't have a say in anything, for his wife married all their children into her clan. I learnt from him that a man can make an utter fool of himself, if he pays too much attention to his wife. Such women are capable of riding roughshod over their husbands. That sister-in-law of mine did! She controlled my brother, just by one tilted eyebrow, and then brazenly flaunted it in all our faces.

'One day I stood up to her, angrily telling her that she shouldn't treat my brother like that. Do you know what she did, my son? She peered closely into my face and laughed, her own face screwed up into a sneer. She poked at my chest with her fat finger. "Mind your own business! If you want to practise domination, do it on your own wife – that is, when you manage to get one. Not on me, you little upstart!" she snarled.'

'I hated them both. I learnt from him, just as you learnt the contrary from me, that I would never become a slave to a mere woman. No female was going to have a chance to dominate and humiliate me. My misfortune was that I spent all my life doing that to my wife and yet never quite succeeded. Your mother was so different from my sister-in-law; but she had guts and stood up to me!'

'Uncle was probably happier than you in his marriage,' Habib couldn't help adding quietly. 'He probably led a more fulfilling life than you did with our

mother. I am the master in my household, Father, just as you taught us to be. But luckily for me, I had no wife whose spirit needed breaking. Shahzada has always been a loving, kind and supportive wife. A wife from whom I have become tragically estranged, because I gave into our desire to keep the land in the family.'

'My son, if you have come here to sing songs of your wife, then you have come to the wrong place. Remember this: you are the master and head of your home – its abiding foundation. If that goes, then the whole building will fall at your feet. Do not become weak, my son! Your wife will forgive you, with time. I agree with you that one good thing your mother did amongst other things was to match you with Shahzada. She is a fine daughter-in-law and always has been. My Zarri Bano is a lovely granddaughter. I am proud of her and I am proud of you too. You are a good son.' To Siraj Din's utter horror, he saw tears form in Habib's eyes. 'Hey! Don't cry.' Leaning forward he patted his eldest son on his shoulders.

'My life is so empty, Father,' Habib wept, his shoulders doubling over as he gave free rein to his grief. 'Jafar has gone. Zarri Bano has gone. Ruby doesn't look at me. Shahzada shuns me. I am not like you, Father. I want and need my family. I cannot live this life. I just wish that Jafar had never died and that I never forced Zarri Bano to become a Holy Woman.'

'Oh, my son, I am so sorry. Forgive me! You are very sad inside. I forget that you are not like me – thick-skinned. You were always the sensitive one of my four children.' Siraj Din's earlier irritation now gave way to concern for his son's anguish. Habib's words had pierced him.

Chapter 26

IBRAHIM MUSA, A young man of twenty-nine years, sat in his study in the family apartment in Cairo, over-looking the River Nile. His hand moving over his closely cropped black beard in a gesture of meditation, he looked through some research papers. Deep in thought, he heard a car door close – their guests had arrived. He stood up and, taking off his reading glasses, rubbed his tired eyes.

Leaving the study, he looked out of the dining-room window balcony, down at the small courtyard where a car had come to a halt. He saw his parents climb out, followed by his sister, Pakinaz, and then two women dressed in long black veils. His eyebrows raised, he peered further over the balcony railings. He hadn't expected this. Believing in the veil himself, he was highly pleased.

Leaving the dining room, he went down a set of stairs to stand in the hallway, to welcome the two guests. His interest now keenly aroused, he was espe-cially curious to meet the young Pakistani woman who had come to study at Cairo's Al-Azhar University, where he taught. The door held wide open, Ibrahim stood with a smile of welcome on his handsome face and uttered the Arabic words of welcome: '*Ehlan Sehlan Marhaba!*' First his parents entered, then the two women, followed by Pakinaz.

'This is my son, Ibrahim Musa.' An indulgent smile played on his father's face, as he introduced his son to their two guests. 'I am very proud of him. This is Zarri

Bano, my friend Habib Khan's daughter, and this is her companion, Sister Sakina.'

'*Assalam-Alaikum*!' Zarri Bano addressed Musa, taking a quick look at him.

'*Wa Laikum-Salam*, you are most welcome to our home,' he replied in English, his dark eyes on her face. Feeling rather shy, she followed Pakinaz into the dining room.

They all sat down on a sofa suite, generously piled with plump home-made cushions in rich colours.

'Would you like to take off your *hijab*?' Pakinaz asked awkwardly, not sure whether she had done the right thing in asking.

'It's all right,' Zarri Bano reassured her, noting the girl's unease. 'We wear it at home all the time.' From the corner of her eye, she was still conscious of the young man's presence. She knew he was surveying her from behind his glasses at the other end of the room. With him hovering nearby, they had no intention of removing their *burqas*!

'I see,' Pakinaz replied after a pause, hoping that they didn't expect her to wear it or to follow suit.

Then there was an exchange between the mother and daughter in rapid Arabic as Pakinaz's mother couldn't speak either English or Urdu.

'I hope you won't mind us speaking in Arabic,' Pakinaz apologised, turning towards Zarri Bano. 'She says that you are welcome to stay as long as you like and hopes that you enjoy your time in Cairo. Are you hungry enough to have dinner?'

'I think we are. We didn't eat much on the plane. We just fell asleep,' Zarri Bano laughed.

Pakinaz's mother spoke again. This time her son quickly translated for her.

'Our mother hopes and wishes that you will enjoy our Egyptian cooking. Obviously it is different from yours.' He stood up and politely guided them into the dining room.

Musa stood aside for the two black-cloaked figures to pass. There weren't many women, apart from the rural Egyptian peasants, who wore a veil like this. Wishing there were more, he was nevertheless surprised by an inexplicable urge to see what the woman with green eyes looked like in conventional female clothing.

He didn't know how it happened, but Musa somehow found himself sitting directly in front of Zarri Bano. As he sat down, Zarri Bano had looked up and then dropped her gaze. Not wanting to have anything to do with any young men, she hadn't bargained for living in the same house as this one. The feeling of disquiet somehow communicated itself to him, for when he saw his sister enter with a tray full of cooked lamb on a bed of boiled rice, he quickly got up, vacating the seat for her.

'Pakinaz, you sit and eat with our two guests. I'll eat later.' He spoke in English for Zarri Bano's benefit. As he stood up, he caught her grateful glance. Now she smiled at him for the first time, appreciating what he had done. He stared at her face, noting the attractive dimple suddenly peeping in her left cheek.

Zarri Bano and Sakina saw Ibrahim Musa the next day, just as they returned from a visit to the Giza pyramids with Pakinaz. Back from the university, he decided to join them in the dining room for a cool drink and politely asked the guests whether they had enjoyed their outing. He addressed Zarri Bano, as she was the one who could speak fluent English.

'The pyramids are a tremendous sight, but I found the descent into the tomb very claustrophobic. I don't think that I will be eagerly rushing down those steps again very soon, Brother Musa!' she told him, laughing.

'Yes, those passages are very narrow in the pyramids at Giza, I agree, Sister Zarri Bano.' He, too, laughed. 'The other tombs in the Valley of the Kings have much wider passages. Perhaps I can arrange for us all to visit the Valley of the Kings and the Queens, as well as Luxor and Karnak. Sadly, I have to go now. I will see you later. *Assalam-Alaikum.*'

'*Wa Laikum-Salam.* Thank you for your suggestion, we would like that very much, once we have settled in. My first priority, however, is to enrol at the University and make a start with my academic work.'

'Yes, of course. If you like, Pakinaz and I can take you to the University to show you around, as well as letting you see some of the other sights at the same time.'

'Oh, that is very kind of you, but we do not want to put you to any trouble. We know how busy you both are teaching and preparing for your lectures.'

'Not at all, sister, you are most welcome. But I must go now.'

'Of course,' Zarri Bano answered politely. She watched him return to his study.

Three days later Zarri Bano telephoned her parents and sister in Pakistan. She spoke at length with Ruby.

'It is hot here, but quite nice. The apartment that we are living in overlooks the River Nile. Imagine, Ruby, from our balcony we can watch the boats sailing to and fro on this legendary river. I can picture Queen Cleopatra floating in her ship in ancient times.

You really must come and visit us in Cairo as soon as you can.'

'I should be so lucky,' Ruby snorted crossly at the other end of the line. 'I miss you, Zarri Bano.'

'I miss you too, Ruby, I still cannot come to terms with where I am and what I am doing here, and why I am doing it.'

'I know, sister. Tell me, what kind of people are they?' she asked, wisely changing the subject.

'Oh, they are really very nice, Ruby. As well as the parents, there are two unmarried children living at home. The rest are married and live either in Cairo or Alexandria. Tomorrow Pakinaz, that is their unmarried daughter, is taking us to visit the oldest University in Cairo, the Al-Azhar, and to meet her sister. I am really looking forward to that.'

'Are there two sisters? You said children.'

'No. One is their son. He is a lecturer at the University where I will be studying.'

'What is he like?'

'Oh, he is OK. I hope that he will be able to assist me a little, once I start on my course. I will be joining his department. He has already passed me a couple of books on how to learn Arabic. It is very handy having him as a resource. I am trying to get my tongue around Arabic.'

'Is he good-looking?' Ruby's voice had dipped to a teasing banter.

'Ruby! Yes, he is good-looking, for your information. He has a black beard and a dark wide pool of eyes that you disappear into. Does that satisfy you? To be honest, I wish that he didn't live with the family. I have to wear the *burqa* all the time because of him. I only take it off in my room.'

'Oh, you poor thing. You must be suffocated. It is supposed to be so hot there. How is Sakina?'

'Sakina is enjoying herself tremendously. She has done a lot of shopping already and has bought at least a dozen beautiful glass perfume phials. I'll send you some, when Sakina returns in two weeks' time. Give my love to everyone.' Zarri Bano ended her first conversation with her sister from Egypt.

Later that day, Ibrahim drove them all to the old University and showed them around, explaining some of its colourful history to them.

Zarri Bano glanced up at the papyrus calendar, with a painting of the Egyptian tree of life, pinned on the wall of Ibrahim's study. Three months had already passed. In that time she had enrolled at the University. The second semester had begun and she was now making headway with her studies. She had chosen as the theme of her thesis *The Travels of the Early Arab Historians Ibn Khaldun and Ibn Battuta*. Finding it difficult to master classical Arabic, she had learnt enough of modern Arabic to cope with her everyday needs for shopping and for conversing in the streets. Although she had a room of her own, with a desk unit, Ibrahim Musa had given her permission to use his study when he wasn't using it himself. Zarri Bano marvelled at the wall-to-wall shelves of books on Islam, religion and Islamic history.

She enlisted Pakinaz's help for interpretation of words and making sense of Arabic colloquial phrases and idioms. Ibrahim Musa offered to spend some time with her every other day to oversee her study and to help her with her acquisition of classical Arabic.

After the first few days, Zarri Bano began to relax in

his company, addressing and regarding him as a brother. He, for his part, respected and addressed her as 'sister'. Enjoying her company immensely, he was gratified to share his enthusiasm in his subject with Zarri Bano. Pakinaz and his parents weren't interested in his studies. Here, however, was an intelligent and vivacious woman from halfway across the world making the most of his learning.

'Sister Zarri Bano, I am most impressed by how much you have mastered in such a short time,' he said, praising her progress one day, leaning back in his chair and surveying her from behind his glasses, his dark eyes resting on her face. Zarri Bano felt her forehead to check that no strand of hair had escaped from her *burqa* hood.

'Thank you for the compliment, Brother Musa. I find all the subjects I am studying very interesting. I feel as if I am a sponge. I want to absorb as much knowledge as possible. It is my goal to become a very learned woman on religious matters, and in as short a time as possible. Of course, as you well know, much of my progress is due to you, Brother Musa. If I didn't have you as my mentor, tutor, or whatever you would like to call yourself, I could never have progressed to such an extent.'

'You are welcome. It really is a pleasure to have your company, Zarri Bano,' he replied warmly, leaning forward. She noticed, with a sinking heart, that he had dropped the word 'sister'. A physical awareness had suddenly crept between them that had not been there before.

Zarri Bano leaned back and pensively looked down at the book in her lap. Then she stood up, keeping her eyes carefully averted from his. 'Excuse me, Brother

Ibrahim. I think that we are both tired. I will leave you in peace.'

Taken aback by her abrupt manner he watched her go with a thoughtful look in his eyes.

Chapter 27

IT WAS A Friday morning and Ibrahim's family had gone on holiday to Alexandria, on the Mediterranean coast, to visit their relatives for a week. They had asked Zarri Bano to accompany them. Thanking them for their kind invitation, she had graciously declined, saying that she had so many books to read for her research.

Having showered for the *Juma* prayers, Zarri Bano decided to put on a long red cotton Egyptian dress, which she had purchased from Cairo's central souk market. She sat by the open wooden-shuttered window, in Ibrahim's study, letting the warm breeze from the River Nile dry her hair, as it framed her face in a riot of natural fiery curls. Eyes closed, she savoured the feel of the warm breeze on her face while she thought about her assignment on twelfth-century Muslim scientists and mathematicians.

Hearing steps outside the study door, she sat upright, eyes open and very alert. Who could that be? Everyone was supposed to be in Alexandria. Next minute, the study door was thrust wide open. Zarri Bano stared up in shock as Ibrahim Musa entered the room.

'*Assalam-Alaikum!*' he greeted her, startled to see a strange woman in his study. It was only for a few

seconds, but his eyes behind his spectacles had blinked and quickly clicked the image of her firmly onto his retina. The short sleeves of her dress revealed her arms above her elbows. Her throat and the rest of her feminine beauty was apparent to his gaze in all its glory.

Colour sweeping high in her cheeks, Zarri Bano eventually came to her senses. Her arms rose and crossed over her chest, shielding herself from him and his gaze. She turned her back to him, and looked down at the Nile.

'*Wa Laikum-Salam*, Brother Musa.' She returned his greeting in a shaky voice. 'I thought you were in Alexandria visiting your eldest sister.'

Ibrahim Musa had instinctively looked away as he saw her gestures of female modesty. He felt both ashamed and embarrassed, in causing her to be caught in such a compromising situation. And it was all his fault. He had just walked in, while she had thought she was all alone in the house and had thus availed herself of the comfort of moving around without the veil. He, Musa, had robbed her of that comfort, by invading her privacy.

'Forgive me, Sister Zarri Bano. I must sincerely apologise. I just hadn't realised you were here . . .' His voice trailed away, waiting for her to say something. His eyes focused on her slim back and shoulder-blades highlighted by the cut of her dress. He was still finding it difficult to come to terms with the image of the vulnerable-looking woman standing in front of him, to the strong woman constantly enveloped in a long baggy veil.

'It is all right, Brother Musa. It is your home,' Zarri Bano answered quietly, still unable to recover her poise

after having been seen by this young unmarried man; without her *burqa*, she felt naked under his gaze. Her back throbbed, imagining his male eyes roaming on it. 'I thought you had gone to Alexandria and wouldn't be back until tomorrow night,' she said again still with her back to him.

'I decided to come back early, as I had a meeting with my colleagues at University. I am sorry to disturb you, sister. Please forgive me if I have upset you in any way. And please feel free to move at your leisure in this home. I assure you, you will not be disturbed again. I am going to visit my second sister, here in Cairo, later, and I will stay with her for the night. I will see you tomorrow evening when the rest of the family return. I apologise once again, sister. *Assalam-Alaikum.*'

'It is all right. *Wa Laikum-Salam*, Brother Musa.'

He left, closing the door firmly behind him. Zarri Bano remained standing by the window until she heard the outside door close and the sound of a car driving away. Only then did she let her arms fall to her side and turned to sit again at the desk.

She looked at her open book on the desk, but it was no use! Ibrahim Musa had spoilt it all. She was angry with herself for being caught like this. 'I should always be in my *burqa*!' she scolded herself. What if she had had an accident, and there was nobody around to help her except Musa. Could she stand him touching her body without the veil, while helping her?

An hour later she returned to her room and ritually pulled the *burqa* over her body. It was only then, sitting behind the protection of the veil, that she was able to concentrate on the book she was reading. She knew in her heart though, that she would never feel the same in Musa's presence again. She wished to Allah, over and

over again, that he had either not come, or that she had been wearing her *burqa* at that time.

Ibrahim Musa drove through the late-afternoon traffic of the densely populated city centre to his sister's home. As he passed the central souk market and saw one of the traditional Egyptian dresses hanging on the stall amidst the rest of the wares, he recalled Zarri Bano in her red dress. Ashamed though he was to voice the thought to himself, it couldn't be denied that Zarri Bano was a very attractive woman. He had suspected it, from her face, hands and eyes. Now having seen her without the veil, his eyes had sinfully learnt to appreciate what lay behind the black garment. At the same time he was angry with himself. He had done wrong. He had no right to look at a woman without her veil. That was a privilege only available to her family or her husband to enjoy – and he was neither. In this way he had shamed both her and himself. He just hoped that she would forgive him, and learn to trust him again and not build up any barriers in the light of that incident. He wanted nothing to mar the warm relationship which they already shared.

With dismay he recalled how she had kept her back to him all the time while he was in the room. Perhaps she would always be on her guard now and would maintain her distance from him. If she did, he had no choice but to accept it, and respect her for it.

The image of Zarri Bano in her red dress and her crown of curls around her face flashed a number of times in front of his eyes that evening, as he played with his sister's children.

Chapter 28

MADAME, THE FORMER Headmistress of the village girls' high school, had now retired and Firdaus, to everyone's delight, was unanimously elected by the school management committee as the new Headmistress.

Firdaus sat in her office preparing important documents for a presentation for the special guests she was expecting later in the afternoon. A principal from a women's college in a nearby town was interested in building links with girls' high schools in the villages. Firdaus flicked through the last page, satisfied with the paper she had prepared, when she heard footsteps in the veranda outside. 'Are they here already?' She rose from her seat. Without the customary knock, the door was pushed abruptly open. Firdaus blinked at the person standing in front of her and sat down in her armchair.

Kaniz's tall frame dominated the room. For the next electrifying few seconds, both women stared at one another, speechless. Kaniz's cold dark eyes were insulting in their appraisal.

'*Assalam-Alaikum*, Chaudharani Kaniz Sahiba,' Firdaus managed to offer, having recovered her poise and remembering her social graces. 'How can I help you? Please do sit down.' Firdaus nodded towards the chair.

Kaniz darted a look of utter disdain at the chair, then back to Firdaus's face. The 'chit' was ordering her about!

Firdaus glanced at the wall clock. Any minute now the guests were due to arrive. She had no desire

whatsoever for either Kaniz's company or a confronta-
tion with her. It was only too apparent that Kaniz was
itching for the latter. Firdaus thus quickly debated
with herself as to how she could get rid of her without
any unpleasantness. Why was she here anyway?

'Is there anything I can help you with? I have some
guests arriving soon, Auntie, you see.' Firdaus
explained politely, calmly looking Kaniz in the eye.

'Yes, you can definitely help.' As frosty as the icicles
on the Kashmiri mountains, the words ricocheted
around the room. 'Why did you and your mother target
me and my son to wrap your evil web around?'

Taken aback, Firdaus closed her eyes behind her read-
ing glasses and mentally counted to three – an effective
habit she had adopted a long time ago, in an effort to
contain herself and her temper, which was foul when it
erupted.

'I don't understand. We have set no evil trap or web
around you, your son or family. It must be that wild
imagination of yours that makes you think that,
Madam Kaniz,' Firdaus replied coldly.

'Don't you "madam" me,' Kaniz hissed, her dark,
almond-shaped eyes narrowing with fury. 'You and
your mother have destroyed me and my family.'

Firdaus's heart was now thumping away uncomfort-
ably in her chest. The conversation was getting more
and more out of hand and she didn't know how best to
deal with the situation.

'I repeat, Auntie, I don't know what you mean. I
have nothing to do with your son,' Firdaus tried, fear-
ing that she was fast being sucked into the eye of the
hurricane of Kaniz's twisted imagination.

'You have nothing to do with my son, you say! You
wicked, conniving women. You and your mother have

been after him for years. God knows how many glasses of milk with *tweez* you and she have toppled down his throat. He has left home because of you, you bitch!'

'That is enough!' Firdaus shot up from her chair, thoroughly shaken by the woman's venom. Her brown cheeks now a shade of bright red and her hands spread flat on the desk, Firdaus leaned all of her slender five-feet body towards Kaniz and through gritted teeth ground out in her most authoritative voice – the one she used on her pupils.

'If you please, Madam, out of my office and out of my life. You have no manners, but I will not sink to your debased level, by matching abuse with your abuse. However, let me tell you that I wouldn't touch your son, or any other member of your family with a barge pole, let alone marry him. You can keep your precious Khawar. Make jam out of him, for all I care,' she ended viciously, surprising even herself. Kaniz had apparently brought out the worst in her.

'How dare you say that! Keep your evil mouth shut, you slut. He has left home because of *you*. I don't know what he sees in you. You are such a plain creature!' The look of insulting disgust on her face and the way in which her lips curled down in contempt at the corners made Firdaus's hands tremble on the desk.

'He has not left your home because of us, but because of *you*. He couldn't bear to be near a viper of a mother like you!' Firdaus had now dispensed with social proprieties, having decided that this woman deserved no respect. 'I have not plied him with any evil amulets – I do not believe in them. It is only ignorant, superstitious and evil women like yourself, who believe in them. I never had designs on your son and never will. I am ashamed to admit that my mother would have liked

such a match, but she is foolish, like you. No, Chaudharani Kaniz, I would never marry your son, even if you crawled on your hands and knees and begged me to.'

'That will be the day!' Kaniz shouted, scandalised. 'Me – crawl to ask for a washerwoman's daughter's hand in marriage.' Her eyes almost rolled in their sockets.

She was abruptly cut short by Firdaus's hand stamping down three times on the bell on her desk. Itching to strike the woman, Firdaus was shocked by her own feelings of violence towards Kaniz.

The school caretaker, the *chaprassi*, came running into the room.

'What is it, Madam Headmistress?' Respectfully addressing Firdaus, he fearfully looked from one angry woman to another.

'Please, Baba Jee, show this unwanted visitor out of our school. In future make sure that you are on duty at the door. We don't want any *nathu pethu*, any unwanted guests, to crawl into our school.'

Shocked by her own stream of venom, Firdaus nevertheless felt better for it. Kaniz gulped back a retort. Bursting to give Firdaus another mouthful, she found herself almost blindly and mutely following the *chaprassi* out of the room.

Leaving the room a dazed, humiliated woman, Kaniz felt as if she had lost a full three inches from her height. 'Thrown out by a *chaprassi*! I, Kaniz, *chaudharani* of the village! And by whose orders? A mere washerwoman's daughter!' she screamed in her head, wanting to run away and hide somewhere.

As she crossed the school courtyard, she saw a group of women, smartly dressed in designer *shalwar kameze* suits, enter through the gates. Firdaus, having followed

Kaniz out of the office, moved eagerly forward to wel-
come and greet her guests. Kaniz looked, with bitter-
ness, at Firdaus's outstretched hands and arms. Now
totally ignoring her, Firdaus led her guests to her room.

Feeling defeated, Kaniz slinked away, pulling her
shawl further over her forehead, hiding her face.

There were two shiny cars standing outside in the
school's small car park. Those important-looking
people had evidently come to visit the washerwoman's
daughter! Kaniz's mouth tightened again in disgust
and rage.

Her head was still reeling. By the time she was a few
yards away, Kaniz wasn't sure who she was any more. It
was as if Firdaus had somehow stripped her of her iden-
tity as the *chaudharani*. The sickening image of Firdaus
being hugged one by one by those women, with smiles
of pleasure on their faces would stay with Kaniz till the
day she died. Firdaus had really turned the tables
on her. She had succeeded in making her, Kaniz, feel
like a washerwoman while she preened herself as the
chaudharani of the school.

Chapter 29

AS HE WALKED by himself in one of his vegetable
fields, Siraj Din bent down and prodded the dry earth
with his walking stick to check how moist it was
underneath. The irrigation system was definitely work-
ing. A tractor, driven by one of his workers, Faisal,
passed him by. Siraj Din continued with his leisurely
walk, heading back towards the village.

Passing the girls' high school, he didn't notice the

woman sitting on a large boulder on the edge of the path, until he was only a few yards away from her. With her head bent and her *dupatta* partially concealing her face from his sight, he couldn't make out who she was. Was she a visitor from the city or from another village? But there was no luggage in sight.

As he approached, the woman heard the tapping sound of his walking stick and looked up. Siraj Din was very surprised.

'Kaniz, my dear, what are you doing here sitting in the middle of the path?' he asked, stopping in front of her. It was so unlike her; she always travelled about in her car. The village path and a dusty boulder were the last place anyone would think to find Chaudharani Kaniz.

Kaniz stared back blankly. Siraj Din's shrewd old eyes recognised the pinched look about her mouth. Her normal poise was missing; the expression on her face was an unfamiliar one. Lost for words, she continued to stare up at him. Her lips struggled to say something, but failed to move apart, as if sealed with cement. Siraj Din was now mildly alarmed on her behalf. He saw that there were two other women passing by, one with a large bundle of sugar cane on her head. They inclined their heads in respect as they met his eyes and bade him 'Salam'. He bent his head slightly in acknowledgement and leaned forward to pat the shoulders of the women. He knew both of them by name, and their family backgrounds.

'Are you all right, my dear daughter?' he prompted gently as he turned once more to Kaniz. Siraj Din addressed all the women in the village with the term 'daughter', with the exception of those three who, because of their age, he addressed as 'sisters'.

Kaniz was never ever known to be at a loss for words.
If anything, Siraj Din chuckled to himself, she was a
great mistress of speech, adept at keeping it flowing
and putting people in their place.

'She had me thrown out, Baba Jee,' she whispered, so
quietly that he almost didn't hear. Turning her face
away from his gaze she looked down to the ground.

'Who had you thrown out, my dear?' Siraj Din
coaxed.

Kaniz glanced up sharply, anger dancing in her eyes,
indignant that he hadn't understood who she had
meant by 'she'.

'She! She! That witch! That *charail*, who has got my
son wound round her little magic finger. That washer-
woman's daughter!' The stream of words had now
jetted out with all the innate vehemence and hatred she
bore in her mind and heart for Firdaus.

'You mean Firdaus?' Siraj Din guessed astutely.

'Yes! While she welcomed with open arms, hugged
and kissed her "elevated" guests from the city, she
ordered the *chaprassi* to throw me out like a beggar. Can
you believe it, Baba Jee? Me, the *chaudharani* of the
village, being shown the door by that chit of a woman
who isn't worthy enough to clean my shoes.'

'My dear Kaniz, don't get carried away now.' Siraj
Din tapped his stick gently on the ground, a discreet
smile crossing his face.

'Baba Jee, I felt as if I had been robbed of my iden-
tity, when I walked out of the school gates,' Kaniz
confided as if she hadn't heard him. 'I have sat on this
spot since the afternoon. My head reels in disbelief.
Who am I? I keep asking myself. Tell me, Baba Jee,
aren't I the village *chaudharani* any more? Is this the
way to treat a respectable older woman? She has done it

deliberately, to humiliate me and rub my face in the mud. She has turned my son against me. He has left his home. Now she had me evicted from the school. Who is she, Baba Jee? She is nothing but an upstart. Her mother's hands are still greased with the grime of the dishes she scours in your son's home!'

'Kaniz, my daughter, take it easy. I think you have got carried away with your imagination. I am sure Firdaus would never have you thrown out.'

'But she has, Baba Jee. Why are you taking her side? I am sure I am going to have a heart attack from this.' Kaniz's cheeks flamed red in pique.

'I think I know what you mean,' he said thoughtfully 'what you must have gone through. I experienced something similar once in my life. I have learnt that we are kings and queens in our small, self-centred domains. What is hard for us to believe and accept is that outside the perimeters of those domains, we are nothing, Kaniz. I, too, had a rude awakening myself, when I was treated shabbily at Makkah by someone. I, too, reeled back in shock, my ego totally bruised. Like you, I began to doubt my own identity and sanity. At the end I realised, and it was brutally brought home to me that it was a good experience for me, to look outside my self-created, self-centred world. Here in the village I am the master of all things. In the city, I am just a senile old man.'

'You are *not* a senile old man! And I am *not* getting carried away, Baba Jee. She did have me thrown out,' she asserted impatiently.

'Never mind. Don't upset yourself further. Why don't you come to terms with everything? I do know what has been going on. Why won't you let your son marry Firdaus?'

'Never!' Kaniz shot up, thoroughly outraged, her eyes glowing red with anger.

Siraj Din's mouth curved into a ghost of a smile, his brown bushy eyebrows well arched in amazement. This was the Kaniz he knew: loud, volatile, always sure of herself and infinitely domineering. He didn't say anything for a few seconds, judiciously remaining silent – letting her calm down. Kaniz remained standing, her body stiff.

Siraj Din began to walk using his stick. Kaniz joined him and silently they walked side by side towards the village. Siraj Din knew he hadn't endeared himself to her by his words, but he persisted, nevertheless.

'You never forgave Fatima, did you?' Siraj Din stated softly.

Kaniz froze, stopping in her tracks. Her face turned accusingly towards him eyes wide and mouth slightly open. Siraj Din stopped too.

'What do you mean?' she asked in a barely audible voice.

'You know what I mean. I know everything that has gone on in this village, Kaniz.'

She stared in disbelief at the wiry upright old man, with his thick cap of henna-dyed white hair and beard. Her eyes stood out large in her face.

'I don't know what you are talking about, Baba Jee.' Kaniz pretended ignorance, in an attempt to bluster it out. She was surprised and shaken that the old man knew, even after twenty-nine years. 'Why do I have to forgive Fatima?' she continued, injecting a false note of sarcasm in her voice, as a smile lit her face.

Siraj Din's lips twitched with laughter. Kaniz had an impeccable knack of recovering her poise quickly. The smile on his wrinkled face grew prominent.

Nothing, and nobody could ever keep Kaniz down. She bounced back with a vengeance.

He continued to walk for a few more yards, tapping his walking stick on the way. Kaniz walked by his side, waiting for him to say something, her body tense. Siraj Din stood still in the middle of the dusty path, his stick drawing a circle, and turned to the woman by his side.

'You are being deliberately obtuse, Kaniz. You know very well what I mean. You haven't forgiven Fatima for jilting Sarwar, your husband. Now you see the pattern being repeated, with your own son interested in Fatima's daughter.'

Colour flared high in Kaniz's fair cheeks. Throwing social etiquette to the wind, she forgot the code of respect for elders.

'Baba Jee, I think in your old age, your imagination has got the better of you. What . . .' she was about to shout out the word 'nonsense', but she just about managed to pull it back in time, knowing that it would be too offensive to the elderly man.

Just then, Siraj Din's loud laughter rang out through the air, startling her. Perplexed, she watched helplessly as his tall slim body shook with mirth. Only Kaniz had the temerity to stand up to him and say what she liked without mincing her words, and then get away with it. His own daughter-in-laws, particularly Shahzada, wouldn't even have dared to look him in the face, while speaking to him – let alone insult him by saying that his imagination had run away with itself!

'*Khudah Hafiz*, Baba Jee, I must go home. My sister is waiting there for me and I have no time to waste in discussing the washerwoman or her chit.' Siraj Din's words had put the life back into Kaniz. Finding the subject of his allusion too unsavoury, she wished to be

gone before he said anything else, and before she herself said something she might later regret. Straightening her shawl around her shoulders, she scuttled off leaving Siraj Din behind.

Siraj Din continued his stroll back to the village with a smile still hovering around his mouth. He was immensely glad that Kaniz wasn't *his* daughter-in-law. God forbid, he would have been in his grave by now. She would have led them all quite a dance if they had to put up with her waspish tongue night and day. Her self-centredness, her arrogance and volatility would have destroyed the domestic harmony in his son's household a long time ago. Siraj Din was so grateful to his wife, Zulaikha, for choosing such suitable daughters-in-laws, like Shahzada, for example.

The thought of Shahzada, brought Habib to his mind. His son had still looked very unhappy when Siraj Din had last visited them in the town. It was over a year since Zarri Bano had become a Holy Woman. His daughter-in-law, Shahzada, was still not as forthcoming towards him as she used to be. Outwardly, he couldn't fault her. She appeared the same. She paid him due respect, served him his meals and made the right remarks when he visited them in their home. What was the matter then? Siraj Din mused.

He knew the answer, just as his son had painfully come to know it. 'She has closed the doors to her inner self and has left us outside. She will never let us in again.' He wondered sadly whether Shahzada would ever forgive them. Surely time was meant to thaw hearts?

Zarri Bano, Habib had told him, had gone to England, on the invitation of one of her university friends.

Siraj Din missed his eldest granddaughter. He shook his head. She was definitely not the Holy Woman that he had envisaged. He was beginning to wonder whether it would have been better to have allowed her to marry Sikander. At least then she would have stayed at home, and led a normal life, rather than roaming around the world on the pretence of attending one convention or another.

His mind, no matter how broad he tried to make it, couldn't yet digest the idea of his beautiful granddaughter all alone and in the vicinity of strange young men. It wasn't safe for a woman to be without the protection of male kin. Their Zarri Bano was totally alone in Egypt! Siraj Din feared for his granddaughter. Men could mentally rape a woman just with one look, even if she was covered from head to toe.

He recalled the sight of his son's solitary figure, as he paced the grounds of his estate. Habib's words: 'Have we done the right thing by Zarri Bano, Father?' sprang into his mind.

'Of course we have!' Siraj Din spoke aloud to himself. Zarri Bano was destined to inherit all her father's wealth and to become the *Bibi* – the Holy Woman! It was her *kismet*.

Chapter 30

KANIZ AGGRESSIVELY PUSHED the white wrought-iron gate open with her foot and let it bang loudly behind her, heralding her arrival to all. She immediately went in search of her sister. 'Sabra!' she bawled. Neesa came running out of the bedding storeroom on

the ground floor. Catching sight of her mistress, she hurried to take the shawl off Kaniz's shoulders.

'Where is my sister?' the *chaudharani* demanded. Neesa flinched. Anger appeared to exude from her mistress's every pore.

'She is resting, Sahiba Jee,' Neesa informed Kaniz timidly moving away; wisely she wanted to place as much distance as possible between the other woman and herself. Kaniz was well-known for her tantrums and throwing and breaking things.

It was a good two hours later when Sabra came down from her afternoon nap. Still yawning, she hadn't bargained for the verbal onslaught that hit her as soon as she saw Kaniz lying on a *palang* on the veranda.

Kaniz was fanning herself vigorously with a bead-studded hand fan. The electricity had just gone off; the generator wasn't working either. The late afternoon's heat and her hot flushes had literally lent more fuel to Kaniz's anger. 'Twice in one day! What is the use of paying thousands of rupees for air conditioners, when there is no electricity available to use them?' she fumed, barely waiting for her sister to sit down on a cane chair before beginning to rant and rave.

Then: 'She had me thrown out, Sabra!' Kaniz exclaimed, her arms outstretched dramatically.

'Who, Kaniz, dear?' Sabra ventured innocently, totally unprepared for the molten lava of words ready to erupt from the crater of Kaniz's beautiful mouth.

'That witch Firdaus, of course – who else!' Kaniz rasped, throwing her sister a murderous look. Trust Sabra not to understand!

Now wide awake. 'What do you mean, she had you thrown out?' Sabra asked gently, very anxious to calm her sister and to lower her own blood pressure,

which had a habit of rapidly shooting up when Kaniz shouted.

'When I went to visit her, she told her *chaprassi* to show me the door,' Kaniz hissed, breathing fire. 'She was entertaining her special guests – principals and all the top nobs. While she eagerly flew to hug them, she had me thrown out like a *fakir* by her minion!'

'What, just like that? You must have said or done something, surely?' Sabra knew all about the animosity her sister bore towards Fatima and her family.

'I only told her what she rightfully deserved to hear: to leave my son well alone!' Kaniz swung the hand fan in front of her face in long, heavy strokes. The heat was bursting out of her cheeks.

Studiously avoiding her sister's eyes, Sabra lifted the second fan from the table and began to fan her own face languidly. She was not quite ready to get herself embroiled in Kaniz's petulant outburst as yet. Well conversant with her sister's erratic behaviour since childhood, she could read her moods and degrees of volatility like the back of her hand.

'She has left your son well alone,' Sabra eventually placated, now looking frankly into her sister's eyes.

'Oh no, she hasn't!' Kaniz was scandalised by her sister's temerity in disagreeing with her. 'It is he who has left me! Me – his mother, who gave birth to him! He has abandoned me and his home for that chit. What in Allah's name does he see in her? She is too short and plain – a nobody,' Kaniz spat, her nose in the air.

Sabra looked calmly at her elder sister, wondering whether she should be honest for once – and therefore speak very bluntly indeed – or whether to humour Kaniz, as she usually did, by keeping quiet.

In the end, honesty won the day – she owed it to her

sister, after all. Sabra's heart sank at the prospect, 'but it has to be said,' she told herself firmly. 'In fact, it is time someone spoke out.'

'Kaniz, my dear sister,' she began, taking the plunge, 'why don't you let Khawar marry this young woman, if he really wants to? Then you could have him back at home.'

There was complete silence. Kaniz blinked at Sabra, unable to believe her burning ears – feeling totally betrayed. Her own sister, mouthing such infamy!

Kaniz's almond-shaped eyes stood large in her face, her lower lip quivering with emotion.

'You too, Sabra?' she said, her voice incredulous. 'It seems I am living amongst a nest of vipers and traitors. I have already had a lecture from the old man, Siraj Baba. I definitely do not deserve one now from my baby sister, my own blood. Has that chit got round to feeding her *tweez* to everyone? To you too? I tell you, sister, that I will never let that washerwoman's daughter step over the threshold of this house. As long as I live, this house is *mine*. Do you understand?'

Sabra sighed. She had already dipped her foot in it, so she might as well dive straight into the dangerous deep end of her sister's pool of wrath.

'Have you ever considered, Kaniz dear, that that "washerwoman" as you like to call her, could have been *chaudharani*, in your place? If she had married Brother Sarwar *she* would have been mistress here. But Fatima turned him down: only then did you get the chance to become the *chaudharani* yourself.'

At that moment, Kaniz could easily have strangled Sabra. If she had been younger she would have leapt at her sister and pulled out her hair from her chunky thick plait.

'First it was Siraj Baba, now you!' she hissed. 'Is everyone going to abuse and humiliate me?'

'I just don't understand why you bear such a grudge against them! You see, you have gained in every way, sister. You are the mistress of this place and of acres of land. Fatima, on the other hand, has to work hard at an uncongenial job to support her husband and her family. Firdaus could have been Sarwar's daughter. She could have been a sister to Khawar.'

'Khawar is my son, Sabra. Your imagination is running away with you.' Kaniz's voice was now threaded with steel.

'Please, sister, don't get yourself all worked up. Remember your blood pressure. You are both respected families. The girl is educated. Firdaus and Khawar apparently want to marry each other. Then why are you preventing it? I will tell you why sister. It is all due to your pride, which one day will prove your downfall. I am not going to mince my words any more to please you. I know you do not like hearing the truth and you can go purple as beetroot in the face, but if I don't say it, nobody else will.'

Sabra looked her sister right in the eye as she told her straight: 'If you don't let this marriage take place, you will regret it to the end of your days. You have only one son, and if you lose him, you will lose everything. Love is what you are fighting here, my dear sister. It makes people do crazy things. People have murdered for love; kings have been known to abandon their thrones for love. I tell you, sister,' her voice lowered, 'you are at the losing end here.'

'I already am. He has left home for that witch,' Kaniz said despairingly.

'Why do you hate them so much?' Sabra wanted to

know. 'I don't understand it! She is a very nice girl, this Firdaus, from what I have seen of her. I tell you, sister, she is a good catch. If she goes to the city, she'll be one of the most eligible of young educated women. I would have thought that you would love to have a Head-mistress for a daughter-in-law – one who earns thousands of rupees in salary. People will come flooding to your door out of respect. Later, she could even become a Principal.' Sabra beamed at her sister.

But Kaniz was in no mood to listen. 'I don't want to hear another word, Sabra. You, my own sister, have turned traitor!' Her fingers were now held to her burn-ing ears, trying to block out the unwelcome words.

'No, dear sister, I am not a traitor,' Sabra said solemnly. 'Your jealousy and hatred have eaten away all your commonsense.'

'Jealousy! Of whom, may I ask?'

'Of Fatima, of course. You cannot forgive her for turning your husband down. You cannot bear the thought that you were second best, that he really wanted to marry Fatima, but she refused. What you seem to forget is that if she *had* married Sarwar, where would you be? In a miserable three-room apartment in the inner city bazaar area of the town, in our parents' home. You would certainly not be the *chaudharani* of all this!' Sabra ended passionately, having lost both her fear and patience with her sister.

Insulted beyond belief, Kaniz stood up and strode away into the house, flinging the fan on to the marble floor. It fell with a sharp crack and broke into two pieces. Sabra shook her head resignedly. She had def-initely done it now. Kaniz would throw her out, for sure.

When Neesa came to ask where they wanted to eat, whether inside in the dining room or outside on the

balcony rooftop, Sabra ruefully told her that she had better bring her a tray in the courtyard; she didn't think her mistress would be eating with her today. 'I am afraid,' Sabra continued, looking sheepishly at Neesa, 'I am in her bad books at the moment. You might as well pack my bags; I will be leaving soon. I have definitely overstayed my welcome this time!'

Neesa flashed a conspiratorial smile at Sabra and nodded in understanding. It didn't bode well for her either. Today she would no doubt be taking the brunt of the *chaudharani*'s anger, but she had spent twenty-nine years of her life doing just that. So what was another day? She sometimes wondered why she put up with her mistress's tyrannical ways, but in her heart, Neesa already knew the answer: it was for love of Khawar, the young master she had helped to raise with Kaniz.

Chapter 31

SIKANDER SAT WITH his parents in their drawing room in Karachi. Over twelve months had passed since Zarri Bano had become a Holy Woman. They had learnt from some friends that Zarri Bano was now studying at Cairo University. Sikander had forbidden his parents to mention her name in his presence. 'I can never forgive her, Mother!' he had raged.

An idea had, however, been germinating in Bilkis's head. Having toyed with it for so long, she found it difficult to give up. This evening, with both her son and husband in a notably relaxed mood, she gambled and took the plunge.

'Sikander, do you know I can actually see some white hairs near your temple?' she remarked. Sikander laughed. 'It's not funny,' she remonstrated fondly. 'As a mother I am concerned, not about your white hair, but about your single status. Your two sisters hardly ever visit us these days. My heart hungers for the sound of children in this large, lonely place. I want grand-children, Sikander. I think it is time you decided to marry and settled down, my son.'

Sikander, working on his business accounts, moved them aside from his lap and respectfully paid heed to his mother's words. He was about to make a concili-atory remark when his mother quietly slipped in, 'What about Ruby?'

The words died on Sikander's lips. He stared at his mother in stunned silence, as though receiving an elec-tric shock. Thrusting the papers onto the floor, he stood up. 'Never!' His grey eyes dark with emotion, he strode out of the room.

Raja Din turned to his wife, his own eyes mirroring his surprise. 'When and from where did you get this preposterous idea in your brain, my dear? That wasn't very clever, or very sensitive of you. You know how he still feels about Zarri Bano. To tell you the truth, I can't forget her myself,' he told his wife with a wistful look in his eyes.

'Well, Ruby is her sister,' Bilkis began defensively. 'She is just as nice and nearly as beautiful. I know you are both partial to Zarri Bano's beauty, but in looks you can hardly tell the difference between the two sisters apart from Ruby's hairstyle and the colour of her eyes. If Sikander cannot marry Zarri Bano, what is to stop him from marrying Ruby? After all, she is not a Holy Woman – is she?'

'No, Bilkis! Sikander wants nothing more to do with that family. Marrying Ruby would only evoke memories of the past for him. You are right, of course, Ruby *is* a very attractive and eligible girl – but it doesn't seem right. What would Zarri Bano think? What would Ruby herself think?'

'Well, if she had any sense, Ruby would be pleased. Our son is so eligible, wealthy and such a good-looking man. As far as Zarri Bano is concerned, she now belongs to another world. From what I gather, she will be forever on her religious tours, seminars or pilgrimages. It is nothing to do with her, who her sister marries.'

'But she still has feelings,' Raja Din persisted.

'She has no right to object. She gave up Sikander and marriage to become a Holy Woman,' Bilkis stated firmly.

'My dear, you argue everything so plausibly, but in the end it will all depend on Sikander. He is not keen on that family at all – you know that.'

'Well, my heart is set on Ruby and I am not going to give up. I want to exorcise Zarri Bano's ghost from my son's heart, once and for all. I know in my bones that woman lives in his mind and heart all day, as much as he will deny it.'

And Bilkis didn't give up. In fact, she kept on battering away at her son's reserve. After three tries, she managed to get him to listen to her again.

'I know what you felt for Zarri Bano, but that is all in the past now, my son. She is part of another world and another life. You must learn to forget her. She is out of your reach. But her sister isn't, and Ruby is such a nice girl.'

'Mother, this is my life you are talking about. It was Zarri Bano I wanted to marry, not Ruby. How can I

suddenly think of Ruby as my wife? Also, she would always remind me of her sister.'

'Zarri Bano is the past, my son,' Bilkis repeated firmly.

'I know, Mother – so you keep reminding me. I have tried to remove her from my mind and heart, I really have. But linking myself to Ruby will bring it all back again. I will never be able to get away from her or her family. Don't you see?'

'No, my son, I do not see. You need to adjust yourself to the idea, that is clear, but Zarri Bano is the past while Ruby is the present and the future. She is a person in her own right. She also has the qualities and looks that you found so attractive in Zarri Bano. She is not Zarri Bano, we know that, but she is a wonderful woman. Give her a chance, my son, please. She is an intelligent, beautiful, graceful woman and has a warm sunny personality.'

'But with no sparkle,' Sikander added mentally to himself, recalling that one vivid quality in Zarri Bano. He knew he would not find it easily in another woman. The new Zarri Bano, the Holy Woman, had lost it too. It was buried with the old Zarri Bano, behind the *burqa*.

'Mother, have you ever thought of what Ruby might have to say, or how she would feel on this subject? After all, I was her sister's fiancé once. I find it an abhorrent idea. I am sure that she will find it even more so, especially as it is her sister I should have married in the first place. If you want the truth, Mother, I hate the idea. As a matter of fact, I hate that family.'

'Forget about Zarri Bano and her father! Do you hate Ruby?'

'No, of course not.'

'Then why don't you marry her?' Bilkis persisted doggedly.

'Mother! Please stop!'

'I am not going to stop until you agree to at least think rationally about it and allow me to get in touch with Ruby's parents, rather than dismiss it rashly because of your prejudice.'

'All right, Mother, I'll think seriously about it. Now can we change the subject?'

Bilkis stopped and triumphantly lowered her gaze, hiding her pleasure from him. She had partially reached her goal.

Sikander did think about it. He thought about it as he lay in his bed at night-time and as he walked in the orange orchard. In fact, he thought of nothing else. A few days later he announced to Bilkis that he had capitulated.

'Mother, you may go ahead and approach Zar— Ruby's parents,' he said a week later. He had decided that it was time to bury the past and make a fresh start. Zarri Bano had, hadn't she? Now he was entitled to do the same. She had forgotten him. It was time for him to forget her.

'I will, my handsome son,' said Bilkis, hugging him, her cheeks warm with pleasure. 'You don't know how happy you have made me. You'll not regret it, I assure you. Ruby is a wonderful girl, my darling.'

'That is to be seen, Mother. She'll never be Zarri Bano, will she? I won't kid myself, but I am a fool for wanting to get involved with that family again and for listening to you.'

Bilkis wasted no time in setting the wheels in motion and two weeks later Sikander was formally engaged to

Ruby. Bilkis had telephoned Ruby's parents that very evening, when Sikander had given her the go-ahead. Shahzada and Habib were very surprised by Bilkis requesting Ruby's hand for her son in marriage. Since Zarri Bano's ceremony it had been an awkward affair for both the parties. Wanting to make amends for having broken their ties over Zarri Bano's engagement, Habib agreed in theory – even before approaching Ruby.

When Shahzada gently broached the subject with her daughter, Ruby's face went scarlet in embarrassment. She was expecting to marry soon, but not her sister's ex-fiancé, and she recoiled inwardly. Of course she was very flattered by the proposal, but there was something not quite right. Sikander was very wealthy, educated, good-looking and of a high social standing, she told herself – but he was to have been her sister's husband. How could she marry him? He was the only man her sister had ever wanted to marry, and he was the one her sister had been prevented from marrying. How could she ever face Zarri Bano if she were to marry Sikander? She would be betraying her in the worst possible way. She felt like a traitor for even harbouring the thought in her mind. Luckily Zarri Bano was not around. She was now in India, at Ajmeir Sharif, visiting the famous Indian Darbar. How would Zarri Bano react? What would she say?

And what about her own feelings? Ruby mused. Twinges of awareness had already alerted her to the fact that she did find Sikander attractive. And yes, she would like to marry him; after all, which woman would not? She argued the pros and cons with herself. The only obstacle and problem was Zarri Bano and her reaction when she found out.

After two days of wrestling with her conscience, Ruby accepted the proposal. As yet Sikander and Ruby had not come in direct contact with each other. Sikander didn't drive over immediately to meet his fiancée. 'I already know her. I have seen her,' he told his parents, dismissively and gave them permission to act as his go-betweens.

The engagement was formalised by Sikander's parents a fortnight later. They brought presents for her, including a very expensive engagement ring. Sikander accompanied them to Ruby's home, only agreeing to it after finding out that Zarri Bano was not in Pakistan. Otherwise he would have preferred the engagement party to take place at his home.

After a short, formal meeting in the lounge, with everyone taking refreshments, Ruby and Sikander were left alone to get to know one another better – prompting Sikander to bitterly recall another time, when he and Zarri Bano had been left alone to take a walk in the fields.

Both Sikander and Ruby felt uneasy in the other's presence. The last time Ruby had seen him, he had been a prospective brother-in-law and now she had to view him as her own fiancé.

Sikander's eyes swept over Ruby. Undeniably, she was an attractive woman. In terms of looks he couldn't fault her, apart from the colour of her eyes. He accepted, however, that she was no match for Zarri Bano and never would be. She would never kindle the fire in him like Zarri Bano had.

Sikander gave himself a mental shake. He must stop comparing Ruby to Zarri Bano. 'She means nothing to me any more!' he told himself angrily. Then why did his heart always trip over when he heard her name

mentioned, or when an image of her face came startling fresh before his eyes?

It was an awkward repartee with Ruby constantly dropping her gaze before his.

'Are you happy with this match, Ruby Sahiba?' he asked.

'Yes,' she answered, finally meeting his eyes, a blush suffusing her cheeks. 'And you? Are *you* happy to go ahead with it?' There was a solemn expression on her face, replacing the earlier shyness.

'Yes,' came his firm answer. He had seen and felt her reserve and that, in turn, had melted his own. His attractive mouth now curved into a spontaneous warm smile.

Ruby blossomed under it – caught. She forgot her sister but instead welcomed the union with this good-looking man with all her heart.

As she stood up to return her tea plate to the table, Sikander's eyes followed. 'She is Ruby, not Zarri Bano,' he told himself. Zarri Bano had to be exorcised from his heart, and he now felt happy and confident in the belief that Ruby would certainly help him to do that. The sisters were so alike and yet so different. As he smiled into her brown eyes, Sikander vowed that he would never compare the two in his mind again.

Ruby returned with a cup in her hand, a tremulous smile still playing on her lips. Feeling his eyes sweep over her, her woman's intuition signalled to her that this was the first time Sikander was seeing her as a woman in her own right and not as Zarri Bano's sister. A triumphant glow lit up inside her and she exulted in it.

They talked for a long time. There was not the electric awareness, the powerful desire that he had

harboured for Zarri Bano on his first encounter, Sikander mused, but he had begun to enjoy Ruby's company and felt happier for it.

When the parents returned they found the couple relaxed and laughing. Both sets of parents exchanged glances and smiles, knowing that a marriage between Ruby and Sikander would indeed be imminent.

That same evening, a date was set for the wedding – a month later. By that time Zarri Bano would be back from India. If anybody felt any tension in the room when Shahzada mentioned Zarri Bano's name, nobody gave any indication of it.

Sikander and his parents declined to stay overnight as Sikander was flying off to Malaysia on a business trip early the following morning. They left late that same night.

Shahzada joined her husband in their bedroom, after they had seen Sikander and his parents off. She sat on the sofa facing Habib, who was sitting on his bed.

'Do you know, it is going to be my Ruby's wedding, but I do not feel at all happy about it, Habib,' she began solemnly.

'As parents of a daughter we are not culturally meant to feel happy, my dear. We will be losing a daughter. Well, at least we shall still have Zarri Bano, once Ruby leaves us . . .' He stopped, noting the expression on his wife's face.

'That is just it, Habib – Zarri Bano.' Shahzada hoped that she wouldn't have to digress further.

'What about her?' he asked, not meeting her gaze.

'We should never have agreed to this match with Sikander. Have you considered Zarri Bano's feelings on the subject?'

'She is a Holy Woman now, Shahzada. What does it matter to her who Ruby marries?' came his sharp reply. Habib was annoyed with his wife for referring to that matter and spoiling it all.

'Sikander was the man Zarri Bano was supposed to have married, Habib! Surely you remember that? Don't you think that you've done enough damage as it is, without hurting her more? Can't you be sensitive enough to see it from her point of view?'

'Shahzada, you are delving too much into Zarri Bano's feelings. We have no idea what she'll think. As she is not marrying anybody, what will it matter to her who Sikander marries? She is too busy with her new life to give any of us much thought. Anyway, I feel happier that I have been able to make amends to Sikander and his family. What is the difference between Ruby and Zarri Bano, anyway? To me they are both the same.'

'Are they though, my dear Habib?' Shahzada asked curtly. 'Would *you* like to be the one to tell Zarri Bano when she returns that the man you stopped her from marrying is to become her brother-in-law?'

Disquieted by her words, Habib said nothing. Put like that, he definitely didn't want to be the one to break the news to Zarri Bano, or even to face her. He had suddenly recalled, all too clearly, his eldest daughter's passionate words: '*I want to marry Sikander.*'

Chapter 32

THE PREPARATIONS FOR Ruby's trousseau were in full swing. The jewellery had been chosen and commissioned from their family jewellers. Three master tailors

in their exclusive boutiques had received orders to pre-
pare an array of outfits in various designs, styles and
fabrics. Ruby, Shahzada and Fatima made daily excur-
sions to the shopping plazas and bazaars to buy items
for Ruby's dowry. Ruby chose while Shahzada and
Fatima ordered. Almost like a ritual, every day they left
home early in the morning and returned late in the
afternoon, exhausted and carrying numerous bags of
goods.

Sikander telephoned Ruby often in the evenings
following their engagement. With a light spring to her
heels, Ruby would sprint to the telephone, when
Fatima informed her who it was. Her face often split
into a full smile as she chatted to Sikander. Fatima
watched her with mixed feelings. On one occasion,
Ruby caught the expression on their housekeeper's face
as she turned away from the telephone.

'Fatima, are you all right?' Ruby asked, the smile
slipping from her face.

'Yes, my dear. Why do you ask?'

'Nothing. I . . . Fatima, you do not approve of me
marrying Sikander, do you?'

Fatima stopped in her tracks. A long silence
followed, while the older woman debated with herself
as to what to say.

'Ruby, of course I approve! I am very pleased for
you. Sikander will make a fine husband.' She tried
not to pay heed to the inner voice saying, *'He would
have made a finer husband to Zarri Bano.'* Her heart wept
for her princess, Zarri Bano. She would never say any-
thing to anybody, not even to Shahzada, who confided
almost everything in her. She would mourn for her
beloved Zarri Bano alone. The inner voice said so
loudly she was almost afraid that Ruby would hear:

'Sikander should have been Zarri Bano's husband, not yours!'

It was a weird twist of fate, Sikander marrying the other sister. What sort of a father *was* Habib? she thought disgustedly. He could have rejected the marriage proposal if he had wanted to. Preventing one daughter from marrying Sikander, then encouraging another to do so. It wasn't right in Fatima's way of thinking – it was immoral!

Sikander telephoned Ruby on the afternoon when Zarri Bano was expected back from India. A momentary pause and tension ensued on the line when Ruby told him that her sister was returning home that night.

'I see,' was all he said. In normal circumstances he would have received and welcomed Zarri Bano at the airport, as her future brother-in-law. Because of their past relationship, he wasn't quite ready to meet her yet. Therefore, he said nothing. Instead he asked what Ruby had brought from the bazaar that day.

'It is such a foolish thing to do, to buy all these items, Ruby.' He laughed, a lighter note entering his voice on hearing that she had acquired a silver cutlery set.

'I know,' she responded, warming to his laughter. 'I am well aware that you have everything in your household, and yet it has become a custom for parents to give presents to their daughter, from a fridge down to a toothbrush. What about Zarri Bano? She had a trousseau and she wasn't going anywhere.' Ruby stopped, her cheeks smarting with heat, regretting the words as soon as they were out. Once again she felt the tension at the other end of the line. Was she forever to suffer the pangs of guilt on behalf of Zarri Bano? 'It isn't fair!' she cried to herself.

'I have to go now, Ruby. My manager, Ali, has come in. *Khudah Hafiz*.' And Sikander abruptly rang off without telling her whether he was going to call the next day.

In his office, Sikander flicked through the accounts of the computer parts he had received from Singapore. His mind, however, was with Zarri Bano. She was due to arrive that afternoon at Karachi Airport. He hadn't seen her since the ceremony, nor did he harbour any desire to see her. He had had his fill of Zarri Bano. He could never forgive her for what she had done to him. He could not help wondering, however, what her reaction would be to the news of Ruby's forthcoming marriage. His lips twisted. 'This is my revenge, Zarri Bano!' he said bitterly, wishing he could be there when she found out that he was to become her brother-in-law . . .

Habib and Shahzada went to meet Zarri Bano with their chauffeur at the international airport in Karachi. They saw her coming through the customs in her long black *burqa*, accompanied by Sakina and two other women. The latter were dressed less severely than the two Holy Women.

'How was Ajmeir Sharif, my daughter?' Habib began as soon as they settled in their car. Sakina and the other two women had left with their respective families.

'It was great, Father. There were so many people to see. We actually spent our time in a house next to the *darbar*. The people we lived with were so hospitable. Every day, at that *darbar*, it was like a festival. There were recitations from the Holy Quran, lasting for hours, and offerings of food made in the afternoon and into the night. A lot of people came flocking to the holy

premises seeking advice, moral and religious guidance. I was on the floor for almost eighteen hours a day, only getting up to offer prayers. I was so busy, I just couldn't get away from there. Women clamoured to get near me. My limbs ache all over.'

'My poor daughter. You can relax now that you are at home. You can take walks around our village fields and get lots of fresh air. You've been on a long journey, and away from home for so many months. We have missed you!' Shahzada squeezed her daughter's arm in affection.

'Do you know, Mother, women came with different desires and hopes, seeking my audience. They had heard that I was a Holy Woman, and therefore they treated me with great reverence. I offered prayers for them all as well as for myself.

'I tell you, sometimes I cried with them in their need. That in turn made them cry more. I think they appreciated me empathising with their pain and their inner hopes. Many of the women came begging to me to pray to God to provide them with children. Others wanted me to offer prayers for their physical health. They desperately required medical help. I knew that what most of them probably needed was to see their doctors. But it was their belief in their faith, and in us as "go-betweens" between Allah and themselves that made them come to us. Doctors apparently gave them no incentives. Another woman or another man, could have taken advantage of their vulnerability, as I am sure they do and have done. It is so easy for all of this to go to one's head, to one's ego – but I was upset by it all.' She looked at her parents and tried hard to explain.

'At times I felt as if I was a fraud. For I had no cures or miracles for them, only prayers and my faith.

My reputation was built up to such an extent that they felt I merited special attention and worship. There were some women who kissed, not only my hands but also reached for my feet, Mother. Horrified by their action, I drew my feet away and wanted to shout out to them: "Look, I am a mere woman like you," but my lips remained sealed; I found I was reluctant to disillusion them and turn them away from their inner belief that my prayers could help them. I also had Hindu and Sikh women coming to see me for the same purpose, as well as the Muslim women.'

'You are not just a mere woman, my beloved daughter,' Habib replied sharply. 'You are a *Shahzadi Ibadat!* That is why they come to you. Not just to seek miracles but also knowledge and guidance. You are an educated and now quite a learned woman in religious matters. With time you'll become the most knowledgeable woman on religious matters in our community. Therefore you must not denigrate yourself or ever think of yourself as a fraud. What a word, my dear. You should have faith in your own ability. Never doubt yourself, Zarri Bano!' he told her proudly.

'Enough about me and Jajmeir Sharif. I still have so much to tell you about Egypt and Cairo, but later. How is Ruby and everybody else?' Zarri Bano asked innocently, missing the look in her parents' eyes, as they exchanged surreptitious glances in the car mirror.

'Ruby is fine and so is everybody else, my daughter. We missed you so much, Zarri Bano,' Shahzada replied, putting her arm around her daughter to clasp her in a semi-embrace.

'And now tell us about Cairo!' Thus Shahzada steered Zarri Bano away from the dangerous topic of Ruby.

Chapter 33

'ZARRI BANO IS due any minute now!' Ruby anxiously watched Fatima putting frantic finishing touches to the vase of flowers on the dining table. Her eyes fixed on the clock on the wall, she was feeling more and more like a traitor by the minute.

Just as Ruby had anticipated, Zarri Bano swept into the room in her flowing black *burqa*, and embraced her younger sister in a tight hug. She did not notice that Ruby had avoided any eye contact with her.

During their evening meal, after she had showered and refreshed herself, Zarri Bano asked innocently if anything of importance had happened while she was abroad.

'I feel that I have been away not just for one year but for a decade. What have you been doing in my absence, Ruby?' Zarri Bano turned innocently to her sister. Ruby dropped her gaze.

'We have got some good news for you, my dear,' Shahzada answered smoothly, feeling the scalding warmth of both Ruby's and Habib's eyes on her face.

'What has happened? Tell me, Mother,' Zarri Bano enquired pleasantly.

'We have set a date for Ruby's wedding.' Ruby and Habib now held their breath, waiting anxiously for Shahzada to continue.

'What a wonderful news! When and with whom? You never said anything to me on the phone.' Zarri Bano looked at them both with surprise.

'I will tell you all about it later, after you have

rested,' Ruby intervened before her mother or father could say anything – her heart going out to her sister, wanting to give her privacy.

'Is it somebody I know?' Zarri Bano asked softly, unaware of the charged atmosphere in the room.

'As Ruby said, she'll tell you later.' Licking her dry lips, Shahzada stopped her husband with a look. 'It is Ruby's privilege, Habib Sahib, to tell her sister. You must be feeling tired, my daughter, why don't you go to bed?'

'It is true that I am tired, Mother, but I am dying to know who my sister is going to marry. It must be Khawar, am I right? Chaudharani Kaniz must surely have succeeded by now. Well, you all kept it very quiet. You make me feel like an outsider now. What a secretive goose you are, Ruby!' Zarri Bano teased, laughing at the warm blush spreading over her sister's face. She stood up to leave the table. Habib and Shahzada exchanged a glance, both breathing more freely.

'Ruby, come up to my room and tell me all about it!' Zarri Bano beckoned to her sister before closing the door behind her.

Ruby sat frozen on her seat. The moment of reckoning had come. On legs that felt as if they were suddenly shackled to lead weights, she stood up, darting an appealing look at her mother to come to her aid. Shahzada, however, shook her head sadly at her daughter, deeming the matter deserved privacy between the two sisters.

'Don't worry, dear,' Shahzada urged gently, as Ruby looked at her before leaving the room.

In her bedroom, Zarri Bano glanced around with enormous pleasure. It was so good to be back. She looked

out of the window at the lawn and the rose beds in full bloom in the courtyard.

'It is Sikander!'

Zarri Bano didn't hear Ruby enter, but the three, softly spoken words sliced across the room, freezing her on the spot. A paralysis of some sort attacked her body, depriving her of all feeling and sensation; her eyes grew wide.

Ruby waited for Zarri Bano to face her. The seconds ticked away on the wall clock. Sitting awkwardly on the corner of Zarri Bano's bed, she wondered bleakly what to do.

'I wasn't the one who desired this match,' she pleaded, feeling as if she had just sunk a machete into her sister's back. 'Zarri Bano, it wasn't me! Please forgive me. I know how you must be feeling.' Hiding her face in her hands, she began to cry.

Her sister's weeping echoing around her, Zarri Bano forgot about herself and moved towards the huddled figure.

'Don't cry,' she whispered against her sister's hair, gathering her in her arms. 'There is nothing to forgive, my princess. I am so pleased for you.' And yet the quivering voice belied the words drawn out from the depths of her being.

'But he was your fiancé. I *do* feel guilty, Zarri Bano,' Ruby countered, raising her tearstained face up to her sister's.

'Yes he was.' Zarri Bano managed to keep her expression neutral. 'That was the past, my dearest sister. You have nothing to apologise for. Never feel guilty on my account. It was my *kismet*, my destiny. I gave up Sikander, remember, when I decided to become a Holy Woman. I forfeited all rights to him. It doesn't matter

to me or, more to the point, shouldn't matter to me who he marries: you or any other woman.'

'Oh my dearest sister, you are so generous. Thank you, Zarri Bano, for being so understanding.' Tears shone out of Ruby's eyes.

It was at that very moment that Shahzada entered the room and saw her two daughters locked in an embrace. Zarri Bano was taller than Ruby, and saw her mother first over her sister's shoulders.

Shahzada immediately glimpsed the naked pain in Zarri Bano's eyes; she had hidden it from her sister behind her words of assurance, but she was unable to conceal it from her mother.

How did one deal with a pain of this kind? Shahzada wondered wretchedly, her heart leaping out in sympathy to her eldest daughter. There were no solutions to this situation. The only avenue open was total negation of oneself and one's longings.

'Ruby, you have told your sister?' Shahzada asked in a dull voice.

'Yes, Mother, she has.' Zarri Bano let her sister out of her embrace. Ruby decided that it was an appropriate time to retire for the night and thankfully left.

Alone, mother and daughter stared across the room at each other. Zarri Bano moved to stand near the window. Lifting the net curtains she looked down at the courtyard and the lawns below, through a blurred vision. Her beautiful home had suddenly become a fortress of pain. Silence stretched between the two women.

'I am sorry, Zarri Bano.' Shahzada went to stand next to her daughter. 'It wasn't us – you must believe me. It was Bilkis's suggestion. I was against it, Zarri Bano. Before we knew what had happened, the

engagement took place.' She prayed that her daughter understood.

'Mother, you don't have to explain to me how it happened. Nor do you have to apologise.'

'Zarri Bano, why are you holding yourself back? You don't have to pretend to me, or safeguard my feelings. Why don't you just say what you feel? Remember, I am not Ruby, I am your mother. I know it was both insensitive and wrong of us to allow the engagement to go ahead. I told your father so.'

'Mother, please leave me alone. What is done is done. I can never marry, so what does it matter to me who Sikander marries? He was bound to marry someone one day. I am a *Shahzadi Ibadat*, I am not supposed to care.' But she was unable to hide the despair in her eyes.

'You are not only a Holy Woman. You are a woman first, with feelings.' Shahzada reached out and shook her arm.

'Then as a woman tell me how I can fight this, Mother!' Zarri Bano cried in anguish. 'Show me how I can come to terms with this, the greatest emotional hurdle in my life – to triumph over my female feelings. It is a God-sent task, Mother, but I *will* triumph. I tell you – I will! But first tell me how. Show me how I can stop this knife spearing through me and ripping me apart inside.'

The anguish in her daughter's voice brought tears springing to Shahzada's eyes.

Holding her arm tightly against her chest, Zarri Bano doubled over and leaned down on the arm-chair, hiding her ravaged face from her mother in shame.

'Hush, my darling. Cry, if that's what you want to

do. You can trust me with your feelings, my daughter.'
Shahzada's own voice broke with tears.

'Cry, Mother?' Zarri Bano accused, with tears of
agony glimmering like green mysterious gems in her
eyes. 'Please, *Allah pak*, help me!' she beseeched.

She let herself be drawn into her mother's arms,
leaning on her shoulders. 'He said . . . He said . . .'
Her voice broke, tripping and choking over the
words. 'He said that I will remember him till the
day I die, Mother. Now I'll never get away from him.
How I fooled myself! I thought that I had killed
and buried the old Zarri Bano behind the folds of this
burqa, this black shroud – but she lives, Mother. She
lives! Oh, *Allah pak* have mercy! I never knew my
parents could be so cruel. Tell me, Mother, how I can
kill this woman inside me, still passionately in love
with this man.'

Moving out of Shahzada's arms, Zarri Bano tried
desperately to retrieve the tatters of her self-control.
She stood up tall, angrily brushing away the tears from
her cheeks.

'I should like to rest now. Forgive me, Mother, for
this outburst of a weak woman. I am so ashamed. You
never thought to see the day when your proud Zarri
Bano wept for a man. I never knew love could be so
painful. This is Allah's way of punishing me for turning
away all those poor suitors. I should be congratulating
you, Mother. I am so sorry.' Her body wracked once
more, Zarri Bano turned her face away and closed her
eyes.

Helpless, Shahzada stared at her daughter's back for
a long time. Afraid to touch. Afraid to say anything
that might break Zarri Bano's fragile control and push
her over the precipice of mental breakdown.

At the end she quietly left the room – her eyes brimming with tears. She went straight down to the kitchen, where Fatima was scrubbing a large silver pot at the sink.

'She knows, Fatima. She said, "I never knew my parents could be so cruel",' Shahzada murmured quietly behind her housekeeper's back.

Fatima's body went still. Her soap-sudded hand remained poised in mid-air. 'How did she react?' she half whispered, without turning.

'As can be expected – she is totally devastated. It is a wicked thing we have done, Fatima. I never thought to see the day when my daughter would lose complete control of herself. She has always been so strong. But she went to pieces, Fatima. Allah help us and my daughter. She hasn't yet got over him.'

'It is both unkind and unethical for her sister to marry the man that Zarri Bano loved and wanted to marry,' Fatima said forthrightly. 'It is going to be a very painful experience for her, Shahzada Jee.'

'Please, Fatima, don't say any more. As she says, we must remember that she is a Holy Woman. She cannot marry anybody, so must learn to trample on those feelings.'

'Even if it kills her emotionally in the process?' Fatima questioned.

'Hush, Fatima! That we already did, the day we made her into a Holy Woman. Don't say any more. If your master hears you . . .'

'So what if he does? What more can he do than he's done already?'

Fatima returned to scouring the pot, with a long hard sweep, venting both her grief and rage on it. The pot was thus assured of an extra layer of shine.

Tears swam in her eyes, which Shahzada would have seen, if she hadn't left the kitchen. Fatima sighed.

'Habib and Kaniz are two of the same kind. They both know how to destroy their children's happiness.' Fatima's mouth curled bitterly. Feeling hot she shrugged the heavy Kashmiri shawl angrily off her shoulders and let it fall to the floor in a heap.

Chapter 34

HER ROOM SOAKED in darkness, Zarri Bano sat on an armchair, her hands folded in front of her on her lap. Eyes squeezed shut, she rocked herself to and fro, desperate to block out images that threatened to topple the wall of her inner world, the wall she had constructed after the veiling ceremony.

The past, however, in all its colour and radiant glory came thundering back with a vengeance, as if the last year of her life had never taken place. Sikander and his face flitted everywhere in her mind. She capitulated, letting the scenes roll lovingly before her closed eyes, ending with the one of her fingertips tracing the shape of his mouth. As her body grew warm with longing, Zarri Bano recoiled, shaking her head in a desperate attempt to dislodge the thoughts and images that plagued and ensnared her.

'I hate you, Sikander!' she cried aloud. Then:

'Oh *Allah pak*, please help me. This is the worst test You could have devised. You are testing my willpower and purity of mind and heart. In this test I can never hope to win! How can I be pure of mind when the thought of Sikander with my sister slices through me

like a knife? I bleed from the shattering pain. Also I hate and despise myself for what I have been reduced to. For my female weaknesses.'

An hour later, still in her *burqa*, she crept into bed. How she had longed for this bed, after the uncomfortable nights she had spent in Ajmeir Sharif. Tossing and turning she smothered her face in the pillow, attempting to block everything from her mind.

She had known that Sikander would marry one day. Thus she had been mentally prepared for that eventuality. So why was she feeling as if the last breath was being snuffed out of her body? The answer came in an agonising moan.

'It is because she is my sister. I will have to witness her life, and imagine what it might have been if *I* had married him.' Was it sheer envy she felt? '*Yes!*' the inner voice cried out, loud and clear. She didn't want her sister to marry him. Any other man, yes, but not Sikander! It was the cruellest of all blows.

'He will share his life and raise a family with my sister.' The knife twisted inside her again as she thought of the marital intimacies they would enjoy. Had he swapped one sister, one body, for another? 'Sikander, is this the revenge you promised? How could you do this to me?' she wept, sinking her face once more in the damp hollow of her pillow.

Some time later she sat bolt upright in her bed. She looked at the clock on the wall: it was nearly 2 a.m. How could her family sleep peacefully when they had thrown a thunderbolt like this at her and snatched her very sanity from her?

'*Allah pak*, help me!' she beseeched again through dry, quivering lips.

She stood up resolutely to say her late-night prayers.

She believed in her Allah pak and in Him she would seek peace and solace. She knew she would get it.

As she stood on the prayer mat, she had to concentrate hard, making sure that she had recited the correct verses and number of cycles in prayers. In her concentration she forgot all about Ruby and Sikander. When it came to offering her personal prayers, her *du'ah*, Zarri Bano raised her hands high in front of her and appealed with all her heart.

'*Allah pak*, please heed the prayers of a weak woman, a sinner. Guide me back onto Your path of peace and religious devotion. Tear out this ugly human emotion that is renting me apart and torturing my soul. Douse this longing, this fire that is engulfing my body. I am supposed to be a pure woman. How can I be that, while I harbour such base feelings? Enfold me in Your holy mantle of female modesty. Rid my mind and heart of this man who haunts me at this moment. Show me Your path; for that is the path I seek.

'I thought I was on that path, the road of peace and female innocence. I thought I had happily parted company from the old Zarri Bano. Today I have not only lost my identity, but also my way. I have been thrown asunder. I do not know which way to turn – where my destination lies. I don't want to neglect my *Shahzadi Ibadat* duties and role. Help me to keep these ugly thoughts and feelings at bay, to purify myself and exorcise all traces of my past life, so that I can begin again, in a new state of utter purity. Rinse out of my heart the passionate feelings I still harbour for Sikander! Give me strength so that I can rapturously rejoice in my sister's marriage. Instil in me a sense of indifference, so that when I look at him, I will feel nothing for myself, or for him but only joy for my sister. Please help me to reach

this state of mind! Otherwise I am a lost soul. I will not be able to bear this torment or face my sister.'

Depleted of energy and ending her fervent prayers, Zarri Bano stepped off the prayer-mat and sat in her bed. Leafing through the pages she read two chapters from the Holy Quran and a few pages from the Hadith. Rolling her rosary beads five times mechanically between her fingers gave her a distinct purpose, and took her away from the havoc of her inner world.

Finally at peace with herself, Zarri Bano fell asleep and woke up at about eleven o'clock in the morning, thus missing her early morning prayers. As she washed and dressed, she mused over her present state of mind, for now she felt indeed calm and peaceful.

When she beheld her sister downstairs, in the lounge, the smile Zarri Bano gave to Ruby was warm and genuine. Zarri Bano glowed inside, in the knowledge that now she could meet her sister and share her joy with no reserve on her part. Faced with her sister's smile, Ruby basked in the warmth of it and let the cobwebs of worry blow away. She hadn't slept either, dreading this meeting with her this morning.

It was only Shahzada who saw the haunted look in her elder daughter's eyes. Apart from that, there was no sign to show that Zarri Bano had clawed her way up a mountain in the night and had claimed victory, triumphing over herself, and her longings.

To prove this to herself, Zarri Bano immersed herself in her religious devotions as never before. At the same time, she also took a keen interest in the preparations for her sister's wedding.

As yet Zarri Bano had not come across Sikander. He didn't visit. On the day he was expected, Zarri Bano

took herself off on a religious errand, leading a prayer meeting in a nearby *darbar*.

'One day I will have to meet him, but not now, not yet.' Her female intuition warned her clearly that she was still too emotionally bruised to come face to face with him so soon.

In fact she didn't have to face Sikander until the day of the *mehndi*, the party organised for Ruby, three days before the wedding day. Meant for the women and young girls, the party included singing and dancing to popular music, as well as the traditional wedding folk songs to the music of a *dholki*, a small drum.

The girls' cousin Gulshan had arrived a week earlier to help with the preparations and to join in everything. On the morning of the party, Gulshan had approached Zarri Bano with a twinkle in her eye and made a special request. 'My dear, I will not let you appear in a *burqa* at the party. There will only be women and girls there.'

'I must wear the *burqa*, Gulshan,' Zarri Bano blurted out.

'Please forget your *holy* self for just one night. I want you to dance at your sister's party.' The trace of sarcasm was not lost on Zarri Bano.

A hushed silence followed as a stunned Zarri Bano took in what her cousin had suggested.

'Me, dance! Now that is utterly out of the question, Gulshan. When have you seen a Holy Woman dancing?'

'I don't know any Holy Women, apart from you. You are also my cousin and a woman like me. I will make you dance – just see if I don't,' Gulshan teased, laughing up into Zarri Bano's scandalised face. 'But first come upstairs to Ruby's room. I have a surprise for you. Ruby and I have sorted out an outfit for you. It is red

and white, we definitely do not want you to wear black, although it has become your favourite colour. Only bright colours will do for your sister's wedding.'

'I cannot go through with it. You must understand, Gulshan!' Genuinely upset, Zarri Bano tried to free her hands from her cousin's grasp, as she led her up the stairs.

'Look, Zarri Bano, today we want a glimpse of the old glamorous you – all right? How can it be a crime for you to dress up or to dance in front of us women? Why do you behave like this? You don't have to deny yourself the pleasure of dancing or dressing up. Both gave you a great deal of pleasure once, as I recall.'

And that was that. Zarri Bano couldn't get out of it. At about six o' clock, she was ushered into Ruby's room, and was shown the outfit. In the end, Gulshan helped Zarri Bano to get dressed in her own room. There was no tall mirror in Zarri Bano's room any more, therefore she had no idea what she looked like in the flowing *shahrarah* outfit, with a long red chiffon skirt and white matching tunic, with sequins embroidered on to it. Gulshan had skilfully made up her face, and her hair, which had now grown abundantly to her shoulders, was allowed to swing around her face in bouncy curls. A necklace complemented the outfit.

Gulshan stared at her cousin in satisfaction. How petty it seemed now that she had once envied Zarri Bano. She couldn't wait to show Zarri Bano off, and to announce her entrance theatrically, knowing that everyone would be amazed and all heads would be turned. She thus went ahead of Zarri Bano into the large hall where music was being played and the clapping of hands could be heard, punctuating the movements of one of the women dancers.

After a few minutes, Zarri Bano stepped out of her room, feeling as if another woman had taken over her body. These clothes felt so strange and cumbersome. The ornaments clawed at her skin. The urge to go back and wipe her face clean was very strong. The make-up made her feel as if she was wearing a heavy mask. The weird sensation of having her hair swing openly and wantonly around her face made her long to sweep it all back and hide every single strand under her *burqa* hood. Instead, she carried her *burqa* over her arm.

About to descend and holding up her skirt awkwardly from the floor with one hand, Zarri Bano heard footsteps in the hall below. She glanced down and then stood transfixed on the top step of the long curving staircase.

Standing at the foot of the stairs, Sikander gazed up at her. He smiled, mistaking her for Ruby. Then his eyes narrowed as they focused on the black garment on her arm, and he gasped. It was Zarri Bano!

For a split second, the world stood still for Sikander. His heart pounding with a dull beat, the smile slowly ebbed from his face. Seeing the beautiful picture she made standing at the top of the stairs, the ache he had managed to suppress in the last year rose in him with a gigantic leap. A sob of longing caught in his throat.

Zarri Bano continued to stare down at him, caught up in a spell. The last year of her life of religious devotion peeled away from her mind. Only the present mattered. Oh, how powerful was this spell! The world stood still.

Then a sound from a nearby room drew Zarri Bano painfully back to reality. Gave a great ragged sigh then, sweeping round, she disappeared from sight.

Sikander stood rooted to the spot. 'We haven't

exchanged a single word,' he mourned. This was the first time he had seen her since the day of her veiling ceremony.

He was still standing in the large hall, but away from the stairs, when he heard her come down. He looked up expectantly, ready to greet her.

She was dressed in her black 'holy' *burqa* again. The contrast to her earlier appearance could not have been more poignant. Holding her head high and looking ahead, she swept past him. The only words of greeting in reply to his were, '*Assalam-Alaikum*, Brother Sikander.'

The words sent a chill through him. The spell was broken: Zarri Bano was back in her religious shell. His attractive mouth curved in a bitter line. He was certainly going to be her brother.

For a moment, Sikander nearly gave way to despair. He was betrothed to Ruby, a loyal, loving girl . . . but still in love with her sister, his true betrothed. And he didn't know what to do about any of it.

Chapter 35

'ZARRI BANO, WHY are you still wearing the *burqa*?' screeched Gulshan, catching sight of her cousin in her black veil.

'I have to wear it. A man could walk in here, at any time,' Zarri Bano offered defensively as she came to stand next to her.

'But there aren't any strangers here, and apart from our family members there is, of course, only the groom himself. He will soon be your brother-in-law, therefore

he cannot be a stranger for long. Here, let me take it off!' Swiftly Gulshan pulled the *burqa* off.

Zarri Bano stood awkwardly in the middle of a circle of seated women, noting both their in-drawn breaths and amazed stares. It was as if she was in a freak show.

'Gulshan, I will deal with you later,' Zarri Bano hissed as she quickly sat down. 'I feel terrible! What will people think of me? Do you think that they will ever respect me again? I am dressed in such a vulgar fashion – almost like a lady of the night!'

'Don't be silly,' her cousin scoffed. 'You are dressed in the height of fashion and you know it. Just as you also know that at this moment and in this room, you are the most attractive woman here.'

Colour ebbed from Zarri Bano's cheeks. 'What is the purpose of all this?' she asked simply.

'The purpose? To enjoy life, of course. To celebrate beauty! To take pleasure in this moment in time – which happens to be your sister's *mehndi*. You won't have this opportunity again, Zarri Bano.'

'Gulshan, it is true what you say, but please remember, I am a Holy Woman.'

'So you think your sister's party is frivolous?' Gulshan accused. 'Come on, forget your holy self for once. Give us back the old Zarri Bano just for one evening. Please come and join us in the fun to celebrate our Ruby's wedding. Come!' Grabbing hold of Zarri Bano's hand, Gulshan dragged her into the empty space left for dancing in the middle of the circle. Flushed with embarrassment, Zarri Bano tried to draw her hand away from her cousin.

'Please, Gulshan,' she appealed, panicking. 'Don't do this to me – this is most unseemly.'

'Right, girls, Zarri Bano and I are going to dance to

pakeeza's song "Cheltah cheltah". Please start the music, and everyone can join in by clapping!'

In high spirits the women started to clap. Gulshan began to sway to the music, moving her supple body in elegant movements, her chiffon skirt billowing out around her. Zarri Bano looked at the crowd of women sitting on the floor. She caught her sister's eye. Ruby was sitting on the raised platform, waiting to have her hands painted with henna patterns. 'Please,' Ruby's eyes begged.

Zarri Bano surrendered, entering the dancing arena. Slowly her arms, hands and legs began to sway in graceful fluid movements around the circle. The *Shahzadi Ibadat* was forgotten as her body remembered how to weave magic in movement and rhythm. The rhythmic clapping spurred her on. She responded to the tune, smiling and dimpling down at the women. Rising and dipping with ever more elegant movements of her body, finally reaching a crescendo to the sad music.

At last the song ended and her body swirled to stop. Her eyes slowly focused on the faces of the women, watching enthralled. Then they stumbled upon one face. She froze. It was Sikander, sitting hidden in the shadows at the far end of the hall.

Zarri Bano felt faint as the realisation hit her that he had been there all the time. She dropped heavily down on the cushioned seat next to Gulshan. Twice in one day he had seen her without her *burqa*, this time in an even more compromising situation – dancing in open abandonment. It was his wedding and she had performed like a *kanjari*, a dancing girl in front of him. Colour flooded her cheeks in shame – no man had seen her like this.

With trembling hands she dragged the *burqa* back

over her body, fixing the hood neatly over her hair. Even if the women begged her on their knees, she would not get up and make a fool of herself again. Remembering the exact, sensuous movements of her dance, her body went cold again in embarrassment. She hadn't worn any *dupatta* nor a shawl to cover her front.

Once in control of herself, Zarri Bano ventured to glance around at the assembled group and thought wryly: I suppose, at least, I have made Ruby and Gulshan and all these women happy. Renowned for her dancing skills, at *mehndi* parties she was often dragged to the dance floor and normally not allowed off it, until she had danced to at least five popular songs.

For the remainder of the ceremony she let Gulshan take the lead in the celebrations. Later in the evening, she ventured to look in the corner where Sikander had been sitting. The space was empty. Breathing more freely, she promised herself that she was going to avoid him as much as possible. There would be times, of course, when she would have to meet him and talk to him, but never would she willingly seek his company. She had already made plans to immerse herself thoroughly in her new role, in an effort to distance herself from her past life and in particular from him, the serpent gnawing away at the delicate petals of her rose garden of religious devotion.

On the day of the wedding, Zarri Bano, like her parents, was kept busy and thus had little time to dwell on Sikander. The guests had all duly arrived and had to be seen to. All the wedding arrangements had been carried out. The hall was decorated for the reception and the ceremony. The morning passed in a hectic

whirl of different activities. Ruby was locked away with
Gulshan and the beautician.

Zarri Bano helped her mother with the last-minute
errands. At about eleven o'clock she decided to check
up on her sister to see how her bridal preparations were
progressing. Beholding Ruby's breathtaking appear-
ance, a lump caught in her throat. 'Oh my dear, you
look wonderful!'

At precisely twelve-thirty, the groom and his party
arrived for the ceremony from Karachi. Most of Zarri
Bano's clan were assembled in the front courtyard to
receive and welcome them. Young girls holding small
china bowls were waiting to shower rose petals over the
heads of the groom and his party.

Alone, Zarri Bano watched from her bedroom
window – the line of cars, the accompanying band
of musicians, on foot, gaily playing wedding tunes.
Heading the procession was the groom on a white
horse, leading the way, following the centuries-old
custom.

Zarri Bano hardly recognised Sikander dressed as a
groom, with a traditional bead-studded *khullah* on his
head and a long white jacket with a matching *shalwar*.
Zarri Bano's eyes rested on his face. The horse cantered
to a stop outside the gate.

'*Kismet*, you are so cruel.' Zarri Bano turned from the
window, wondering how many other women and men
had experienced this nightmare scenario. 'How do they
came to terms with it?' she murmured.

Then: 'I am a *Shahzadi Ibadat!*' she bitterly reminded
herself. 'A woman who has denounced marriage and a
normal life. I am the one who turned him away.' Yet
she was paying for it now. His words mocked her: '*You
will die for me on my wedding day.*'

She had prayed to Allah and had kept herself busy. Today, however, the mere sight of him had shown her that beneath it all she was still a vulnerable human being – just another victim of life's pains and triumphs.

'I *am* dying for you, Sikander. You've had your revenge.' Zarri Bano brushed the tears angrily from her cheeks. Through gritted teeth she promised herself, 'Zarri Bano will never cry for a man again! I am going to lock away, bury forever, these vulnerable parts of me. I will show myself and the world that I am indeed the pure one, the holy one! To do this I have to first unearth Sikander from the essence of my being.'

She fumbled open one of the drawers of her dressing table and drew out three seashells hidden in a small trinket box. Nestled against the palm of her hand, Zarri Bano looked at them for a long time. Lifting the net curtains, she threw the shells through the open window, far over the wall of her home. Her last link with Sikander was gone.

During the wedding ceremony, Zarri Bano remained in the background. The 'milk greeting' ceremony, with the sisters traditionally offering a glass of milk to the groom, in exchange for gifts of money, Zarri Bano had delegated to Gulshan. She couldn't have stood in front of him. As she watched her sister sitting next to Sikander on the stage after the wedding ceremony and laughing up into his face, Zarri Bano knew that the ties of the past would be truly severed that night.

Hungrily, she watched Sikander's eyes. 'They once glowed into mine too!' she grieved. He couldn't see her, but she feasted her eyes on him for the last time.

Unable to bear any more, Zarri Bano left the hall and walked out into the rear courtyard. Sitting on a chair on

the patio she stared dejectedly at the rose bed. Hearing a sound behind her, she hastened to assume the mask-like expression on her face.

Fatima stood behind her. 'I too found it hot in the hall, my dear,' she volunteered.

'Yes, Fatima.' Zarri Bano stood up to leave.

'Take a rest, my dear. You've been very busy.' Fatima gently pulled Zarri Bano into the chair, a deep silence of understanding hovering between them. 'He is not worth it,' the woman said sadly.

Zarri Bano's eyes widened. 'I don't know what you mean, Fatima. If you are referring to Sikander, then you have no need to worry on my account – but he is definitely worth my sister marrying. I am so happy for her. Remember I am a Holy Woman. How can you harbour such a thought? Really . . .' Zarri Bano's nervous laugh made her feel light inside. 'Come, we need to show Ruby's trousseau to all the women. Gulshan has been doing everything. You and I will take on this task between us.'

Years later, Zarri Bano realised that it was at that moment, in the garden, that the hurdle she had craved so badly to jump had been managed, at the end, thanks to Fatima's sympathetic words. To prove to herself that nothing mattered to her any more, Zarri Bano had even volunteered to accompany Ruby to Sikander's home.

'I am a strong-willed person and will prove to myself and to the world that I am indeed a Holy Woman. I hope Sikander finds happiness with my sister. There will be no more suitors in my life ever again!' She offered this personal prayer, as she knelt on her prayer-mat on the night of her sister's wedding day.

Chapter 36

FATIMA HIRED THE *tanga*, the local horse and carriage, to take her from Chiragpur to the house where Khawar was living in the neighbouring village. Tipping the driver generously in advance, she told him to wait outside for her, for there were no taxis around in the village. Even the *tangas* were a scarce commodity at times.

Built on the outskirts of the village, Khawar's large homestead stood alone, amidst green fields. He had inherited two such homes when his father died. He kept two male servants to look after the house and Rani, an old woman helper, to cook and wash for him on a daily basis. It was Rani who let Fatima in, ushering her into the drawing room, telling her to wait for Khawar's return.

'No more dreams,' Fatima bitterly scolded herself. 'It is all over.'

She had learnt her lesson, well and truly. Her daughter's happiness and welfare meant more to her than her own foolish dream of seeing Firdaus as the Headmistress of the school and the future *chaudharani* of the village. The latter post being the one she herself had forfeited some thirty years previously when she had decided to marry Fiaz instead of Sarwar.

Scolding oneself didn't, however, make it easy to part with one's dreams. For a long time, Fatima's heart had indeed been set on Khawar, as her eldest son-in-law.

She could still recall the look in Kaniz's eye when

one woman guest had loudly and tactlessly whispered to the new bride: 'There is Fatima, the woman that Sarwar wanted to marry, but she turned him down.'

Blushing, Fatima had quickly glanced up and found Kaniz's piercing gaze on her face. Feeling for the new bride, Fatima's heart had gone out to her. Later she had admonished that woman with the loud mouth.

Kaniz, however, had neither forgotten nor forgiven Fatima for simply being 'the other woman'. Fatima, in turn, had to revise her own early opinion of Kaniz, for the new *chaudharani* soon made it abundantly clear, by various means, that Fatima wasn't at all welcome in her house. Later, she had used her servant, Neesa, to tell her bluntly that she had no right to come there. It was then that the animosity had begun, only to increase over the months and years to follow.

When Fiaz had his accident and Fatima joined the staff in Siraj Khan's household, Kaniz had her sweet revenge.

Welcoming every opportunity that came her way, she had publicly and indiscriminately sneered at the 'washerwoman' Sarwar had originally wanted to marry. Fatima, for her part, had neither the time nor the patience for Kaniz or her petty taunts. She was faced with the task of keeping her family going and caring for her disabled husband. She had found a confidante and a friend in Chaudharani Shahzada instead.

Fatima was still lost in her own and Kaniz's entwined past, when she heard Khawar's footsteps outside on the veranda. She glanced up, marvelling at the young man's even set of white teeth and the ever ready smile on his face.

She didn't return the smile.

'*Assalam-Alaikum*, Auntie Fatima. What a lovely

surprise!' Flicking the dust from his boots with a handkerchief, he came forward into the room.

Fatima stood up. Her gaze dwelt on his tall, well-built frame.

'Come and sit down, Auntie Fatima, and tell me all your news. How is everyone?'

'Everyone is fine, Khawar. What about yourself? You seem to have settled down here permanently, my son.'

'Yes, I am quite happy here, Auntie,' he offered politely, uneasy at discussing the matter of his separation from his mother.

'It is not right that you should be here,' Fatima quietly commented.

'Why, Auntie?'

'Well, your poor mother is on her own in the village. You are her only child, Khawar my son, and you should be staying with her.'

'How is Firdaus?'

'She is fine, but she is leaving the village for good, my son.'

'*What?*' he asked sharply, standing up.

'Yes, my son. She wishes to leave us and the village. She has been offered a new post as the Vice Principal of a girls' college in the town. I cannot persuade her to stay on in the village. It is all over, my boy.'

'What do you mean, Auntie?'

'I mean that she wants nothing to do with either you, your mother or your home. She is adamant that you are the last person she wants to marry.' Fatima almost immediately regretted her words. It was the second time that a man had been jilted in his family.

'I am so sorry, Khawar,' she said, more kindly. 'I have tried my very best, you know that. But things are beyond my control.'

'It is my mother, isn't it?' Khawar's harsh voice matched the steel glint in his eyes.

'Your mother hasn't helped, I am afraid. Her recent visit to Firdaus's school has definitely made matters worse. She probably has reasons to behave as she does. But all I want to say to you, Khawar, is to return home to your mother. I do not want you to be seen to be estranged from her on our account.'

'I don't want to go home!'

'You must, my dear. Your mother loves you dearly. I have come to request that you return home and put Firdaus and us aside from your mind and heart.'

'It is not as easy as you suggest, Auntie. And why should I have to, just because you and my mother say so. Can I see Firdaus?'

'I wouldn't recommend it, my son, not at the moment. She is in a very volatile mood. Your mother and I haven't helped matters. Her pride is sorely wounded on both counts.'

'What about the future, Auntie? I'll not let her go without fighting for her.'

'That is up to you, my son – but I personally wouldn't recommend it to you, as much as I would want you to. You know yourself, Khawar dear, how I have always wanted you my eldest son-in-law. But it looks as if Firdaus is destined for another home. If you have any respect for me, I hope to see you back in your family home in Chiragpur with your mother within the next few days.'

Fatima left, declining both lunch and refreshments. Her *tanga* thankfully was waiting for her, the driver still munching on his *paan*. Fatima had achieved her task – to talk plainly to Khawar.

Chapter 37

IT WAS A BEAUTIFUL Saturday morning with the sun high up in the sky over Chiragpur. The village sparrows were singing in the trees. Yet Fatima didn't relish the forthcoming afternoon and the unpleasant task that loomed ahead of her. She let the morning pass on her rooftop.

Finally, after two o'clock Fatima forced herself to leave her home. Resignation was stamped in each step she placed on the cobbled lanes, leading her inevitably to Kaniz's home.

'So many years wasted,' she mourned. If she had only known! Personal selfishness was a hard thing to contend with. For so long she had desired the match between her eldest daughter and Khawar and had actually begun to believe in it as a foregone conclusion. And now Firdaus had already left for the town to start her new job.

Today Fatima intended putting an end to all those years of dreaming, and allow Kaniz to triumph and crown herself as the winner. As for herself, the inevitable loser, it was a day for her head to be lowered in humiliation and for Kaniz's barbed taunts to find their true mark. 'Even if that woman's lips spill venom,' Fatima reminded herself firmly, 'today I will willingly gulp it all down with dignity and bow out of Chaudharani Kaniz's life, with honour, and for good.'

Outside Kaniz's gate, Fatima's chapped finger hovered above the doorbell – not quite ready to touch it. When eventually she pressed the small round

button, her heart started to hammer away in her chest, startling and disconcerting her. Neesa opened the gates and led Fatima into the central courtyard with its alabaster pillars, to the canopied sofa on the veranda.

Bemused, Fatima stared around at the variety of pot plants lining the veranda, creating an attractive arena for the courtyard. It was indeed a beautiful place. Fatima recalled the occasion when top architects had been enlisted from Karachi by Sarwar's father to design it. Fatima had secretly envisaged her daughter Firdaus roaming merrily around the scores of rooms on the two floors or sunning herself on the trellis-lined balconies on the rooftop. Fatima shook her head sorrowfully. It was time to part with her dream.

Kaniz was enjoying her afternoon siesta in her large air-conditioned bedroom. When Neesa gently touched her on the arm, she was not at all pleased to be woken from a pleasant dream. Her brain, somewhat befuddled by sleep, didn't register straight away Neesa's words that 'Fatima Jee' was here to see her. She sat up on her *palang*, and started to straighten her *chador* around her shoulders.

On spotting her 'enemy' enter the room, Kaniz's almond-shaped eyes first screwed up into tiny slits and then flapped wide open, her body utterly still. Her mind went completely blank. Why is this hated woman here in my bedroom? she thought perplexed.

Fatima remained poised in the doorway, her face straight and her eyes steadily fixed on Kaniz's face.

'*Assalam-Alaikum!*' Her cool confident voice echoed strangely in the semi-shaded quiet room, startling its occupant.

'*Wa Laikum-Salam!*' Kaniz replied stiffly, still unable

to look at Fatima. Social and village etiquette demanded that she treat Fatima as a guest. The nearest she could stoop to, however, was to nod at Fatima, and gesture towards the chair for her to sit on. The snub was not lost on Fatima; it was a gesture akin to the one Kaniz threw at Neesa, her servant. Apparently Fatima was no different.

Her heartbeat quickening, Fatima took rapid stock of herself and the situation. She hadn't come to pick a quarrel with the *chaudharani* but to act in a restrained and mature manner. She thus grandly and magnanimously decided to ignore Kaniz's petty insults.

Instead, she merely padded two steps forward on the cool marble mosaic floor, declining to sit on the chair. Signalling thus to Kaniz that she wasn't here 'to do her bidding'.

'What has brought you to our home, Fatima Sahiba?' The heavily laden ironic use of 'Sahiba' wasn't lost on Fatima.

'I thought it imperative that you and I had a chat.' Fatima said with quiet dignity.

'Concerning what?' Kaniz hated her shrill voice and for being on the verge of losing her poise so quickly and particularly in front of the enemy.

'Our children and our past, Kaniz Sahiba,' Fatima replied quietly.

Kaniz turned away. Picking up her mirrored fan, she began to fan the long column of her neck, pulling her muslin *chador* off her head and shoulders. Swivelling her head around, she darted a fierce gaze at Fatima.

'I didn't know that we had anything in common. You are very presumptuous,' she commented disdainfully, her cheeks now very warm.

'I disagree, but if you insist, then I will agree that we

have nothing in common. However, I have not come here for your insults or to bandy words with you, Kaniz.'

'Then what *have* you come for?' Kaniz retorted, her fair cheeks throbbing with an ominous shade of red.

'I have come to inform you that my daughter has left the village. She has got a post as a Vice Principal in a college . . .'

'So you have come to boast, have you?' Kaniz sneered.

'No, I haven't!' Fatima snapped in return. 'I have come to tell you that my daughter is adamant that Khawar is the last person she wants to marry. She is saying goodbye to the village for good. I will not pretend to you: I will admit that I had entertained hopes for her and Khawar. Luckily I have now come to my senses. Is there any point, I ask myself, in placing one's face in the mud over and over again, just to have it smeared with filth. My daughter deserves better. You and your son are not worth wiping her shoes on. I was foolish, oh so foolish, for wanting my Firdaus to marry into your household.' She sighed heavily.

'Thank goodness, that at last I have woken up, Kaniz. I have decided that I'll do whatever my Firdaus wants. Through your stubbornness and selfishness you have lost your son. I will not lose my daughter the same way. I have spent years of my life working to give my daughters a good education and a standard of life. I will not let all that go to waste.' She looked sternly at the other woman.

'I didn't have any money to look after my son, unlike you. I could have, of course, if I had married Sarwar – but you know that, don't you? You have never thanked me, have you? You are a *chaudharani*, but only because I

declined to marry Sarwar. You are a *malika*, the queen of this village, who treats everyone like dirt, but don't forget I know who you are and from whence you have sprung. You have forgotten your humble roots – your shabby home with *charpoys* piled on top of each other, and your brothers and sisters falling over each other because of lack of space. You are an ungrateful and thankless woman. A woman who doesn't know how to digest riches. You have to be born to them to do that.'

By now Kaniz had bolted up from her *palang*.

'How dare you come here to insult me in my own home!' Her mouth opened and closed – aghast.

'I am not insulting you,' Fatima continued calmly, keeping her eyes steady on Kaniz's face. 'Just giving you a wholesome dose of what you always mete out to others. Today, I will wipe the slate clean between us, once and for all. There will be no going back, for either you or me, Kaniz. It is true, as you delight in telling the whole village, that my hands are "greased", but tell me, who was on a par with Sarwar in the first place? Me or you? You know that my family are a land-owning family, and it was my pride that wouldn't let them help me. I wanted to support my family myself. My weakness, unlike yours, Kaniz, is pride in my own achievements and work. I didn't want to extend a begging hand to anyone.

'Have you known, or can you imagine, what it is like to work, to support one's family? You have no idea, have you? You, who are used to barking at your servants. I married my husband, not for his wealth, but for love. You married yours for wealth. That is the difference between us.' Her voice grew stronger.

'It is true, in your book of social etiquette, that I have done demeaning work. I have brushed, washed and

carried things for other people. But it is good honest work. It is very different from your lazy lifestyle, where you are totally dependent on other people. I have made my daughters self-sufficient too. All this I have achieved from my own efforts. Can you tell me what *you* have achieved? Apart from giving birth to one son?'

'Enough!' Kaniz shouted, totally scandalised. 'I will not listen to any more of your insults. You mad, vindictive woman – get out. Neesa!' Her eyes were now practically rolling in their sockets.

Unperturbed, Fatima merely smiled, showing a row of even white teeth. 'Have no fear – I am going. You will not have to listen any more. I have said more than I had planned or wished to, but you deserved it, Kaniz. The chapter of your animosity towards me and my family will end today. My daughters and I decline to have anything to do with you, or your son. You can keep it all. It is beneath us. Goodbye.' With a dignified gait Fatima strode out of the room, leaving the *chaudharani* of the village with her mouth half-open, standing in the middle of the room – near hysterical.

Fatima met Neesa in the courtyard, carrying a tray with a jug of iced lemon juice and a glass.

'You must stay for a drink, Sahiba Fatima,' Neesa politely insisted.

'Thank you, Neesa. I am afraid I don't feel inclined to drink even a drop of water in this house at the moment, nor would your mistress thank you for offering it to me.' She flashed a knowing smile at the woman before she walked out of the property, closing the gates firmly behind her.

Inside, mixed feelings vied. She was triumphant, because she had had her say. Miserable, because it was a

hollow victory, and knowing that Khawar was never destined to marry her daughter. If only . . . No more foolish thoughts! Angrily, Fatima thrust open the gate of her home.

Part Two

In my dark nights they brought me
The good tidings of the morning,
Put out the candles, turning me
Towards the rising sun.

Mirza Asadullah Khan Ghalib (1797–1869)
Translated by Ralph Russell
From *Selection from the Persian Ghazals of Ghalib*
(Pakistan Writers' Co-operative Society, 1997)

Chapter 38

DURING THE *EID-UL-FITR* holidays, Ibrahim, Pakinaz and Zarri Bano cruised down the River Nile from Cairo to the ancient city of Luxor in the south. They spent the first two days resting, after an exhausting tour of the city of Aswan and its ancient monuments. On the third day they visited the Valley of the Kings. Crossing the Nile by ferry, they took a taxi to the Temple of Ramses. Zarri Bano marvelled at the tall majestic façade, carved into the reddish rock and, at the beautifully preserved hieroglyphic paintings and inscriptions on the walls, pillars and ceilings.

Outside, the afternoon sun beat down on her head. Sweltering in her long dark *burqa*, she was glad to climb back into the air-conditioned taxi and head towards the Valley of the Kings.

King Ramses' tomb was their first destination. All three happily entered into the shade of the long, wide corridor. Fascinated by the magnificent multi-coloured hieroglyphics painted on the walls, they walked along to the large chamber housing the King's sarcophagus, listening with rapt attention as the Egyptian guide recounted the history of the tomb.

Outside again, they crossed the road and went down into the much smaller tomb of the legendary King Tutankhamen. It was packed with tourists, and Zarri Bano found it difficult to get a good view of the boy-king's sarcophagus. His remains and treasures were housed in the Cairo Museum.

'It is very impressive, Brother Musa,' Zarri Bano said

to Ibrahim, as he stood aside to let her view the tomb in the semi-darkness of the chamber. 'Where is Pakinaz?'

'Gone to the souvenir shop to buy a present for our niece. Do you want to stay a little longer and savour the moment?'

'No, I think I have seen enough. Shall we go back outside?' They retraced their steps, keeping well to the side of the road, allowing the many sightseers, mainly Europeans and Americans, to pass by.

'Let's wait here for Pakinaz,' Ibrahim suggested 'it is cooler here under this shade.'

'Thank you.' Zarri Bano moved gratefully to the place he indicated, by his side.

As they both watched the tourists coming out of the tomb, an awkward silence stretched between them. It was broken by Ibrahim's words in Arabic.

'Marry me, Zarri Bano.'

Startled, her eyes flew to his face, thinking she had imagined him saying it but, like her, he was wearing dark glasses, which both shielded his eyes and also hid his expression. She waited – her pulse racing, hoping she had misunderstood.

'I am sorry, Brother Ibrahim – did you say something?' she ventured hesitantly in English, staring at the dry rocky mountains beyond his shoulders.

'Yes, I did, Zarri Bano. I believe that you heard me, but are probably too shocked to absorb what I have just said. I am sorry. I will repeat it in English, just in case you thought you imagined it. I am asking you to be my wife, Zarri Bano. Nothing would give me greater pleasure.'

Zarri Bano gasped in dismay and she stumbled away from his side.

As Ibrahim watched her, his spirits sank. This was

not the reaction he had expected. Discomfited, he followed her to the shops and saw her go up to Pakinaz and stand next to her. He understood her signal. She was apparently distancing herself from him. Waving to his sister, he walked down the road and climbed into the taxi waiting for them there.

Pakinaz happily showed an alabaster cat she had bought for her niece to Zarri Bano. Pretending to admire it, Zarri Bano's thoughts were not on the cat, but on the man waiting in the taxi. Pakinaz climbed into the front passenger seat, leaving her friend with no choice but to sit in the back with Ibrahim. They drove off, in silence, to take the ferry over the Nile, heading for the temple complex at Karnak.

'Hey you two!' called Pakinaz from the front. 'You are very quiet – has the heat got to you both? I bet it has in your case, Zarri Bano. You must be baking in your black *hijab*.'

'I think that it has, Pakinaz, for the heat makes us say and do such irrational things.' Zarri Bano cast a meaningful glare at Ibrahim. His mouth tightening, he let the moment pass, however, and said nothing.

After crossing the Nile, they walked towards the Karnak complex. When they reached it, Ibrahim told his sister. 'I will show Zarri Bano around, Pakinaz, as I know the history of this place so well.' He then switched from English to Arabic and Pakinaz listened and nodded. Zarri Bano stood nearby, feeling helpless and trapped. She had no wish to see the ancient complex alone with Ibrahim.

'This way, Zarri Bano,' he beckoned, walking on and not giving her time to refuse.

She noted with dismay that it was the third time he had dropped the word 'sister' when addressing her.

Silently she followed him along the passage between the majestic pillars reaching high into the sky, their ancient surfaces scarred with forgotten inscriptions. Animal shapes of Egyptian gods lined the entrance to the complex.

With the rest of the tourists from all over the world, Ibrahim walked slowly, letting Zarri Bano absorb the splendour of the place, and mull over the atmosphere of the remains of Egypt's glorious past. She imagined what it must have been like in the time of Queen Hatshepsut and King Ramses, who had built this huge complex. A cool breeze wafted through the tall pillars, soothing her heated blood, billowing the dark folds of her *burqa* against her body.

Ibrahim led her to one of the secluded rooms, away from the crowds, and sat down on a boulder, fallen from one of the pillars.

'Would you like to take a rest, Zarri Bano?'

Seating herself on a similar-shaped boulder a few feet away from Ibrahim, Zarri Bano looked around the stone chamber, taking in the symbols and the half-animal shapes.

'Would it be very impertinent of me to ask what your answer is to my earlier question?' Ibrahim said quietly. 'I gather you were shocked by it, as it resulted in your rapid flight from my side.'

Zarri Bano's heart sank. The peace of the afternoon was shattered and she felt hedged in. She debated with herself how best to respond to him.

'I am very honoured by your proposal,' she began cautiously, 'but I am also very surprised. I hadn't suspected, you see, Brother Musa.'

'No?' His voice caressed her in its softness. 'I thought I was quite transparent in some ways.

My family have known for a long time but you, the woman that I want to marry, unfortunately have not.'

At his words 'want to marry', Zarri Bano shuddered inwardly.

'You are a very pleasant, attractive woman,' he continued huskily, seeing the image of her in the red dress in his mind. 'You are intelligent and have a sunny personality. Over the last few months I have got to know you well. You are just the type of woman I admire, need, and wish to have by my side for all time. We have so much in common. We share the same passion in books and religious history, Zarri Bano,' he said earnestly.

'Please stop, Brother Ibrahim,' she appealed to him.

'Oh don't call me Brother, Zarri Bano, I beg of you. For I harbour no brotherly feelings towards you – particularly I am ashamed to say, since that day I saw you without your veil.' He let his black eyes now openly spell out his feelings for her.

Colour crept into Zarri Bano's face as she realised the deep waters she had fallen in. How on earth could she retrieve the situation without hurting herself or him in the process?

'I am very sorry, Brother Ibrahim, but that is how I will always regard you,' she said in a low voice and looked down at her feet once more.

Unable to believe that she had refused him, Ibrahim stood up. With his fists balled in his trouser pockets, he closed the distance between them, and peered down at her bowed head.

'May I presume to ask why you cannot see me in any other light than as a brother? Do I lack anything, Zarri Bano? Have I done something wrong?' There was a trace of anger in his voice.

'No!' Zarri Bano too stood up. Opting for honesty, she looked him directly in the eye. 'No, Ibrahim Musa, you lack nothing.' Her eyes appraised his face and body, seeing him for the first time with a woman's eyes. 'Another woman would give anything to be courted by a man like you. You are very good-looking, very caring, highly intelligent and fun to be with.'

'Another woman – but not you!' he said dryly. 'What requirements do you have? May I know how I fail to measure up to those?'

'I don't have any requirements, Brother Musa. You are everything a woman could dream of – but I cannot be that woman, ever.'

'Why not?' A frown marred his high forehead, his hand moved thoughtfully on his beard.

'Because I have renounced marriage.' She spoke so quietly that he almost didn't hear her. The subject of her marital status was a painful one and a closed book to everyone. It took a few seconds for her comment to register in his mind.

'I don't believe it, Zarri Bano! What are you saying? Is it that you cannot marry – or won't?' His frown intensified.

'Both.'

'Are you by any chance *teasing* me, Zarri Bano?' he asked hopefully.

'No, Ibrahim, I could not and would not tease you on a subject like this.' She winced. 'I find it difficult to explain. All I can say to you is that I have decided to devote my life totally to religious studies and to teaching. I have no wish to marry—'

'But that is nonsensical,' he interrupted. 'You can marry as well as devote yourself to religious studies. I can think of nothing better than having my wife share

the same Department in the University, as well as my home and life. You already do that, to some extent,' he pointed out.

'It can never be! Please believe me, Brother Musa. I came to Egypt with that purpose, to become a learned woman. Perhaps if we had met at another time and in another place or another life, it might have been possible. I am honoured by your proposal, but what about Selima? She will make you a wonderful wife. She is Egyptian and shares your language and culture. I don't even do that.'

'That is immaterial. You have learned the language anyway. You are a Muslim, that is all that matters, and a woman whom I would like very much to marry.'

'Please, Ibrahim, do not say any more.' Zarri Bano was reaching the end of her tether. 'I can never marry you, and if you want me to be very plain, I will be, just to make you understand. Even if I hadn't renounced marriage, I would still not have married you, because in the end I would have chosen someone from my own country, culture, background and class. It is true we share a common culture of Islam, but I would never anticipate, nor would my family, my marrying someone who lives thousands of miles away from my home and country. If you don't mind me saying so, at the end we are still strangers.'

'I do not accept your reasoning, Zarri Bano. You are not giving us a chance. Many mixed marriages have taken place. The world is a small place now. The differences you mention can easily be overcome. The main affinity between us is our faith, which is supposed to unite all races, all nationalities. I am surprised at you. I know many people who have married Western women, from a totally different culture. Think of your

own countryman, Imran Khan, married to Jemima Goldsmith, a Western woman from a different religious background, and they are happy. Their marriage is successful. Our union would have much to support it.'

'Those marriages you speak of are between people who fell deeply in love and were prepared to surmount any barriers to be together. You are talking about a different situation, Ibrahim.'

'I suppose love plays no part in *your* life,' he muttered.

Fearing she had wounded his ego, Zarri Bano felt compelled to bare her soul in order to offer salve to his.

'What can I say, Brother Ibrahim? If I had been another woman at another time, I would have said yes. *Yes!* But I have no feelings for you, apart from friendship and respect. Nor will I have feelings for any other man. You see, I have become a Holy Woman – and part of the equation of being a Holy Woman is that I can never marry any man. I have no wish to marry anyway. You are right – love plays no part in my life. At the moment I harbour no feelings towards the opposite sex, save those of friendship.' Her voice sank to a whisper. 'I did love someone once – but I had to give him up. It was so hard, Brother Ibrahim, but I managed to do it. Now I have begun to think of him as a brother. Therefore, what feelings could I have for you? None, I am afraid. For I have trained both my mind and heart towards a life of total devotion – *ibadah*. I have learned to divorce my life from things like marriage and men. I am truly sorry. I just don't know what more to say,' she ended, her eyes beseeching him to understand.

Ibrahim was silent for a long time. Zarri Bano watched a group of Japanese tourists pass by, thinking that her companion was never going to speak to her again.

'Then there is definitely no hope for me, ever?' he ventured at last.

'No, never. My life has been charted out for me, Brother Ibrahim. I could never be any man's wife. I am married to my faith,' she stated, her voice devoid of any feelings.

They started to walk silently together through the temple complex, both locked in their own thoughts. The day was spoiled for both of them.

'You will understand, Ibrahim,' Zarri Bano began, turning to face him once more, 'why I cannot stay in your family's home after this. With this subject on our mind, it would not be right for me to remain in your house – for you no longer regard me as a sister.'

'That is true, but I do not want you moving out of our home, Zarri Bano. Surely we can be friends?' He dreaded the thought of her leaving.

'In the present circumstances that can never be, for the only friendship we should have is that of a brother towards a sister. As we do not share that, according to you, therefore it is wrong – *haram* – for me to be under the same roof. I am very grateful to you and your family for your hospitality, but when we return to Cairo, I will find another apartment. Of course, I will still liaise with you on the subject of my studies, if that is all right with you?'

He inclined his head politely then, on seeing a smiling Pakinaz approach them, he just said one word: '*lay*'. No. His sister's face fell. Hastening her pace, Zarri Bano walked ahead of them, letting Ibrahim explain to Pakinaz why she had turned him down.

The man who bounded into her mind, all of a sudden, was thousands of miles away on the other side of the world. The mortal ache she had suppressed

months ago on her sister's wedding day now came back to haunt her. It is a strange world, Zarri Bano mused. Here I am, standing on the ancient remains of Egypt's glorious past, proposed to by an Egyptian man, when the person I have given up is happily married to my own sister. Why have I thought of him today? Does he ever think of me?

Zarri Bano brushed away the water in her eyes. 'Sikander, where are you?' she called out in silent anguish, staring down into the green depths of the Nile as they returned to Karnak, a sadder, more subdued trio than when they had set out that morning.

Chapter 39

IT WAS A hot, humid night in Karachi. The man in Zarri Bano's thoughts couldn't sleep. Getting up from his bed Sikander went to the en-suite bathroom for a drink of water then returning to his room, he walked over to the window and gazed out at the shining stars in the night sky and the lightspeckled city in slumber.

Sikander turned to look at his bed. In the semi-darkness, he saw his wife's profile and her dark hair spread out on the pillow. Squeezing his eyes shut, he blocked out the image of another woman's face on his silk pillow.

He hadn't thought of her for two whole weeks. Zarri Bano's name was taboo – never uttered by anyone in his presence.

In the last few months he had concentrated hard on making his marriage a success. Ruby was a delightful woman, sweet and caring, always seeing to his every

need. An ideal partner, in short. He craved two things in life. To perfect this relationship with his wife and bury the image of the woman who had stolen his heart and then cruelly jilted him. Yet still she continued to haunt him!

Ruby stirred. Her hand automatically crept to the empty space beside her. She opened her eyes and raised her head to peer in the darkness, seeking her husband. Seeing Sikander watching her from the window, she smiled, feeling shy all of a sudden under his intense scrutiny.

Sikander came over and sat beside her on the bed. His eyes flickered tenderly over the face of the woman he had married, grown to love, and had shared his life with for the last six months.

His fingertips lightly caressed the planes of her cheekbones. An answering smile lighting her face, Ruby reached up and tentatively began to trace the outline of her beloved husband's face with her fingers.

'I hope I am not going to be sick again in the morning. It is terrible!' she confided, jokingly.

'You won't.' She revelled in the warmth of his deep voice.

'Should I tell Zarri Bano when she phones next time from Egypt?' Ruby then asked, and instantly felt her husband's mood change. When he answered her, the tenderness had gone.

'Not yet,' he said harshly. 'It is too soon. You are only three months' gone – wait for another few weeks.'

'Oh, but I am so excited. I can't wait to tell her the news. After all, she is my sister you know.'

'Yes I know,' came the bitter response. Sikander climbed into bed, laid his head on the pillow and turned the other way.

Discomfited, Ruby slid down under the cotton sheet. Was her imagination running away with her again? She and Sikander were happily married and expecting their first child. Zarri Bano had nothing to do with her husband. She was literally in another country now. Why then do I still feel jealous of my own sister? Ruby miserably questioned herself.

She moved her hand slowly over her lower abdomen. 'I would like to call him Haris, if it is a boy,' she whispered into her husband's shoulder-blades, trying to reach out to him.

'That's a nice name. I like it,' he responded. Behind his closed eyelids there loomed and beckoned a smiling tantalising woman with sparkling emerald-green eyes.

How will she take the news? he wondered sadly. Will she be delighted, as Ruby innocently assumes? Or will she ache with longing for a child of her own?

His advice not to tell Zarri Bano for another month or so had sprung from his innate sensitivity about other people's feelings. He hated his ex-fiancée for jilting him and becoming a Holy Woman, but he still felt strongly for her – enough to want to shield her from any emotional pain.

His love for her was a constant torture. He longed to rid himself totally of Zarri Bano's shadow. At times he forgot her totally, absorbed and happy in his new life. Then suddenly, out of nowhere, her face would beam through his mind, leaving an ache in him – an ache for what could never be.

Does she ever remember me? he wondered now. Or is she truly lost to her holiness and rosary beads? *Allah forbid!* Sikander shouted to himself in his mind. She is my sister-in-law! How can I think of her like this? The hunger for her, however, wouldn't go away. He could

still recall the feel of her fingertips tracing his lips in the courtyard of her home . . .

He opened his eyes to feel the warmth of Ruby's breath on his neck.

'Do you love me, Sikander?' The scared whisper signalled to him that she knew instinctively the times she lost him completely.

Sikander melted in a cauldron of guilt. 'Of course, my darling Ruby.' Tenderly he pulled her into his arms, burying his face in her hair.

'Damn you, Zarri Bano! May you rot in a similar hell to the one you have thrown me in,' he cursed silently, into the night, hours after his pregnant young wife had fallen asleep in his arms.

Chapter 40

IT WAS THREE months since Fatima had visited Khawar in the neighbouring village. Khawar had finally decided to return to his mother's home in Chiragpur as Fatima had advised. Kulsoom had already informed him that Firdaus had left for the city, to take up a post as Vice Principal in a women's college.

Having sent his belongings ahead in a steel trunk in his jeep, Khawar rode on his white horse through the green fields of Chiragpur. There was no joy in this homecoming. The farmers were busy ploughing their fields on their tractors. Sardara's milk buffaloes were enjoying their afternoon wallow in the village pond. The cowherd was keeping a close eye on the new beast which had a habit of running back home to its previous owner in the neighbouring village. Chiragpur lay in

a quiet slumber in the warm afternoon of early spring.

Once outside the gates of his father's *hawaili*, Khawar's face set into a grim expression. Heading first for the rear courtyard annexed to the stable, he tied his horse to a tree. The young man who had been hired to milk and look after their two buffaloes was sluicing down the redbrick-lined compound with buckets of water, after slopping away the cow dung in a separate aluminium bucket to be collected by a couple of women who used cow-dung cakes as fuel for their cooking. On seeing Khawar, the servant jumped to his feet, bidding his master, 'Salam.'

With firm steps, Khawar strode through the large wrought-iron gates and into the main central courtyard of the *hawaili*. Here he found Neesa on her haunches, washing the marble-chip floor of the veranda with a plastic hose. Hearing his distinct booted footsteps, her wrinkled face split into a smile as she sprang up to her full height to pat him on his shoulders. He hadn't been home for over a year.

'Welcome home, Master Sahib! I am so happy to see you.'

Khawar nodded, trying to relax enough so that he could smile at their housekeeper, who had raised him up in her loving arms since he was a baby.

'I'll tell the Chaudharani Sahiba. Oh, she'll be so pleased!' Neesa scurried up the stairs, unable to contain her joy.

At the mention of his mother's name, Khawar's face once more became forbidding. Climbing slowly up the stairs after Neesa, he followed her into his mother's bedroom.

*

Kaniz was combing out the waves of her long, thick hair with a hairbrush, when Neesa charged into the room without knocking. 'Khawar Sahib is here, Chaudharani Sahiba,' she gabbled. 'Isn't it great?'

Kaniz glanced into her mirror, to see her son's large body hovering stiffly in the doorway. She stumbled up from the dressing-table seat.

'My son is home!' She wept with joy.

Urgent strides took her to his side. Drawing him into her arms, she hugged her beloved child against her body. But Khawar remained unyielding in her arms. Disconcerted, Kaniz peeped up into his unsmiling face. Her arms falling to her side, she walked unsteadily back to the dressing table. So he hadn't forgiven her.

Sitting in front of the mirror, Kaniz began to braid her hair with trembling fingers, into a long thick plait.

'Are you just passing by, my son, or have you come home to stay?' she asked nervously.

Khawar didn't deign to reply, but took out his handkerchief, bent down and began to polish the dust off his boots.

'Are you staying, or not?' Kaniz rapped out. She was not at all amused or pleased by his behaviour towards her.

'I am not sure – for I do not regard this as a home,' he said loftily. 'It used to be a home in my father and grandfather's days. Now I just see it as a large, empty – *barren* place. A home, Mother, is supposed to be full of love and harmony. This place, on the contrary, is dominated by a tyrannical, selfish woman who cares for no one but herself.' His dark eyes flashed with hatred.

Dumbfounded, Kaniz just stared. Then a strange

thing happened – her eyes fell before his. She was unable either to look him in the face or to retaliate.

'Yes, I have come home,' he said finally 'but only for appearance's sake and because there is all the land business I have to deal with. Please don't think I have come for you. You are not fit to be a mother!'

'You are cruel, my son!' Kaniz choked her lower lip quivering.

It was true. Khawar *was* in a savagely cruel mood and had no qualms at all about making his mother suffer. Any love he had ever felt for her had been snuffed out long ago.

'Guess who I learned my cruelty from,' he jeered. 'At your knee, Mother dear. For only a truly heartless, selfish woman would stand in the way of her son's future happiness. You succeeded in driving Firdaus away from the village, and no doubt feel very pleased with yourself. For that I can never forgive you! Even if you begged her she'd not marry me now. Therefore, you stupid woman, you had better reconcile yourself to dying without ever seeing any grandchildren. For I will never marry, or bring any other woman as a bride into this house. You can now sing all your lullabies to yourself and to these empty walls that you worship. I am going to live here not as your son but as a stranger. You deserve no better.' Khawar was driven to punish his mother; he had no desire to come back home but had done so because it was his duty – as Fatima had pointed out to him.

'No, my son, no!' Kaniz wept.

At one time, the sight of his widowed mother's tears would have pierced him right through to his soul. Today he turned away in disgust, striding out of the room without giving the stricken woman another

glance. In the courtyard, he ordered Neesa to prepare the afternoon meal for him and his chauffeur. 'I am back home now,' he informed her dully.

Inside her room, Kaniz stood bereft. The world had simply given way beneath her. Tears of self-pity gushed down her cheeks as her son's harsh words echoed through her head. *How could he say those things to me? I am his mother!* She wept in bewilderment. *Does he hate me so much that he can abuse me in such a manner?*

Kaniz turned away from her distraught reflection in the dressing-table mirror. *Am I such a terrible person,* she asked herself fearfully, *that my beloved and only son has turned against me?* For the first time in thirty years Kaniz began to doubt herself, the power and influence she supposedly held in her fair hands and rightfully enjoyed as the village *chaudharani.*

Afraid of bumping into her son she stayed in her room for the remainder of the afternoon, hiding her swollen red eyes from Neesa as she brought her tray of food to her room.

'Neesa, has Khawar eaten anything?' she asked shakingly. 'Make sure you cook his two favourite dishes tonight: *matr pilau* and *kheer*. He has not tasted your cooking for a long time. I don't know what that old hag has been cooking for him. Bundles of spinach every day from the fields, I guess. Have you noticed my son has lost weight?' Kaniz kept her ravaged face averted from her housekeeper.

'No, mistress. He looks fine to me,' Neesa answered politely before withdrawing, deep in thought, from the room. Something had obviously happened between mother and son. Her mistress hadn't left her bedroom

all day. She normally spent the entire morning on the rooftop balcony.

Half an hour later she came up to tell her mistress that her sister Sabra had arrived on a casual visit. Brightening up, Kaniz quickly glanced in the mirror. The red eyes didn't matter. She had nothing to hide from Sabra.

'What on earth is the matter?' Sabra cried in alarm as soon as she saw her sister's swollen eyes.

These sympathetic words acted immediately on Kaniz, affording her the luxury of bursting into tears for the second time that afternoon.

'What's wrong? Please tell me,' Sabra said, in alarm, as Kaniz's large frame trembled against her slight body.

Sabra pulled her down and they sat together on the *palang*.

'Tell me the truth, Sabra!' Kaniz implored 'Am I cruel and selfish? Khawar definitely thinks I am. He hates me so much! His insults have killed me. He is back, but I think I have truly lost him. Sabra – please, *please* tell me what to do.'

There was a long pause, as the younger woman's eyes hovered uncomfortably over her sister's face. 'There is only one thing you can do, my dear sister,' she quietly informed her.

Kaniz's almond-shaped but very puffy eyes stood huge in her face. 'Never! Never!' she shouted.

Sabra politely edged away from her sister's trembling body. She hadn't travelled all the way from Punjab to Sind just to quarrel with Kaniz – hence she deftly changed the subject.

'Have you heard about my brother-in-law, Yousuf? The poor man died last week!'

Chapter 41

ZARRI BANO WAS among a group of Muslim women gathered in the female section of the Regent Park mosque in Central London. They had just finished saying their midday prayers. Saira, the friend, with whom Zarri Bano was staying, had invited her friends to meet and to consult Zarri Bano on all sorts of religious matters. Zarri Bano was happy to oblige. It gave her an opportunity to meet other Muslim women from around the world, living in England.

'May I begin?' asked one woman. The group were sitting in a semi-circle near Zarri Bano, on the carpeted floor.

'Of course,' she assented with a smile.

'Thank you, Sister. My name is Dudiya. I am a Muslim refugee from Bosnia. I would like to ask you: what constitutes a "true Muslim"? For you see, in Bosnia, living as a minority in a Communist country, we knew ourselves just as "Muslims". There were no differences within our community. Here in England, however, I have met and made many Muslim friends and often they ask me which sect I belong to. Am I Shia, they ask, or Shafai or Hanafi or Ismaili? I look back at them, puzzled. I just don't know. These friends keep encouraging me, pulling me towards their particular group's beliefs and thoughts. I don't know what to do, Sister Zarri Bano. Which group should I follow?' The rest of the women smiled in understanding – they knew what she was trying to say.

'Sister Dudiya, you do not have to follow a particular

group or school of thought or sect, if you do not want to. Just follow the words of Allah from our holy book the Quran and the Hadith, the sayings of our prophet Mohammed, may peace be upon him. Islam, like other religions has, over a period of time, evolved and become subdivided. It would be beneficial for you to learn about the differences and the similarities of these various groups, then you can decide which one, if any, you wish to join – according to your own personal beliefs,' she ended with a broad smile at Dudiya. The latter, smiling back, nodded her head.

'Your turn, Sister.' Zarri Bano beckoned to the young Pakistani woman sitting on her right.

'I find it embarrassing to raise this issue in this company, but my husband complains that I spend too much time on prayers and on reading religious books. It often leads to having quarrels. He sometimes stops me from reading the Quran in the evening, when he is around. I am very shocked and distressed by this because I believe I am not doing anything wrong. What should I do, Sister Zarri Bano?'

Zarri Bano paused to reflect. 'It is a complex situation,' she began, dimpling a warm smile at the woman. 'There is no doubt that you are *not* doing anything wrong and that your husband shouldn't stop you from reading the Holy Quran. On the other hand, I can't help thinking that perhaps he feels neglected and imagines that you are not giving him enough attention. Have you thought about doing your *ibadat* when he is not around? Allah Pak wants us to remember Him always, hence we have the five prayers in the day, but at the same time, however, He expects us to lead our normal daily lives too. He definitely doesn't expect us to neglect our family and our loved ones or our work,

which places food in our mouths. He best appreciates one who is healthily able to combine both and lead a very normal life. As you know, my sister, Islam is about a *complete* way of life. You cannot divorce the spiritual side of your life from the material world around you.' Zarri Bano turned to another woman.

'My question concerns myself, and is probably representative of the second generation of immigrants, brought up and bred in the West. I find that our lives are full of compromises. For instance, our faith promotes the segregation of the sexes, yet it is practically impossible here. We have to interact at all stages of our lives with men, especially in the workplace. You do understand the situation I am describing?'

Zarri Bano nodded, smiling, and stopped to think for a few seconds before answering. 'This is a very important issue, of great concern to Muslims all over the world. There are, of course, places such as Saudi Arabia where it is possible to segregate the sexes, however, this luxury is not widely available nor practically possible in most places, especially in countries where you are a minority.

'All I can say is that you should know instinctively your social, ethical and moral parameters as a Muslim woman. At work you are naturally likely to interact with men at all times. If the relationship is truly professional and platonic and you are able to regard the man as a brother or father figure then it is harmless. It is when there is a chance of it developing into something else that you need to step back. Theses things can have dire consequences. Your instincts should signal to you the difference between what is right and what is wrong. Learn to regard all men as brothers, uncles or father figures and address them as such, if they happen to be

Muslim. In the case of non-Muslim men, friends and colleagues, explain to them about your faith and its traditions – so that they cannot misunderstand you, but instead learn to appreciate and respect your behaviour, beliefs and way of life.'

'Thank you,' the young woman replied with a smile.

'You are welcome,' Zarri Bano replied.

Later in the afternoon, Zarri Bano went with Saira to a café, where they were joined by one of Saira's friends.

'This is Jane Foster,' Saira said. 'She was particularly keen to meet you, especially when I told her how you had taken the veil.'

The young English woman held out her hand to Zarri Bano, who took it warmly. 'Thank you for coming, Sister Jane.'

'I was fascinated by your story, Zarri Bano. Saira told me about your university days, when you studied with her. She showed me a photograph of you in a pair of Levi's with only a short blouse on top. Now seeing you wrapped in this veil, I am unable to put the two pictures together in my mind. I want to ask you whether you found it difficult to wear the *hijab* at first and why did you do it anyway? I hope you don't think I am being too personal.'

Uneasy about discussing her past and the *burqa* with a virtual stranger, Zarri Bano did, in fact, feel cornered by Jane's question. She wished that Saira hadn't been so generous in showing old photos of herself and discussing her.

'It is true that I found it very strange at first, Jane, when I began to wear the *hijab*. Two years ago I wanted to tear it aside: now I cannot live without it. The veil has given me a sense of my self-worth, respect and

dignity. Above all, it has freed me from vanity. I never thought it would be easy but I have been able to shed myself of the trappings of female vanity. You must not misunderstand me, Jane. I am not saying that all Muslim women lead very simple and unglamorous lives – that would be a misconception. On the contrary, behind closed doors and behind the *hijab*, most of the women here could compete with any woman in Knightsbridge, in the art of looking good.'

'And you, Zarri Bano, are you still dolled up behind your veil?' Jane asked with a speculative gleam in her eyes.

'No,' Zarri Bano answered quietly. 'Not any more. I have passed that stage in my life – a stage that now, in retrospect, seems so trivial. Once my whole life was devoted to looking good, and presenting a glamorous smart image to the public world. Now I am content with my simple *burqa*. I do not dress to please others and in deference to them. Thank you for your question, Sister Jane. The veil has always perplexed and tantalised the Western world, both men and women alike. It is a disconcerting phenomenon for them as much now as it ever was. Westerners have always misunderstood the reason why women wear it. To add insult to injury, they see it as a symbol of male oppression – a widely accepted stereotyped myth. They think that women are forced to wear it by their menfolk.

'I can assure you, my friend, that in the current climate, there are more women now in the *hijab*, by their own free will, than ever before. There has been an international scarf revolution, a symbol of Muslim women's unity. My father has criticised me for wearing it at home. Now I feel bare without it.'

Zarri Bano stopped to drink her coffee, deciding she

had said enough on this controversial issue. Jane
Foster's expression had changed from mild interest to
amazement. It was not the answer she had been
expecting.

'We are not freaks,' Zarri Bano could not resist add-
ing, 'just women who like to dress in a modest fashion
and believe in covering ourselves well. All we ask is
that people respect us and our dress code.'

'Of course,' Jane Foster said quickly, a blush spread-
ing across her cheek.

'Saira, I wish you hadn't told everything about me or
showed those shameful photographs to a complete
stranger,' Zarri Bano confronted her friend, as they
walked out of the café. 'Please don't use me as food for
entertainment and sensationalism.'

'I am sorry, I didn't think you would mind,' Saira
replied guiltily, as they walked through Piccadilly
Circus.

'I suppose,' after a short pause, 'that you also told her
about my ceremony?' Zarri Bano fixed an accusing glare
at her friend.

'No,' Saira lied, thinking it prudent not to tell Zarri
Bano the truth. Jane Foster was a journalist and Saira
had told her everything. 'Are you coming home with
me or going to visit your sister in the hotel?' She asked,
wanting to steer Zarri Bano away from the subject of
the *hijab*. She herself didn't wear it and thus found it an
awkward topic.

'I'll go to the hotel to see Haris again. He's so lovely,
I can't wait to hold him. I have promised Ruby that I'll
go with her and Sikander to the theatre tonight. They
want to see a play in the West End.'

'Don't be too late. Remember that they are

expecting you at seven-thirty tomorrow evening to give the lecture at Manchester Metropolitan University. Before that we are stopping over at Birmingham. I don't want you to get too tired,' Saira reminded her friend in concern as they reached the underground station.

'I won't be, *Allah Hafiz*!' Zarri Bano waved Saira off as she went down into the station, then walked along to the traffic lights, and crossed over the road to the hotel where her sister's family was staying. Ruby and Sikander with their one-year-old son Haris had been on a trip to Europe and had decided to spend three days in London to coincide with Zarri Bano's three-week tour of England.

As she entered the foyer through a side door, she saw Sikander lounging on a large sofa, his eyes on the revolving doors. Zarri Bano blinked, looking away. She pulled the hood of the *burqa* further onto her forehead, feeling for any missing stray locks of hair. He was waiting for her to walk in!

Sikander watched her glide across the carpeted floor to stand near him. Still avoiding any eye-contact with him, she admired the large Turner oil-painting of a ship on the wall behind him.

'*Assalam-Alaikum!* Where are Ruby and Haris?' she asked politely, sitting down on the sofa opposite him and wishing he would take his eyes off her face.

'Mother and son are waiting for you upstairs. Ruby wants you to go to Harrods with her.'

Zarri Bano chuckled, as she recalled her sister's life-long wish to shop at Harrods. Sikander's face relaxed and he too laughed. Then with a serious expression he asked. 'What are your plans, Sister Zarri Bano? Will you be returning to Pakistan with us or staying longer?

We are heading for Singapore. I – we were wondering whether you would like to join us.' He looked down.

'I am sorry, Brother Sikander.' Zarri Bano stood up abruptly. 'I have other plans. Will you excuse me? I shall go upstairs to see Ruby and Haris.'

Her eyes blurring, she walked quickly away from him and into an elevator. Singapore was where he had promised to take her for their honeymoon.

Chapter 42

HUSBAND AND WIFE laughed as their grandson Haris jumped off Habib's lap and ran out of their bedroom, to go down to his own parents and Aunt Zarri Bano.

'Shahzada, please ask Zarri Bano to come and see me. I cannot rest until I have unburdened myself to her,' Habib informed his wife. 'The cancer has been eating away at me for the past three years,' he sighed.

'What cancer?' Shahzada asked in alarm, straightening up. Although she didn't love her husband anymore, she still cared for his physical well-being.

'My guilt,' he whispered, 'from forcing my daughter to become a *Shahzadi Ibadat*. I shouldn't have done it.' He was unable to look at his wife.

Shahzada's indrawn breath disconcerted him. She said nothing – for she felt absolutely nothing for her husband. Thus the words of understanding and support that Habib so yearned to hear failed to leave her mouth.

'I know that you have never forgiven me,' he went on. 'Have you?'

She was sitting on his bed, while he lay resting

against the headboard, his hands crossed behind his neck. Shahzada got off the bed and walked towards the door.

'Have you, Shahzada?' His raised voice stopped her short.

'Does it matter whether I have forgiven you or not?' She turned round, but her hand remained firmly on the door handle.

'Of course it matters! You were right all along. I lost a wife and a beloved close friend the day my Zarri Bano became a Holy Woman. You act as normal, yet you have kept me at arm's length. I never knew my Shahzada was capable of such hardness. She was a gentle, warm person. In which grave have I buried her? The rapport we had has gone, your love, your respect . . . all gone. I can't cope with it any more! Forgive me, Shahzada – I beg of you!'

What happened next startled both of them. Habib jumped off the bed and went over to Shahzada, kneeling in front of her on the floor, clasping her feet in supplication. She froze, looking down at her proud husband bent meekly over her feet, his hands clutching the strap of her sandals.

It was appalling to see Habib abase himself like this. Although she empathised with his pain, she could not respond to it. It was all too late.

'Habib, please stand up,' she said irritably. 'Do not humiliate us both. It is not seemly for you to touch my feet. You know you cannot turn the clock back. What is done is done. You killed your beloved wife the day you threatened her with three divorces – and the dead do not return. Be happy that Zarri Bano has become the woman you wanted to shape her into.' Her face was marked with deep lines of pain.

'I wish to God that I had never forced our daughter into it,' Habib cried. 'Seeing Ruby happily married and with a son, I shrink inside myself with horror. "What have I done?" I ask myself over and over again. I cry bitterly in my sleep and prayers. I have deliberately prevented my daughter from having a normal life like Ruby's. Who am I – a god? Shahzada, what right did I have to change another person's destiny? I cannot go on this holy pilgrimage to Mecca without asking for Zarri Bano's forgiveness and yours. Allah will not accept my *hajj* rituals until I do this. Prophet Mohammed, may peace be upon him, has said that he who goes on *hajj*, must first reconcile himself or herself to everyone and ask for their forgiveness. As *hajj* is going to be my spiritual journey, I must come back as a person newly born. I have learned to transcend my male ego, Shahzada, and to be humble. It is that humility which has reduced me to come crawling to your feet. No man, no husband of my calibre would ever do that. You must recognise, and appreciate that! You talk about dying. Well Habib too died on the day Sikander entered my home, for I haven't been the same man since.' His eyes never left her face.

'So you see, I have to beg for Zarri Bano's forgiveness and to free her from the oath never to marry. What I hadn't bargained on was that I would lose you too in the process. Allah Pak will never forgive me for treating you the way I did four years ago. I now cannot live without your respect and love, Shahzada. Don't shut me out of your mind and heart, please! I hate myself and what I stand for. When my mind compares Zarri Bano with what she used to be like, I recoil. I wanted the world for my daughter, but we lost her to books, to

religious conventions and to a black *burqa*. She is so remote, so inaccessible.'

There were tears of remorse in his eyes. He went on, choking with emotion as he spoke: 'That dimple in her cheeks, which I used to delight in seeing and touching when she was a child . . . I have not glimpsed it for three years. She hardly ever laughs or smiles any more. Oh where is our beloved Zarri Bano? My mind and conscience will not rest, Shahzada, until I have laid bare my soul to her. I want my daughter back,' he ended passionately, then waited for his wife to speak to bring him the comfort he so desparately craved. But Shahzada's bitter words now lashed back at him.

'It is all your fault. You had wanted to keep your beautiful daughter, your beloved possession, at home. You didn't want to part with either her or the fields. You couldn't stand losing her to Sikander, your rival for her affection, so you thought. Your jealousy has devoured our whole family! You wanted homage and reverence at your daughter's doorstep? Well, now you've got them! People travel from far and wide in Pakistan to seek her moral and intellectual guidance on religious matters. So there should really be no regrets, Habib.' Shahzada didn't bother to disguise the contempt that had suddenly surfaced, in both her eyes and voice.

The light of hope in Habib's eyes died and he rose to his feet. Shahzada was right. He *had* killed his beloved wife that terrible afternoon when he had threatened her with divorce for questioning his decision about Zarri Bano's fate. To be offered three *thalaks* for no apparent reason would emotionally kill any woman, especially someone of Shahzada's gentle nature who had worshipped him. It was too cruel a punishment, merely for standing up for her daughter's rights.

'I will go and get Zarri Bano for you,' Shahzada told him coldly. 'I think she is in the lounge with Ruby and Sikander.' She left her husband standing in the middle of the room, the look of a lost man in his eyes. The padlock still clutching at her heart wouldn't let her utter any words of consolation. As she closed the door behind her, Shahzada wondered sadly if she was ever going to be able to forgive him.

As soon as Zarri Bano walked into the room, Habib came directly to the point. 'My dearest daughter, something has been bothering me lately. In fact ever since you became a Holy Woman.'

'What is it, Father? What's worrying you?' Zarri Bano said anxiously.

'I have to ask your forgiveness, for I cannot go on this holy pilgrimage without doing that.' His voice was husky with emotion. 'I have already asked your mother for hers. You see, I sinned against you both. Please forgive me, Zarri Bano, for forcing you to give up Sikander, marriage and the life you previously had. What we did was wrong. I do not know how to turn the clock back. My dear daughter, I would give anything to have the old Zarri Bano back again.'

'Father, there is nothing to forgive,' she said gently. 'You shouldn't feel guilty. I have gained so very much from my new role – in fact, all the things that you said I would.'

'Is that the truth, my dear,' Habib interrupted, eagerly. 'Or are you saying it just to make me feel better?'

'No, Father. As Allah Pak is my witness, I speak the truth. By your action, you opened the door to another world for me. I am, I hope, a good Muslim now. I hope

I perform all my duties well. I also now have the knowledge to show and direct others along the same path. I have met people that the old Zarri Bano would never have met. I have visited places that in my old life I would never have had the chance to see. It is true my life is not like Ruby's, but mine is fulfilled in its own way. Therefore, you have simply nothing to worry about,' she ended with a forgiving smile on her face.

Zarri Bano's words were like pearls of water falling out of her beautiful mouth onto Habib's thirsting soul, offering a precious salve to his conscience. He gratefully drank them in.

'Her words are not enough,' his conscience prompted, however. Half-heartedly he tried again. 'My daughter, I have thought long and hard about this issue, and I know that I have done wrong. No matter what you say, I want to make amends. If now, or in the future, you ever wish to marry, you will have my full blessing.'

'Father, why do you say such things!' Zarri Bano cried in disbelief, wondering if Habib had become deranged. 'I don't want to marry, ever. I am a Holy Woman now!'

'You wanted to marry then, as I remember clearly – so why not now? I have committed a crime not only against you but also against our faith. I have read the books on Islam and the words of condemnation jump out at me!'

Zarri Bano listened to her father in silence, then answered without any trace of bitterness. 'I, too, have studied those books and read the jurists' interpretations, from Imam Malike and Shafia's school of thought on this precise issue. Marriage is to be encouraged and not prevented. The family unit and the raising of a family is at the heart of our faith. But I

absolve you of that guilt. I accept your blessing, your permission, as my guardian, for me to marry, if I ever so wish.

'Marriage, however, has no relevance in my life now, Father. I am truly happy with things as they are. There should be no compulsion to marry if one is really against it — that, too, is written, Father. There is no man I want to marry.' She quashed the inner whisper: *'There was one a long time ago — but you prevented me from marrying him.'*

'If you are sure? If you ever change your mind, then you have my blessing, my child, remember that!' Habib pressed earnestly.

'Never, Father!'

He nodded his head in understanding. Smiling, she stood up to leave.

'How are the preparations for the *hajj* going?' she asked. 'I was just talking about our *hajj* downstairs with Ruby and Brother Sikander. The tickets are sorted out; our clothing has been prepared. I am going through the book on *hajj* with Ruby, so that she knows what she has to do once she gets to Mecca, and also knows what to expect. I have read two or three books on the subject already. Sister Sakina has been filling in the gaps for me. She was saying that it is best to go to Medina first and say our forty obligatory prayers in the Prophet's Mosque, before the *hajj*. Apparently it is quieter there at that time, than after *hajj*, when most of the pilgrims decide to visit Medina all at the same time. When you went, Father, did you go to Medina before or after the *hajj*?'

'We went before. Sakina is right — it is not such a rush then. One has plenty of time to visit the holy places, and it's easier to find a good hotel.'

'Well, we have booked our tickets so that we have
two weeks before the *hajj*, and one week after. That
gives us about six days in Jeddah and Mecca and then
eight days in Medina before returning to Mecca on the
day before the *hajj* begins. Brother Sikander has con-
tacts in all three places. He has booked us rooms in
good hotels for all of our stay.'

'I am pleased that he will be going with us,' Habib
approved. 'We need a young man on a journey like this.
Anyway, with four women, there is need of another
male escort for the *hajj*.'

'Yes I am glad he is going with us as well. Haris will
miss his parents, though.'

'I know, that's the only problem – we'll all miss *him*.
I can't wait till next month, Zarri Bano,' Habib said
enthusiastically. 'It will be our first *hajj* together as a
whole family.'

'I am looking forward to it too,' she told her father
warmly. 'Right, I had better get downstairs. Brother
Sikander was sorting out the paperwork for our visas;
they are going back to Karachi in half an hour.'

'Aren't they staying the night?'

'No. Goodnight, Father. *Khudah Hafiz*.'

When Zarri Bano had left, Habib went to lie down
on his bed feeling happier than he had been for a long,
long time. He was so glad that he had had this chat
with his daughter, and she had relieved him of some of
the burden.

Chapter 43

THE PLANE RESOUNDED with the chanting of the *hajj* salutations, *Talbiya*, by devoted pilgrims.

'Here I am, O Allah, here I am in Your presence! You have no partner, here I am! You alone deserve all praise and gratitude! You alone can bestow favours and blessings. Sovereignty is Yours and You have no partner,' Zarri Bano happily translated to her sister as they sat together on one side of the aisle and Sikander, Habib and Shahzada sat on the other side.

It was a spectacular sight with the plane full of pilgrims, dressed in their special loose white *hajj* robes, all chanting enthusiastically: 'Here I come, oh Allah', and heading for the house of God, the holy *Al Kaba*, in Saudi Arabia in Mecca Sharif. One pilgrim stood near the cockpit of the plane, and using the plane's intercom system led the chanting for their pilgrimage.

'Have I got the words right, Zarri Bano?' Ruby asked anxiously. She had learned the *Talbiya* by heart at home, but now in the excitement of the journey she seemed to have jumbled all the words yet again, and had to keep on glancing at the small guidebook.

'Yes you have, darling.' Zarri Bano smiled indulgently at her younger sister. An expression of pure joy lit her face all of a sudden. 'Isn't it exciting? I cannot wait to get to Mecca. People from the four corners of the world are converging onto Saudi Arabia. Dressed like this, Ruby, you too look like a devout, religious woman!'

Zarri Bano's eyes slid over the white robe covering her sister's whole body from her head to her feet. Ruby was very uncomfortable in the cumbersome clothes and head covering, but there was nothing she could do about it. All the other women were dressed in a similar fashion. Her hair, like theirs was tied back and hidden under the head covering, for it was wrong to let even one wisp of hair be seen, or for a single hair to fall in the Holy Mosque, the *Al Kaba*. 'Even one hair littering the Holy Mosque would be a desecration of the highest sort, so be very careful,' Zarri Bano had drummed into Ruby, frightening her at first, until she saw the amused expression on her older sister's face.

Ruby hoped she could keep up with everybody in the prayer sequences, which they all seemed to know by heart and which she was trying to learn. She caught her husband looking at her. He was smiling and also chanting the *Talbiya* whole-heartedly.

'Allah must be very busy listening to everybody's prayers today at the holy site of Arafat in Saudi Arabia,' Ruby chuckled to herself. 'When all the pilgrims come from every corner of the world . . .'

The stars shone brightly in the night sky over the small town of Muzdalifah, a few kilometres away from the holy site of Arafat in Saudi Arabia. Like their million fellow pilgrims, Zarri Bano and her family had offered a special afternoon prayers at Arafat and had become *kjajjis*. Following in the footsteps of their Holy Prophet Mohammed (PBUH), they were duty bound to spend a night in Muzdalifah.

Lying on her jute sleeping mat, purchased in Jeddah, Zarri Bano stared up at the sky above them with its

stars winking down at them, acknowledging their holy presence in the small town.

'This is what *hajj* is all about, my dear Ruby!' A trace of excitement still bubbled in her voice. It had been a very eventful day. She turned to face her sister, half-asleep on another mat, only a foot away. 'Have you ever spent a night like this in your life? I know I haven't. My bones ache, but my heart feels joyous and is still throbbing with the excitement. Look at the stars above, Ruby, they are greeting us and saying "Salaam. You are a *hajen* now." Can you imagine, how on this very spot, over the centuries, every year, thousands of pilgrims, from all over the world have slept here? For one day each year, this place becomes the centre of the universe. Are you listening, Ruby?' Zarri Bano raised her head to look at her sister.

'Hmm, I am,' the other girl replied, yawning. 'You are right, this *is* a unique occasion. I am so glad we came. I don't even mind the small pebbles digging into my back through my mat. You had better try to get some sleep, Zarri Bano. We have a very busy day ahead of us in Minah tomorrow. Look, I can hear Mother and Father snoring soundly, although Sikander Sahib is still tossing and turning.'

'I bet the pebbles are digging into *his* ribcage!' Zarri Bano joked. 'Do you remember we have to collect seventy-two pebbles for the "Devil's" *shaitan* site? So these under your mat and your husband's will come in handy!'

When Zarri Bano turned on her other side, she came face to face with a hefty young Nigerian woman saying her late night-time prayers, only a few paces away. The woman's husband was sitting near by, loudly reciting *surahs* from the Holy Quran. Zarri Bano closed her eyes,

totally content to share the moment with people from all over the world. Knowing she would never forget this night.

By the time Ruby got up, her sister had already read three chapters from the Holy Quran. She stood up, feeling embarrassed. Everybody was saying their prayers. She felt as if she had been sleeping in the middle of a mosque amidst strangers.Queues for the public toilets and ablution places grew longer. Makeshift taps had been installed wherever possible every few yards for the benefit of the pilgrims. Stalls were already set up for breakfast.

By six o' clock in the morning, the sun had risen and everybody was up. Soon after breakfast, gathering their belongings together, the pilgrims all headed back towards Minah, and their tents.

Ahead of them lay the third important day of *hajj*, to be spent on the open plain of Minah in their tents. It was a day to be celebrated by Muslims everywhere – culminating in *Eid-al-Adha*, the second most important festival.

'On this day, centuries earlier,' Zarri Bano explained to Ruby, 'Prophet Ibrahim turned his back on three consecutive occasions and spat on the *shaitan*, the Devil. In his footsteps we are to throw pebbles at the marked spot, to show our rejection of him. The *shaitan* had tried to dissuade Prophet Ibrahim from sacrificing his son Ismail.'

Reaching their tents by late morning, Zarri Bano, Ruby and Shahzada were told to take a rest by Habib, while he and Sikander, went to arrange the next holy ritual, the animal sacrifices, in the makeshift abattoirs nearby. By late afternoon, trays of meat began to arrive.

All pilgrims were duty-bound to distribute a portion of it to their neighbours, to eat a certain portion themselves and give the remainder to the Saudi government officials, for it to be frozen and sent to needy families all over the world.

After their ceremonial baths and change of clothing, the women cut off strands of their hair. The men either shaved or cut a portion of their hair, as a sign of humility and spiritual rebirth.

After dinner, Zarri Bano decided to take a walk around the plain of Minah with Ruby. They walked amongst the rows of tents, sheltering the pilgrims from the afternoon sun. People were roaming everywhere. Zarri Bano couldn't believe her eyes when by chance she happened to spot Pakinaz and Ibrahim Musa, walking straight towards them. They, too, were just as amazed and delighted as she was.

'*Assalam-Alaikum*, Pakinaz and Brother Musa. What a lovely surprise! You are performing *hajj* this year as well? I can't believe it!' she said in English.

'Yes, I cannot believe it either. Our parents are with us – wait until they find out that you are here as well!' Pakinaz hugged Zarri Bano, kissing her fondly on both her cheeks. Zarri Bano looked at Pakinaz's white veiled figure with amusement. 'Strange we didn't bump into you earlier anywhere else,' Pakinaz then commented.

'My family is here too,' Zarri Bano told her. 'This is my sister Ruby.'

Greeting Ruby, Ibrahim inclined his dark head towards her.

Zarri Bano explained to her sister, in Urdu, who these people were and how she had stayed with them in Egypt.

'Oh, how nice. Let's take them to meet the rest of the family,' Ruby urged excitedly.

'What a good idea.' Zarri Bano turned to her family. 'Would you like to meet my parents? They are in that large tent, with a green star on top – that is our symbol.'

'Yes, we would like that very much,' Pakinaz replied warmly.

Habib and Shahzada were delighted to meet the Egyptian brother and sister who had made their daughter so welcome in Cairo. After some refreshments and conversation, Ibrahim stood up to leave excusing himself. Zarri Bano decided to go with him to visit his parents.

'Are you coming too, Pakinaz?' Zarri Bano enquired. Her eyes, for some reason, had drifted towards Sikander. He had remained totally silent during their visitors' stay.

'I will follow you in a minute, Sister Zarri Bano. Just let me finish my drink.'

'OK.' Zarri Bano left the tent and followed Ibrahim Musa.

Pakinaz drained her cup then looked around and smiled at the four people in the tent.

'I had better get going too,' she said shyly. 'It's lovely to meet you all and to see Zarri Bano again. We missed her dreadfully when she left Cairo. My family really took to her presence. We all did, including my brother Ibrahim. Did she tell you that he asked her to marry him . . . '

'And what did she say?' Sikander asked sharply, speaking for the first time, his body coiled like a spring all of a sudden. Ruby turned to look at her husband, her eyes on his face.

'What is she saying, Sikander dear? I cannot

understand a word. Don't keep me and your father-in-law in the dark.' Shahzada looked from Pakinaz's innocent face to Sikander's brooding expression.

'She says, Mother, that the man who has just left the tent wanted to marry your princess of worship, your *Shahzadi Ibadat*,' Ruby told her parents.

Habib and Shahzada stared at one another in surprise.

'But she cannot, she is a Holy Woman,' Shahzada voiced, smiling awkwardly at their Egyptian guest. 'Ruby, please ask our visitor what Zarri Bano said when this Ibrahim proposed to her.'

Ruby translated her mother's request into English and addressed Pakinaz.

'Oh, she refused him,' the girl said easily. 'We were all very sad. We had all wanted Zarri Bano to marry our Ibrahim. My brother took it very badly. He liked her very much and probably still does,' Pakinaz ended.

'Did Zarri Bano tell your brother,' Sikander directly addressed Pakinaz in English, 'that she is a Holy Woman and has renounced marriage?'

Ruby was surprised by the hostility she glimpsed in her husband's grey eyes.

'Yes, Zarri Bano did tell us but we didn't believe her,' the girl answered pleasantly. 'We were very disappointed. Sadly my brother is still single. We are trying our very best to get him engaged. This year we have almost succeeded!' Pakinaz stopped as she saw Sikander stand up and march out of the tent.

Outside the tent, Sikander stretched his leg muscles which were stiff. He was wearing a long white cotton Arab robe similar to those worn by thousands of other pilgrims.

People were walking in all directions around the

tents. Sikander scanned the scene in front of him until his eyes fell on Zarri Bano's dark veiled head. She was standing just a few yards away, near a rock, talking to the tall bearded Egyptian in Arabic.

Sikander's grey eyes glinted coldly in the sunshine. The Egyptian had said that he was going to take her to meet his parents, yet here they both were having a cosy *tête-à-tête*. Even in profile Sikander could see that Zarri Bano's lips were curved into a smile as she chatted to her friend. The Egyptian was looking down at her and smiling. From where Sikander stood, their exchange had all the trappings of a very intimate scene between a man and a woman.

Jealous rage burst through his body. His mouth in a tight line, Sikander strode angrily up to Zarri Bano's side. His tall shadow fell ominously across the pair in the hot afternoon sun.

Zarri Bano turned, the smile still hovering on her lips and her dimple clearly visible, Sikander noted bitterly. Ibrahim Musa also turned, reading instantly the look in Sikander's eyes and recognising the raw male energy behind the clear message: Keep Off. Ibrahim cast a questioning glance at Zarri Bano.

The smile deserted Zarri Bano's flushed cheeks. In front of her stood two men, both of whom had once proposed marriage to her. She had never anticipated seeing them together in one place and at the same time. Her dimple disappeared. She looked from one man's face to the other, before mentally distancing herself from both. The look in Sikander's eyes made her feel guilty, all of a sudden – as if she had done something wrong. He had somehow sullied the pleasant moment with his presence and the accusing look in his eyes. The urge to explain herself grew strong.

'Brother Ibrahim,' she blurted out in English, deliberately laying the emphasis on the word *Brother*, so that both men noted her use of it and knew where they stood, 'Brother Ibrahim was just telling me that he is getting engaged to Selima when he returns to Egypt. I have met Selima, she is a very nice woman. I was congratulating him.'

'Congratulations, Brother Musa. *Mubarak.*' Sikander politely extended his hand to Ibrahim, his eyes still cool although his words tried to express warmth.

'Thank you. Shall we go to our tent? It is just over there. Would you like to join us, Brother Sikander?' Ibrahim Musa politely suggested, leading the way.

Sikander joined them, albeit reluctantly, and was introduced to Ibrahim's family. They stayed there for nearly two hours. In that time Pakinaz had joined them. They talked about Egypt and the time they had spent together. Not saying much, Sikander listened politely, sitting beside Zarri Bano on the floor cushions in the tent. To the rest of the group, he distinctly gave the impression that he was Zarri Bano's *mehram*, her male escort.

Walking back together in silence towards their tent, Sikander quietly tossed at her: 'Pakinaz told us earlier that that Musa man wanted to marry you.'

Zarri Bano stopped walking. 'I . . . Did she? She had no right.'

'Why not? And why did you refuse him?' he pressed, his voice dangerously low.

'Brother Sikander! As you well know, I cannot marry nor do I *wish* to marry any man – that is why!' she reminded him hotly, a blush seeping through her cheeks.

'Ruby tells me that your father has released you from that oath,' Sikander doggedly cut in, still not looking at her.

Zarri Bano stood still on one side of a portable chemist cabin, ignoring the queue of pilgrims buying medicine. Sikander stopped too. Their bodies taut, they faced each other. She scrutinised his face, blinking in surprise at his combative stare.

'I don't know what Ruby or Pakinaz has told you. The fact remains that I am a Holy Woman and do not wish to marry *anyone*. It is offensive of you even to suggest it or to make an issue of it.' Her own eyes were now icy cold.

'It didn't look very offensive to me when you were having your cosy little *tête-à-tête* with that unsuitable fellow.' Sikander shocked both himself and Zarri Bano by the words that leaped viciously out of his mouth.

'Brother Sikander!' Zarri Bano was scandalised. 'How dare you insult me. What has come over you? What is it to you anyway?' she taunted, her stare matching his in hostility.

'You dare to ask me that!' he hissed under his breath. Leaning forward, oblivious to the human throng milling around them, he ground out: 'I am the man you jilted, Zarri Bano – in case you have forgotten. *That* is what the matter is with me.' He grabbed hold of her arm and shook her, hard. 'As your ex-fiancé it is natural I should be interested in your love life!'

'Get your hands off me!' Zarri Bano nearly screamed into his face. 'Don't you dare touch me! I will not listen to any more of your madness. I think that the afternoon sun has got to you. You do not know what you are saying or doing. A love life – me? How dare you insult me so!'

He dropped her arm as if it burned him. 'Do you think I enjoyed watching you making eyes at him?' he said passionately. 'Him! A man who any fool can see is still in love with you, not as a holy sister but as a woman.' Sikander was quivering with suppressed emotion, his body all a-tremble.

'Stop right there!' Zarri Bano's tall, slim frame behind her *burqa* also trembled – but with rage. 'You have trespassed all barriers of decency, Sikander Sahib! I didn't imagine that you could stoop so low. I am a Holy Woman, in case you have forgotten. A woman who has renounced marriage and one who has no interest in worldly relationships, let alone with men and *love*!' She spat the word as if it was acid burning her tongue.

Then she took a deep breath and said more calmly 'I will forgive you this time, Brother Sikander, but do not ever, *ever*, talk to me on this topic again! You have no hold over me, any more than Ibrahim Musa does, that stranger from another country. Except, of course, that you are my brother-in-law. Husband of my beloved sister and father of my beloved nephew. We have nothing between us, Sikander,' she said painfully. 'We never had. No other links – save platonic ones. Our past that you delight in referring to and the woman you thought you knew are both buried six feet deep in my brother's grave.' At the thought of Jafar, tears came into her eyes and she swallowed hard. 'We are performing *hajj* here, Brother Sikander. It is a holy pilgrimage, supposedly taking us on to an elevated plane. Do not thus debase our holy spiritual journey with your base insults and innuendoes and sick imagination.' Anger reawakened in her.

'Furthermore, I do not need you walking by my side. You are not my chaperone, my father is. You are Ruby's

husband and that is where you should be – by her side, not by mine! You are with the wrong sister, Brother Sikander! The wrong woman, in fact!' Then gathering her black robe around her body and pulling the hood lower over her forehead, she strode away from him, her head held high.

As the pilgrims walked around Sikander, some still carrying trays of meat to their tents, he watched Zarri Bano disappear, fighting an insatiable urge to grab hold of her and wring her slim neck. Somehow she always brought out the worst in him! He let out a long, slow breath. Needing to take a walk around the camp he set off, only returning much later to their tent.

During the evening mealtime, Zarri Bano and Sikander didn't exchange a single word or look but resolutely maintained a stony silence towards one another. Zarri Bano had managed to erect an almost tangible barrier between them. Resignedly Sikander let her. Apparently, as she had said the past was indeed buried and the woman he knew with it. He recalled the evening on the beach collecting seashells in Karachi. 'When was that? Where has that carefree girl gone? Did that joyful occasion ever take place?' Sikander sadly asked himself as he looked at the woman who stead-fastly refused to acknowledge his presence in the tent although she was lying on a rug only a foot away. He was vexed for betraying and making an utter fool of himself.

Pakinaz, Ibrahim Musa and his parents came to visit Zarri Bano's parents later in the evening, but Sikander left the tent soon after they arrived.

Chapter 44

ON THE MORNING of the last day of *hajj*, a mood of melancholy and nostalgia hung over Minah, compelling some pilgrims to wonder whether they were destined to return to the plain again in their lifetime or if it was to be their last visit.

The sun beat heavily on the shaved heads of the male pilgrims as they threw pebbles at the Devil's site for the last time. In Zarri Bano's party, Sikander volunteered to throw pebbles for everyone. In the human mass of pilgrims congregating around a small site, it sometimes turned out to be a contest of the fittest and the sturdiest being able to survive the crush.

By the late morning, pilgrims and their guides had begun to gather their belongings together and to dismantle their tents. Ahead of them, they all had one important *hajj* schedule: to go to Mecca to the Holy *Kaba*, to pay their respects. Zarri Bano had visited Pakinaz's family early in the morning and exchanged phone numbers and addresses of their respective hotels in Mecca.

Coaches, buses and cars crawled along the road to Mecca. The highway was a hive of activity, with horns blaring away all day. On reaching the city, Habib's party went first to their hotel to freshen up and to deposit their belongings before they departed for the Holy Mosque. In the Holy *Kaba* they joined the throng of pilgrims in the long corridors and the large square courtyard of the mosque, to perform their final devotion.

Entering via the doorway known as 'Bab Ibrahim', their eyes met a spectacular sight. The courtyard was swollen with pilgrims. With not half a foot apart, the *hajjis* clustered around the *Al-Kaba* like a swarm of bees, the chanting sound and rhythm of their prayers resounding around the mosque.

Habib told his family to perform *umrah*, starting first with the *safa-marwa*, by walking up and down the long corridor seven times. After this ritual they rested together in the balconied corridor and watched the other pilgrims walking around the holy *Kaba* seven times.

'Mother,' Zarri Bano suggested, 'I think you should perform your *Tawaf-e-Ziarat* in the upper corridors. It will be less crowded and much cooler up there, although obviously it will take you longer.'

'Yes, I think I will do what you suggest,' Shahzada told her gratefully. 'Just look at that crowd! What about your father?'

'Oh don't be silly, I will be fine.' Habib shrugged disdainfully.

'But that crowd, Habib Sahib – how are you all going to get in? Don't, for goodness sake, try to kiss the *Hajar-e-Aswad*, the holy black stone today, Zarri Bano and Ruby.'

'No, we won't attempt it. Not today, Mother.' Ruby pulled at her father's arm. 'Come on, Father, let's go in.'

Ruby stepped down the white alabaster marble steps and advanced eagerly towards the crowd of pilgrims. Habib took hold of her hand. Zarri Bano, too, stepped down, closely followed by Sikander. He didn't touch her or hold her hand but stood directly behind her, shielding her from the crowds with his arms. They then joined the *tawaf* circumbulation, reciting *surahs* from

the Holy Quran as they walked around the black square building that was draped in a beautiful, new, gold cloth, embroidered with *surahs* from the Holy Quran, lovingly hand-stitched by hundreds of women each year.

Shahzada watched her family anxiously, standing against a marble pillar for a few seconds before turning to go up to the second floor to perform her own *umrah* where it would be less crowded.

'Are you all right, Sister Zarri Bano?' Sikander murmured into her neck, his arms held out protectively on both sides of her, preventing her from being jostled by other men.

It was the first exchange between them since their bitter outburst in Minah. Pushed from behind, Sikander grasped hold of Zarri Bano's arm and held onto it tightly. Drawing closer to him, she accepted his protection knowing that it was for her own safety.

Being very tall, Sikander kept a close watch also on Habib and Ruby. They were three rows ahead of them. Turning, Ruby caught her husband's eye and smiled. He smiled back, his eyes crinkling at the corners with pleasure.

As Ruby turned back, a nightmare began to unfold as one pilgrim suffered a heart attack and fell to the ground. Those immediately around the man, including his wife, tried to pull him up but they, too, stumbled in their turn and fell on top of him. Panic spread through the crowd like a flame. People struggled to flee and found themselves trapped in the crowd unable to go anywhere.

Zarri Bano was thrust forward, away from Sikander's side. His arm snaked out to reach her, but already three pilgrims divided them. Before his horrified eyes he saw

her disappear from sight. Then he found himself trip-
ping over the bent figure of an older Turkish woman.
He grabbed her arm and pulled her up. Panic-stricken,
she smiled her thanks – her lips trembling badly.

Helplessly carried along with the crowd, Zarri Bano
fought against her terror and tried to stay calm. A
young, strong Nigerian woman fell against her chest,
crushing her lungs. Unable to breathe and with the
instinct to survive uppermost in her mind, Zarri Bano
pushed her aside with all her strength. The woman's
face now pressed against Zarri Bano's. 'Please!' Zarri
Bano shouted in Arabic, and the woman, using her
elbows, managed to heave aside the Indonesian man
who was wedged against both of them. Finding a small
space between the pilgrims, Zarri Bano cautiously
eased herself away from the congested area. Those
around her were dispersing in all directions. The cries
and screams tore at her soul.

Clinging to a pillar, Zarri Bano anxiously scanned
the faces and heads of the pilgrims she saw below,
hoping they belonged to her loved ones. Standing on
tiptoe, and afraid of tumbling down, she leaned over to
look. 'They should be here! Where are they?' she
screamed out loud.

Miraculously, before her eyes, she saw Sikander. She
would recognise that head anywhere! He was still stuck
amongst the crowd of rioting pilgrims. 'Sikander!'
Zarri Bano found herself shouting, tears of relief pour-
ing down her cheeks.

To her joy he heard her. A look of sheer relief flashed
across his face, as he saw her standing in safety against
the tall marble pillar of the corridor. She had not
realised how dear that handsome face was, until this
moment.

'Stay there!' he bellowed, over the head of an elderly woman in a black *chador*.

Sikander knew where to go now. He pushed his way urgently between the packed bodies, ignoring the cries of protest, very much afraid for Zarri Bano's safety. She was standing against the pillar. One little shove and she could be crushed against it. To Zarri Bano it seemed like an eternity before he inched his hand slowly towards her, reaching over the shaven head of an old Bedouin. Their fingers touched. He then grabbed her whole hand in a tight grasp. The next minute he was standing directly in front of her.

His breathing ragged, Sikander looked into her eyes. 'Zarri Bano! Zarri Bano!' he whispered. 'I thought I had lost you for good!'

With rivulets of tears trickling down her face she whispered back, 'I thought when that big Nigerian woman fell on top of me, that was my last moment, Sikander.'

'I know,' he answered gravely, realising how close they had both been to death.

'Do you know where Father and Ruby are?' she asked fearfully. 'I can't see them anywhere. Please find them.'

He scanned the crowd of pilgrims swarming around the *Al-Kaba* building.

'Of course I will. But come – let's get you out of here first.' He towed her behind him into the relative safety of the large corridor. Other pilgrims too were swarming towards the sanctuary of the upper corridor.

Turning to Zarri Bano he advised, 'Stay here. I'll go and look.'

The fear of separation evident in her face and voice, Zarri Bano objected. 'No, Sikander, I want to go with you!'

He smiled tenderly down at her. 'OK,' he breathed, his hand aching to caress her cheek. His face sobered as he glanced up. 'Look, the police are going in. Where is Ruby? I must go and find her and your father.'

He couldn't mask the fear in his voice as he saw the police supervising the proceedings in the holy mosque, hurriedly pushing their way towards the scene of the tragedy. Waving their batons menacingly in front of the crowd they made pathways to the *Al-Kaba* building. With Zarri Bano by his side, Sikander went along the corridor, peering over the shoulders of the pilgrims, looking for Ruby and Habib.

As he looked at the large square-shaped central courtyard, Sikander's heart turned to stone. The policemen were carrying out the dead and the injured.

'Just stay here, Zarri Bano!' Sikander ordered her roughly, before hurrying away to see what the police were doing.

The bodies of the dead had been laid out in one section of the corridor, on the carpeted floor. Shocked pilgrims with fearful glances peered over them, unable to take in the tragedy.

On reaching the spot, Sikander looked down in dread; his gaze skipping over the faces of the victims. His heart stood perfectly still as his eyes fell on a body lying beside that of a Chinese pilgrim. He squatted down on his haunches over Habib, the man he had once hated.

Zarri Bano reached his side, peering over his bent shoulders.

'Father,' she uttered in horror. Her hand pressed to her mouth to stop the scream, she fell to her knees beside the corpse. 'Oh *Allah Pak*, no! Surely it can't be!'

With dread in his heart Sikander searched for his

wife, hoping that she wouldn't be among the dead.
Then before his stricken gaze, he saw two policemen
carrying Ruby out to the corridor.

'Ruby! Ruby!' he cried. His wife's eyes opened and
she stared vacantly at him.

Upon hearing her sister's name, Zarri Bano looked
up in hope. Leaving her father, for whom she could do
nothing, she rushed to her sister's side. But Ruby's
breathing was ragged. Her white headscarf had fallen
off. Bending down over her, Sikander felt her chest and
began to press, desperate to revive her.

'Ruby! Ruby! My darling.'

Ruby just softly uttered her son's name: 'Haris!' It
was the last word on her lips. Then her head rolled
backwards, her mouth and eyes open.

'*No-o-o-o!*' Sikander's agonised roar reached through
to Zarri Bano's numbed state. Tears blinded her gaze.

'Brother Sikander, what has happened to us?' she
sobbed, glancing at the lifeless bodies of her beloved
father and sister on the carpeted floor of the mosque
corridor. Pilgrims crowded around, staring down at
them in horror, before moving away.

Squatting on her knees Zarri Bano held her sister's
beloved face in her hands.

'My darling sister, you cannot die. We haven't fin-
ished our *umrah* yet. What about Haris? He is waiting
for you in Karachi. Oh *Allah Pak*, why wasn't it me,
instead of you? You have a son, Ruby! You cannot die!'

The policemen returned with a medical team and
lifted Ruby, Habib and other victims onto the
stretchers. Sikander clamped down on his personal
anguish, knowing he had to think and act fast. There
were the funerals to arrange. As was the custom,
pilgrims who died on the premises of the Holy Mosque

were buried in the holy city of Mecca. It was a secret dream cherished by many pilgrims, who prayed: 'Let it be there, in the Holy Mosque.'

'Zarri Bano, I must go with these men,' he told her compassionately. 'They cannot leave your father and sister here. You will need to tell your mother. Go and find her, but let her finish her *Tawaf-e-Ziarat* first. Take her to the hotel and I will meet you there later. I will also have to phone Pakistan. The funeral arrangements will take place here. You must finish your *umrah*.'

'What has happened to our loved ones, Brother Sikander?' she asked again, and turned a horror-stricken face to him. Sharing her pain and wanting to comfort her, Sikander didn't know what to say or what to do. He could barely control his own grief.

He followed the policeman out of the Holy Mosque and into an ambulance, where they had placed Ruby and Habib next to each other. Once the doors had closed, he put his head in his hands and wept.

As if in a dream, Zarri Bano watched them go. The silence after the pandemonium was deafening. Her head throbbing with the words, 'Oh my God. What am I going to tell Haris and Mother?' she quietly left the scene, remembering Sikander's instructions, telling her that she must finish her *umrah*.

Chanting the words, '*Labbaika Allahumma Labbaik*,' through chattering teeth, Zarri Bano stepped once more into the human circle going around the *Al-Kaba* building. 'How is it possible that my father and sister have already reached Allah?' she queried, brushing the tears from her cheeks.

When it was over, she climbed the steps leading to the top corridor with a heavy heart, to search for her

mother. Was it all a nightmare? she asked herself again, feeling dazed. If so, when would she wake up?

The air hostess removed the untouched trays of food from the three passengers. Zarri Bano looked out of the plane window and watched the white fleecy clouds below. Shahzada sat next to her, silent with grief. It was left to Sikander to comfort both mother and daughter, and to see to everything in the last two days. He had telephoned his own family and Siraj Din in the village – gently breaking the news to them all.

Exhausted, Shahzada finally fell asleep. Zarri Bano, sitting beside Sikander, turned a tearful glance at him. 'I am so sorry, Brother Sikander. I wish we had never come to do *hajj*.'

'No, dear sister, it was fated to happen. Get to sleep now. You haven't slept for two nights. Here, let me clean your face,' he offered, and, taking a napkin, he gently wiped her tears away, almost like a father touching a child's face.

She let him.

Then closing her eyes she slid down into her seat, unable to accept that she would never see her father or her sister ever again. Sikander dabbed at his own wet eyes with the napkin, crying inside, 'What am I going to tell poor Haris?'

He watched Zarri Bano fall asleep. Some time later, her head fell against his shoulder. Gently he moved her back onto her seat. A lock of her hair had escaped from her *burqa*, and he tucked it back into place. 'Thank you,' she murmured in her sleep. The tragedy had in a strange way drawn them into a closer bond. She trusted him with her life.

Sikander moved to an empty seat on the other aisle.

Tears of anguish for his motherless son blinded his eyes again. 'Oh Ruby! My dear wife!' he wept, closing his eyes tightly. Never to see her lovely, smiling face again! It was too much to endure.

Chapter 45

SIRAJ DIN RECEIVED the news of the death of his loved ones with a stony silence, betraying hardly a flicker of emotion on his age-creased face. Inside, however, his world fell apart. It was so unfair to have a young granddaughter and a beloved son die – all gone before him.

He immediately sent a message to Fatima, asking her to come and organise everything for the *hajjis'* arrival from Saudi Arabia, and for the guests who would be coming from all over Pakistan to mourn and pay their respects. He also summoned Naimat Bibi and Kulsoom Bibi to install themselves full-time in his home for the entire mourning period of forty days.

His thin lips issued crisp orders to his servants, but inside he was a lost man. Only years of breeding and built-in stoicism prevented him from giving in to the luxury of displaying his emotions in public and wailing out aloud, which was what he yearned to do. As a role model for the younger men in the village to emulate, Siraj Din had no choice but to cling to the tough façade he had adopted and act the part that was expected of him.

The news had travelled like wildfire across the village and the town where Habib had lived. Within an hour the household was swollen with people come to

offer their condolences. Siraj Din received them with a
simple nod of his head as he remained sitting on the
woollen mat in his courtyard. He had ceremoniously
abandoned the luxury of his *palang*.

While the men sat quietly on jute rugs in the large
courtyard, the women chanted and mourned amongst
themselves inside the rooms. Chaudharani Kaniz was
one of the first to arrive. She took it upon herself to
receive and preside over the women guests.

Annoyed with the racket coming from the women's
rooms, Siraj Din had sent word by his servants that he
didn't want any chanting in his home. 'They should
read the Holy Quran and offer prayers for my loved
ones' souls. Chanting and wailing will not help them,
but the prayers will,' he angrily instructed Fatima.

Siraj Din managed not to shed a single tear for a
whole day. That is, until later in the night when
Sikander's parents arrived with Haris in the village. It
was when he saw Haris skip in lightly through the tall
gates, pushing them wide open with childish force as
he always did with his two small hands, and then turn
to stare interestedly at all the men assembled in the
courtyard, his small mind unable to fathom what was
going on, that Siraj Din lost his grip.

Tears flooded his weather-beaten cheeks as he
embraced Raja Din.

'You have lost a daughter-in-law, my friend. I have
lost a son and a granddaughter, mother of my great-
grandchild, our precious Haris,' Siraj Din wept aloud.
'What sort of welcome are we going to offer them when
they return from their holy pilgrimage? Tell me,
my friend!' Wiping his face with a cloth, he led them to
the gathering of men sitting on the rugs in the
courtyard.

Bilkis was ceremoniously led weeping by Fatima into the large guest room where Chaudharani Kaniz made space for her by her side on the floor rug. She was trying her best to read a chapter from the Holy Quran, but her eyes flickered up every time Fatima entered the room. 'She is in her rightful place now, performing menial duties in this household,' Kaniz snorted bitchily to herself as she saw Fatima bring in a jug of water to serve to the woman who had fallen in a semi-faint while crying. That 'chit' – the so-called headmistress with her arrogant airs – had come in for a short time to offer condolences to Siraj Din's other daughter-in-law and then had left. 'Who does she think she is?' Kaniz sniffed, remembering Firdaus's appearance earlier in the day.

In exasperation Kaniz looked down again at the page of the Holy Quran. The words were beginning to swim in front of her. 'I must concentrate,' she told herself irritably. This was the third time she had lost the thread of her reading because of that woman and her daughter.

Later that evening, Zarri Bano, Shahzada and Sikander were picked up from Karachi Airport by Khawar. The whole village was now in mourning and waited for their arrival, with all the relevant rituals. No open fires or gas stoves were lit that day. Naimat Bibi's village *tandoor* remained cold and forgotten, as she supervised the cooking for the guests.

As soon as they got out of the car in Chiragpur, Shahzada and Zarri Bano ritually embraced and wept over the shoulders of the queues of women waiting to pay their respects. Outside the gates of his *hawaili* stood the bereft lone figure of Siraj Din.

'We meet you not with garlands of flowers to place around your neck, to welcome you back from the pilgrimage, but with arms held out in mourning for our beloved ones, my children,' Siraj Din cried over Shahzada's shoulder. She was drawn away by a weeping Bilkis.

Followed closely by the entourage of mourners, they all went inside. It was when Haris looked at his father and then beyond, seeking his mother everywhere and asking, 'Where is Mama?' that the walls exploded with cries and mourning chants as never heard before in the entire village. Even Kaniz's dry eyes were moist. Zarri Bano gently led her nephew away, cradling him to her body and sobbing bitterly over his head. The child simply looked up at her, unable to understand what was happening around him.

When she saw Sikander watching them, Zarri Bano's heart leapt to his in sympathy. Reaching his side she handed Haris over to him and then cried in the open arms of her Cousin Gulshan.

Inside Siraj Din's household, a large crowd of women mourners were gathered, waiting expectantly for Chaudharani Shahzada to arrive. Accompanied by Fatima, Shahzada stood uncertainly outside the house under the verandah.

'Come on, Sahiba Jee, they are all waiting to pay their condolences. You have to meet them, I am afraid,' Fatima said gently, pitying her, knowing fully well that her mistress was in no state to cope with the chanting and the wailing.

Shahzada nodded and entered the large room, emptied of all its furniture. As if her legs were shackled to heavy weights, she hovered awkwardly on the

threshold. Her eyes dreamily fanned over the white shawled heads of the women sitting around the room on the floor.

Dressed mainly in white, some were reciting *surahs* from the Holy Quran. Others were counting some holy Arabic words over the date stones and then collecting them into large basins.

On spotting Shahzada, most leapt to their feet, to offer their condolences and to pay their respects to her, as the widow of Habib Khan and Siraj Din's most respected eldest daughter in-law. Unanimously as a sign of respect, they accorded Chaudharani Kaniz the honour of rising and being the first to embrace Shahzada.

Exhausted from the plane journey, Shahzada stood woodenly in their arms, accepting their hugs, embraces, chants and tears shed on her head shawl. Finally, when the last woman had drawn away from her, Shahzada moved forward into the middle of the room. The village women looked up expectantly, wondering what Shahzada was going to do.

With a glazed look in her bloodshot eyes, Shadzada suddenly burst out with a chant of her own. There was no need to devise it. It simply erupted from her trembling lips and heart.

'Tell me, my sisters in mourning, what crime have I committed? Am I such a sinner, that Allah Pak had to punish me like this? I have lost all of my family. My beloved son Jafar, my gentle sweet Ruby and my noble husband. All gone! I must have done something bad to be punished like this – to have my beloved grandson Haris orphaned. Tell me, my sisters in mourning, how have I sinned?' Shahzada's wild gaze fixed intently on her best friend. 'I know why I am being punished,

Fatima. It is because I am such a bad wife. I didn't forgive my husband!'

'Hush! Mistress, please sit down.' Afraid of Shadzada embarrassing herself further, Fatima gently urged her to sit down on a pile of cushions, next to Chaudharani Kaniz. Fatima had not missed the sparkle of interest that appeared in Kaniz and Kulsoom's eyes, as Shahzada berated herself as a 'bad wife'.

'You have been a wonderful wife and mother, Chaudharani Shahzada,' Kaniz offered generously, giving a comforting hug to her fellow Chaudharani and rival, thus surprising all the women in the room.

'Yes, I should know. I have lived with you for nearly twenty years, Chaudharani Jee.' Fatima joined in her praise, sitting protectively on the other side of her mistress.

Shahzada turned a bewildered look at her woman helper.

'Fatima, some evil force entered my home the day Sikander and his father came here five years ago. Nothing has been the same since. I became alienated from my husband that day. My son died that very month. What happened, Fatima? I tell you, I am suffering from someone's evil eye. I was so proud of my family and my husband. Now I have no one except one daughter and she is lost to me.' Shahzada automatically reached for the comfort of Fatima's shoulder, and sobbed contritely, 'I didn't even forgive him, and Habib Sahib touched my feet.'

'Hush! Hush, Mistress,' Fatima whispered anxiously, knowing full well that her mistress was beyond caring about appearances or village gossip. It was too late anyway. Fatima shrugged cynically, seeing Kulsoom

get up. By the time the village matchmaker reached her bed that night, almost all the village homes were sure to be fully acquainted with the fact that the proud Habib Khan had touched his wife's feet! Now that was an incredible event, even to her ears, and she was part of that household.

'Allah Pak will never forgive me.' Shahzada continued her broken chant on Fatima's shoulder. Fatima saw the look on Kaniz's face and knew that the other woman resented Shahzada turning to Fatima instead of her. After all, she had so uncharacteristically reached out physically to her.

'I didn't even tell him I loved him!' Shahzada wailed, blissfully unaware of the gathering tension between the two women sitting on either side of her.

Stretching out her stiff legs on the verandah, Kulsoom decided to see how her friend Naimat Bibi was coping with the preparation of the mourning feast for the guests. As she reached the corridor leading into the large kitchen, the thought occurred to Kulsoom that at least Naimat Bibi was working in the pleasant surroundings of a well-equipped kitchen, including being blessed with an air conditioner. How many kitchens in the village, apart from Chaudharani Kaniz's, could boast one of those?

She put her head around the door, and silently watched her friend fast at work on the feast. Standing next to the large cooker and heavily stirring a pot full of meat, Naimat Bibi was oblivious of the other woman's presence. Her face was flushed, and beads of sweat were trickling down her face. As she reached for the towel to wipe them away, she glimpsed her friend in the doorway.

'When did you come in, Kulsoom?' she accused. 'You are always creeping up on me.'

'Well, Naimat Bibi, despite the sweat, you can't argue that this job is something you could do for life, especially as Baba Siraj Din is very generous. I am sure he is going to pay you handsomely.'

Hearing the trace of envy in her friend's voice, Naimat Bibi replied tartly, 'You should try cooking fifteen kilos of lamb some time, Kulsoom Jee! Your bony arms would have cracked in two with five kilos of meat, never mind fifteen. I earn every penny with my sweat, as you can see. The other cook who has been hired is a real lazy one. She has only cooked the rice and prepared the dough, and walked off leaving me with all this meat to cook, and also over a hundred chapattis to bake as well. Can you imagine her cheek?'

'She probably thinks that as you make a living out of cooking chapattis, it would be a doddle for you!' Kulsoom joked.

'*Doddle*! My grey hair! I have been slaving away non-stop since morning. The guests just keep pouring in from all over Pakistan and they all have to be fed, and on time. The breakfast is barely finished when it is time for the afternoon meal, and as soon as the dishes are cleared away it is time for the evening meal. And do you know what else?'

'What, Naimat Bibi?' Kulsoom's cheeks plumped out with laughter.

'Have you noticed how some of the villagers just seem to arrive to offer their condolences, at the time when the dinners are being served?' The old woman burst out indignantly.

'Well, if you are going to be counting rice grains on

everyone's plates, I had better get home and eat my meal there,' Kulsoom said huffily.

'Don't be silly, I wasn't talking about you. Baba Siraj Din has ordered enough food for the whole village. Seven lambs have been slaughtered. He expects everyone to eat here.'

'You should be very pleased with the work. In fact, I am beginning to wonder whether I am in the wrong business. A month of cooking here, as well as a normal chapatti-making business, would tide me over nicely. I don't earn that much in my matchmaking business,' Kulsoom Bibi stated ruefully.

'Come on, Kulsoom, I am not that simple, no matter what you think. I know very well that this mourning period is a heaven-sent opportunity for you to entice new clients into your matchmaking webs,' her old friend chided her. 'As we all know, quite a lot of marriages are arranged during this time, because with everyone gathered together it is a golden opportunity for people to cement relationships and build up rapport amongst themselves. And this is where your role comes in.' Naimat Bibi was well aware that, during the period of Jafar's mourning, Kulsoom had managed to arrange three matches, earning herself three fat fees.

'That may be so, but this time, things are different. It must be your evil eye,' Kulsoom teased her friend. 'All the women I have met so far either have married children, or they are too young or just don't happen to need my services. There are over thirty women here at the moment and I have been with them for two days, but nothing has come of it. Nobody needs any marriage arranging.' Kulsoom grimaced and sighed heavily.

'I am sorry,' Naimat Bibi offered insincerely, turning the other way to hide the smirk on her face.

'I had better get back to the gathering. Did you know Habib Khan touched his wife's feet before going to *hajj*? Now that is what I call wifely devotion.' Kulsoom's eyes were beady with mischief and speculation.

'Pity neither of us have got a husband to touch *our* feet,' Naimat Bibi tittered.

Both the friends laughed. Before Kulsoom left, she had deigned to taste two bowlfuls of meat from the two cooking pots. In recompense she had ended up rolling seventy small balls of dough ready to make chapattis as a way of helping her friend.

Zarri Bano left the room full of women, wanting to get away from them, unable to cope any longer with their dramatic mood swings. From a well-synchronised chorus of chanting and wailing on each other's shoulders one minute, the next moment they were happily gossiping amongst themselves, as to who had recently got married – how many *tolas* of gold the bride had inherited, and who had died.

She went on the verandah, and looked around, catching sight of Sikander in the far corner of the courtyard. He stood alone with his son in his arms under the grapevine. Something caught in Zarri Bano's throat. Her eyes filled with tears, aching for her sister. With her vision blurred she crossed the courtyard and joined Sikander under the tree. They stood together in companionable silence, joined by their grief. His chin on the head of his sleeping son, his eyes rested on the tears shining on her cheek.

'I am so sorry, Brother Sikander.' The words tripped over the painful lump in her throat. 'Please forgive me. I should never have let you two go to *hajj* together.

It was my idea. If Ruby had not gone, my nephew wouldn't be motherless today.'

'Don't, Zarri Bano. Please don't blame yourself or anyone. It was fated to happen.'

'If only you had been with her – by her side – I am sure you would have saved her.' Zarri Bano couldn't help voicing her regrets, nor control the fresh flood of tears as she saw his arms tighten protectively around his son.

'Don't punish yourself or me – please, Zarri Bano,' he appealed. Then his hand unable to help itself, reached out to her face, tenderly wiping the tears from her cheeks. He could never bear to see Zarri Bano cry. 'Please don't cry. We have all our lives to weep,' he whispered sadly. Then he left her standing alone as he walked out into the night, with his son in his arms. He wandered alone in the village fields, staring up at the sky, mourning for his beloved wife.

In the other corner of the courtyard, in the shadows of the verandah, Siraj Din was reclining on a bolster on his portable bed. He had watched his granddaughter standing and talking to Sikander under the tree and seen the young man's hand reaching out to her face. His green eyes glittered coldly in the night.

Later that night, when all the guests were sleeping soundly in their allocated beds, Shahzada went to pay her nightly respects to her father-in-law, before going to her own bed. He asked her to sit and talk with him for a short time.

'Shahzada, I heard your chant this evening with the women. I was not pleased. Why do you blame yourself, my dear, and say all those things about you and Habib in front of a group of village gossipmongers?'

'I meant every word, *Aba Jan*. They are all true,' she replied unrepentantly.

'No, my dearest Shahzada, they aren't true. You are being very harsh on yourself. You were a good wife – always have been. Habib did wrong by you; he threatened you with *talaks*. He was in the wrong. You were sinned against.'

'*Aba Jan*, you are very generous, but I wasn't a good wife. I am so ashamed to say I never forgave him. He even touched my feet.' She began to sob quietly. 'I will carry the burden of this guilt inside me for the rest of my life.'

'Oh Shahzada, daughter – you talk of the burden of guilt, but you don't know the meaning of the word! If you were to look through the dark window of my soul, into my heart, you would soon learn that there is a scale of sinning, and my soul happens to top the lot. In our own ways we are all sinners, Shahzada. We all carry guilt or dark secrets inside us. Your Habib just threatened you with a divorce and you were shattered, unable to forgive him. Imagine what it must be like for an innocent woman to be divorced from a beloved husband, who didn't *want* to divorce her.'

'I don't understand.' Shahzada was confused.

A bitter laugh escaped Siraj Din's mouth. 'I forced a woman to be divorced with three *thalaks* on the spot, by a husband who didn't want to divorce her. I did that! Tell me now, Shahzada – who bears the greatest burden in life? Do you think Allah will ever forgive me for all this? I sleep in fear of nightmares, of the haunted look in the wretched woman's eyes. I sometimes think my family is cursed because of her sighs and tears!'

'Who was she?'

'A beautiful young woman with long black hair.

I will tell you about her one day. All I know is that I need to see her again and ask for her forgiveness. I couldn't die without doing that. You must find her for me. I haven't seen her for twenty years.' Siraj Din's voice petered away, lost in thought. Just as she rose to leave him, he stopped her with the following words.

'I saw Sikander touch my granddaughter on her face, Shahzada.'

The words hung awkwardly between them in the night. Siraj Din with his eyebrows raised turned to look at his daughter-in-law – waiting for and expecting an explanation.

Shahzada sat down heavily on the edge of his *charpoy*. With a serious look in her eyes she explained, 'He was probably wiping away her tears, as he has been doing for the last three days. He is a very tender, caring person.' Then when she saw the speculative look beaming at her from his eyes, she added, 'Sikander cares very deeply for my daughter.' There was nothing else left in her life but honesty.

Siraj Din was silent for a long time. Eventually he asked. 'And Zarri Bano?'

A tortured laugh escaped Shahzada. She looked away into the night, at the shadows of the trees in the courtyard.

'My daughter is now too afraid, too emotionally bruised, to care for anyone. Everything she cared about and the people she loved, she lost. Now she herself is lost – to a life of religious contemplation.'

Tiredly she got up to go to bed. It had been a long, long day.

Chapter 46

FROM HER BEDROOM window on the top floor of the *hawaili*, Kaniz's forlorn gaze followed her son's white horse as it cantered out of the village. She saw Khawar stop and talk to one of the farmers near the village well. Then he took the path towards the brick-making *bhatta* complex, with its two smoke-belching kilns.

As her son disappeared from sight Kaniz's vacant stare fell on the sugar- cane crop, circling the village. Razed to the ground, the sugar cane was stacked into huge bundles, before being taken by truck to the nearest town and sold to the factories to make sugar.

Kaniz was slowly wilting away, barricaded behind a wall of humiliation. 'A full year has passed and Khawar hasn't said a single word to me!' Her piteous voice echoed around the room as she turned away from the window. Barely civil to her when they were together, at other times Khawar avoided his mother completely. The longing for one warm smile, for one kind word from him had grown deeper with each day that passed.

Kaniz tried her best to ignore the situation, but the estrangement was slowly eating her away, making her lose interest in all things, including her passion for running the *hawaili* and business accounts for the land. Kaniz's grip on normal life was fast disappearing. She cared not for films, clothes or gossip. Nor did she bother to seek suitable *rishtas* for her son. She had even stopped sniping at Neesa. In short, nothing mattered any more!

It was Neesa who noticed the gradual change in her

mistress. Happy with her lot, now that Chaudharani Sahiba was no longer quite so verbally abusive, she nevertheless cared for Kaniz's well-being and ached on her mistress's behalf. Bravely she decided to voice her misgivings to Khawar, one evening while serving him his meal.

'Khawar, my young Sahib, I am worried about your mother. She is not the same woman any more. You must spend more time with her. You are her only son,' she beseeched respectfully.

'Neesa, this is between my mother and me. Please don't presume to discuss her with me!' he admonished, standing up from the table, his meal unfinished. The subject of his mother was a thorny one. It perplexed him that his heart, instead of softening towards Kaniz, seemed to be hardening with time.

His Aunt Sabra had endeavoured many a time on her numerous visits to thaw her nephew's manner towards his mother. Like Neesa, however, she learned to her dismay that neither cajoling words nor reasoning would do the trick. He was simply unable to find it in himself to forgive her.

'Oh Sabra, Khawar and I are like two strangers,' Kaniz had tearfully confided in her. 'I want to hold my son against my chest, but I can't even look him in the eye. All I see in them is so much resentment. What have I done that is so terribly wrong that my Khawar treats me so shabbily? It's been over two years since we last had a proper conversation, can you believe it?' Kaniz's pleading tone tore at her sister's heart.

'It's all right,' Sabra soothed, embracing her sister tightly in her arms.

'That witch, Fatima, was right all along. I *have* lost my son. They have taken him away from me – if not

physically. Fatima took everything from me. My hus-
band – he was hers. And now her daughter has tricked
my son away from me.'

'No, my dear sister, she hasn't. Your son is still with
you. She has departed. It is she who doesn't want your
son.'

'I tell you, Sabra, I am going to die from this
estrangement.' Her lower lip quivering with distress,
Kaniz tried to make her sister understand the situation.
'I only have one son. I live just for Khawar. I remained a
single woman for his sake. As you know, I turned down
Younas Raees, the landowner, when I was twenty-seven
years of age. You have other children. If one doesn't
speak to you, you can easily turn to the others. To
whom shall I turn, apart from you, Sabra? I have no one
else!'

Sabra debated with herself about what she could do
to help her sister. It was time for honesty. Drawing the
other woman against her shoulder again, she whispered
compassionately, 'Then as a mother, decide with your
heart what you can do for your son.'

Feeling her sister go still in her arms, Sabra con-
tinued in the same tone, hoping that her sister under-
stood her meaning. 'Sometimes in life we have to gulp
down cups of poison for the sake of our children's hap-
piness. That is one of life's wicked dances. We may have
to deny and sacrifice our own happiness *for their sake.*'

Understanding her meaning only too distinctly,
Kaniz's heart sank in dismay and then turned to stone.
She moved out of her sister's arms and sat down heavily
on the *charpoy* on the verandah. Sabra stood and
watched her sister's reaction with disappointment, her
arms still open, telling herself sadly, 'I had to say that.'

For the remainder of the day, Kaniz refused to speak

to Sabra. Her face was stormy, signalling to everyone that 'Chaudharani Kaniz was in one of her moods'.

At night-time, Kaniz tossed noisily on her bed, her sleep disturbed with one particular dream. She was standing in the courtyard of her *hawaili*. Khawar stood on the opposite side, his face wearing a harsh expression. In the middle of her courtyard was Firdaus, a bewitching smile on her lips, her arms held out to Khawar . . . Agitated, Kaniz bit her lips together, waking up and tasting the salty blood on her tongue.

'I'll do anything to get my son back – anything! Even drink poison, as Sabra suggested. I'll even let that dreadful woman into my home!' she told the dark walls of her room, the love for her son burning through her.

Sitting up in bed, she wiped the beads of sweat from her forehead and the blood from her lips with her muslin *chador*. Leaving her room, she went up to the rooftop gallery and let the cool night air sway against her body. Feeling defeated she glanced across at Fatima's house two streets away, recalling her sister's words, 'Life's wicked dances.' Life was about to make Kaniz perform one of those dances. Restlessly she padded barefoot to and fro on the rooftop gallery of her home, lost in thought and shivering now with the night chill. When Kaniz decided on something, she never looked back.

After she saw her sister off, the very next afternoon, Kaniz told her chauffeur to get the car out. 'I am going shopping in the town bazaar,' she told him loftily.

Once they had left the village road, Kaniz directed the driver to take her to the town's local women's college. On arrival, she instructed him to wait outside the college gate for her. Finding the entrance, she went

to the reception and asked the young secretary if she could see the Vice Principal, Madam Firdaus. She was offered a seat on the comfortable chairs in the carpeted reception area, while the Vice Principal was contacted over the phone.

Kaniz waited with her heart beating a slow tattoo. Hearing steps come down the concrete corridor, she looked up expectantly.

An astounded Firdaus stood in front of her. Kaniz held her gaze steadily. Firdaus turned and was on the point of leaving the room, when the older woman's arm shot out and grasped her.

'Please wait. Don't go.' She stood up.

The hint of a plea in Kaniz's voice took Firdaus by surprise. Turning she looked pointedly down at the hand restraining her. Gently but firmly, Firdaus pulled her arm away from her visitor's grasp.

'I need to see you. Please spare me a few minutes, Firdaus,' Kaniz pleaded, her voice breaking.

Firdaus couldn't quite believe her words or the fact that the proud Chaudharani was here. Then she hardened, recalling the scene in her school office. It is because of this woman I had to abandon my school and the village, she thought angrily. Why won't she leave me in peace! Is she here to heap further abuse on my head?

'I don't blame you for fleeing from me,' Kaniz said with quiet dignity, 'but I have come so far, Firdaus, so bear with me for one minute.'

'Very well. Please come this way to my office,' Firdaus threw crisply over her shoulder at Kaniz.

Her heart growing immeasurably lighter with each step, Kaniz trailed behind Firdaus down the college's pillared verandah to her office. Everything will be all

right now, she thought contentedly. I will soon have my son back. A smile glowed on her face.

Standing aside, Firdaus politely let the elder woman step into her room. Kaniz scanned it with interest, noting the tasteful furnishings that showed the high status of its occupier. The washerwoman's daughter was indeed a Principal!

Perching herself awkwardly on the leather chair Kaniz gazed at Firdaus, sitting across from her behind the large walnut desk. Firdaus stared coldly back from behind her reading glasses, waiting for Kaniz to say her piece and wondering whether she had done the right thing in giving the detestable woman her valuable time.

Kaniz tugged nervously at the corner of her *chador*. The moment of reckoning had come, but she didn't know quite how to begin, especially in front of this woman – the 'chit'. Her son's face flashed before her eyes and made Kaniz swallow the bitter pill and do something she had vowed she would never do in a thousand years. Her mouth went totally dry. She licked her full lips.

'Firdaus, I have come to ask for your hand in marriage, for my son.' The words fell quietly and scattered around them.

The eerie silence that followed was shattered by Firdaus's shrill laughter. She couldn't believe her ears. Discomfited, Kaniz stared up at the daughter of her enemy.

'Am I to be honoured, that our gracious Chaudharani has come to ask for my hand in marriage? Certainly it cannot be because of my physical attributes, Sahiba Jee, for you have always reviled me on my colouring and height. Nor could it be because of my mother and

family, for you hate us all – as you have always made the point of broadcasting to the whole world. And now you have the audacity, the *gall*, to ask for my hand. Get you gone, Chaudharani Kaniz! I don't know what game you are playing, but I have neither the time nor the patience to join in. Moreover, I want nothing to do with you, your son, or your home – *ever*.'

'No Firdaus! Please don't say that.' Kaniz began to panic. 'Don't turn me away. I have come in good faith. I want you to become my daughter-in-law, really.'

'Really – but why? Because your son desires it?' Firdaus sneered, leaning forward in her chair.

'Yes. Yes!' Kaniz's voice broke. She hadn't bargained on this reception from Firdaus.

'Then hear me clearly. I definitely *do not want to marry your son*, Chaudharani Kaniz. Remember what I said three years ago. I wouldn't marry your son, even if you begged me on your knees.'

Desperation born out of love for her son, made Kaniz part with the last ounce of her pride, and she did now what she thought she would never do in her wildest of nightmares. Bitterly she performed one of 'life's wicked dances'. Sacrificing her pride, she went down on her knees on the carpeted floor of the office and held up her two hands in supplication to Firdaus.

Stunned, Firdaus fell back against her seat.

'I beg of you, on my knees! Come home, Firdaus, and marry my son. He loves you so much. Please forgive me. Return my son to me. I give up, he is all yours.'

Firdaus continued to gape. The spectacle of this hitherto proud and arrogant Chaudharani on the floor in front of her made her feel ill.

'Please, Sahiba, get up! I do not like people begging on their knees – especially older people. I was only

joking. What you ask for is impossible, and holding your hands up to me will not help. I am sorry, but I have no wish to do what you say. Please go!'

Firdaus held the door open, wanting to usher the older woman out of her room as quickly as possible. It was all too much for her to cope with. Kaniz stood up. Numb and humiliated, she walked out of the room, down the long corridor and out of the college. Wordlessly she let herself into her car and lay back on the seat staring into space.

She didn't utter a word on her journey back to the village. Nor did she return Kulsoom's greeting when she met her in the street outside her home. Indoors, she went directly up to her room and remained there for the rest of the day. Neesa discovered her mistress was at home by chance when she went to clean her room.

She returned, bringing a tray of food. Politely Neesa enquired what her mistress had bought from the bazaar. Kaniz didn't answer. When Neesa came to collect the tray, Kaniz was still sitting in the same position, staring vacantly into space – her food untouched. Alarmed, Neesa sent the errand boy to find Khawar, to see if he was in the fields.

When at last Khawar returned home, Neesa hurried over to him. 'Khawar Sahib, you must call the doctor! Your mother is not well. She has not spoken all evening.'

'Don't be silly, Neesa, Mother doesn't have to speak all the time.'

'No! No, Khawar Sahib, you don't understand. She is just staring into space. Please come and see.'

Khawar followed her reluctantly into his mother's room but Kaniz was in the bathroom. He immediately left and later on, forgot all about his mother.

Chapter 47

IT WAS THE holy month of Ramadhan, the month of fasting. The village mosque rang with the sound of the bell in the evening, telling the villagers that it was time to break their fast. Kaniz sat on the flat rooftop of her *hawaili*, a tray of food in front of her, not bothering to break her fast. Instead she continued to stare at the far horizon.

Neesa, returning a few minutes later with a jug of iced lemon juice, seeing her mistress sitting in stony silence with the food still untouched, was alarmed and thought it imperative to warn her Master Khawar that his mother was acting strangely again. So strangely in fact, that she hadn't even started the *Eid-ul-Fitr* shopping – a ritual that normally took her two weeks. Now there were only two *days* to go! She had made no preparation, nor sorted out the presents she distributed every year to all the young women in the village – excepting Fatima's daughters, of course.

Khawar again ignored Neesa's warning with a laugh, but then, when he happened to go up to the rooftop himself and saw his mother sitting staring vacantly, a tray of food untouched in front of her, he stopped in his tracks and Neesa's words came ominously back to him. Not having spoken to his mother on a personal level for over a year, Khawar didn't relish the prospect of having to talk to her now. He hovered awkwardly in front of her, wondering what to say and how to say it. He still had to ask her what groceries he should purchase for *Eid* from the town. The tall shadow on the sunny floor told

Kaniz that her son stood in front of her, but she felt no inclination whatsoever to lift her head and look up at him.

'Mother, the flies are all over the food! Why aren't you eating? Don't you want to break your fast?' Khawar asked at last.

Her face expressionless, Kaniz slowly lifted her head. She seemed to look right through him. Then she shifted her gaze to the marble pillar in the far corner of the rooftop, and the washing draped on the balcony wall and the green ivy from the earthen pot winding attractively around the pillars. Khawar turned impatiently on his heel and marched off. His mother was apparently sulking for some reason. That was all.

The following day, Khawar casually asked Neesa whether his mother had eaten her evening meal the previous night.

'Not a morsel!' the servant fretted. 'I am so worried about her. She fasts, yet she doesn't eat anything. You must call your Auntie Sabra. I am sure she will get her to talk and to eat. She totally ignores me. Have you seen her face? Her cheeks have gone hollow and her eyes are sunken. Look, *Eid* is around the corner. She needs to sort everything out.'

'All right, Neesa. I will telephone my auntie,' Khawar replied heavily. Now he, too, was beginning to experience pangs of anxiety. Whatever she had done the fact remained that Kaniz was still his mother.

Alarmed on her sister's behalf, Sabra promptly arrived from Lahore the following morning with her eldest daughter and her two grandchildren by plane. She had decided that the sight of the children might affect Kaniz in a pleasant way, especially as they had come to

celebrate the festival of *Eid-ul-Fitr* with her. As the children flew into her arms, Kaniz accepted their hugs mechanically. Returning her niece and sister's hugs in a similar manner, Kaniz sat down woodenly on her chair, staring vacantly into space in front of her.

Sabra exchanged a quick glance with her daughter, alarm bells ringing in her head. She beckoned to her to take the children away. Something was obviously terribly amiss here, for Kaniz hadn't even greeted them.

Sitting down heavily next to Kaniz on the sofa, Sabra put an arm around her shoulders and gave her a warm hug. 'What is the matter, *Baji Jan*? You are acting so strangely. Your son, can you believe it, phoned me last night? And I have hurried here on an aeroplane because I just couldn't bear hours of journey on a train. Khawar is worried that you are not eating anything. He tells me that you fast – but you don't *break* your fast. Nor do you talk to anybody. I can now see with my own eyes what he means, if you act like this towards your own young sister, your niece and her children,' she ended jokingly.

Her heart beating nervously, Sabra waited for Kaniz to say something. The other woman, however, continued to stare back at her with the same vacant look in her eyes.

'What is the matter, sister? Please tell me!' Sitting down on the carpeted floor of the guest room, in front of Kaniz, Sabra held the cold hands in her own and rubbed them, now very much concerned.

The sight of Sabra kneeling on the floor at once cleared the fog in Kaniz's mind. Panicking, she screamed, 'No! No! Get up from the floor!' Snatching her hands away she leaned back, her eyes horror-struck.

Thoroughly shaken, Sabra was afraid to touch her sister again. 'Kaniz, please. I'll get up, don't worry.'

Sitting back down on the sofa, she tried again. 'My dear sister, please tell me what is the matter with you.'

The seconds ticked away on the wall clock in the cool, air-conditioned guest room. At long last Kaniz swung her gaze at her sister. 'You told me to compromise, and give in. To drink poison. I have done so Sabra, and reached the ultimate degradation. I have performed one of "life's wicked dances" that you talked about. I went on the floor, Sabra. My knees touched the ground. I held up my two hands together in front of her. I begged her, but she . . .' Kaniz pinched at the crocheted lace of her *chador*, snapping the white silken thread with her nail into tiny shreds.

'Who did you beg?' Sabra demanded.

Kaniz didn't hear her sister. 'She opened the door and told me to leave.'

'*Who?*'

Moistening her dry lips with her tongue, Kaniz shot an accusing glare at her sister. Her large body shaking, hysterical laughter tumbled inside her and then spilled out of her mouth.

'You don't even know who I am talking about!' Kaniz accused in distress.

Fear gripped Sabra, a sudden thought darting into her mind. 'You don't mean Firdaus?'

Kaniz's head fell forward on her chest as the fog descended once again like a woollen curtain across her mind. Her eyes traced, with hypnotic fascination, the green peacock pattern on the silk lounge carpet.

Tears springing to her eyes, Sabra's heart swelled with overwhelming love and pity as she imagined her proud sister on the floor, begging in front of that 'chit'.

'Who told you to beg? I only meant that you should ask for her hand in marriage – I didn't want you to

beg!' Sabra cried, wiping the tears from her cheek with
her *chador*. Angrily she gathered her elder sister in her
arms. Melting in this loving tight embrace, Kaniz
finally wept too, on Sabra's comforting shoulders.

'I don't know who I am any more – tell me, Sabra.'
Kaniz's agonised voice broke between the tears, pier-
cing her sister's heart. 'Am I the village *chaudharani*, its
headwoman? Does a *chaudharani* go on her knees to a
mere slip of a girl? Do you know what it cost me to go
to her? I battered my pride for that young woman. I
drank the poison you directed me to – I gulped cupfuls
of it. I did it all. I danced to her tune. She had taunted
me about going on my knees. I did so. I went on my
knees. I, the same woman who is known to beckon
everyone around with her eyes. I, Kaniz, Queen of this
village held up my hands to her like a beggar, with a
begging bowl. I asked for *beekh* – I asked for her hand.
But she . . .' Kaniz stopped, horrified by the scene star-
ing at her in her mind. Her voice dipped to a mere
whisper. '. . . She went and held the door wide open,
telling me to go. Tell me now, Sabra, is my life worth
living? How can I respect myself? My face has been
cruelly smeared into the mud. What bigger dishonour
can one face in one's life? What more "wicked dance"
can one dance than the one I have chosen?

'She has won, my sister, in every way. I have lost my
son to her and gone crawling to her on my knees –
something that I would never have done in my wildest
dreams if it wasn't for the love of Khawar. She had said
that she would never marry my son, even if I begged
her to. Well, I begged her to. She had her wish fulfilled.
How she and her mother must be laughing!

'I hate myself, Sabra. All I want to do now, is to sink
into a mental vacuum, to dive into some deep, dark

well where I can hide for ever. Neesa keeps putting on videos for me to watch. Ironing new suits for me to wear. I have no heart for videos or clothes. Sabra, I cannot live with myself and with what I have done! Help me, please!' Kaniz twisted out of her sister's arms and rushed, maddened, from the room.

Sabra stood, shaken and dismayed, in the middle of the room, Kaniz's words ricocheting around her head. Then she went after her, hoping to persuade her to eat something, and ease her anguish.

Kaniz was standing in her bedroom, a glass of water in one hand and the other hand cupped tightly.

Catching sight of a bottle of tablets on the dressing table, fear lent wings to Sabra's feet. She flew to her sister's side, clawing the tablets away from Kaniz's tight-fisted palm. Falling on the marble floor, they rolled under the bed.

'Oh God! What are you doing, Kaniz?' Sabra screeched. 'Khawar! Bano! Neesa! Please everybody come!'

Hearing the commotion, Neesa came running into the room.

'Call Khawar and the doctor immediately!' Sabra ordered, and Neesa ran to do her bidding.

Panic-stricken, Sabra's heart thumped away behind her ribcage. What was happening to them? This was the worst scenario she had ever envisaged. Her sister on the point of committing suicide! It was unthinkable!

Drawing Kaniz tenderly against her body as if she would never let her out of her arms ever again, she asked, 'Why, sister, why?' in a voice hoarse with emotion.

'I have nothing. Everything has been snatched from me.' Kaniz lifted her pain-glazed eyes to the other woman. 'No son, no self-respect – nothing. I am just an

arrogant, evil, middle-aged bully. That is how everyone
sees me. My mirror delights in winking a tarnished
picture at me. I cannot disregard it any longer, Sabra.
My life is simply not worth living!'

'No, you are not an evil woman. That is ridiculous!
Now listen to me, Kaniz,' Sabra said firmly, taking
charge of the situation. 'As Allah is my witness, I am
not going to let you out of my sight or allow anything
to happen to you. I promise you, you will have your son
back and that Firdaus – that "chit" – will beg your
forgiveness. Your self-respect will return. Do not ever –
I repeat, *ever* – contemplate doing anything so stupid
again. My beloved sister, don't you know that in our
faith it is *haram* to commit suicide? No one has the
right to take their life!' Sabra took a deep, shuddering
breath.

'Firdaus is not worth committing suicide for,' she
said quietly. 'She is just a foolish young woman who
didn't appreciate what it had cost you to beg in front of
her. You triumphed over your pride and I am so proud
of you. She is a petty-minded, hard-hearted person.'
Sabra pressed kisses over her sister's face, sweeping her
hair lovingly back into place. They remained locked in
a tight embrace for long poignant minutes.

After supervising Kaniz's meal herself, Sabra put her
sister to bed and stayed with her until she fell asleep.
Unable to find Khawar, Neesa sent the errand boy for
the local doctor.

When Khawar came home later in the evening, the
doctor had already been and gone. Sabra had hovered
anxiously by the bedside while he examined Kaniz and
asked her questions about her health.

Gesturing to Neesa to stay with Kaniz, Sabra took
the doctor to the guest room.

'I am worried about her, Doctor sahib,' she burst out. 'My sister was about to swallow a whole bottle of tablets before I happened to come by chance into the room.'

'She is suffering from what I think is an acute form of depression of some sort. Something is bothering her, apparently, and it goes deep. She needs a lot of support from you and the rest of her family.'

Sabra listened quietly, nodding her head in agreement. Love for her elder sister made her start to cry again. She didn't care about breaking down in front of the doctor. She promised herself that she would not leave her sister's side until she got better.

'It is time to bring the animosity between mother and son to an end.' Sabra spoke firmly to Khawar. 'It has nearly cost my sister her life!'

As soon as Khawar walked in, Sabra had begun her verbal assault.

'Do you realise, my arrogant nephew, that your mother is mentally a very sick woman? Earlier today she tried to commit suicide!' Here, Sabra faltered, but gained control of herself. 'She doesn't talk or eat – as you very well know. And I blame *you*! What sort of a son have you become? Are you so lovesick over Firdaus that you callously neglect your own mother? My sister may have her faults, but she doesn't deserve this sort of treatment!

'She has been pining for your affection for so long, and finally she did something that I personally couldn't imagine her doing in a hundred years. But she did it for your sake, Khawar! She went to Firdaus and begged for her hand – on her knees! Can you believe that?' Sabra ended, her dark eyes glittering coals of angry fire.

'What! What nonsense is this, Auntie?' Khawar demanded, unable to make sense of what his aunt was telling him.

'Surprised, are you? And do you know what that horrible woman did, she opened the door and told your mother to get lost and said that she would never marry you! Can you begin to comprehend the extent of the humiliation your mother has suffered, the depths to which she has sunk? Can you imagine it? On the floor! Your mother – holding up her hands to the daughter of a woman she has always hated.'

'Why did she do it? I didn't tell her to,' Khawar lashed out sulkily, his nostrils flaring in rage as he listened to his aunt's account of the disgraceful incident. Repentant and guilty he immediately went to his mother's quarters where, worn out, Kaniz was fast asleep. Sitting near her bed, Khawar watched over her for most of the evening.

Early next morning, Sabra kept a vigil over her sister, reassuring Khawar that she was going to stay until her sister recovered her normal spirits. Offering special prayers for Kaniz's health, Sabra promised herself that she would have her sister's sparkling, albeit waspish, self back in place by the time she had finished with her. Her daughter and grandchildren she sent back to Punjab the following day.

Khawar accepted his aunt's help gratefully. All night while he had sat watching over his mother, his thoughts turned to Firdaus. 'How dare you do this to my mother? I will see to you!' he vowed, his jaw stiff with rage.

Chapter 48

TWO DAYS LATER, Khawar paid a surprise visit to Firdaus's college. He was taken directly into her office and told: 'The Vice Principal is in a meeting, but she will join you soon.'

Khawar glanced around the opulent furnished room. For some reason, he did not relish seeing Firdaus here, on her own territory. Returning to the college reception, he informed the young smartly-dressed secretary that he preferred to wait outside and would therefore be grateful if Madam Firdaus would see him there. When asked who he was, 'Tell her an acquaintance from the village,' Khawar said shortly. He followed the secretary out of the building to the semi-secluded verandah.

Declining to sit down, he leaned against the tall stone pillar and looked out at the green hockey lawn.

'*Assalam-Alaikum*!' A voice he recognised broke into his thoughts a few minutes later. His shoulders stiffening, Khawar took his time in turning round. When Firdaus saw his expression she blinked in shock. His eyes stared unsmiling at her. His body, though giving the appearance of lounging indolently against the pillar, was a tight coil ready to spring on her.

'To what do I owe this pleasure?' Firdaus asked politely, her eyes on his shirt collar. Afraid, somehow, to meet his glance again.

Khawar lifted his eyebrow at her innocent question.

'The pleasure is all on your part, Madam Principal. For I experience none in being here in your company.' Firdaus paled at his insolence. Then, to her astonished

gaze, Khawar stooped down theatrically on his knees and held up his two hands together in front of her. Shocked, Firdaus jerked back.

'Khawar Sahib, what drama are you playing?' she asked, bemused.

'I am replaying the drama with you and my mother in it, Madam Principal,' he jeered. 'That is what my mother did, isn't it? She held up her hands to you like a beggar with a begging bowl – *didn't she*? My proud mother! The Chaudharani! One who has never been known to apologise to anyone, let alone *beg* from someone. Well, she fell from the lofty sky to your lowly feet, pleading for your hand, didn't she?'

'I never asked her to. I didn't want her to beg.' Firdaus's quiet retort hit back at him.

'But you threw her out, didn't you?' There was a dangerous thread of steel in his voice.

Cornered. 'Yes, I did! So what?' Firdaus screeched, now unable to hold on to her temper or her dignity.

'Well done!' Khawar cried, his mouth twisting in a sardonic smile. Getting up he clapped his two hands together, the sound vibrating strangely in her ears. 'That is definitely the sort of treatment my mother deserves – so much so that after she had left you, she tried to commit suicide!' he finished bitterly.

'What?' Firdaus's head shot up.

'Yes, Firdaus Principal. Her death would definitely have been laid at your door.'

'I do not know how your mother's mind works, but please don't use me as a scapegoat.' Shrinking from the look of raw loathing in his eyes, Firdaus tried to defend herself, her lips quivering in anger and distress.

'You may not know my mother's mind, but I know mine well enough. She must have been insane to resort

to begging for your hand. You are not worth it, Firdaus. For your sake I shunned my mother and left my home. I haven't spoken to her for over a year. In desperation she swallowed her pride and stooped this low. I tell you this because for someone of my mother's stature, it is indeed a noble gesture. But she got nothing in return from you, did she? Just dishonour. Because of you, she is now suffering depression, crying all the time, not eating anything and staring into space. She has wanted to put an end to her life.'

'I am sorry,' Firdaus said tritely, her eyes lowered to the ground.

'I haven't finished yet.' His voice sliced through her. 'In the end you have proved yourself worse than my mother. I do not wish to marry someone who has no respect for my mother. You are a cold-hearted and a proud woman. I am a fool for having wasted years over you. At the end the gold I thought I was chasing was all the time brass. Dross, in fact! But then in your book, in your elevated stature as a principal of a college, Madam Firdaus, *we* are the brass, the village bumpkins from whom you were so desperate to escape. Well, you are free from us all now, Firdaus. We will not be troubling you ever again. Good day to you! Madam Principal.'

Stunned, Firdaus watched him leave. The colour had long since flown from her face. Shakily, she sat down on a chair on the verandah, her mind ablaze with thoughts, her heart thudding with shock.

Khawar disappeared through the double doors leading into the college corridor. With angry strides he reached his Jeep. The driver quickly opened the door for him and, seeing his master's thunderous expression, forbore from attempting to make small talk.

Khawar's spirits were low. The episode of his desire

to marry Firdaus was over. It would take him a long time to recover, but his masculine pride was at stake. 'She is welcome to those urban *Sahibs* who probably flock to her side every evening,' he scoffed inwardly, then dismissed her from his mind.

Chapter 49

ZARRI BANO HAD taken Haris to the village to visit her grandfather and to familiarise him more with village life. Siraj Din loved to hear the chatter of his great-grandson in his *hawaili*.

Arriving on Friday to take Haris back to Karachi, Sikander hid his disappointment at not seeing his son. Sitting out on the verandah of the rear courtyard, Shahzada and Sikander talked generally for some time and about Haris in particular. The young man wondered how best to approach the subject he had had on his mind for the last few months.

'Auntie,' he uttered softly, avoiding her gaze, 'I hope very much that you will not be offended by what I am going to say.'

'What is it, my son?' Shahzada looked up in concern, placing the rose china teapot on the white wrought-iron patio table in front of her.

'I . . . I wish to marry your daughter, Zarri Bano!' Shahzada darted a quick look at him, her eyes wide with surprise. 'I know she is a Holy Woman,' Sikander went on before she could say anything, 'but I also know that Uncle Habib Khan, over a year ago, released her from the oath never to marry. He personally gave her his blessing to marry if she so wished. Ruby told me all this.'

It was a very pleasant surprise for Shahzada. A smile curved the contours of her lower face but words failed to leave her mouth. Sikander waited anxiously and then hastened to explain.

'I do not mean to offend you, Auntie. Please will you forgive me? You must appreciate that it is for Haris's sake. I need a surrogate mother for him. This to-ing and fro-ing from Karachi to here will have to stop some time. It is tiring me out. It has been going on for over a year. I want my son with me, but he is also very close to his aunty and you. He regards Zarri Bano as his second mother. If I were to marry her, that would solve everything, wouldn't it?' His voice was earnest.

'I am not at all offended by your suggestion, my dear son. Nothing would give me greater pleasure than to have my Zarri Bano happily married and also to become a mother to Haris. I am keenly aware of your situation. At the end you have to remarry some time. I am just surprised it hasn't been sooner. But tell me, my son, why do you want to marry Zarri Bano? She is not the same woman as the one you saw five years ago. Are you really marrying her entirely for Haris's sake, or for personal reasons?' This time Shahzada's gaze remained steady on his face.

Sikander looked down at the cup he was holding, letting his fingers trace its gold rim. He took his time in answering, but finally opted for honesty.

'I will not pretend to you, Auntie, it is very much for personal reasons. I do not know how to talk about this to you. After all, you are the mother of my dead wife.' He sighed sadly. 'All I can say in my defence is that I want to marry Zarri Bano very much – just as I wanted to marry Ruby. I have loved both of your daughters. I don't know how it was possible to love both sisters, but

I have and did. Please do not get me wrong. Zarri Bano is the one I wanted to marry originally, but it was Ruby that I ended up with.

'I can truthfully say that Ruby and I were very happy together. I loved her as deeply as it is possible for any husband to do so, when you have shared four years of life together. The love just grew with time. The place she has in my heart will always be there. She was the mother of my child, the woman I shared my life with, twenty-four hours of the day. How can I forget her? If I close my eyes, I can still see her before me with her warm brown eyes and gentle smile.' Shahzada watched Sikander's face fold with the pain. His eyes closed as he continued.

'I can still hear her footsteps on the marble stairs or in the orchard. Her clothes, still hanging in the wardrobe, bring forth aching memories every day of the week. I miss Ruby so very much, Auntie – but she has gone. I cannot bear the thought of a strange woman with my son. No other woman could be his mother in the way Zarri Bano can. He simply adores his Auntie Zarri Bano and she adores him in return. There is a chance that with her at his side, he will not ache for his own mother so much.'

'Yes,' Shahzada agreed quietly.

'You asked if I want to marry Zarri Bano for personal reasons? Well I do, and not just for Haris's sake. I am being totally honest with you. As you well know, Zarri Bano is the woman I originally intended to marry, the woman I fell in love with at first sight. It was at the *mela* . . . ' His eyes softened, as he recalled the instant.

'She was standing under a tree in a black chiffon outfit, her hair swinging free around her face, and then she caught sight of me. Something happened between

us. Across the crowd of men gathered at the fair, our souls seemed to leap to one another. She looked so breathtakingly beautiful. I was a lost man. Nothing like that had ever happened to me before. It was not the same with Ruby, I am sorry to say. I knew from the first moment that Zarri Bano felt something for me. She has always attempted to deny it, but I know she did. The rest is all history. It was too late for us, another life was carved out for Zarri Bano by your husband. I am laying bare my soul to you, Auntie. I haven't even come to terms with it fully myself – because it is such a personal and a painful topic.' There were tears in his eyes as he spoke of these secret matters of the heart.

'In all those years, I never forgot Zarri Bano,' he told Shahzada. 'I tried, but she was always there in my head and thoughts, haunting me. In Saudi Arabia, I was out of my mind with jealousy because of that bearded Egyptian. I couldn't bear the thought of him looking at her or being linked to her in any way. I have also hated her, too,' he confessed in a low voice. 'I have still not forgiven her for turning her back on me and our love.'

He looked imploringly at his mother-in-law. 'I have undergone the bad *kismet* of loving not just two women but also two sisters, married to one but still aching for the other. As their mother, I don't know what you will think of me.'

'Thank you, my son, for being so honest.' Shahzada was deeply moved. 'I am very aware of how painful and embarrassing it is for you to confide your feelings to me, but you have proved to me the true feelings you have for both my daughters. You are right, I do not know how I ought to feel on this topic because they are both my daughters, born from the same womb. I am glad, my son, for your sake, for Haris's sake, for Zarri

Bano's sake above all that you wish to marry my eldest daughter. As a grandmother of Haris, I would wish no other woman to take my dead daughter's place.'

Now it was time for Shahzada to bare her soul to Sikander. 'But it is not just for Haris's sake,' she said. 'I have been plagued by guilt since the day Zarri Bano became a *Shahzadi Ibadat*. I wanted her to marry you and lead a normal life. She says that she is very happy with her current life, but in my heart of hearts, I know we did wrong both by you and especially by Zarri Bano. The day she learned that Ruby was going to marry you, I will never forget the look in her eyes, Sikander. It was the look of a woman devastated and toppling over the edge of reason. I saw my daughter nearly die before my eyes, but she battled with herself and won. My Zarri Bano always does. I am so proud of her. She is good in overcoming and facing crises, but at what cost? We'll never know. We have killed her emotionally in the process.' For a moment, Shahzada allowed her feelings to overwhelm her. Sikander remained quiet, instinct telling him to let his mother-in-law take this moment at her own pace.

'Until the day we went on *hajj*, I never forgave my husband,' she continued. 'Sikander, the day my Jafar died, all our lives became shrouded by a *chador* of doom. I supported my husband, yet I betrayed my daughter. Now you tell me, my son, how can I forgive myself for betraying Zarri Bano? I was helpless to do otherwise. There was no way out for us two women. No way of defying my father-in-law and my husband's joint decision. We are proud, yet obedient women, and for our clan's sake, we bowed and gave in.

'You must forgive her for turning you away. She simply had no choice, Sikander! Zarri Bano makes

herself out to be happy and has forgiven her father. She has found a new lease of life in her adopted identity and has discovered a new world on an international scale. My daughter admirably suits the role. I, on the other hand, lost respect for both myself and him. I built a wall against my beloved husband that he could never batter down. My heart became a cold shell. Empty! He could batter away, and did so – but all to no avail. I knew he was lonely – but I couldn't bring myself to forgive him. That is my bad *kismet*, my son. I wish that I hadn't been such a cruel wife to him.

'If you were to peep inside my heart, you would see nothing but heartache and suffering. Two of my beautiful children have died. I have lost a husband, and my grandson is motherless.

'Therefore, dear boy, nothing would give me greater pleasure than to have you marry Zarri Bano. I want my daughter to lead a normal life, the life that she was denied five years ago. I want to see her hands painted with henna patterns, a young baby in her lap. All the dreams I cherished for her, I want to come true. Let me speak to her first, my son. I need to break it gently to her. For you see, she now has no place for marriage or men in her heart nor in her mind.'

Chapter 50

ZARRI BANO DIDN'T return that evening. She sent a message that her grandfather Siraj Din wanted her and Haris to stay a couple more days in Chiragpur. Finding the quietness of the house unbearable, Shahzada decided to join them in the village.

When her mother arrived, Zarri Bano was alone in the drawing room of their village family home. Delighted, she hugged Shahzada warmly.

'Where is Haris?' Shahzada asked, desperate to hold her dead daughter's son in her arms.

'He has gone for a walk with his great-grandfather. He is probably having a ride on the tractor in the fields or playing around and swinging the tails of the milk buffaloes on our farm. He loves it here, Mother. It is good for him with all the fresh air and open fields. The village women adore him, taking him in turns to their houses. He has been invited twice to Chaudharani Kaniz's house.'

'I can well imagine. Our Haris is a gorgeous child. The village women used to do that to you when you were young. So you have decided to stay for a couple more days.'

'Yes. Grandfather keeps insisting that we should all move back here in the village. He wants me to head the village *madrasa* that he and I are opening for young women to receive high quality religious education.'

'I know he does, darling, but he can't have his way, I am afraid. Haris already has a home in Karachi, with his father. We are being too selfish in keeping him with us all the time. By the way, Sikander came last night to collect Haris, and he was quite disappointed not to see him.'

'Well, he could have come here to visit us,' Zarri Bano answered sharply.

'He had to go. You see, he gets tired with all the travelling. He'll be returning in two days' time. Or perhaps we could take Haris back to Karachi. It has been so long since I have been to that big city and visited its shopping plazas.'

'I cannot go, Mother. You take him, if you like. I am quite happy here in the village. In fact I am thinking of taking up Grandfather's suggestion and setting up a *madrasa* here.'

'Could you really spend your whole life here, Zarri Bano? You are a city girl – I thought you didn't like the country scene?'

'I don't know. It is so peaceful here, Mother. I have travelled a lot in the past few years and got it out of my system. I now want some peace in my life. Also the women here need me. I am training one of the teachers from Firdaus's school to head the *madrasa*.'

'What if you were to marry, Zarri Bano?' Shahzada softly slipped in. She had been on the lookout for such a cue.

The book from which she had been making notes for the seminar fell from Zarri Bano's hands with a thud on to the marble-chip floor.

'Mother!' Zarri Bano stared at Shahzada as if she had taken leave of her senses.

The ceiling fan purred away above them, the only audible sound in the room. Leaning back against on the soft cushions of the sofa, Shahzada calmly watched her daughter. Zarri Bano was sitting on an armchair, opposite her mother.

Shahzada leaned forward, her eyes steady on Zarri Bano's face. 'To Sikander!' she added in a low, even voice.

Zarri Bano gaped, speechless. Surely she had mis-understood? Her mouth opened and then closed.

'For Haris's sake, my daughter,' Shahzada quickly explained, dismayed at her reaction.

The notebook lying on Zarri Bano's black *burqa*-clad

lap also fell to the floor as she stood up. So she hadn't misheard!

'Mother, how can you say this?' Her body was shaking, and her eyes glazed with pain. 'I am a Holy Woman. Marry my dead sister's husband, you say? Have you no feelings or respect?' Zarri Bano clamped one hand to her mouth and the other on her stomach, as nausea spiralled up to her throat and her abdominal muscles heaved.

Before Shahzada's bewildered eyes, Zarri Bano ran out of the room and out into the open courtyard, where she stood gulping fresh air into her lungs. She was trembling like a leaf.

Back in the house, Shahzada slumped wearily in defeat. If that was her daughter's reaction to her suggestion, it didn't seem likely that Zarri Bano would ever marry Sikander. Who, then, would become stepmother to her beloved grandson? Sadness overwhelmed Shahzada, shattering all her hopes at one go.

Looking ahead at the clear blue horizon, Zarri Bano walked alone on the narrow, tuft-lined path through her grandfather's fields. The wind teased and billowed her black *burqa* around her body. The words burned themselves into her mind. 'Marriage! To Sikander!'

The vision of herself, Ruby and Sikander, set her stomach churning again. This time, she couldn't hold back the waves of nausea. Wiping the beads of sweat from her forehead with her handkerchief, she walked on.

She reached the village well, where Khawar, Firdaus and she used to play together as children and throw small stones down into the water. Sitting on the brick ledge of the well, she shouted, 'Never! Never!' down

into the dark pool of water. The words echoed against the damp brick-lined wall of the well. 'I smothered and killed the wanton woman that you drew out of me, Sikander. She bled for you. Never again!' Getting off the well ledge, Zarri Bano walked towards her grandfather's farm. Listlessly she walked around the hen pens, watching the milk buffaloes tied to their iron posts, munching away at the green fodder placed before them in purpose-built wooden troughs.

When she returned to the *hawaili* much later, she saw her mother sitting and chatting to her grandfather. Shahzada quickly inspected her daughter's face, noting her closed expression and refusal to return her mother's smile.

Wordlessly, Zarri Bano went to the bathroom to cleanse herself for the afternoon prayers. Even during her prayer sequence, she couldn't keep her mother's words at bay, or the unwelcome images they conjured up.

Later Shahzada joined her daughter and, with her heart tripping over, she got ready to try again. I have to, for everyone's sake, Shahzada told herself vehemently. Reaching forward to take hold of Zarri Bano's hand, she rubbed the back of it gently with her own. She looked at her daughter's soft skin with pleasure and pride – they had never known the kitchen sink.

'Is it so bad, such a sacrifice, to become a mother to your orphaned nephew that the mere mention of it leads you to flee from the *hawaili*?' Shahzada gently reprimanded.

'Mother, not again!' Zarri Bano appealed, closing her eyes tightly. 'Please do not say anything more.'

'Why not?' Shahzada queried incredulous.

'Have you forgotten?' Zarri Bano hissed. 'I am a

pakeeza woman. How can you thus suggest marriage to me? And with my own sister's husband!' Anger danced in her emerald-green eyes.

'Remember that your father has released you from that oath.'

'How convenient of you to remind me now, Mother. Now that it suits all of you, I am asked to marry. Do you think I am a wax doll, a *phutley*, that you can mould to dance to your tune when and however it suits you? *I am a human being!* A woman who can never contemplate wedlock!

'Now you are requesting that I should forget all of that and marry who? A man who has had a physical relationship with my sister for four years. Am I a vege-table, on a market stall, then, that Sikander can swap for another? Have you no sensitivity, Mother, no ink-ling of what you are suggesting? I cannot marry any man. And above all not Sikander! Never, Mother, *never!*' she hurled at Shahzada, her cheeks throbbing with red-hot colour.

'I understand how you are feeling, my darling, but you will change, you'll see. We are thinking mainly of Haris.'

'Yes, I can see you are thinking mainly of Haris. I will never change, Mother, I can assure you. You, Father and Grandfather transformed me the day you made me into a Holy Woman. There is no turning back for me now. I can live no other life. If you want me to be blunt, I will be, as long as you understand that the topic is closed and never to be opened again. I am a religious woman, therefore I could never, I'll be immodest and say it, sleep with any man! Let alone one who has already had an intimate relationship with my sister. That you expect me to slot into Ruby's place fills me

with horror and revulsion. You must never again use Haris to blackmail me.'

Agitated, Zarri Bano withdrew her hand out of her mother's grasp. Rising to her full height, she left the room, her black *burqa* swishing angrily around her body. Shahzada remained huddled on the prayer-mat, a forlorn figure. Going by the intensity of Zarri Bano's feelings and words, there appeared to be no chance of her ever marrying Sikander.

Her daughter was right, of course. They could no longer force her to do anything. As a mature adult, she knew what was right for her. 'Except she doesn't,' Shahzada sighed. 'How does she know what marriage and life is like with children and a partner? She has never experienced it, or tasted that life, but she has conditioned her mind against it.'

Shahzada sadly accepted the fact that her daughter had indeed become a real *Shahzadi Ibadat*. And in the process had truly bartered away her womanhood. The role she had recoiled from in horror five years ago, she had now taken to whole-heartedly and with a lifelong commitment.

That evening, Fatima came to visit her Chaudharani Shahzada. Both were very pleased to see each other, and hugged warmly.

'How is your family, Fatima? I'll come to visit them soon. How is Fiaz?'

'He is fine, Chaudharani Sahiba.'

'And what about Salma's *rishta*? How far have you got with that?'

'Well, Kulsoom our village matchmaker and I have been to see the boy and met his family. They are really nice people, Chaudharani Sahiba. They have come to

meet Salma. We are all pleased with each other. They came again and placed a *segan* for her hand in marriage. My Salma and the boy have been introduced and apparently got on very well. As you can see, I am going to be very busy with Salma's forthcoming wedding. I'll definitely need to pick your brain.'

'I am delighted for you, Fatima. Of course I will help you. If only my Zarri Bano were to get married to Sikander.'

'Have you mentioned it to her?'

'Yes I have, but she is totally against the idea.'

'Shall I have a word with her, Chaudharani Sahiba?'

'You can try. But she is like a heavy rock that will not be moved. Do you know, Fatima, she actually found the suggestion nauseous. It is not so strange, is it? It is not the first time that men have married the sister of their dead wife. It is mainly for the children's sake, of course.'

'Of course, it is so convenient for everyone,' Fatima quickly agreed. 'Especially for the husband and the children. The husband, because he has peace of mind, knowing that his children's stepmother will look after them well, by virtue of her being an aunt. The children, because they can relate to an aunt, who is like a second mother. So all round, it would be so beneficial for Zarri Bano to marry Sikander. But it is not just for Haris's sake. I personally believe they were fated for one another. I have always wanted my princess to marry Sikander, just as I always wanted Firdaus to marry Khawar. Do you know, Chaudharani Sahiba? I have still not been able to forgive Habib Sahib for what he did. Even though he is dead . . .' Fatima abruptly stopped, feeling embarrassed.

'It is all right, Fatima,' Shahzada said sadly. 'I have

only just learned to forgive him myself. But you must also realise that he wasn't the only one to be blamed. The other person behind it was my father-in-law, Siraj Din. He was the one who started the whole affair.'

'If that is the case, why don't you have a word with him, Chaudharani Sahiba? See if he can persuade Zarri Bano. I will try to talk with her myself.'

After dinner, Fatima left. Zarri Bano didn't dine with them as she had eaten earlier with her grandfather and nephew.

Fatima chose her moment with care. It was two days since her chat with Shahzada. Zarri Bano was sitting with her nephew in her lap, smoothing with loving strokes his hair from his forehead, as she watched a TV drama serial in the lounge.

'Beautiful, isn't he?' Fatima sat down next to Zarri Bano.

'Yes, he's like our Ruby.' Sorrow flitted across Zarri Bano's features.

'He could easily pass as your son, my dear. You two girls were so alike. However, he is like his father too and Sikander is very good-looking. It takes two to make a child's looks. I don't know what will become of Haris once his father remarries . . .' Fatima waited for a response from Zarri Bano. When none was forthcoming, she bantered on. 'Sikander is bound to remarry. It is very difficult for men to stay widowed for long. My mother always said that most men remarried even before their wives were cold in their grave. It's been a year since Ruby died. If not for themselves, men end up marrying for their children's sakes. That is the excuse they always give, of course, although we know otherwise. So my mother told me. Celibacy is a

problem for all of them.' Fatima stopped in embarrass-
ment. She could have bitten out her tongue for carrying
on in such a vulgar vein. This was Zarri Bano, the *pure*
one – the Holy Woman, she was talking to.

'Why are you talking about Brother Sikander,
Fatima?' Zarri Bano ventured to ask.

'I just wondered what will happen to Haris when he
marries again,' the other woman offered lamely.

'Haris can stay with us, as he is doing now. Good-
night, Fatima.' And Zarri Bano neatly ended their
conversation, having astutely surmised the direction it
would take.

Chapter 51

OFTEN, AT NIGHT-TIME, a group of five older
village men came to visit and pay their respects to
Siraj Din. Carrying their hookahs in their hands, they
strolled into the *hawaili* courtyard and stayed long into
the night chatting away. With their hookah topped up
with fresh tobacco by Siraj Din's servants, and with
delicious sweetmeats to eat and nuts to chew with their
old teeth, the village elders peppered the marble court-
yard with the pistachio shells, studiously ignoring the
plates placed near them. Why bother with plates, when
the floor was going to be swept and washed early in the
morning? They enjoyed the friendly banter amongst
themselves and listening to Baba Siraj Din's ideologies
and tales of old India. How, for instance, Siraj Din and
his family had fled to Sind in Pakistan and started a
new life after Partition.

Under the cool breeze of the ceiling fan Shahzada sat

at a discreet distance on a *charpoy* away from the men,
hidden in the shadows of the tall potted plants on the
verandah. She listened unobtrusively to their lively
conversation. When she saw them leave, strolling out of
the courtyard with their hookahs held in front of them,
Shahzada dutifully went up to Siraj Din, to ask if he
needed anything before she went to sleep.

'*Aba Jan*, shall I bring you a fresh hookah? I'll pre-
pare it for you myself.' She volunteered her service,
although the servants usually performed this task.
Standing next to his portable bed in the courtyard, she
drew her cashmere woollen shawl tightly around her
shoulders and head as a sign of respect to the old man.
Siraj Din had never seen her bare-headed – a fact he
acknowledged to himself and boasted about to others
with much delight.

'No, my daughter. What I do desire, however, is your
company. Sit down, my dear – here, near me.' Siraj Din
curled his long legs up beneath him and made space on
his *palang* for Shahzada to sit.

'It is so nice to have you all here, Shahzada. I wish
you and Zarri Bano could stay here for all time. It
reminds me of the old days, when you used to live here
and this place was alive with people and children.
There was so much going on – your mother-in-law
Zulaikha was still alive then. Do you know, I can still
remember Zarri Bano and Ruby, may she reside in
Jennat, fighting together, pulling each other's hair, in
this very courtyard. Zarri Bano always had a problem
covering her head,' he chuckled. 'Ah well. It is five
years since I have seen her hair now. How things have
changed!' His mood altered. 'Sometimes, Shahzada, I
feel so sad that I am still alive. It is almost like a pun-
ishment. It is not fair to lose young grandchildren and a

son – all gone. I feel so sorry for you, my daughter. You have lost them all. Husband, son and daughter.'

'Yes, I have lost them all,' Shahzada agreed quietly.

'You looked very sad today. I note everything, Shahzada, my daughter. I may be getting old but nothing misses these eyes. Is everything all right?' She was touched by the marked concern in his voice. He leaned forward, pulling the long hookah pipe to his mouth and puffing on it, but his eyes were on his daughter-in-law's face – carefully surveying her. She looked down.

'I am all right,' she finally offered, with a sigh.

Dissatisfied with her answer, Siraj Din reckoned that it was an appropriate time to refer to the matter that had cut his family adrift.

'You never forgave my son Habib for making Zarri Bano a Holy Woman, did you? He died a sad and a lonely man. Therefore, how can you forgive me, your father-in-law, the one who encouraged and supported him.'

Shahzada pretended ignorance. 'I don't know what you are talking about, *Aba Jan*,' she replied.

'Shahzada, my dearest of daughter-in-laws. Why do you dissemble? If you hate me for making Zarri Bano a Holy Woman, then have the courage to show your hatred. Shout at me, if that is what you want to do! But do not dam it up inside you! I have committed a crime against you. Don't make it worse for me by being too nice. This battered old heart still has space and the strength to hear your screams and curses, if that is what your heart and lips crave to utter.' Siraj Din's eyes gazed tenderly down on Shahzada's shawled bent head. Waiting patiently for her to say something, he pulled the hookah pipe to his mouth again.

'I am over fifty years old, *Aba Jan*,' Shahzada uttered

in a clear voice, raising her dull eyes to him. 'A
grandmother, but still I have had the training, the
upbringing to know that I must respect you for all
time. Therefore, how can I scream and curse even if I
wanted to? I have been a dutiful and dumb prisoner of
female etiquette for so long, how can I now open my
mouth to you, *Aba Jan*?

'I placed a heavy padlock and chain on my mouth
and heart and sealed both for good, when Habib Sahib
and you decided upon and held my daughter's fate in
your powerful, masculine hands. You didn't think to
consult me then. I was, of course, of no consequence.
Instead I received chastisement from you for letting
Zarri Bano stay in Sikander's home. Neither of you
considered a mother's feelings of any importance, let
alone my daughter's feelings. You see, we women are
just dumb servants to grace your household – obedient
vessels. So how can I now confide my feelings to you?'

It was the longest and most heartfelt speech she had
ever made in front of her father-in-law. Siraj Din's
hollow laugh rang eerily in the semi-darkness of the
courtyard, silencing the sound of the night crickets
momentarily. 'No, my dumb daughter-in-law is not so
dumb. On the contrary, she is blessed with an agile
brain. She doesn't scream or curse, but she knows how
to sharpen her words, and how to prick with them
where they wound the most.'

Blushing, Shahzada looked up and decided to be
honest with him as he had requested. 'You asked me to
speak and thus I have spoken. Today this dumb vessel
has spoken out of bitterness. You must forgive me
because, *Aba Jan*, you have touched me on a sore point
in my life – my daughter, Zarri Bano. It is true what
you say. I changed the day you all imprisoned my

daughter in this holy role. I lost and buried a daughter that day, *Aba Jan*, the Zarri Bano I knew and loved. I have never recovered from that loss – I am faced with a stranger. I feel sad today because I want my daughter to marry Sikander. I consulted you on this and you gave us your blessing. But the truth of the matter is that none of us bargained on what Zarri Bano has become. She truly *is* a Holy Woman. She is adamant that now she will never marry Sikander or any man! It is for this reason I am so sad. I do not know how to persuade my daughter. I want her to revert to being a normal woman again – to have a husband and a family. I want Haris to have Zarri Bano as his new mother, not some strange stepmother that his father may happen to marry. I know Sikander has always loved Zarri Bano. She, how-ever, recoils from the very idea of getting married to him.'

Overcome by emotion Shahzada stopped. The anguish in her voice wounded Siraj Din. Reaching out his arm, he gently patted her shawled head. It was too much for Shahzada. She fell on his shoulders and burst into tears.

'Hush, my daughter. Don't cry, or you'll make me cry too. I will try to sort something out with Zarri Bano. Unfortunately, I cannot turn back time, Shahzada. If only I could. I don't know if you'll ever forgive me. Sometimes I wish you were like Gulshan's mother – petulant, disobedient and wilful. For if you had been like that, you would have fought for your daughter by tooth and nail. But you are too good a daughter-in-law, too perfect, too submissive to ever think of rocking our patriarchal boat. For this you have a very special place in my heart. My daughter, I cannot make amends for the past, but let me try by asking for your forgiveness.'

He gently shifted Shahzada away from his shoulder. Then, sitting up straight he held up his two hands together in front of her, in a manner reminiscent of traditional begging for forgiveness.

'No, *Aba Jan*!' Shahzada shrieked, her eyes stricken. She jumped off his bed as if she had been stung and grasped his hands tightly in her own. 'Why are you doing this?' she asked, her voice breaking.

'Forgive me, Shahzada. I know my son touched your feet. We committed a crime against you and your daughter. I don't know if you'll let me touch your feet, but will my hands do instead?'

'Please, *Aba Jan*! Do not insult me or yourself by this act,' she cried. 'I cannot bear it! You don't need to do this. I forgive you. But please, put your hands down. You are making me tremble.' She printed kisses all over his gnarled hands, touched to the core of her being, holding his hands against her face.

'All right, Shahzada. I will put my hands down, but let me say, you are aptly named a princess indeed – a "shahzadi", a woman of noble bearing. I am and have always been honoured in having you as my daughter-in-law. May you have a long life and may Allah give you the peace of mind you so crave. I will pray for you in all my prayers. Go and rest, my child. I'll have a word with Zarri Bano tomorrow morning.' He gently withdrew his hands out of her tight grasp.

'*Khudah Hafiz, Aba Jan*.' Bidding him goodnight, and turning the hookah pipe back to his mouth, Shahzada got up. She returned to her portable bed on the verandah, but couldn't sleep. It was a long time since she had had such a heart-to-heart chat with her father-in-law. Her own parents lived far away and she very rarely saw them. She closed her eyes in stunned

disbelief as she thought of her father-in-law's hands held out in supplication, asking for her forgiveness. That, from such a proud *zemindar*! She shuddered, ashamed on his behalf. To have stooped to such a level as holding hands up to his daughter-in-law. It was unthinkable! 'And he did it for me! I forgive you, *Aba Jan*,' she cried generously in her sleep.

Next morning, after breakfast served by Naimat Bibi on the open verandah, Siraj Din asked his grand-daughter to accompany him on his daily walk in the fields.

'Yes, of course, Grandfather. Haris and I will love that. Come along, little one!'

She had just supervised her nephew's meal after getting him dressed and combing his hair. She followed her grandfather out of the house and took the path through the village, greeting all the women she met. They indulgently watched Haris hopping in front of them on the narrow, dusty path.

'You love your nephew very much, don't you, my dear?' Siraj Din began, with his eyes on the ground and prodding it with his ivory walking stick.

'Yes I do, Grandfather. He is very precious to me.' A smile lit up her face.

'You, too, are very precious to us, both to me and your mother. You do understand that, don't you, Zarri Bano?' He smiled back at her.

'Yes, of course, Grandfather,' Zarri Bano laughed, keeping pace with his stick.

'Your mother was talking to me last night. She was very sad on your behalf.' The easy bantering tone was gone.

'Was she?' A wariness entered Zarri Bano's voice.

'Yes, and you know why, don't you?' Siraj Din said.

Zarri Bano held her breath. 'If you know why, then I can tell you that I cannot do what she asks,' she answered coolly, looking ahead and keeping a careful eye on Haris.

'Not even if your grandfather requested it of you?' Siraj Din prompted softly.

Zarri Bano stopped walking and she turned to face her grandfather. He saw the grim line of her soft pink mouth. Siraj Din stopped too and leaned heavily on his stick. Granddaughter and grandfather stared at each other with equal determination.

'You and father used moral and psychological pressure to make me into a Holy Woman,' she told him now. 'I obliged and submitted then. I will not do it this second time, Grandfather, not even if you went on your knees. I am not a wax doll that you can mould to your whim. Moreover, I have no wish to marry any man, ever! Please do not raise this subject again. It is very painful for me. Forgive me for my rudeness, Grandfather, but I cannot oblige you. You see, I cannot do it as my own individual autonomy is at stake.'

If Siraj Din was disappointed, he hid it well. Zarri Bano's refusal was understandable. He swallowed his wounded pride, but felt sorry for Shahzada. He had promised her. He tried again.

'Zarri Bano, my dear, forgive us for what we did,' he began.

'There is nothing to forgive, Grandfather. I am very happy with my life.' She walked briskly away.

'I know you are, my dear, but now I think that marriage would be good for you.' As soon as he had uttered the words Siraj Din regretted them.

'How gracious of you to think so,' Zarri Bano said

sarcastically. 'Marriage is good for me now, is it? But it wasn't good for me five years ago – why? Do you know, Grandfather, I was engaged to be married to a man I really wanted to marry, but you and Father tyrannically vetoed it. I did what you wanted me to do. Not now, not this time, Baba Jee.'

'Well, you can marry him now, Zarri Bano,' Siraj Din hastened to offer.

'No, Grandfather, I cannot. It is five years too late. For you see, in case you haven't noticed, I am a different person now. I have no desire for marriage – with or without your gracious permission. My father black-mailed me into becoming a Holy Woman by refusing to give permission for me to marry. I didn't need any-body's permission, I was a grown adult, but I became a prisoner of our female and filial sense of duty. When I gave into that, I sacrificed my soul and happiness and peace of mind. I will not do the same again. To do so would be to lose the essence of my individual autonomy. If I lose that, then God forbid, I might as well be a dummy – a *phutley*.'

'I don't know about souls or individual autonomy or *phutleys*. All we are asking you, Zarri Bano, is for you to become a mother to Haris,' Siraj Din stated, his voice hardening.

'I am sorry, Grandfather, the answer is still no.' Her voice matched his in hardness. She swept round to follow Haris.

There was nothing further to say. Silence reigned between them – a unique experience for Siraj Din. He was used to people running to do his bidding. His granddaughter's flat refusal was a bitter pill for him to swallow.

Why couldn't she have refused them five years ago?

In his heart he knew the answer. Zarri Bano had had no chance in the face of four strong males. What could a mere slip of a girl, only twenty-seven years of age, do when faced with a father, an uncle, a grandfather and an elder? She had had no option but to submit, to bow down before them all.

Chapter 52

'IT IS TO no avail, Sahiba.' Fatima had gone straight to her mistress in her bedroom as soon as she had had a talk with Zarri Bano. 'She will not listen, and is adamant that she doesn't want to marry him. You are right; she feels genuine revulsion against the idea.'

'Thank you for trying, Fatima.' Shahzada sighed heavily. 'I don't know what to do. She will probably avoid me even more now. Today she didn't even come home for lunch, but remained at the *madrasa*, pretending that she had to organise an important meeting. I will have to tell Sikander tomorrow when he comes for Haris. I am dreading it. Do you know, a week goes so quickly, Fatima. It seems only yesterday that Haris came to stay with us.'

The following evening, Sikander arrived to collect his son. 'Where is your aunt, Haris?' he asked after taking some refreshment and cuddling the child.

'She is still at the *madrasa*, Sikander my son,' Shahzada replied.

'I see. It's very late, isn't it? Shall I go and walk her home, or has the chauffeur gone to collect her?'

'No, it's all right, don't worry. I have sent Ali to accompany her,' Shahzada told him, knowing

instinctively that Zarri Bano had deliberately stayed
late at the *madrasa* so that she wouldn't have to meet
Sikander. Shahzada had made up her mind to be honest
with him and let him know exactly what had happened
between her daughter and herself.

'Sikander, I liked your suggestion very much,' she
began. He looked up at her sharply. 'You know what I
am talking about, don't you? Well I have talked to
Zarri Bano about it and I am very sorry, my son, but she
wouldn't listen or consider it. She is totally against it.'

Sikander tried to mask his disappointment. 'I see', he
commented after a while.

'You can understand her situation, can't you?'
Shahzada appealed for his understanding.

'Yes, I can, Auntie,' he replied flatly.

'She is a changed person these days. She accused us of
treating her like a wax doll, moulding her when it
suited us and our circumstances.'

'Yes, I can imagine Zarri Bano saying that – and
thinking that. That is probably what I would have
thought in her shoes. I remember her telling me a long
time ago that above all she would not be moulded, yet
ironically she *has* been.'

'Also she feels guilty over her sister's death. The
thought of replacing Ruby is abhorrent to her.'

Again Sikander listened intently but didn't reply
immediately.

'Come on, son. We must go home,' he said at last,
and stood up to leave. Then turning to Shahzada again.
'Is it all right for me to talk personally to her about it?
Do I have your permission?'

'Of course, my dear, please do. I would like you to
marry my daughter very much.'

Sikander smiled his thanks. 'Rather than me

bringing Haris over, is it possible that you could persuade Zarri Bano to come over to Karachi in a week's time to collect him? I would like to see her there very much, and so would my parents.'

'I don't know if it is the right thing to do,' Shahzada worried. 'The way Zarri Bano is at the moment, she runs at the mere mention of your name. I will try my very best or I will come myself.'

'Good. Please do that. *Khudah Hafiz*, Auntie.'

He walked out into the darkened front courtyard. Just as he approached his Jeep, he saw Zarri Bano in her long black cloak, come into the courtyard with Ali.

Zarri Bano stopped on seeing him. She was caught, undecided whether to go back or forward. Common sense spelt that it had to be forward. Sikander remained standing under the canopied verandah, with his son held tightly in his arms, waiting for her to approach him.

'*Assalam-Alaikum*, Brother Sikander,' she ventured, laying deliberate stress on the word *Brother*.

'*Wa Laikum-Salam*, Zarri Bano,' he replied quietly, his eyes glittering in the semi-darkness of the verandah. She noted his omission of the word 'Sister'. For the last four years, during his marriage to Ruby, he had respectfully addressed her as 'Sister Zarri Bano'. Her cheeks flared with colour in the dark.

'I am taking Haris home.' Sikander had now walked up to her.

'I see. Is Auntie all right?' Zarri Bano asked politely, trying to keep to the banal level of social pleasantries. She still hadn't looked him in the eye, but had her eyes on Haris, who leaned forward and took hold of her arm.

'Auntie, will you come to pick me up next week in Karachi?' he piped. 'Grandmother said you would.

You must come and stay with us for two days.' Haris was blissfully ignorant of the tension crackling between the two adults.

Zarri Bano caught her breath, trapped by Haris's question. 'No, darling, I can't. I am going to a meeting in Multan next week,' she replied truthfully.

'Well, come when you've been there. You never come to our Karachi home, Auntie, do you?' Childish petulance spilled out of his small mouth.

Zarri Bano felt herself falling deeper into the trap.

'My son issues invitations for me. I don't have to do it,' a smiling Sikander uttered softly in his deep voice.

Zarri Bano stepped back, an expression of panic on her face. This time she looked him directly in the eye. The idea had to be nipped in the bud. She couldn't pretend ignorance any more.

'I am sorry, Brother Sikander, but I really will have to decline that invitation. Perhaps later, when you remarry, I will attend your wedding.'

'You will,' he replied cryptically, before moving away with his son in his arms. Once he placed Haris on the passenger seat of the Jeep, he turned once again to give Zarri Bano another sweeping look. She stood watching, shaken by the strange tingling awareness entering her body.

She entered her home, disgusted with herself and her feelings, and quashed them with two sharp words: 'Never Again!' That chapter of her life was over – never to be lived again.

Over the next few days, Shahzada tried very hard to hint to Zarri Bano that they should go to collect Haris next time. The girl declined. 'Mother, you go! There is no need for me to be there. You can send Ali to pick

him up.' Now she was beginning to think there was a conspiracy to send her to Karachi and throw her into Sikander's company.

'Mother, why do you persist? You know that I am not supposed to meet a *gheir merd*, an outsider.' She turned on her mother angrily.

'But Sikander is not a *gheir merd*,' Shahzada insisted.

'Oh yes he is. He is no blood relative of mine, thus he is *gher*. Until he remarries someone, I don't want to have anything to do with him *or* his family. Please do not plot on my account behind my back, because the answer will always be the same.'

Three days later Zarri Bano reluctantly ended up accompanying her mother to Karachi. She had postponed her visit to Lahore because Haris had been taken ill, and wanted to have his Aunt Zarri Bano and his other grandmother with him. Trapped, she agreed to go. If Haris really was ill, it would be so unkind of her to stay away. He had said over the telephone in his groggy voice, 'Auntie, please come. I miss you so much. I love you. Will you come?'

'Yes, darling,' Zarri Bano had said resignedly. Haris was the epicentre of their world, a living remnant of her sister. She could never refuse such a heartfelt request. 'I will deal with Sikander when the time comes,' Zarri Bano told herself firmly.

Looking at Haris a few hours later in his bed in Karachi, Zarri Bano was ashamed of her selfishness. 'It is all right, my darling. Aunty's here to stay with you,' she promised, gathering the feverish little boy into her arms and printing kisses on his hot forehead. A lump suddenly arose in her throat for her dead sister. With Haris still in her arms, she gave in to the urge to weep.

'Auntie, are you crying?' Haris said, looking up inquisitively at Zarri Bano.

'Yes, I am, my darling. I am crying for your mummy, because I miss her so much.'

'I miss her too,' he sniffed in his small voice.

'We all miss her, but crying will not help,' Sikander chipped in, having come into the room. Zarri Bano wiped her eyes with her hands and turned to look. Sikander and Bilkis stood together, warmth in their eyes, as they beheld the aunt and nephew wrapped in each other's arms.

Zarri Bano patted the little boy's cheeks with a tissue. 'Haris, won't you drink a little of the soup that your Dadi Ama has brought for you?' She took it from Bilkis and tasted it herself first. 'Oh, it is yummy! You try it now.' Spooning some of it into Haris's mouth, she concentrated hard on the soup, because her body was aware of Sikander sitting on the other end of the bed, leaning forward and watching them both intently.

'You are lucky to have your aunt to spend so much time with you,' Sikander told his son. 'Your other two aunts, my sisters, live so far away and are so busy with their own children that they cannot come at such short notice.'

'I may live nearby, Sikander Sahib,' Zarri Bano explained curtly to Sikander, 'but as you know I, too, lead a very busy life and have little time to spare. I only came because Haris was ill. I'm especially busy now that I am hoping to set up the publishing company, as I intended to do five years ago.'

'Yes, of course, Sahiba. I didn't mean to imply that you had nothing to do,' Sikander quickly amended. 'We know you have a very busy life. I am also aware that you postponed your visit to Lahore. We are all very

grateful that you have spared so much of your time for this visit. Were you thinking of Karachi as the base for your company?' he asked with keen interest, a light coming into his eyes.

'I am not sure yet, but I am hoping to specialise in academic and scholarly books, perhaps in Hyderabad or Islamabad,' she answered evasively, having already purchased the land in Karachi for the company. He didn't know, nor did her mother – only her grandfather.

Zarri Bano went downstairs for the evening meal and joined her mother. Soon afterwards, she returned to Haris's room and decided to sleep with the little chap. Ever since his mother's death, Haris had always slept with Zarri Bano when he was staying with her. Slipping out of her *burqa* and pulling on her night *kurta*, Zarri Bano climbed into the large bed, pulled Haris into her arms and fell asleep.

Sikander called in a little later in the evening. As he saw his son cuddled up against his aunt, something caught in his throat. He stood for a long time staring down at them both. It was the first time that he had seen her sleeping in his home. 'I'm not going to let her go! I must talk to her very soon; each day is a wasted day,' he told himself in exasperation, closing the door behind him.

Sikander found his opportunity to speak to Zarri Bano two days later. She was out in the orange orchard, playing with Haris. The child's health had improved over the last forty-eight hours. Zarri Bano wasn't aware of Sikander's presence for some time as she was totally engrossed in playing hide and seek with her nephew, delighting in his healthy childish giggles.

'Oh, there is Daddy!' Haris cried, running towards

Sikander. When Zarri Bano turned to watch, the smile had left her face. Sikander caught his son in his arms and watched her closely over the little boy's head.

His scorching gaze captured hers fully. The words, 'Haram! Haram! It is a sin!' thundered through her mind as she hastily looked away. 'I mustn't look at a gheir merd,' she mumbled to herself.

For a few seconds he had succeeded in straddling her in the two worlds: of her past and that of the present, with her as the Holy Woman. To her dismay, she saw that she was standing on the very same spot as five years ago, when he had proposed to her. His eyes played over her face, coaxing and forcing her to remember that time and to acknowledge it – making her raise her eyes to him once more.

The bundle in his arms moved, releasing Zarri Bano to return to the present world. She bent down to pick up the ball from the ground.

'Haris, your grandmother is calling you inside,' Sikander told his son, putting him on the ground.

'OK! See you in a minute, Auntie,' Haris shouted, running gaily along the garden path leading into the villa. Zarri Bano watched him go, wishing and wanting to follow him, but unable for some reason to do so.

She turned to Sikander with a polite smile, pulling the hood of the burqa further onto her forehead, check-ing that no strand of her hair was visible to his gaze. 'Haris is getting better, Brother Sikander. After a few days I could take him back to Sind with me,' she offered, for want of something to say.

'Yes, he is getting better, but I would prefer him to stay here. This is his home. He has got to stay here, Zarri Bano. I miss him too. This to-ing and fro-ing between Karachi and your home has to stop. It's been

going on for over a year. It is not good for his health, nor for his education.

'I know.'

'Could you come and stay here with us for a while?' he asked carefully, taking the first tentative steps to his goal.

'I . . . I . . .' she stammered, looking him straight in the eye. 'Sikander Sahib, I have only come because Haris wasn't well. I have no right to stay here. I have a life of my own to turn to.'

'I know you are a very busy person. Tell me why don't you have the right to stay here? Are you not related to Haris? You are his aunt.'

'Sikander Sahib you know it is not seemly for me to stay here, particularly as a single woman and you are now a single man.'

He neatly took the cue offered by her stiff words. 'I see. Well perhaps we can remedy that, Zarri Bano. Why don't we legitimise your stay here with us. Haris needs you – we need you, why don't you replace Ruby?'

As soon as the word 'replace' left his mouth, he knew he had made a terrible mistake.

Zarri Bano couldn't pretend to misunderstand him. She stood on the spot – thunderstruck.

'Replace Ruby? Never! I have no wish to replace Ruby ever, *Brother*.' She enunciated the word with a whiplash clarity.

'Why?' he asked, wincing at her word 'brother'.

'Why?' she echoed dumbfounded. 'Have you no feelings of decency, Sikander Sahib? She was my sister, your wife, and I am a Holy Woman! What you are suggesting is impossible – it is both degrading and utterly loathsome.'

'I am only thinking of what is best for Haris. There is

nothing *degrading* nor *loathsome* about that suggestion,' he bit out, his voice hardening.

'Yes, everyone is bent on thinking about Haris, but what about me? My mother, my grandfather have been at me. Don't I count? Aren't I a person who has a say in anything? Haris needs the care of another female. He can get that from any source, not necessarily from me. I wouldn't make a good mother anyway, my life is far too busy. I have a number of projects that I am overseeing at the moment. I have no experience of children. I have renounced marriage; that is what I was made to do—'

'I didn't make you!' Sikander coldly cut in.

She ignored his interruption and continued, her eyes fastened on his face. 'Now it suits everybody. I am asked to fall in with everyone's wishes. You are a brother to me, Sikander Sahib. That is how I have seen and beheld you for over four years. You are my dead sister's husband. How can I join my life with yours? Moreover, I am not an ordinary woman any more. I have become a true Holy Woman, in every sense of the word that my father and grandfather envisaged – and much more.

'Five years ago, my life was turned upside down. I surrendered then. I learned to turn my back on you and the prospect of marriage. And I survived. People change with time, Brother Sikander. In my case I underwent a personality change. For a few weeks I did not know who I was. Now I am at peace with myself and happy in my present role. I have no wish to recall my previous life or connections.

'You are an old connection, as I told you in Minah in Saudi Arabia. It is *haram* to link my name with a man, let alone my sister's husband. I am wedded to my faith. So please don't mention anything about this again.

I have had my fill of what can never be. Our paths, though they have crossed yet again, are never destined to merge, my dear Brother Sikander. Ruby must be turning in her grave.'

'No she wouldn't.' The quiet words came out force-fully. 'She would have wanted you to be Haris's mother. You know that she always felt guilty about marrying me. She didn't talk openly about it – but I knew. She thought that she had stepped into your shoes. I was your betrothed once, remember, not hers.'

'We are women, Sikander Sahib! Not vegetables that you can swap at your will,' she said in a low and agon-ised voice. Before his very eyes she began to shudder, recalling images of another time in the orchard when he had almost imprisoned her in his arms near a tree and had proposed to her. He had touched her hand then and she had let him! She wanted to banish the memory totally from her mind. She found it easier instead to escape from his presence than the past images – thus she fled. Sikander watched her go sadly.

He remained in the orchard long after she had left. His hands balled in his trouser pockets, he strolled around the fruit trees, going over in his mind what Zarri Bano had said. As he recalled her vehemence and that look of distaste on her face, he felt his spirits sink. He had never anticipated such a change in Zarri Bano. From a passionate woman she had turned into one who recoiled at the thought of human relationships. 'How am I ever going to win her?' he asked himself in frustra-tion. If she really saw him as a brother, then what hope had he of marrying her?

He now wished with all his heart that either he had never set eyes on Zarri Bano, or Ruby hadn't died. Was this to be his ultimate fate? To pine forever for this

woman, who rebuffed him totally? A woman who would remain inaccessible to him for all time!

Yet although he understood and empathised with her feelings, that didn't quell the longing in his heart. She was always there and would always be there, locked away in the secret recesses of his soul – shaming, haunting and tantalising him.

In the following two days he avoided her company totally. She had made her feelings very clear. What was the point of pursuing it all? Zarri Bano spent her entire time in Sikander's home with her nephew, playing with him and reading him stories. After a week she left.

Chapter 53

SABRA STAYED WITH Kaniz for a further two weeks, keeping a constant vigil over her sister – even to the extent of sleeping in the same room; she had another *palang* moved into the large bedroom. She talked constantly about different things, in the hope that it would somehow bring a smile to Kaniz's sad face.

Khawar told no one of his visit to Firdaus. He was now trying his best to make it up with his mother for all his past neglect. Like his aunt, he stayed with her as much as he could. Kaniz, now humbled to her very core, thirstily drank in her son's attention. The odd panic attacks and bouts of depression that had swept over her since that scene in Firdaus's office still, however, continued to plague her.

Nothing made her laugh any more. It was almost as if the joy of life was snuffed out of her. On the contrary, she wanted to cry all the time. Sabra found

her cowering in an armchair and crying discreetly into her shawl, one afternoon as she sat by herself on the rooftop, basking in the afternoon sun.

'Sister Kaniz, why are you crying? Everything is all right! Please don't cry. Come and sit here and I'll massage your head with almond oil,' Sabra offered.

Looking up with puffy eyes, Kaniz sat obediently on the *charpoy* in front of her sister and leaned her head back on to Sabra's lap. Pulling her sister's cotton shawl off, Sabra began to nimbly unbraid her long, chunky plait. She noticed that Kaniz had worn the same cotton *chador* for the past three days, and felt her eyes fill with tears. Changing her clothes twice a day had been the norm for Kaniz ever since she was eighteen years old, this self-neglect showed clearly how low she had fallen.

Sprinkling some of the oil from the bottle onto her palms, Sabra dabbed the drops on the crown of her sister's head, and began to rub it into the scalp with long, soothing strokes. Her eyes shut tight, Kaniz began to enjoy the massage.

'Why were you crying?' Sabra asked softly, leaning over her sister's shoulder.

Kaniz's eyes fluttered open nervously, but she didn't reply immediately. 'I was remembering my wedding day and my wedding night.'

'Why did that memory make you cry?' her sister wanted to know. She continued the massage, hypnotic and healing bringing forth hidden feelings.

'I was trying to forget the type of person that I have since become,' Kaniz uttered, her voice full of pathos.

'I do not understand. What has your wedding day got to do with anything?'

'Everything, my young sister. It was on that day I

embraced the shroud of humiliation which I am still wearing thirty years later and cannot shed.'

'Shroud of humiliation? What are you talking about?' Sabra peered into her sister's face. Kaniz remained silent for a few moments, her eyes tightly closed as if running away from the image.

'I have never talked about this with anyone,' she said in a low voice. 'Sabra, can you imagine what it is like to be an unwanted wife? To learn on the very first day that you are only second best.'

'Is this true?' Sabra ceased her massage.

Sitting up, Kaniz turned away from her sister's incredulous stare and began to braid her thick long hair, tugging at it in nervous jerks.

'On my wedding day I learned that Sarwar had really wanted to marry Fatima. You know about this, don't you? The scene is indelibly printed on my mind for eternity. I was sitting in my red Shanghai bridal gown, on the sofa – a proud new *chaudharani*, full of life and herself. There was a small group of young women sitting around me. Some were local village women, others were relatives – but I don't know who *she* was – that *charail*, that witch. I have not clapped eyes on her since that day.

'Fatima was there too. I didn't know who she was then, not until this woman opened her evil mouth. In a clear, loud voice, although she made pretence of whispering it to her friend, she said: "There is Fatima, the woman that Sarwar *really* wanted to marry, but she turned him down and is now married to her cousin." She went on to say that she wouldn't like to be in my shoes – as I was only "second best!"

'Stunned, my ears burning with hurt and shame, my eyes dropped to my bejewelled and hennaed hands.

Inside, I was trembling like a leaf with humiliation. I had quickly glanced at the woman she pointed to and saw Fatima. She for her part looked back at me sheepishly. I knew intuitively then who she was. She had heard it too and had turned quickly away, her cheeks pink in embarrassment. At that moment, I could have jumped into a lake, my sister Sabra, and have drowned myself. I prayed for the ground to open beneath me and swallow me up, away from the stares of the women.

'I didn't dare to lift my eyes up again, imagining that everyone was talking about me and probably sniggering and ridiculing me. I knew that I was being compared to that woman and I recoiled in shame. Belittled by the whole affair, my heart banged with hatred for the woman who had shattered my dreams and my whole world and had robbed me not only of my happiness but also of my *skoon*, my peace of mind in one mere flicker of an eyelash.

'I had come to my new home full of happiness and with my pride sky-high. That woman with her spiteful tongue had whipped it all away from me. From the lofty heights of exultation I was hurled into the murky depths of humiliation. I hated Fatima for no other reason than that she was *the other woman* – the one my husband had desired and had originally wanted to marry. Also because she, too, had heard and had thus witnessed my humiliation. Tell me, my sister, can any wife bear the thought of another woman being linked to her husband, and to know that she would always be the second best in his affection?'

'But he was a wonderful husband,' Sabra said sincerely. 'I know, I witnessed how loving and good he was.'

'Yes, he was. But he, too, humiliated me on my

wedding night. If only he had pretended for my benefit. If only he had said what my fragile, vulnerable heart had craved to hear. But men are such straightforward creatures; they do not possess the wiles to dissemble like we women can. Least of all not my Sarwar, may he reside in heaven.'

'What happened?' Sabra asked, her senses alert, now very much piqued on her sister's behalf. This bit she didn't know.

'On the wedding night, still shaking from the typhoon of feelings that the words of that woman aroused, I couldn't help asking my husband about Fatima. I needed to know if he *had* wanted to marry her – and he told me straight away that it was true. I next asked him if he had loved her and again, without a moment's hesitation, he said that he had.

'He denied nothing, Sabra, little guessing that my woman's pride desperately demanded and needed a denial – but it never came! I had sought a salve for my injured pride, instead I got poison – heaps full. From that moment on, I shrank into myself. My confidence, already at zero, totally deserted me. It appeared that everything and everybody in the *hawaili* was suspect. I imagined them all laughing at me behind my back. Jealousy tore at my guts. Apparently Fatima still held my husband's heart in her hands. Although we consummated our marriage, for me there was nothing real any more. The joy of becoming a *chaudharani* had barely lasted one day. I cried quietly to myself in the pillow, long into the night.

'The next morning I talked to no one. I kept my eyes down all the time. The shame of being the unwanted bride covered me like a white shroud. Women, including his relatives, tried to talk to me, to tease me,

as women are generally wont to do after the wedding night, but I couldn't and wouldn't respond to them. I felt alienated from them all. I liked no one. They were all suspect in my mind. In the end they gave up and left me alone, probably imagining that I was a a ungrateful, ungracious sort of woman.

'On the morning of the fifth day after the wedding, I was standing on the upper balcony drying my long hair out in the warm breeze when I saw Fatima down below in the courtyard with another woman, talking to Sarwar's aunt. As my eyes skirted the *hawaili*, I saw Sarwar descending the stairs from the rooftop. Jealousy, again, ripped through my veins. I didn't think, but acted irrationally. I didn't want Sarwar and Fatima to meet, not in my presence or not in my home, anyway. I couldn't bear that! Neesa was sitting on the balcony with me, ready to braid my hair. She had been assigned as my personal maid.

'"Neesa," I said, "go down and tell that Fatima, the one in the green suit, in her ear, that she is not welcome in this house from today. Tell her that the *chaudharani* has said this!"'

'Surprised by my message, Neesa did as she was told. She ran off down the stairs. Sarwar, fortunately, had gone into our bedroom on the first floor, so he didn't see Fatima. From the balcony I watched Neesa approach Fatima and whisper my message to her. Fatima glanced up and saw me looking down at her from the rooftop balcony. It was at that moment, Sabra, I rose tall out of my humiliation, I glared my signal of triumph down at her. I was the Chaudharani, Sarwar's lawful wife. Who the hell was she? She had no right to come barging into my *hawaili*. Our *hawaili* – my home!

'I think that moment was the turning-point in my

life. Whole-heartedly I changed and gained confidence in myself; I embraced the role of what a *chaudharani* should be. I kept everyone at arm's length. Not that anybody dared to come too near me. Most were too frightened to attempt it. Their fear and awe gave me strength and encouragement. I practised it on Neesa first. I was hard on her. I still am, I am sorry to say.' Kaniz sighed deeply. 'One day I am going to ask for her forgiveness – I have been so cruel to her all these thirty years. That is the sort of person I have become. I have been wearing this ruthless and selfish façade for years. Yet it was that which helped me to keep my sanity and gave me confidence. Without it I was a lost soul.

'Can you imagine the terrible depths to which I had sunk? When I learned about Fiaz's accident, I felt not a moment's pity for *her*. My husband had already died, but I was still jealous of her. Can you believe it? I still could not forgive her for being *the other woman* and secondly, for having rejected him. When she began to work in Siraj Din's house my heart literally sang with joy. Here was my sweet revenge, it seemed. I just wished that I could find out who that other woman was, the one who had shattered my wedding day and my whole world. For now I could trample *her* face in the mud and say to her, "Is that the woman Sarwar had wanted to make his *chaudharani*? This miserable wretch who has become a washerwoman?" I was desperate to find that woman. Unfortunately I have not laid eyes on her since. Just as well, for her sake! I have hated her for so long.

'Then Fatima had *her* sweet revenge. Just as she had ensnared my husband in her small dark hands, her short, dark daughter then stole my son from under my very nose. In front of my very eyes! Here was the cycle,

repeating itself. I could never accept that woman's daughter into my house.

'The rest you know, the agony that I have gone through. I have lost an only son who has lived away from me for over one year. Then lived for another year with me, during which he has hardly glanced at me nor said a word – all because of that chit's sake.

'For my son's sake, I sank low, sacrificing my pride and descending to new depths of humiliation. Begging on my knees for the hand of a woman I couldn't stand, offspring of a woman I have always loathed – and what was my reward? I was thrown out.' She shuddered and seemed to find it hard to speak. Then:

'Each time I recall that scene, I am swamped by memories of my wedding day, for the feelings are the same. On the outside, people see this big, bulky body, and a hide like that of an elephant. Inside, my dear sister, I am a fragile, tottering, wreck. A little knock, a bruise of any sort, sends me reeling. I don't know what to do, Sabra, how to make myself strong again. You cannot stay with me all the time, although I wish you could. You are the only one who can save me from myself. Otherwise, Sabra, there are times when I still want to end it all. Even my son's smiles don't have the same magic. I keep remembering myself on my knees with my hands outstretched to her. I have died a hundred times, each time I think of it. It will haunt me to my dying day.' Kaniz then began to sob again, into the folds of her shawl.

'Hush, my dear. I will stay with you as long as you like,' Sabra promised her. 'I will not desert you. There is nothing more important to me than my sister. Hush now. Do you want me to wash your hair for you?'

'No, I can do it myself. Neesa will be there to help,

if I need it. Thank you, my sister – for listening to me.'

'You must dress yourself smartly, the way you used to. Please look after yourself. All these blemishes on your fair skin! You've been sitting out too much in the sun. You always had a lovely skin tone and prided yourself on it.'

'What does it matter, Sabra?' Kaniz said drearily. 'It is not as if I am in the flush of youth. I am over fifty. What does it all matter?' She shrugged, dismissing Sabra's concern. Her skin was the least of her problems.

Kaniz stood up and went in search of Neesa, so that she could sort her things for the bath and iron a new suit for her to wear.

Sabra remained on the flat rooftop balcony looking over the village fields, her mind going over her sister's words.

Chapter 54

ZARRI BANO THRASHED restlessly around on her bed, her mother's words of appeal ringing in her ears.

'It could be a marriage in name only, at first,' Shahzada had suggested. 'Sikander has agreed to this. Just for Haris's sake. At least think about it, Zarri Bano. Could you become a full-time mother to Haris and spend half of your time in Karachi? Would that be too much to ask?' Shahzada had stopped short as her daughter stormed out of the room.

Now Zarri Bano pressed her face in her pillow, tortured by conflicting emotions. 'I am not ready for this new upheaval in my life. Allah Pak, what am I going to

do?' she prayed. 'I love my nephew but I cannot cope with this. I want to have nothing to do with Sikander – ever!'

During the next few days, she managed to put the whole affair out of her mind. Shahzada hadn't mentioned it again and Zarri Bano avoided meeting Sikander when he came to drop Haris off for his weekly trip.

After leading the Friday prayers for the women in her *madrasa*, Zarri Bano led a seminar for her regular group of students.

Sitting cross-legged on the carpeted floor of the large seminar room, the young women discussed the sayings of Prophet Mohammed (Peace be upon him), and the writings of the Holy Quran. A table piled high with textbooks in English, Arabic and Urdu stood near Zarri Bano.

On this occasion, they were debating the issue of women and inheritance, according to the Islamic *Shariah* law.

'Our faith says we have distinct rights of inheritance, yet in reality it is the men who end up getting most of it,' one young woman complained angrily, starting the debate off.

'You are right, Nargis. Unfortunately, that does tend to happen in our society, especially if the woman is ignorant of her rights,' Zarri Bano agreed, fingering the page on the issue of inheritance in one of her textbooks. 'If you know your rights and are conversant with the *Shariah* law, and consult these books, you may be able to change things. You can take the matter to our *Shariah* court.'

'What you say is true, Sister Zarri Bano, but in reality how many women, whether young or old, will

actually stand up and confront their male kin, or fight for their rights, let alone take the matter to court? It is easily said, but difficult to achieve in reality. The male kin also come up with insulting the woman, saying that she is greedy, especially as they have already spent a great deal on raising her up as well as on her dowry.'

'Can I stop you there, Nargis. There is some truth in what you say about dowry. Say, for instance, a property is in question – a house is to be divided up between five brothers and a sister. If the brothers have already spent a lot of money on the sister for her wedding (note, the brothers, *not* the father), then I think we have a moral and ethical problem here. Is the woman in question entitled to the same share of the inheritance as her brothers? Is it right for her to claim it, if she personally has no need of it and if her brothers have already spent a lot on her out of their own pockets? I think it is a grey area, which makes the situation complicated. That doesn't mean, however, that fathers can go ahead and aggressively disclaim their daughters' rights, by harping on how much they have spent on them.' She paused, then went on.

'The issue of inheritance is a very sore point with me personally. As you know, I have inherited the bulk of my father's estate. I had no desire for this inheritance, but as the eldest daughter and with no brother, my father decided to pen almost everything to my name. As I have no children, nor am I likely to . . .' Zarri Bano paused again, losing, for a moment, the thread in her thoughts, '. . . I will pass my inheritance to my nephew Haris. Inheritance is a major issue for landowning families like ours. Brothers have killed each other and had lifelong feuds over land. Some end up applying

their own brutal law, that of the fittest, and the one with the most influence ends up winning everything.'

Zarri Bano suddenly stopped, fearing that she had said and revealed too much. She glanced up at the assembled women, listening to her with rapt attention. 'Let's turn to page seventy where this issue is discussed . . .'

Zarri Bano looked up as she saw her Cousin Gulshan come into the room.

'Gulshan, how nice to see you. Please join us,' Zarri Bano said warmly.

Gulshan looked around awkwardly at all the women on the floor, with opened books lying in their laps.

Zarri Bano moved aside and made space beside herself for Gulshan, pulling the *burqa* hood in place on her head. Dressed in cool pastel shades of pink and blue lawn fabric, Gulshan felt frivolous amidst the severely dressed students surrounding Zarri Bano. With an awkward movement, she pulled the pink chiffon *dupatta* over her hair, feeling that she should cover it up too, out of respect for the group, although normally she never did this in front of other women. Then she sat back and listened to Zarri Bano leading the remainder of her seminar session.

Zarri Bano's performance and knowledge impressed Gulshan. She appeared to speak authoritatively on different issues and explained everything in a very balanced, intelligent manner. Gulshan looked at her cousin, marvelling at her. She couldn't believe that only five years ago Zarri Bano never had an inclination to say a single prayer in one day, yet here she was, supposedly the local female authority on all religious matters. 'She knows everything,' Gulshan mused in awe, becoming more and more aware of her own ignorance.

Eventually the session ended and the women left. 'How do you manage to sit cross-legged for so long on the floor?' Gulshan asked, standing up and stretching her own stiff legs. 'I definitely can't.'

'You get used to it after a while,' Zarri Bano replied with a laugh, also standing up. 'Remember the daily prayers are not only meant to be a spiritual union with Allah but also the best form of exercise. The *wudu*, the daily ablutions, is the best form of hygiene. There is a wonderful purpose for mankind in everything that Allah Pak has prescribed for us to follow. When we say our prayers, especially if you know Arabic, one is directly communicating with Allah Pak, Gulshan.'

'It is all right for you, Zarri Bano, because you know Arabic. For us, ordinary ignorant folk who recite it in a parrot fashion, the rapport you talk of can't always take place. Do you know, I could do with attending one or two of your seminars. I have so much to learn.'

'Of course, my dear, you are most welcome. There is a breed of us women from our background and class who have become totally divorced from our faith. I have only recently realised by how much. I was like a blind person, stumbling in the dark and spiritually bankrupt. Now thanks to my father for directing me onto this path, my life is so different. I have gained so much!'

'But you have also lost a great deal too,' Gulshan prompted softly, remembering the reason why she had sought Zarri Bano out and had come to visit after Shahzada had phoned her.

'I have lost nothing!' Zarri Bano snapped, the smile disappearing from her face. 'Once, I might have thought so – but not any more.'

'Come on, Zarri Bano. Surely you've not forgotten how you were forced into the role. You are not going to

pretend to *me* that you walked into this life freely? You were about to marry Sikander!'

'Let's go home, Gulshan,' Zarri Bano interrupted, cutting her cousin short. It seemed as if everybody was intent on getting her to review her present and past life, and then proving to her that her life was somehow sadly lacking and that Sikander was suddenly the answer to everything! It was absolutely maddening.

Later in the evening, sitting on the verandah at the back of the house, Gulshan resumed the conversation that her cousin had ruthlessly cut short. Haris was playing on the lawn. Zarri Bano watched him with affection shining out of her eyes.

'You love him very much, don't you?'

'Yes, if you mean Haris.' Zarri Bano said. 'He is my Ruby's treasure.'

'Don't you ever get sick of wearing it?' Gulshan teased, changing the subject gently.

'You mean my *burqa*?' Zarri Bano returned. 'No, I never get sick of it. It is like my second skin now. I only feel comfortable when I am wearing it. It also makes my life so simple and carefree. I don't have to worry about what I am wearing underneath, or about my hair and so on. It is an amazing experience, I can tell you. I still remember the first time I wore it. Can you imagine, shudders of horror passed through me? Now I feel naked and vulnerable without it, particularly when I am in front of strange men. Not that I come across many as they all dutifully keep a respectable distance. The old vain Zarri Bano drew whistles from men, this one draws distant courteous respect. My life is so sheltered that men just don't feature in it.'

'What about the future?' Gulshan said, cleverly

steering the conversation her way. 'Do you not visualise a future with a man in it? I know Uncle Habib gave you his blessing to marry if you so wish. You don't know what you are missing. Marriage is a wonderful experience, especially with children — see for yourself, Zarri Bano, please!' Gulshan appealed.

'I see,' Zarri Bano muttered, looking down at the empty cup in her hand.

'What do you see?' Gulshan prompted, after a long silence between them.

'I can see that my mother has been talking to you too. It seems that, these days, someone is forever trying to marry me off. Only last week Sister Sakina was at it and, before her, my former tutor, Professor Nighat, phoned and tried to persuade me to marry by referring to her own experience. "I wish I had remarried after my husband's death," she said. "I gave up my youth for my daughter's sake. Now I am so lonely. What am I going to do when she leaves? You don't even have children. What will you do when your mother dies? You will be all alone. Loneliness is a terrible thing. Take this chance, Zarri Bano, before it is too late!"

'Suddenly I am asked to forget who I am; to give up what I do and become a *normal* woman to everyone's way of thinking. Gulshan, marriage may agree with you. It may be the answer to what you want in life. I know that you are happily married and now have a family of your own. But what if I say I want none of it and that I love my life too much to give it up?'

'I am sure you can still carry on with all that, but your life will be more fulfilled.'

'How, Gulshan? My life is already fulfilled, not in the way you imagine, but fulfilled nevertheless. I do not need a man in my life.'

'Not even Sikander? Does he not mean anything to you?'

'No, especially not Sikander! Excuse me, Gulshan, it is time for my prayers.' And Zarri Bano ended the conversation, leaving her cousin watching her in bemusement.

Chapter 55

AS ZARRI BANO reached her bedroom she saw Haris talking with his father on the telephone. She quickly closed the door, afraid in case Haris asked her, in his innocent manner, to talk to Sikander. She waited in the corridor for a few moments and then went in. Haris was bidding his father goodbye, his lower lip quivering in distress and there were tears in his eyes. Zarri Bano flew to her nephew's side. Putting the receiver down on its cradle, she caught the little boy in her arms and swung him up into the air.

'Why are you crying, my darling?' she asked, nuzzling her face in his hair, holding him tightly in her arms.

'Daddy said I had to go home tomorrow. But I don't want to go, Auntie. I want to stay here with you,' he cried, snuggling further into her arms.

'But you have to go home, my darling. Your daddy misses you too,' she reminded him gently.

'I like staying here with you. Don't you want me to stay with you, Auntie? You don't love me!'

'Of course I love you, Haris,' Zarri Bano quickly assured her young nephew.

'No, you don't. Nobody loves me! I want my mummy! My mummy!'

'Please stop, Haris. We all love you very, very much.'

'I want my mummy back! Where is she?'

'Oh *Allah Pak*, Haris – I want your mummy back too, but Allah has taken her to heaven.'

'Will Mummy never come back?' he asked in a small fearful voice, looking at his auntie with his thick fringe-lined brown eyes, brimming with tears.

'No, darling Haris, I'm sorry, she won't,' she answered sadly, opting for honesty.

'But I want my mummy!' Haris wailed, his small body trembling as he sobbed.

The anguish in her nephew's voice lanced through Zarri Bano. 'I am your mummy too. Remember you have always called me your second mummy.'

'But my mummy stayed with me. You just keep sending me away back to Karachi!' he replied angrily, turning away from her arms.

Stung, Zarri Bano cried, 'I won't send you away, my darling – ever, I promise. I will never let you cry again.'

Holding him tightly to her chest, Zarri Bano promised herself that she would never let her nephew shed a single tear again. 'Oh, the selfishness of adults,' she chided herself sadly in her mind.

It was as she was putting him to sleep, in her bed, that Haris sought reassurance from his aunt. His small arms around her neck, he pulled her head down. Putting his hand through her hair, he asked, 'Do you mean it, Auntie? Will you always stay with me, even in Karachi?'

Zarri Bano's heart stopped, panic looming in her body. She hadn't thought that far ahead. 'Even in Karachi, I promise!' she quickly reassured him. 'Now, go to sleep.'

Gently massaging his temple and sweeping his hair

away from his forehead, Zarri Bano printed light kisses on his face until he fell asleep.

Rising from the bed, she felt a new weight of responsibility falling on her shoulders. Her sister's son was now her responsibility and she would treasure him for all time.

'They have all won!' she cried inwardly. Yet they were all right. What mattered was Haris and his happiness.

For a long time she stood looking out of the window at the lush green lawns of their courtyard. With a heavy heart, she then went to the telephone and stood by it, gathering her resolve. She knew what she had to do. With a trembling hand, she tapped out the Karachi numbers, hoping that *he* would answer it.

Her wish was answered.

'It's me, Sikander Sahib.' She spoke in a voice so low that she hardly recognised it herself. She had to consciously remind herself not to call him 'Brother' now. There was an awkward pause before Sikander answered.

'Is everything all right? I was speaking to Haris a short while ago, Zarri Bano.' She could tell he was surprised to hear from her.

'He is fine and is sleeping soundly in my bed. He was a little upset earlier when you reminded him that he has to return by Friday.'

'I see, but you do realise that he has to come home sometimes.' His voice was cool.

'Of course I do.'

'Will you be able to bring him yourself?' he asked more pleasantly, after a pause.

Zarri Bano took the cue he had offered.

'Yes, I will. Moreover, I will stay as long as Haris wants me to and as long as I am welcome, of course, in

your home. Haris's happiness means everything to me,'
she rushed quickly. There was a long silence at his end.

'You know you are most welcome, Zarri Bano, any
time. Would that mean indefinitely?' he asked after a
further pause, feeling the tension grow at the other end
of the line.

Zarri Bano glanced down at her hand holding the
receiver. The palm was moist.

'If that is what is best for Haris,' she answered in a
voice that sounded alien to her ears.

Sikander seemed lost for words, then: 'Thank you,
Zarri Bano! Look – you do know what you are saying,
don't you?'

'I do.'

Sikander couldn't leave it at that. He wanted it
clearly out in the open. 'When can *it* take place, Zarri
Bano?' he persisted.

She couldn't pretend to misunderstand him. 'I . . . I
don't know. I haven't thought that far ahead,' she
murmured, her heart going faint, as if she'd been run-
ning for miles in her grandfather's fields. 'I only came
to this decision in the last few minutes. Haris's tears
tore at my heart. I couldn't bear to see them. I do this
for him.'

'As Allah is my witness, Zarri Bano, I will never let
you regret your decision. You'll be free to pursue your
career, your vocation in life. You can come and go
whenever you wish. I demand nothing, only that you be
a permanent mother to Haris and make my home your
home.' She couldn't fail to note the warm earnestness in
his voice.

There it was, all out in the open. The taboo word
marriage had still not passed through their mouths,
almost as if they were both afraid that the tenuous link

that was being forged would snap with that one word. Neither wanted that, at any cost.

'Thank you. I hope you appreciate that I am only doing this for your son's sake. I am not the same person I was five years ago, Sikander. This will not be an ordinary marriage to a normal woman.' She felt it important to remind him.

'Of course I know that you are now a different sort of person from the one I first met – yet, beneath it all, I believe you are still the same woman, Zarri Bano. But I don't want to go into that at the moment. All I can assure you now is that everything will be in your hands. I'll make no demands on you. It will be one step at a time.'

Zarri Bano felt her cheeks grow warm at his word *demands*. Closing her eyes, she tried to shut out the sensuous images behind her eyelids. It was such a long time since her mind had entertained them.

'Thank you for your understanding. I will tell Mother about this tonight. It seems that everyone has won – Gulshan, Fatima, Grandfather, you and Mother.' She shook her head, unable to disguise the bitter tone. '*Allah hafiz*, Sikander Sahib!'

Putting the phone down she returned to the window, and stared out bleakly. 'What have I done now?' she asked herself in dismay.

In Karachi, after ending the conversation, Sikander sat looking at the telephone for a long, long time. Then in a semi-daze, he went to find his mother. Bilkis was sitting on her prayer-mat, offering her *Isha* prayers. He waited until she finished, then bent down and kissed her forehead.

'Say a special prayer today, Mother, for me, Zarri

Bano and Haris. Pray that we shall prosper and be happy together as a family and for our future.'

Bilkis looked up with joy leaping out of her eyes, and standing up she drew his shoulders down to hug him.

'Oh my beloved son. I am so glad for you!' Holding his face in her hands, she kissed his cheeks. 'Has she accepted?'

'No, she proposed herself instead! To start off, it will be a marriage in name only.' Seeing the look on his mother's face, he felt challenged to explain. 'She needs a lot of patience, Mother. Too much has happened in her life. She has received too many emotional knocks. She is only marrying me for my son's sake, not for herself nor for me. It will be hard, but at least my son will have a woman who is like a mother to him, and who will be with him most of the time.'

'What about her work? Will she abandon her new college, the one for women that she recently established?'

'I hope not. We'll see what happens, but it's one step at a time. I need to keep in mind that this is the woman who once beguiled me with one look, five years ago, and who now shudders in distaste at the idea of any intimacy with me because I married her sister. So we have a long way to go. We cannot steam-roller her to our wishes. She has already been oppressed and exploited by her father and grandfather. I am not going to be another male oppressor in the guise of a husband. I will be a friend and companion to her until she decides she is ready for a more fulfilling marital relationship.'

'I will pray for you all. May Allah bless my family . . . and may poor Ruby's soul rest in peace.'

'*Amin*. Yes, Mother, yes!' he said with sincerity in his heart.

Chapter 56

WITH THE COLLEGE closed for the summer, Firdaus returned home for the holidays. She was dreading her stay in the village. The thought of meeting Khawar disconcerted her. She still hadn't recovered from his last visit and verbal attack. Her conscience often pricked her, it made her think and reflect on the scene of Kaniz going down on her knees and begging for her hand. The trouble was, the more she thought of that unseemly incident, the more wracked she became by it. By the second day at home she was shuddering with guilt; the urge to tell her mother all about it became very strong. For Kaniz was only a street away. There was every chance of accidentally meeting her.

Kulsoom had deigned to grant them her presence again. Treated as an honoured guest, she ate a hearty breakfast of two *parathas* and an omelette, finished off with a bowl of creamy yoghurt fresh from Sardara's dairy. When pressed to stay for lunch, Kulsoom made a half-hearted pretence at declining and then readily agreed. Fatima, her cheeks filling with secret laughter, and her daughters took this behaviour with good humour and in their stride. 'After all, it's a small reward for bringing about the match between Salma and the bachelor from the neighbouring village,' Fatima found herself telling her daughters in a conciliatory effort to convince them, and herself, that the amount being lavished on Kulsoom, including the breakfasts and lunches was justified.

Since Firdaus had left the village, having declined to

discuss her marriage plans with anybody, Fatima had decided instead, to concentrate on fixing a match for her other, more willing daughter, Salma. Firdaus wasn't the only one she had to think of. This way, she ensured that at least *one* of her three daughters would be married. 'If Firdaus isn't careful, she will be left on the shelf,' Fatima fumed inwardly. She was beginning to lose patience with her eldest daughter. 'The girl is nearly thirty, for heaven's sake. I had had four children by then. Who is going to want her at this age, despite her qualifications?'

Fatima had already sorted out her Salma's dowry. The furniture had been especially ordered from a prestigious Karachi store. Now all that remained was to set the date for the wedding. Kulsoom had a special purpose for her visit. She had arrived to discuss with Fatima the question of what presents were to be given to the groom and his family. She thought herself duty-bound to bestow upon Fatima, for whom it was a first occasion, some of the knowledge from more than two decades of experience in arranging weddings and preparing trousseaus.

'Listen, Kulsoom, my heart tells me to order a gold earring set and a matching locket. I would like to give that as a present very much. We can afford it,' Fatima justified to Kulsoom, seeing the latter's eyes open wide in surprise.

'You don't have to, you know. You mustn't get carried away now, Fatima Jee. Remember, you still have two other daughters to marry off, and you will have to do the same for them, in all fairness. It is up to you, of course, I would think twice about it. Now, what about the suits? How many were you thinking of giving her?'

'I wanted to consult you and Firdaus on that.'

'I see. Talking about Firdaus, Fatima Jee, I haven't seen much of her today.' Kulsoom allowed herself the luxury of this observation.

'She's probably tired. There is quite a bit of work to do at the end of the college summer term, with exams and so on. However, I too have noticed that she is a bit cagey, not at all her normal, lively self at the moment, Kulsoom Jee.'

'Do you want me to liaise with my fellow match-maker in the town to find a suitable *rishta* for Firdaus?'

'I would like that very much, Kulsoom Jee, but I don't want you to do anything until I have talked to her about it. I do not wish to proceed without her permission,' Fatima hastened to add.

'What about Khawar?' Kulsoom asked quietly.

'That chapter is finally closed.' Fatima shook her head sadly, a wistful look coming into her eye. 'I was a foolish, ambitious woman, wasting both my time and theirs. I have learned to my cost that it is no use pursuing a dead cause.'

'I see,' Kulsoom said thoughtfully, her brain alive with curiosity. 'Have you heard that the Chaudharani Kaniz has been ill lately, and has not been seen by anyone for the last few weeks? Have *you* seen her? She has not called me for over two years, so I don't know what she is doing about her son's marriage.'

'No, I haven't seen her, nor do I *want* to see her – or hear anything about that woman either!' Fatima retorted, recalling the last scene between herself and Kaniz, which was still fresh in her mind. Thank goodness she hadn't set eyes on that harridan since then!

On hot summer nights, Firdaus and Fatima, like many other rural people in Pakistan, loved sleeping out in the

open on the rooftops of their home. Mother and daughter laid out their cool, quilted cotton bedding on their portable beds, which were placed side by side.

Fazeelet and Salma on the other hand preferred to sleep inside downstairs, under the ceiling fans. If it happened to rain, it was just too much bother for them rushing from their beds, to scurry around collecting their bedding and dashing indoors. Their father always slept in the open courtyard downstairs.

Fatima and Firdaus settled down to sleep. Propping her pillow into shape and pulling the thin cotton top sheet over her body, Firdaus lay back and glanced up at the stars. She turned her face towards her mother. 'These pests!' Fatima snapped, as she vigorously fanned away a large mosquito, intent on playing around her face.

'Mother, I wanted to tell you something,' Firdaus began quietly.

'Yes?' Fatima offered half-heartedly. 'Oh, these nuisances! I think I will have to get the mosquito nets out soon. I never thought when we bought one in Hyderabad that we would need to use them in Chiragpur. These pests have even invaded our village. I thought only the cities had them.' She yawned loudly. It had been a long day.

'Chaudharani Kaniz came to see me,' Firdaus announced.

Now she had her mother's undivided attention.

'What? When was this? Why didn't you tell me?' Fatima asked all at once, sitting bolt upright and forgetting all about the mosquitoes.

'It was a few weeks back.'

'My goodness, daughter, why didn't you tell me? What did she say?' she marvelled. The excitement

in her mother's voice both dismayed and depressed Firdaus.

'Well, I have only been home since yesterday, Mother,' she said peevishly.

'So, go on, tell me what happened,' Fatima asked impatiently. Her heartbeat was now racing out of control. She wanted to know what Kaniz had been up to, visiting her daughter.

Firdaus, for her part, felt no pleasure at the prospect of telling her mother all about Kaniz's visit. Fatima's eyes already glowed with sly expectation. How will she react when I describe how Kaniz went down on her knees and begged for my hand in marriage? Firdaus wondered apprehensively. She would probably jump right out of bed with joy! Until she heard the rest of the story.

Firdaus decided to honour her mother with the whole truth. The matter with Khawar was weighing heavily on her heart and nerves. She desperately needed to share her burden with somebody.

'She came to ask for my hand in marriage,' Firdaus stated, staring once more at the stars above her in the dark sky.

'Oh my God. Did she really? I can't believe it!' Fatima's eyes feasted on her daughter's face in wonderment.

The cotton sheet thrown aside, her legs now practically dangled out of the bed, her feet drumming with a dull beat on the concrete floor of the rooftop. Firdaus gulped at the thought of what she had to say next.

'That is not all, Mother. Chaudharani Kaniz went on her knees and held up her hands in front of me and *begged* me to marry Khawar.' Firdaus stopped, dreading the next bit of information she had to impart.

Fatima was now virtually speechless and spellbound.
The image of Kaniz on her knees, begging her daugh-
ter, Firdaus, to marry Khawar was a bizarre dream –
one too good to be true! She didn't know what she
was supposed to feel. Different emotions – triumph,
astonishment, disbelief – battled inside her.

At last, all she said was: 'When did this happen?
Why didn't you tell me? Did she really go on her
knees? I just don't believe it! That proud, arrogant
woman . . . begging.' Fatima's head shook on her
shoulders in wonder.

'Yes.' Firdaus licked her dry lips, before she dropped
the bombshell. 'And I turned her down.'

Khawar's words of condemnation tapped at her
brain. A masochistic urge to punish herself compelled
Firdaus to continue harshly: 'And while she begged,
Mother, and held her hands out to me, I opened the
door and ordered her to leave.'

A hushed silence descended as Fatima wrestled to
absorb the astounding news which her daughter had
carelessly just thrown her way.

Firdaus was painfully aware of the tense silence. Her
mother's breathing was the only sound apart from the
mosquito buzzing around Fatima's face. The insect was
forgotten however, as her thoughts did wild somer-
saults in her head. The twin images of her daughter
standing with the door open and Kaniz on her knees,
hands held out together in front, outraged her every
sense of social decorum and human decency.

At last finding the use of her tongue: 'Firdaus! How
could you?' Fatima screeched out in the darkness of the
night, her voice expressing both her utter dismay and
distaste. 'Where did your sense go, my girl? I cannot
believe that you did this!'

'I know,' Firdaus answered miserably, recoiling from her mother's words. 'But there was nothing else for me to do.'

'Nothing else to do? I don't know what has happened to you. I thought that I had done a good job in raising considerate, well-mannered, intelligent daughters – but I have just discovered, to my horror, that I have a very thoughtless and a hard-hearted woman as my eldest daughter. Do you realise what it must have cost that woman to come crawling to you and beg on her knees, Firdaus? And you – you cruelly threw it back in her face! I have always disliked that woman, but, Firdaus, what you have done is unforgivable. It goes against all the rules of decent human conduct. Nobody deserves what you have done, not even one's worst enemy. Poor woman!' Fatima shuddered at the image of Kaniz on her knees.

'Please, Mother, stop. Khawar has already abused me on this subject,' Firdaus appealed, feeling more miserable than she had anticipated.

'When did you see Khawar? What did he say?' Fatima asked in an incredulous voice. 'You mean to say you have been keeping all this to yourself – and leaving us in the dark!'

'It is nothing worth telling,' Firdaus mumbled, loath now to repeat what Khawar had said to her. The word *dross* still rankled, terribly.

'You said that he abused you. What do you mean?' Fatima demanded, Then angrily: 'Tell me, Firdaus! What did he say?'

'OK, Mother, if you must know, let's just say that he was very angry indeed. He called me . . . things.'

'I am not surprised, my girl. You deserved it all.'

'He said that he was wiping his hands of me for

good,' Firdaus said wretchedly. She knew she had now truly dumped her mother's dream to the bottom of the well.

'Well done, my daughter. Congratulations. You've got your come-uppance well and truly,' Fatima jeered. 'God knows what it cost that woman to come crawling to you, but you didn't have the grace to appreciate it. No, you had to be small-minded and petty about it and throw it back in her face. I tell you, daughter, learn this well and truly: never throw a good thing away! Do you think he will glance at you ever again, let alone marry you, when you have done this to his mother? Firdaus, he might have been besotted with you, but let me tell you: a woman is nothing in a man's eyes, when it comes to his mother. He has sacrificed a lot for you. Quarrelled with his mother and left home on your behalf. And you didn't even have the sense, let alone the charity, to welcome his mother and accept what she came to offer.

'On the contrary, you threw her out. An older woman – a *chaudharani*! A woman who could have been your mother-in-law. Oh Firdaus, I am so ashamed to have you as my daughter. I cannot believe that your pride made you so cruel.' Fatima rocked herself to and fro for a minute. She didn't look at her daughter, couldn't bear to, so she didn't see how Firdaus suffered. Eventually she came to a decision.

'Until you have apologised to that woman, Firdaus, for your insensitive behaviour, and asked for her for-giveness – on *your* knees – I will not forgive you myself. That is my ultimatum. Now have you anymore unpleasant shocks to divulge to me while you are about it, daughter dear?' Fatima clipped sarcastically.

'I am sorry, Mother. I will do as you suggest. Perhaps then I will gain some peace of mind,' Firdaus sighed.

'Huh! My selfish daughter still thinks only of her-self – about her own peace of mind? What about the other woman's mind. You probably turned her world upside down. It is not your peace of mind I care much for at the moment. It is for that poor soul, whose ego must have taken quite a battering at your hand. If your conscience will let you, go to sleep now, if you can. For I will not be able to sleep a wink.' Fatima clucked her tongue in distress! 'First I abused her in her very home, then you did this! It wouldn't be any wonder if she didn't have nightmares about us two!'

Propped up on her pillow, she twisted the head of the tall portable fan, standing near the bed, in her direc-tion. Then she loosened the top button of her muslin nightshirt. Her body was on fire and she was in no mood to go to sleep. Fatima's eyes turned in the direction of Kaniz's *hawaili*, the 'wretched pests' of mosquitoes as they were swept away by the fan's breeze now totally forgotten.

Chapter 57

FIRDAUS SPOTTED THE white horse and the tall figure on top, from the wrought-iron railings of the rooftop. It was definitely Khawar going for his morning ride. He had done this for years. As a young teenage girl, she used to surreptitiously watch him ride out on his horse, early every morning, to return an hour later for breakfast. Sometimes he caught her watching him, even though she used to duck her head down in embar-rassment. He would then slant her a rakish look and give her a knowing smile.

Firdaus knew Khawar would take a good hour for his morning ride. It gave her just enough time to get changed and have breakfast. She went back to the roof-top and waited patiently, keeping an eye on the horizon for a glimpse of the white horse. He was the only one who rode a steed of such a compelling colour and with such a sleek coat. Spotting the pair, she quickly ran down the stairs and called Fatima, who was still having her breakfast in the kitchen, 'Mother, I am going for a walk in the fields.'

Seeing Kulsoom Bibi and Naimat Bibi walking in the village lane, Firdaus hastened her pace. She was in no mood to make small talk with the two village gossip-makers, and just hoped that they didn't follow her. Briskly, she walked out of the village and along the path in the direction she judged that Khawar was likely to take, praying that she woundn't meet anyone else on the way.

Khawar didn't see Firdaus until she reached up and touched him. He looked down in surprise, then immediately jerked his leg away, but her hand remained on his calf.

'Kindly remove your hand, Madam Principal,' he said pompously. 'I am not in the habit of being mauled by a woman during my morning ride.'

At any other time, his words would have made her chuckle, but this was no laughing matter. Colouring, Firdaus removed her hand. She had come to apologise, therefore she would not pick a quarrel with him.

'I was only trying to stop you, Khawar Sahib,' she said quietly. 'Please do not be so insulting. I do not make a habit of touching men, let alone mauling them.'

He heard her, and for a second was tempted to smile, but he still felt very raw and bitter where she was

concerned, after the incident with his mother. He wished to be gone – to put as much distance as possible between himself and this woman.

Firdaus continued to watch him, trying to gauge his thoughts, while Khawar stared back. Firdaus was evidently caught up in the urban glamour process. She had exchanged her long chunky plait for a shoulder cut. Her raven-black hair framed her face most attractively, he was forced to admit. One of the things he had always admired about Firdaus was her long braided hair, reaching below her waistline. He had always reckoned that there was a certain elegance, and an aura of femininity about a woman with a plait hanging down gracefully behind her shoulders. Her blue floral, lawn outfit was cut in stylish urban designer lines and her *dupatta* lay nonchalantly draped around her shoulders, instead of on her head as was the normal village custom. On the whole she presented a very alluring picture, but she wasn't the old Firdaus he had once known. This was the urban, sophisticated Madam Principal.

His hand tightening on the horse's reins, he was about to move on, when Firdaus caught hold of his calf again.

'Am I never to be forgiven?' she beseeched. 'I have come to ask for your forgiveness, Khawar Sahib.' Her eyes didn't waver before the fury of his.

'For what, Madam Principal? For insulting and debasing my mother . . .' he said angrily. . . . 'and reducing her to a mental wreck?'

Bravely, Firdaus stood her ground and continued to smile at him, knowing instinctively that she had to humour him. 'Whatever you say, Khawar Sahib. I am very sorry I acted stupidly – I admit it. I realise now

what I have done. In fact, later today I am going to visit
your mother and apologise to her on my own knees, if
that will assuage your pride, Khawar, or persuade you
to forgive my youthful stupidity. Remember this, I am
doing it for your sake.'

'Oh please, Madam Principal, do not demean your-
self by begging on my account,' Khawar replied stiffly.
'Now good day to you.' Once more he made to leave.

'You are cruel, Khawar Sahib,' she burst out. 'I am
not enjoying this. You are not making it easy for me.'
By now Firdaus was beginning to hate every second of
this encounter.

With rage in his eyes, Khawar retorted: 'Did my
mother enjoy begging for your hand? Did you make it
easy for *her?*' Leaning down, he spat the words into her
face.

Parting with the last vestige of her pride, Firdaus
cried out. 'If she were to ask me now, I would say yes!
Yes!' Her calm exterior had completely crumbled.

Khawar straightened up on the horse. An uneasy
silence stretched between them. His heartbeat had
stood still for a second. Then, looking away, he
delivered the final insult.

'I am not in the habit of taking stale offerings – and
from women themselves! *We* like to do the asking here.
Now why don't you run along and offer yourself to
some city sahib, who would be more compatible with
your new urban image anyway!' With that parting jibe
he rode swiftly away.

Firdaus remained rooted to the spot. Still shuddering
from his insulting tone, she felt soiled and debased, as if
balls of mud had been thrown at her from the village
ditch. She had actually proposed herself – and he had
rejected her, with such biting contempt! What had

come over her? How low could she have stooped? Her cheeks burned red with humiliation.

Walking home in a daze, she felt both crushed and mentally bruised. 'I deserve it!' she kept telling herself. And if cruelty offered one form of salve to his pride, she reasoned with herself, then she didn't mind – as long as he forgave her at the end.

Holding up her head, she entered her parents' home. By that time, she had forgiven him. The thought suddenly leapt through her, 'This is what Chaudharani Kaniz must have felt and experienced, when I turned her away. It dawned on Firdaus that rejection was a bitter pill to swallow. It rent one apart, diminishing one's self-esteem.

For the rest of the day Firdaus avoided her family. She had performed one Herculean task that she now thoroughly regretted. She still had one more to perform, however, and she definitely didn't relish the prospect! Her mother, though, would see to it that she went to visit Kaniz and humbled herself at her feet to ask for forgiveness.

Chapter 58

FIRDAUS PUT OFF the dreaded visit for two more days. She had nightmares about the meeting and what she had to do – to beg forgiveness on her knees. On the third day, putting aside her fear and pride, Firdaus decided to take the plunge. From the rooftop of her home, she kept an eye on Kaniz's *hawaili*. As soon as she saw Khawar climb into his Jeep and drive out of the village with his chauffeur, Firdaus decided to 'honour'

Chaudharani Kaniz and the *hawaili* with her presence.
It would be the first time in ten years that she had
entered that place.

'I am doing this for two reasons,' she told herself. 'To
ask Kaniz for her forgiveness, only because she is older
and therefore it is my duty. For Khawar's sake, because
if I don't do it, he will never forgive me. Then there
will be no chance of a reconciliation between the two of
us, let alone marriage.'

Sadly, she accepted the fact that, through her foolish
pride, she had sunk all her ships. Firdaus now had her
eyes fully opened to her inner heart, which revealed
clearly to her that she *did* really want to marry Khawar
– and deep down had always wanted to – but Kaniz's
opposition had put her on the defensive. Now she real-
ised what she had lost. If the key to winning Khawar
back was in laying herself at his mother's feet, then she
would gladly do it. After all, hadn't that same proud
chaudharani prostrated herself at *her* feet, for the sake of
her son's happiness?

Khawar's dismissive comment that she was 'brass',
and 'stale offerings' still rankled. She was beginning to
learn, to her cost, that pride was an evil phenomenon,
which achieved nothing, but only created chasms
between loved ones.

Dressing herself with care, and appropriately, in a
subdued and dowdy outfit, Firdaus braided her hair and
pinned it down at the back away from her face.
Scrubbed clean of make-up and wearing a large, dis-
creetly coloured shawl fully draped over her head
and around her shoulders, she looked every bit a local
village woman and not a College Principal.

Each step to the *hawaili* was a measured one. 'If only
I could turn the clock back and eat those words of mine

that "I'd die before I would set foot in your *hawaili*".'
Well here she was, very much alive. Not only going to
step over the threshold, but also to beg in the presence
of that woman. Fate was cruel, Firdaus was learning. It
delighted in throwing people's words and actions back
at them. Hadn't Kaniz herself begged when she had
sworn that she would never do so.

Fatima had personally escorted her daughter out of
the house, ensuring that she didn't get cold feet at the
last moment. She had asked Firdaus whether she
wanted her to come along for moral support. Firdaus
declined, wanting it to be a private meeting.

With a fast-beating heart, Firdaus stood outside the
large wrought-iron gates of the *hawaili*, her hand
poised on the bell. There was no turning back. She had
to face the music – even if it cost her both sanity and
pride.

Kaniz was sitting on the carpeted floor of the large
room in front of her sister Sabra, having her routine
almond oil head massage, when Neesa came to inform
them that a Miss Firdaus was waiting in the guest room
to see Chaudharani Kaniz.

An electric silence filled the room. Sabra stopped
dabbing drops of oil from the bottle onto Kaniz's scalp.
Kaniz turned a bewildered gaze up at her younger
sister, as if to ask, 'What is going on?' Panic spilled all
over her face. The hand holding her *chador* in her lap
began to tremble.

Sabra stood up and said to Neesa, 'Bring Miss
Firdaus up here, please. Thank you.'

'Why is she here?' The distress looming in Kaniz's
eyes and voice sent a chill through her sister. 'I don't
want to see her, Sabra. Please.' Kaniz's teeth were

chattering with fear. Even after four months on medication, prayers said on her behalf, almond oil head massages and *tweez* – amulets wound around her neck and ankles – minor incidents still sent Kaniz hurtling into a state of panic and hysteria.

'It is all right, Sister. I am here,' Sabra comforted, patting Khaniz on the shoulders. 'She will not say anything to upset you, I assure you. In fact, I will give her a piece of my mind.'

'No, Sabra, please. I don't want any quarrel in my presence. My heart couldn't stand it – it is already bouncing like a yo-yo. Why is she here?' she asked again, nervously pulling up her *chador* and spreading it around her shoulders and over her open oily hair.

'We will find out soon enough, dear. Here, let me straighten your shawl. Please sit on the sofa. Don't worry about anything, I will handle her,' Sabra reassured her sister.

Kaniz had only just sat down on the sofa, facing the door, when it was thrust open to admit first Neesa, followed closely by Firdaus.

A heavily shawled figure stood in the doorway. Her face held straight, Firdaus bade them 'Salam.' Unabashed, her eyes moved from one sister to the other.

Seeing her sister's eyes drop in fear before Firdaus, pain sliced through Sabra. Her proud sister's gaze had never dropped before anyone's in all her life, yet here she was, sitting nervously with her eyes downcast because of that jumped-up female! Sabra shot a look full of hatred at their unwanted guest, and Firdaus flinched.

'*Wa Laikum-Salam*, Miss Firdaus!' The loud, sarcastic tone grated on Kaniz's overwrought nerves. 'To what do we owe this visit? Is it so that you can insult my sister

in her own home now? Have you not done enough
damage already, young woman?'

Ignoring her Firdaus looked steadily at the silent
figure of the Chaudharani, surprised and moved to pity
by her nervous posture, the hands clutching the edge of
the sofa. Something caught at Firdaus's heart.

It was then a strange thing happened. Firdaus forgot
her own pride. She forgot herself. She even forgot
Khawar – and only saw the lonely, suffering woman,
and remembered Khawar's words that his mother had
tried to take her own life as a result of that unfortunate
episode.

Firdaus didn't have to pretend; didn't need to seek
any prelude – no formalities to be got over. Just raw
feelings of pity and empathy for the forlorn figure on
the sofa cut through Firdaus and, on an impulse, she
flew to Kaniz's side. Squatting on the floor in front of
the older woman, she placed her head in Kaniz's lap.

Kaniz froze. Drawing back on the sofa she darted
first a look of sheer panic at her sister, then looked
down, dumbfounded, at the covered head in her lap,
and the hands touching her bare feet. Kaniz's trem-
bling fingers gnawed at the edge of the seat, gripping
the sofa even tighter.

'Please forgive me, I beg of you,' Firdaus beseeched,
her voice muffled, 'Forgive my youth, Auntie Kaniz. I
didn't know what I was saying or doing. I know I hurt
you dreadfully on that terrible day.'

'What *chal* is this? This game may work on my poor
sister, who is ill, but not on me, young woman,' Sabra
taunted, having found her tongue.

Lifting her head from Kaniz's lap, Firdaus turned a
blank stare at Sabra. Kaniz too looked at her sister.
Sabra stared back at them both – defiant. She wasn't

going to fall for this rubbish. Apparently she had underestimated the young woman. Hadn't the devious creature in one second laid herself at her sister's feet? What a piece of drama! The audacity of the woman!

'I don't know what you mean. What *chal?*' Firdaus stammered.

'There is no need to play games with us, or to act the innocent. You are a spiteful young woman, we all know that. What are you hoping to gain by this act? Do you think that by laying yourself at my sister's feet, you can turn everything rosy again? Did your heart and head take an almighty flight from your body when you humiliated my sister by turning her away. The woman you see in front of you is a mental wreck – the result of going on her hands and feet before you, begging! And, if that wasn't enough, you had to callously throw her out. Not once but *twice!*'

'I . . . I . . .' Firdaus was looking down in embarrassment and shame.

'Lost for words? You, the articulate Principal, the head of a college?' Sabra jeered.

'Sabra, stop.' Kaniz's quiet tone momentarily dammed Sabra's outburst. 'Get up my child,' Kaniz commanded softly, her hand gently propelling Firdaus up from her feet.

Sabra shot a questioning look at her sister. Why was Kaniz behaving like this?

Firdaus stood up and sat on the sofa beside Kaniz. The woman's whole demeanour, her words, the tone and the expression in her eyes signalled to Firdaus that Kaniz bore her no grudge – not at the moment, anyway. Humbled, she dropped her eyes to her hands in her lap. She didn't deserve this treatment. Kaniz had indeed ennobled herself in Firdaus's eyes.

'It is all right, my dear. You are forgiven.' Kaniz spoke gently to Firdaus. 'We all do silly things in our youth and I should know! I am no exception. We all have unfortunate episodes tucked away inside us, that we are ashamed of and which haunt us for life. Welcome to my home!'

At her sister's words, Sabra's eyes grew huge in her face and her lips fell wide apart. She was totally stunned.

'Thank you. You are very kind.' Firdaus looked uncertainly from one sister to the other.

The atmosphere was now highly charged. Having achieved her goal, Firdaus wisely decided that it was an appropriate time to escape. 'I only came to apologise. You are very generous, Chaudharani Kaniz, you have put me and my actions to shame. I will bid both you aunties good day. *Khudah Hafiz!*'

On unsteady legs, and with as much dignity as she could muster under the circumstances, Firdaus walked out of the room. Kaniz's hand rose to stop Firdaus, but then catching the fierce, warning look in her sister's eyes, she let it drop to her side.

Outside the *hawaili* gate, Firdaus rested her hand on her chest, feeling her heart thumping away as if she had been skipping for hours on the village's cobbled lanes. She had climbed a mountain, but oddly she felt no triumph in her achievement. On the contrary, she felt ashamed of herself in the face of Chaudharani Kaniz's generosity. The woman was indeed a changed person. Had she herself caused all that? Firdaus shuddered. She could clearly now imagine Kaniz trying to take her own life.

Inside the *hawaili*, the two sisters stared at each other. Sabra was bursting to rant and rage, but she struggled

to contain herself. Reluctantly, she allowed herself to
simmer down and managed to place the lid on her
pent-up feelings. She just couldn't afford to upset her
sister.

'You are annoyed with me, aren't you, Sabra dear?'
Kaniz ventured timidly. 'But what could I do? She
came to my doorstep. She fell on her knees. I couldn't
bear to hear you talk to her like that, Sabra. I had to
stop you. You do understand, don't you?' she pleaded,
wanting her sister on her side, unable to bear being
estranged from her Sabra.

'No, I don't,' Sabra said frankly. 'Why couldn't you
bear it? She is the daughter of a woman you have hated
for years, the person who grossly humiliated you and
was the cause of your depression and illness. The callous
creature almost killed you!'

Listening patiently to her sister, Kaniz chose her
next words with care, knowing that Sabra would be
surprised by them.

'What you say is all true, or was, my sister, but the
reason I couldn't bear it is because she *is* my son's
destiny.'

Sabra was totally silenced. When still no words left
her sister's astonished mouth, Kaniz felt compelled to
explain.

'I know you are surprised, Sabra. But listen to me,
please, and hear what I have to say. It was because I
knew she held my son's happiness in her hands, that
I went to ask for her hand in marriage. You yourself
advised me to do so – remember?'

'But not after what has happened,' Sabra replied
sharply, having at last found her tongue.

'We all make mistakes, my dear Sabra. Mine
was holding a grudge against her mother for over two

decades. I love my son so much. All I hanker for is to see a smile on his face and a light to enter his eyes. It has been quenched for so long, Sabra. And it is all because of me. I have stood in the way of his happiness, as you have always told me. I care nothing about my loss of face. I know, in my very bones, that my son's heart is entwined with this woman. Who am I to tear them apart, Sabra? I tried to do it, but I learnt a bitter lesson, to my cost. Tell me, where did it lead me? As you yourself warned me, I lost my son in the process.

'Now I want my son back! I want to see him, now, today – this afternoon! This very second! Sabra, a burden has been lifted from me. I feel light-headed and happy. I am so glad she has come – remember, she came herself, I didn't call her. She begged for my forgiveness – I didn't demand it. We can now ask for her hand properly. She will not refuse us now. She dare not, and she will not. She loves my son! You see, I know her so well!' Kaniz ended triumphantly, her eyes alight with pleasure and excitement, scanning her sister's face eagerly.

Nonplussed, Sabra didn't know what to say – whether to rant, rage or to laugh at her sister. In the end she opted for silence, imagining in her mind, her sister blooming with life and joy again as she found herself beginning to believe Kaniz's words.

'Sabra, there is so much to do. Send Neesa for the matchmaker, Kulsoom. I am raring to go! Every minute is precious! I cannot wait to have Firdaus in this house as my daughter-in-law.'

'Sister, I think you have truly become deranged. I cannot take it all in. You are too fast for me, I am afraid,' Sabra sighed, with an answering smile and warmth in her eyes which flashed the answer that Kaniz had sought.

'I know I have knocked you for six,' Kaniz giggled, 'but remember I am the new Kaniz. Just forget the old one. I killed her the day I decided to ask for Firdaus's hand. Now are you going to sit there all day, or will you go for Neesa?' She rubbed her hands together. 'I am dying to have a chat with Kulsoom. The village will see a wedding that it will never forget! After all, it will be my only son's – my beloved's. There will be a trousseau for Firdaus that even Habib's daughter Ruby didn't receive from that Karachi tycoon, Sikander. Also I want the *halwaie*, the sweetmeat chef, to be summoned here immediately to take down the order for the engagement party. I want, not only all the normal sweetmeats, but also the traditional white sugary *pathasay* made especially for the children. The whole village will receive enough food to stuff themselves silly. There is so much to do, Sabra dear, and I am so excited. And I desperately need your help. So, you see, you definitely cannot leave us until after the wedding,' Kaniz ended happily.

Sabra smiled lovingly at her sister. It looked as if the future was indeed going to be rosy for Kaniz, after all. She sat down next to her sister and, removing the chador from Kaniz's head, she began to massage her oily scalp again. There would be no need for almond oil head massages any more. Her son's wedding would give Kaniz back her inner strength.

Sitting on the floor before the sofa, Kaniz tilted her head back towards her sister and closed her eyes. Behind her lids she could still see Firdaus on the floor, with her hands held up in supplication. Then from somewhere else there flashed the hideous scene of herself in a similar position. Kaniz's eyes screwed up waiting for the pain, but nothing happened. Giggling in

her mind, Kaniz opened her eyes. Two silly proud women had both bowed down and touched the ground. Both had had their faces smeared in the mud in equal measure. Chaudharani Kaniz was well and truly vindicated.

Chapter 59

KULSOOM CROSSED THE main village street from Kaniz's *hawaili* into the side lane leading to Fatima's home. Her footsteps were light and hurried. She couldn't wait for the moment when she would break the bombshell to an unsuspecting Fatima and her daughters. Just to see their expressions would be ample reward.

Salma heard the urgency of solid knocks on the door and rushed to open it. Kulsoom was standing outside, holding her arm up and looking at her glass bangles. She had just broken three of them, knocking. Salma opened the door wide and asked her to come in. 'Are you all right Auntie?' she said, wondering what all the excitement was about.

'Where are your mother and sister Firdaus?' Kulsoom asked, letting herself be led into the guest room, while counting how many bangles she still had left on her bony arm.

'Please be seated. I'll go and call them down. They are sunbathing on the rooftop.'

'Wait, Salma, don't call them down, I will go up,' Kulsoom bravely volunteered.

'Are you sure, Auntie?' Salma teased, a smile on her face. She knew Kulsoom hated climbing steps.

By the time Kulsoom reached the rooftop balcony, she was panting heavily. The excitement, however, was still threatening to tear her ribs apart.

On spotting Kulsoom, with her small hand held tightly against her heaving chest and her dark sun-tanned cheeks flushed with the heat of exertion, Fatima laughed aloud.

'Welcome, Kulsoom Jee, but what are you doing up here? You shouldn't have climbed all those stairs. We would have come down.'

'It is all right, Fatima Jee,' Kulsoom replied mag-nanimously, in a hoarse voice and still trying to catch her breath. 'I am not used to so much exercise, like climbing all these stairs at one go,' she explained feebly.

Firdaus quickly removed her book from the chair and pulled it over for Kulsoom. Secretly amused Salma went down again to fetch some refreshments. Scanning their faces, Kulsoom smiled, her small eyes glittering amid her wrinkled face.

'I have great news for you both,' she announced, still panting for breath.

'What is it, Kulsoom Jee? I could tell by looking at your flushed face that you had some important news for us,' Fatima teased pleasantly, glancing slyly at her daughter.

'Fatima Jee, I feel as if my chest is going to burst at the seams. My old battered heart has never suffered so much excitement since this morning. I am sure I am going to die of a heart attack, probably right up here on your rooftop.'

'God forbid if something happened to you, Sister Kulsoom. What would we all do without you?' Fatima said kindly. 'Please tell us, don't keep us in suspense.'

Kulsoom braced herself, standing up straight. She wanted to achieve the right effect. She hadn't sacrificed her heart or climbed all those steps for nothing. Nor did she have any intention of wasting an ounce of this golden opportunity that had generously been turned her way. After all, Chaudharani Kaniz had bestowed upon her a high status as the carrier of good tidings which would fulfil Fatima's lifelong dream.

'Fatima, you are a very lucky woman,' she began as a form of prelude, twitching her earring in place around her small right ear. 'Your star sign is definitely beckoning you.'

The conversation was getting nowhere and Fatima was beginning to feel irritated with Kulsoom, but she managed to hide it. She knew the old matchmaker inside out, with all her flaws and foibles, and was thus able to tolerate Kulsoom's ritualistic way of telling news. Biding her time, patiently she allowed Kulsoom the luxury of talking in riddles, and for as long as she wished.

'I see, Kulsoom Jee,' Fatima replied in a neutral tone, keeping her face straight and pretending not to be interested, while she fanned herself.

Firdaus's lips quirked. She herself had always found the matchmaker an amusing and a grotesque figure. The old lady would never change. How else would she make a living? She did it, of course, by manipulating people's desires and interests, cleverly pulling the right strings at the right time, in the right place and with the right people, as Firdaus well knew.

With her shawl straight in place over her bosom, and her gold locket with the word Allah embossed on it conveniently dangling out of the *chador*, the old woman said portentously: 'I have just come from the *hawaili*.'

She now had both their attention. Firdaus stiffened, dropping her eyes to the book in her lap. Fatima's gaze locked itself on to Kulsoom's lips. The seconds ticked away, and Fatima feared that everybody could hear her banging heartbeat. Then, slyly glancing at them from under hooded eyes, having now ascertained that she had their full attention, Kulsoom plunged forth.

'Chaudharani Kaniz has asked for Firdaus's hand in marriage for her son Khawar. If you find the proposal agreeable, she will come to initiate the engagement ceremony. How about that?' Kulsoom finished with a hearty laugh, scanning their faces with interest.

Total silence greeted Kulsoom's dramatic announcement. The only audible sound was that of the village flour mill grinding away the wheat, and the village tube well sloshing water into the fields of rape and sugar cane, and the chomping of their neighbour's fodder machine. Mother and daughter's glances clashed. The unheard-of had come about. The sky had met the land. The impossible Chaudharani had formally asked – no, more correctly 'stooped' – for her daughter's hand, hers the washerwoman's.

With a sigh of satisfaction escaping her lips, Fatima rested her back against the thick bolster. Years of snubs and abuse by that woman were washed away in an instant. Whether they accepted the proposal or not, the Chaudharani had herself asked for Firdaus's hand. It was done, despite her vehement assertion that she would rather die than do it. Life was strange, making people eat their words, knocking humility into them, Fatima pondered.

Firdaus for her part, felt embarrassed and uncomfortable. How could Kaniz ask for her hand again in the light of what she had done? Also there was the question

of Khawar. Had Kaniz consulted her son? Or was it her own decision? Gratified and humbled by Kaniz's proposal though she was, her pride wouldn't let Firdaus give her permission until she knew what Khawar felt for her. The last time she had seen him, he had treated her like dirt. I am not going to throw myself at him, she decided fiercely. I, too, have my pride. I will not marry him just to please the two mothers. He will have to propose personally.

Fatima was the first to break the silence. 'Thank you, Sister Kulsoom, for such good tidings. I find it so hard to believe. How did it all come about? You know what her opinion has been on this matter. On the other hand, I think she has undergone a change of heart recently.' Fatima shot a meaningful glance at her daughter, causing Firdaus to blush. Her mother would never allow her to forget her foolish act in letting Kaniz beg on her knees.

'You are right, Fatima Jee, it is most unusual. I couldn't believe it when Neesa came to summon me to the *hawaili*. I was very surprised. You see, I have not spoken to her for the last two years, especially since Khawar left home.' Kulsoom stopped, recalling her astonishment at the change wrought in Kaniz's manner and appearance. 'She is a different woman now,' she told them. 'Do you know, her hand actually trembled when she lifted a cup of tea, Fatima Jee! You have seen her recently, haven't you? She has always been a beautiful woman, but now she looks quite haggard. Her manner – I can't describe it.' Kulsoom thought for a moment. 'She actually regarded me, for the first time in her life, as a human being and not just as a servant to do her bidding. There was warmth in her look. She didn't say much, but whatever she uttered bore no resemblance to

the old, demanding Kaniz. She actually looked me directly in the eye, all the time I was there.'

Kulsoom cackled gently. 'Her sister Sabra, who has been staying with her for ever such a long time, warned me that I should be gentle and say nothing which might upset her. As if I would! I never upset people. My job is to please people, not to upset them. How else would my business run?'

She beamed. 'She used to make me quake in my shoes and feel one inch high. To her I was just the matchmaker, one of those many menials who had a subservient role to play in her life. Now do you know what she said, Fatima Jee? She called me "Sister Kulsoom"! Me I tell you, she is a changed person. Have you any idea what might have brought about this change, Fatima Jee?'

'No idea at all,' Fatima replied evasively.

'So what are you going to do, Fatima Jee? What shall I say to Chaudharani Kaniz?'

'I don't know what to say. We are obviously very flattered and honoured. I suppose it depends on the two people who are getting married. You know my view on this. I have always wanted Khawar for Firdaus. He is a wonderful person. But I am afraid, Kulsoom, that things have been very strained between the two families over the past few years and months. I really don't know what to do. Ask my daughter! She is the proud, stubborn one, who once vowed that she would never marry into that family, and would remain a spinster rather than enter that home. That is true, isn't it, Firdaus?'

Fatima's voice lashed at her daughter with anger. Firdaus, who had been listening to everything that had been said, just looked from one woman to the other.

'It is true what my mother says, Auntie Jee,' she said

finally. 'But things change – we all change. I will accept the Chaudharani's proposal willingly and I am very happy and honoured to do so, but on one condition . . .'

'*What?*' Fatima sprang up from her chair, unable to believe her ears. 'Have you lost your senses, my girl?' She didn't care whether Kulsoom heard or not! 'You are in no position to bargain! You proud vixen.'

'Mother, please!' Firdaus hissed under her breath. 'At least let me finish. I was about to say that I will accept on the condition that Khawar proposes to me personally. After all, I will be marrying him, not his mother. It was the *chaudharani* who asked me, not him. How do I know that he still wants to marry me? He might have changed his mind. I do not want to marry a man who would be marrying me just to please his mother and out of sufferance.'

'Oh, you sly girl!' Kulsoom laughed. 'That boy has been besotted with you for nearly fifteen years, and you say that he won't marry you?'

'People change, Auntie Jee. We have just been discussing that very topic,' Firdaus replied stiffly, hedged in both by Kulsoom's innocence and her mother's innuendoes.

'OK,' the old woman said brightly. 'Shall I say to Chaudharani Kaniz that you accept, but would also like Khawar to propose in person?'

'Yes, please Auntie Jee,' Firdaus whispered.

'Also, Kulsoom Jee, tell the Chaudharani that I would personally like to accept it and I will come and visit her shortly,' added Fatima.

'Of course I will. I hope you are going to make me a happy woman, Fatima. I will have fulfilled your dream. This locket and pair of earrings have become rather old

now.' Kulsoom held up her locket from her chest and dangled it meaningfully in front of Fatima.

The other woman laughed. 'If and when my Firdaus marries, I promise you that I will grace your neck with a new locket that will pull your neck down. One with a large ruby in it.'

'That is most generous of you, Fatima Jee. I will thank you by finding a wonderful *rishta* for Fazeelet, your last daughter and, of course, for your son. Tell him to come home from Dubai. You are all rich now. I will look out for a lovely bride for him. A tall, fair one – just like him.'

'Don't forget education, Kulsoom Jee,' Fatima teased.

'Of course. These days all men seem to want educated women – even those with not a certificate to their own name.

'Of course, there are some men, the *very* educated ones, who only want homemakers – *gheraloo* women. Personally, I think they feel threatened by those other dynamic, educated and professional women. It is either that or they want to have power and authority over their wives. I believe education is good for girls, but not for them to work. A home needs a woman to run it. If both husband and wife work, how can the house run?'

'I am afraid, Kulsoom Jee, you are talking to the wrong woman here. I am all for women working. Have you forgotten, I myself have worked for so long and raised a family. My Firdaus works and I do not expect her to give it up once she is married. I didn't pay thousands of rupees on her for it all to go to waste, for her just to stay at home and twiddle her thumbs. No, a woman needs her own life, a sense of independence and to feel valued. To have achieved something.'

'I daresay you are right, Fatima Jee,' Kulsoom replied diplomatically, swiftly changing her tune. It wasn't a good tactic in her business to displease her clients. She always agreed wherever she could, without losing face. And after all, she herself was a working woman.

After refreshments and an early lunch, Kulsoom returned to Kaniz's *hawaili* to deliver the messages. On the way back she had met Siraj Din and told him the good news also.

He was very pleased for everyone. His agile mind at once began to work. If Firdaus married Khawar, then perhaps Firdaus would stay in the village and return to the post in the school. At the moment they had only issued a temporary contract to the new head-mistress. The latter was all right, but she wasn't a local woman. Sometimes he wished his own grand-daughter, Zarri Bano, would become the headmistress. But he knew he was fooling himself. An urban and international life was more her thing. His son was right. Their Zarri Bano was not a '*Bibi*', a woman who barely stepped out of her home. He prayed for happiness and serenity in his daughter-in-law and granddaughter's life.

Chapter 60

FATIMA HAD ASKED Chaudharani Kaniz, via Kulsoom, if it was possible to visit her.

Kaniz replied promptly. Almost an hour later, Neesa came to the house with a message for Fatima that Chaudharani Kaniz and her sister Sabra were looking

forward to meeting her. At Neesa's words a thrill of excitement rushed through Fatima's body.

'Girls, get my blue Shangai suit out!' she barked at her daughters as soon as Neesa had departed. 'Impressions matter and I want to look my best. I think I'll need to, for, if the truth be told, I am dreading this meeting.' She turned to look from one daughter to the other, standing in the middle of the courtyard.

'Why are you dreading it?' Salma asked curiously.

'I'm not exactly sure, dear. It's just that, as you well know, we two women haven't got on for almost half of our lives. So it is a bit strange to consider her as my in-law. Still we'll both have to get used to it, I guess,' she said ruefully.

Fatima looked across at Firdaus, who was crocheting a lace pillow cover while sitting on the veranda! The young girl looked up at her mother, keeping her thumbs on the stitch.

'Don't forget to mention that without Khawar's personal proposal, I will not be able to marry him,' she said firmly. 'In your own feverish delight, do not forget my pride!'

'Your pride,' Fatima almost screamed, her tongue on fire, rounding on her eldest daughter, '. . . nearly cost us everything, you ungrateful girl!'

Firdaus calmly held her gaze, then deftly continued crocheting the lace. Exasperated, Fatima turned away. An hour later she left her home for the *hawaili*. 'These young people don't appreciate anything,' Fatima mumbled to herself, shaking her head in disbelief. The *chaudharani*, the mother of the young man, was asking for her daughter's hand but she, the arrogant miss, still wished to hear it from his own lips. The world had

indeed changed. Fiaz hadn't proposed to *her*. At that time it just wasn't considered respectable. Parents did the proposing and the arranging, the children agreed to or declined the other's hand.

And look what her daughter had done! Thrown a *chaudharani* out of a room! Fatima shivered. In her day, if a village elder even hinted that he sought your daughter for a relative of his or for other people, one was duty bound to accept, because the elder's honour, his *izzat*, depended on it. If he were to place his turban in front of you, refusal was totally out of the question. It was almost tantamount to his laying his honour at your feet.

Nowadays, apparently, the young people cared for nobody's *izzat*. Neither their family's nor their own. Women were now more independent and more assertive, and wished to shape their own destinies. Parents had to now gracefully bow down and in the process become prisoners of their children's whims and fancies.

Fatima stood outside the *hawaili* gate and let her eyes lovingly scan the tall, majestic, white-washed building, looking at it with pride. It was going to be her daughter's home. One could spot this *hawaili* a mile from the village. It was the only one with two storeys. Even Siraj Din's only had one.

She rang the bell, then quaking, recalled her own previous visit. If only she could erase it forever from her mind!

Neesa let her in. She was shown into the guest room, and asked to be seated. The *chaudharani* and her sister would soon be down from the top floor, she was further informed.

Fatima looked curiously around the room, noting that it was furnished to the highest taste. The marble-chip floor, the matching marble tables with sturdy gilded legs, the tall fireplace housing a large electric heater – all shone like mirrors. The curtains with beautiful swags and tails, gracefully draped themselves across the large windows, falling softly to the floor. The place reeked of opulence. There was even a plush woven pure silk rug on the floor in the centre of the room. It is just as well I took my shoes off outside, Fatima thought, feeling the delicate silkiness of the carpet with her toes.

It was a strange experience for Fatima. She was seeing everything from a new angle. Her daughter would soon be living in these surroundings, and one day she would be the mistress of everything. Fatima sighed with pleasure.

Neesa returned and Fatima looked up at her expectantly. 'The *chaudharani* finds it difficult to come downstairs,' the servant told her. 'She fell down the steps yesterday evening. She requests, therefore, that you accompany me upstairs to her quarters, if you don't mind.'

'Of course not,' Fatima answered, her heart suddenly beginning to beat faster. Was this a deliberate snub on Kaniz's part? Was she being summoned up like any menial? Then Fatima dismissed the thought as beneath her. Hadn't Neesa said that Kaniz had fallen? Also, she herself was in no position to pick bones about trivial matters. After all, Kaniz probably still thought of her as a washerwoman. Therefore, in Kaniz's eye, it was right for Fatima to be beckoned up rather than to come down herself.

*

Kaniz was waiting nervously, in her room. She glanced up at her sister sitting next to her, panic in her eyes, and Sabra gave her hand a reassuring squeeze.

The sound of steps outside the room made them look at the door. Neesa entered first, followed closely by Fatima. Sabra stood up to greet Fatima, while Kaniz found herself unable to move.

The sight of her old rival standing in the doorway brought back the memory of their last meeting, and she recalled Fatima's cruel words with painful clarity; they thumped away in her brain. The smile she had pinned up, for Fatima's benefit, deserted her and she found herself staring into the other woman's eyes with a look of pure hatred.

Seeing her remain seated and sensing the hostility that emanated from her, Fatima's joy was quenched. Had Kaniz invited her here merely to humiliate her? Was it all a joke? Her confidence faded.

Sabra quickly put an end to Fatima's speculations as she warmly embraced her and issued words of greeting. '*Bismillah*, *bismillah*, my sister.'

'*Assalam-Alaikum*,' Fatima greeted her between dry lips.

'*Wa Laikum-Salam*. Come and sit down on this sofa. My sister has been ill and finds it difficult to move much. Excuse us for calling you up.'

'That is fine, Sister Sabra. How are you, Sister Kaniz?' Fatima's eyes now focused warily on the other woman's face.

Wrestling with her personal hatred of her rival, Kaniz triumphed by managing to pin back a smile to her lips. 'I am fine,' she answered pleasantly enough. 'How is your family? How is Brother Fiaz doing?' The words sounded alien on Kaniz's lips, and both knew it.

Previously Kaniz had never enquired or even cared a *paisa* for Fatima's family. It was thus a strange new beginning for them both. A new fragile thread being woven into the tapestry of their lives and relationships.

'He is doing well and he sends his good wishes to you. My daughters are fine and Firdaus enquires especially after your health?' Fatima voiced politely reverting to the subject of her visit. Before her surprised eyes, Kaniz's face softened and broke into a smile.

'She came to see me, Sister Fatima, and she laid her head in my lap, like this . . .' Kaniz gestured to her lap. 'She touched my feet.'

'I am glad, Sister Kaniz. That is what she should have done. She told me everything.' Fatima's glance wavered before Kaniz for a second and then she decided to be honest. It was better to bring everything out in the open now. 'I was astounded and very hurt at her behaviour. I think she has been a very stupid young woman. I hope you have it in your heart to forgive her, for I still find it difficult to do so.'

'I have. It is because I have that I have asked for her hand for my son.'

Fatima abruptly dropped her eyes, afraid that they would betray the rush of pleasure that suddenly coursed through her body. So it appeared Kaniz did, indeed, want her daughter as her daughter-in-law.

'I am honoured,' Fatima replied, taking in a deep, uneven breath. 'My whole family is honoured, Kaniz Sahiba. Kulsoom brought your message to us. It came as a special surprise, because we didn't expect it. Especially in the light of our last meeting.' Fatima scanned Kaniz's face warily. 'We often say unkind and cruel things,' she continued in a low voice. 'Things which we do not always mean, Chaudharani Sahiba.'

'If you are referring to *your* words, then, Fatima Jee, I must remind you that you meant every one of them,' Kaniz interrupted quietly. She wouldn't let Fatima get away with that comment.

'Then I beg for your forgiveness,' Fatima replied with a blush. Again her glance dipped in front of Kaniz.

'It is all right, Sister Fatima, I deserved it all, anyway,' Kaniz replied magnanimously. 'But do not let us talk about the past; I do not like to dwell on it. Fatima Jee, I have been ill for some time. During my illness, I had the opportunity to think about everything and had to face some painful facts about myself and others. I now want to put the past firmly aside. I eagerly look forward to the future and to your daughter becoming my daughter-in-law, my son's wife, our next *chaudharani.*'

'You are very generous, Kaniz Sahiba. You have put us both, mother and daughter, to shame.' Fatima was overcome by Kaniz's generosity.

'Please, no more!' Kaniz held up her hand. 'Tell me, is it you who are accepting or your daughter? For it is what your daughter says that matters to me. She is a proud girl, just as I used to be. Is she going to do us the honour of stepping into my home as my daughter-in-law? Is she able to swallow her pride?'

'There is no pride, Sister Kaniz, just the foolishness of youth. She has, however, said . . .' Fatima paused, remembering her daughter's words with disgust. Nevertheless, they had to be said.

'What has she said?' Kaniz asked, feeling her heartbeat accelerate. Sabra noticed the anxiety in her sister's eyes and gave her hand another reassuring squeeze.

'She says that she accepts, but only if Khawar

personally wishes it so. She believes that it is you who now desires the match and not your son. If he personally proposes to her, she will very happily accept.'

'I see.' Kaniz paused and was momentarily lost in her thoughts before speaking and looking directly at Fatima again. 'She is right, of course, right. Khawar *should* personally propose to her. That is the way of the world now, especially with the young people. But you know that it is the respectable thing for the parents to ask first.'

'Yes, of course. But you know what these young people are like.'

'I certainly do. Tell your daughter that Khawar will personally propose to her, then we will set into motion the engagement ceremony. Are you happy with that?'

'Yes, I am. Thank you, Kaniz Sahiba.'

They talked for a short time longer, keeping deliberately to safe topics, whilst they sipped iced lemon drinks.

Her heart singing with joy, Fatima left – a very happy woman. Her mind was buzzing with ideas for the forthcoming wedding preparations.

In the room upstairs the two sisters sat in silence. It was Sabra who spoke first. 'What's on your mind, my dear? Are you perhaps thinking what I am thinking – that you have not yet told your Khawar anything of this?'

'Yes, Sabra Jee. I am wondering what he will say. Will he be very angry, do you think?' Kaniz's face was creased with lines of worry; she pulled nervously on the corner of her head shawl.

'No, my darling sister, why should he be angry with you? How dare he? After all, it is for his sake that you

have done this. Let him dare to say anything . . . I will deal with him!'

Khawar was livid. He couldn't believe what his mother and aunt had done. For a long time he remained silent, with his head lowered and his hands flat on the dining table. Sabra had told him after he finished his dinner. Kaniz was sitting in the other room.

'Well, my dear nephew, you are very quiet. It is what you've always wanted, isn't it?' Sabra demanded.

'It was what I wanted *once*,' Khawar told her, trying to keep a grip on himself, 'but not in the light of what has happened recently, not after what my mother suffered. You had no right to interfere, either of you! Why on earth didn't you consult me first? Do you think I want to have anything to do with that, that *creature* after how she treated poor Mummy? I can never forgive her! She is not worth it, Auntie, You don't honestly think that I would marry her now, do you? No way!' He glared at his aunt.

Sabra stood up from the table and, standing behind Khawar, touched him gently on the nape of his neck.

'Well, it seems that young woman of yours would not accept the proposal anyway unless you proposed personally to her.'

A bitter laugh rang out of Khawar's full masculine mouth.

'She'll have a long time to wait, then. You two can hatch whatever plots you like – but I have no intention of marrying her.' He stood up to leave, towering over his aunt. She restrained him, her hand on his arm and a smile on her face.

'You young people think only of yourselves, never of other people. Now listen to me – and hard.

Khawar, you left home for that woman; presumably you wanted her very much. You had quarrels for her sake. Now how can you tell me that she doesn't mean anything to you! You still want her, my son; do not try to deny it to yourself. Not only that, this marriage means a great deal to your mother. She is overjoyed. I have never seen her this happy before – and she wants to make *you* happy, too, especially since Firdaus came and asked for her forgiveness.'

'She came!' he said in a raised voice. 'Does nobody tell me anything any-more? Why did she come?'

'Well, she came and went on her knees and begged for your mother's forgiveness. Oh, it was quite an act. You missed a treat, Khawar. Anyway, my sister has forgiven her and is now thrilled and ready to have her here in this home as your wife. Do you know what your mother said? She said that Firdaus was your fate and that she holds your destiny in her hands.'

'I see. It looks as if my mother is indeed a changed woman,' the young man said thoughtfully. 'Well then, if she desires it so much, who am I to refuse? If her heart is bent on Firdaus, I will have to start battering on my own, I am afraid.' He laughed. 'To wake it up!' He patted his chest with one hand.

'Huh. Your heart was wide awake already,' Sabra teased him. 'What do you take me for? It was all a pretence anyway.'

'No, Auntie. It wasn't a pretence. My anger allowed me to forget her. I am still angry with her, but if that madam wants a proposal, we'll see what we can do.'

There was a sparkle in his eyes that hadn't been there before. He also looked much more relaxed. Sabra was

happy for him. Just as he was about to move away, she pulled his head down and kissed him on his forehead and cheeks.

'We will not let you go until there is a bride in this house, Aunt,' he vowed and kissed her on the cheeks in return.

'I have no intention of going until then,' she said tartly. 'But you had better get a move on. I have already been here for over two months. My own family is getting restless now. Oh Khawar, I cannot wait for your wedding. This home will be happy once again, at long long last.'

'What about Aunt Fatima?' he asked suddenly.

'Oh, don't worry about her. Your mother and she are getting on like a house on fire. You will have no thorns in your flesh from any quarters, I promise you my son,' she ended, letting him go.

She immediately went up to see her sister. Kaniz looked up expectantly at her, feeling nervous all of a sudden.

'It is all right – he will propose to her. You can relax.' Sabra gave her a reassuring smile.

'You are a wonderful sister! I don't know what I would have done without you. What did he say?'

'Nothing for you to worry about. He is very happy, and he wants to marry very soon.'

'Oh Sabra, I am so happy!' Kaniz stood up and reached to embrace her sister. They remained locked together for a long time. Tears of joy and relief streamed down Kaniz's cheeks.

'Thank you for everything, and I thank Allah Pak for giving me this blessing. Do you know what I am going to do before the wedding, Sister Sabra? I am going to hold a big religious gathering, and invite all the village

women to it. We will ask Zarri Bano to lead the special prayers.'

'I don't know if she'll still be here in the village, Sister, I gather she is getting married herself soon. Have you not heard? She will be marrying her late sister's husband. I have never seen her closely, but they say that she is very beautiful.'

'Well, my Firdaus is very attractive.'

'Isn't she short and dark any more?' Sabra teased her sister, winking at her.

'Don't you dare say that about her! I was just being catty and vindictive then. Her colouring is good, she is almost as fair as you and me, and her height is that of an average woman. Let anybody comment on that and I will pull out their tongue.'

They both burst out laughing. Later, Kaniz insisted on Sabra going to their large storeroom and looking in their steel cases. There was so much to do and to buy. At least they could see if they had enough rolls of fabric for the engagement presents to be given to Firdaus and her family.

Chapter 61

A WEEK HAD PASSED since Fatima had visited Kaniz in her *hawaili*. Khawar still had made no effort to get in touch with Firdaus. He kept promising his mother and aunt that he would do it very soon. Firdaus, for her part, waited nervously for news from him every day. By the fifth day she had given up.

'Well, Mother, I told you, didn't I?' she said cynically. 'Chaudharani Kaniz may desire this match, but

the groom obviously doesn't. If he really wanted to marry me he would have contacted me by now. I find it very humiliating. I told you earlier that he has no intention of marrying me. He has still not forgiven me.' She was rueful.

'I doubt it, my dear. Yet I am a little surprised myself. Never mind, give him another day or two, and then I will intervene.'

'No, Mother. Please — no intervention,' Firdaus begged.

'Whatever you wish, my daughter.' Fatima waved her hand in defeat. Her eldest daughter's *rishta* had given her more headaches and heartaches than her other two daughters put together. She was sure that she was going to die of palpitations before ever she saw Firdaus's hands painted with wedding henna patterns.

Next morning, much to the delight of Firdaus's entire family, a young boy from Kaniz's *hawaili* came with a message. 'Master Khawar wishes to talk privately with Madam Firdaus, if that is OK with Auntie Fatima and Uncle Fiaz, of course? Would she be so kind as to meet him by the old well, just outside the village, later this afternoon. The well where they used to play as children,' the boy elaborated.

Firdaus's first instinct was to refuse. 'Let him sweat it out. Who does he think he is?' she told her mother heatedly.

'Again, I feel duty bound to drill it into you, my headstrong daughter,' Fatima snapped back, 'that you are in no position to let him sweat it out, as you say. On the contrary, he is teaching you a lesson. Letting *you* sweat it out. He is calling the shots, my dear, *not* you.'

As much as she would have liked to call his bluff, Firdaus eventually set out for the old well.

It was a bright sunny afternoon and the black crows were merrily cackling away in the trees. Firdaus had dressed herself with care; her sisters had excitedly helped her to choose the colour and pattern of her suit. They also insisted on curling the ends of her raven-black hair so that it fell like a heavy bouncy curtain around her shoulders. 'We want you to sweep Khawar off his feet,' they teased her.

Draping a *dupatta* casually over her hair and shoulders, Firdaus left her home. She walked through the cobbled village lanes, skipping over the pools of water where the stones had gone missing, then she followed the path through the fields towards the old well. She let the *dupatta* fall to her shoulders as the breeze blew it off.

Nobody was around in the fields. The serenity of the surroundings, the greenish-yellow carpet of the rape fields brought a smile to her lips. This was what she had missed in the bustling, polluted city of Hyderabad – the clean fresh air and utter tranquillity.

Under the shade of a mature tree with its gnarled dry roots spread across the path was the old village well. It was now redundant in use, apart from drawing water for the fields using the buffalo plough. In the old days, it was the focus of the village social activity, as women made daily journeys to it from their homes to draw water. Filling their large earthenware pots, they then swung them up in the air to prop them neatly on their heads, and walked back home, gossiping vivaciously amongst themselves.

Brushing down the one-foot thick edge of the well with an old rag lying nearby, Firdaus sat down on it

and peered into the water. It was a long time since she had been to this spot. Her mind flew back to those childhood days when she, Zarri Bano, Ruby, little Jafar and Khawar used to meet and chase each other around the large tree next to the well. A cool breeze flowing through the branches swept her hair in front of her face.

She looked up when she heard the sound of horse's hooves. Khawar and his white horse were a few yards away. Firdaus turned to look down into the well again, feeling very shy all of a sudden.

'Meditating, Firdaus?' Khawar climbed down from his horse and tied it loosely to the tree.

'No, waiting for you to push me in, as you almost did twelve years ago!' She resented the fact that he had not smiled at her or issued a pleasant greeting. Just offered two cold words like a douche of icy water from the well in the winter.

He walked over and, picking up the sturdy chain with one hand, he threw the well's silver bucket down into the water. It fell with a thud, hitting the dark surface. Khawar pulled the bucket out, now filled with water, and with the plastic container left on the flat well edge, he began to rinse his hands and face.

'Is this your new bathroom? Have you been thrown out of your home?' Firdaus asked cheekily, letting her eyes scan his face, his hair and neck visible from his shirt collar.

'As you well know, I have lots of bathrooms, Madam Firdaus, but there is nothing like drawing water from a well. But you wouldn't know that, would you? Village wells and a Madam Principal just don't go hand in hand together these days, do they?'

Firdaus didn't miss his personal dig nor his scathing look. 'Nobody draws water from a well these days,' she

said steadily. 'I was brought up in the village, as you well know, but I have never carried a water-jug. They were from our grandmothers' days. People have showers and running hot water now, even in the village. So don't try to make me feel guilty, please!'

'I was just commenting.' He wiped his face with a large handkerchief, his eyes in turn moving over her face, hair and clothes, noting everything and not missing a thing.

'You must admit, however,' he continued, 'that this is an appropriate place for our meeting. You obviously received my message. It isn't by chance that you are here, is it?'

'No. I am here because Your Majesty demanded my presence.'

'And you, Madam Principal, deigned to obey. I am honoured indeed,' he said with a laugh and sat down on the brick ledge next to her. His eyes flickered over the neat profile of her face – her chin, her nose, her high cheekbones.

'You know why I wished to see you,' he stated quietly. His face was now very close and she could almost feel his breath on her face. 'You requested that I propose to you myself.'

'Not if you don't want to!' Firdaus said stiffly.

'What do you think I want, Firdaus?' he asked and waited for her reply, but she had none to give him. 'Well?' he prompted her, but still there was no response. 'The articulate Principal is known to have a sharp tongue – has a snake bitten it out now?' His voice was thick with laughter.

She turned and smiled, shyness spilling out of her eyes. He looked deep into them and understood. 'OK! I will spell it out for you, just in case your female

modesty has clamped your tongue, for once. I want you, Firdaus. Just as I have always wanted you for nearly a decade. I wish you to be my wife. You wanted a personal proposal, so this is it. Now, what is your answer? Are you going to be churlish and throw it back into my face, just for the sake of revenge?' he challenged.

'No, of course not! On the contrary I happily accept, but only if you give me the assurance that it is really what *you* want, and that you have truly forgiven me for what happened recently.' Colour crept into her cheeks. 'I am afraid you will be marrying *brass* — is that what you want? Dross in fact.'

'It is up to you, Firdaus, to prove that you can turn brass into the gold I first had,' he replied, his face serious.

'Tell me, Khawar, or my female pride will not let me rest otherwise; are you really marrying me for your mother's sake or do you personally want to?'

'You are a very persistent young woman. I thought I had already made myself very plain. Once again I will spell it out to you. No, I will demonstrate it.' As he spoke, he turned and took her hand in his. 'Look at me, Firdaus. I want you to marry me. I desire that very much because I love you. The fact that my mother desires it also is an added bonus. Now, have I made myself perfectly clear?'

'Crystal clear.' She drew her hand away and stood up. They were not married nor engaged. It wasn't right to be so physically close. She moved, placing a modest distance between them.

'What will you do about your job?' Khawar asked. He needed to know — his happiness rested on her answer.

'I will give up my job in the city,' Firdaus answered promptly, her eyes steady before his.

'I cannot let you do that. I know it is a good job for you,' he objected.

'Jobs aren't everything, Khawar Sahib. Anyway, I would love to return to the village, and if the village school management committee can find me a teaching job here, I'll be happy enough.'

Khawar laughed. 'The job of a headmistress is still yours. The other one is only temporary. The village will be so happy to have you back, my dear girl.'

Suddenly Firdaus spotted Baba Siraj Din coming down the path from his cattle byre. Her cheeks grew very warm.

'Tell your mother she can begin the arrangements. I happily accept. *Khudah Hafiz*! I must go. Baba Siraj Din is here!' She quickly pulled her *dupatta* over her head, out of respect for the old man. He had never seen her hair all open and draped around her shoulders. Blushing she ran off, taking the path leading back to the village.

As Khawar waited for Siraj Din to approach, he untied his horse from the tree.

'*Assalam-Alaikum*, my son. How are you? That was Firdaus, wasn't it?' Siraj Din asked, pointing to her disappearing figure with his walking stick.

'Yes, indeed it was, Baba Jee.'

Siraj Din had missed nothing. Even from a distance he had seen them sitting and talking together.

'Am I correct in thinking that now your two families are reconciled, we will soon be hearing some good news concerning you and Firdaus? There is a rumour around the village that your mother is preparing a magnificent wedding for you.'

'Yes, Baba Jee. *Insha'allah*. With your prayers and blessing, it seems that the feud between my mother and

Auntie Fatima is over. Firdaus and I are getting married – *al-hamdulillah*.'

'*Mubarak*, my son! I am very pleased for you both. Your mother has come a long way. She is to be praised and indeed congratulated. I will visit her. Let me know when the wedding is.'

'Of course, Baba Jee. We cannot do anything without your presence, guidance, and supervision, and of course your blessing and prayers. We have only just started the ball rolling. *Allah Hafiz*.'

Khawar climbed back onto his horse and cantered towards the village.

As Baba Siraj Jee watched him go, his thoughts turned to his own granddaughter, Zarri Bano. He prayed that she would settle down happily with Sikander!

Chapter 62

TWO HOURS AFTER the simple wedding ceremony and reception, her trousseau packed, Zarri Bano left for Karachi with Sikander and his family.

Waving them off from the verandah, Fatima wept on Shahzada's shoulder.

'Don't cry, Fatima. Aren't you happy?' Shahzada said chokily, her own eyes wet with tears.

'Yes,' the other woman sobbed. 'That is why I am crying. I'm going to miss her so much.'

'We must pray for them both, Fatima. I hope their marriage works out. We both know that Zarri Bano has entered it very reluctantly. Only this morning she told me that she would only stay in this marriage for a year.

She had that look on her face, you know the one. Fatima, I am so afraid she means what she says.' Shahzada stared anxiously at her friend and woman helper.

'You have nothing to worry about, Mistress Shahzada. They will work it out, you'll see,' Fatima reassured her *chaudharani* smoothly, with her strong conviction. She had great faith in human chemistry. There had always been magic between her princess and Sikander.

Zarri Bano sat perched in the corner of the car. Haris sat between herself and Sikander. His childish chatter helped to diffuse the tension building up between his father and aunt. Beneath the fringe of the large *dupatta* on her head, Zarri Bano chaffed under Sikander's eyes – they seemed to be roaming everywhere.

'I want to sit next to the window!' Haris demanded during the journey. Everyone thus rearranged themselves to let him sit where he wanted. As they moved, Sikander's thigh accidentally brushed against Zarri Bano's, making her swivel round in panic. Her husband stared steadily back at her, as he saw her inch further away from him. Pulling the heavily embroidered *dupatta* around her, Zarri Bano draped it further over her face to shield herself from his scorching gaze.

Suddenly, Sikander grabbed hold of her hand and held it tightly in his grasp. Shocked, and lost for breath, she tried to pull it away. In a voice too low for his mother or chauffeur to hear, Sikander growled out, 'I'm not going to eat you.' He moved his fingers over hers and began to caress them gently. Helplessly, Zarri Bano let him play with her fingers for a moment or two. Then she pulled her hand away.

Haris climbed back from the window and once again wriggled between them, hugging both adult in turn, he stayed there until the end of the journey.

As the car came to a standstill Zarri Bano stared at Sikander's home in Karachi. The imposing facade of the large villa was garlanded and lit with colourful lights. Inside, a group of women well-wishers and relatives were waiting to welcome home Sikander's new bride. They ceremoniously came forward in turns, as soon as she sat down on the sofa in the drawing room, to give her the 'initial greeting' *salami* presents in the form of money. The women were especially keen to meet the new bride. For they had heard that she was the elder sister of Sikander's dead wife and was reputed to be not only more beautiful than Ruby, but also a very devout woman. She was said to be always in *hijab*. Some believed the rumour that she even slept in it.

Today, however, the *burqa* was nowhere to be seen and she didn't look at all devout. On the contrary she was a blushing picture of a bride and almost like a glamorous actress. They just couldn't visualise her in a *burqa*. Her hair was elegantly styled, her eyes shone like gems. To match the wonderful smiling mouth, Allah had blessed her with a most attractive dimple that seemed to peep out at you every time she smiled.

'As you can see, the groom simply cannot take his eyes off her. He pretends that he is not looking at her, but have you noticed, my friend, he has not looked at a single soul in this room. Nor is it surprising as she is so beautiful. I told you so, didn't I?' whispered one woman to her friend; she had had the pleasure of having seen Zarri Bano's photograph in advance.

'Did you know that she was the one our Sikander

wanted to marry in the first place?' she further elaborated.

'Was she really?' The friend stared in wonder at the good-looking pair. 'Oh, how romantic!' As their neighbour, she was definitely going to cultivate a friendship with Sikander's new bride.

The evening meal was served to Sikander and Zarri Bano alone, on a special table, with only Haris joining them. It was a silent affair, during which Sikander frequently looked at his bride. She, on the other hand, kept her eyes down. It was as if they were complete strangers. God, she looks so vulnerable, he thought. It is almost as if she is afraid of me! He smiled, wanting to reassure her, but didn't quite know what to say.

Later in the evening, Sikander's elder sister Rahat suggested to Zarri Bano that she should go and rest in her room. Awkwardly, holding up her heavily embroidered silk skirt, she followed Rahat up the staircase into the large bedroom. Throwing open the door, Rahat stepped aside for Zarri Bano to enter.

Recognising the room, Zarri Bano froze. A large bed stood in the centre with a canopy of wedding streamers draped becomingly around it. Zarri Bano closed her eyes tight, feeling her legs giving away beneath her. Reaching for a chair, she sat down and looked at the bed with horror dawning on her face and in her eyes.

'Are you all right, dear sister?' Rahat asked in concern. It was just at that moment that Sikander appeared in the room. He looked at the bed and then at Zarri Bano's white face.

'Rahat, please leave us,' he urged. 'I will look after her.'

'All right, Brother Sikander.' Rahat quickly left,

disturbed by her sister-in-law's behaviour and wondering what was wrong.

In one neat movement, Sikander pulled down all the decorative streamers and threw them into a corner on the floor. Angry with himself, his sister and the whole situation, he bent down and spoke to his new bride in a tortured voice. 'Believe me, Zarri Bano, I had no idea they were going to bring you to this room!'

Zarri Bano stared at the bare, forlorn-looking bed.

'This was her room. That was her bed!' she cried out in agony, in a voice full of reproach. 'This was how it was for her. I can't sleep here! You *promised* me, Sikander.'

Then before his very eyes, shudders passed through her body. Her eyes were closed, as she deliberately shut him and the room out of her mind.

'You aren't sleeping here,' he said gently. 'You have your own room. My sister doesn't know of our situation. They have only done what people normally do for any bride. Please forgive her.'

'Ruby slept in that bed, Sikander!' Zarri Bano cried, breaking down and weeping for her dead sister. Her small forehead pendant dangled in front of her face.

Sikander moved away from her, watching her helplessly. She is not the only one with memories. Ruby was my wife! Doesn't she realise that I too am afraid of those painful memories? Sikander thought resentfully. He wanted to comfort her but didn't know what to do. If he touched her, he was sure to send her over the brink, shattering her fragile self-control. Instead, he used his voice to reach out to her.

'Zarri Bano, this is not your room and never will be.

If it makes you feel safe and happy, you can share
Haris's room for the time being. Come on. Let's get out
of here.'

Wiping her tears, Zarri Bano followed him word-
lessly into Haris's room. 'Here, make yourself at home,'
he said cheerfully. You are used to sleeping in this room
with Haris, aren't you? Either Mother or I will bring
you some milk later. Our woman helper will fetch your
suitcases.' Zarri Bano nodded gratefully, and Sikander
left her.

After changing into her night clothes, Zarri Bano
put Haris to bed. Straight after her prayers, she settled
down beside him and planted kisses on his sleepy fore-
head. 'I've done all this for you, my darling nephew,'
she whispered over his yawning face.

Zarri Bano tensed when someone knocked on the
door. Sikander entered with a glass of milk in his hand.
She had hoped that his mother would come rather than
him. In the semi-darkness of the room, his dark hair
gleaming after a shower, he looked tall and very attract-
ive in his dressing-gown over his pyjamas. Zarri Bano
felt a spate of nervousness.

His eyes on her face, Sikander came forward and
placed her glass of milk on the bedside cabinet. He hid
his disappointment from her. She had removed her jew-
ellery, her make-up and bridal suit – thus robbing him
of one of the groom's prerogatives, that of helping her
to remove her ornaments.

He stepped back, away from the bed and smiled
down at her. Zarri Bano blushed. Then she pulled the
quilt up to her neck to hide herself. Noting her gesture,
Sikander turned to look at his son.

'He is fast asleep,' he whispered.

'Yes,' Zarri Bano gladly commented, pleased to say

something to break the tension in the room and praying that he would leave soon.

Sikander moved over to his son's side of the bed and sat on the opposite corner. Zarri Bano relaxed.

'He'll be very happy to find you sleeping with him.'

'So he should be. After all, we married for his sake, didn't we?' Zarri Bano retorted.

Sikander looked down at the attractive appliqué pattern of birds and trees on the quilt cover, not answering her immediately. 'Yes, Zarri Bano, we did marry for Haris's sake, but I am still hoping that at the end it will be a real marriage. I didn't marry you just for Haris's sake, but for my sake too.' He wanted to say so much to her, to open the doorway to his heart, but he knew instinctively that it wasn't the right moment. A wrong move, a wrong step by him and Zarri Bano would surely blow her top. He couldn't risk that and jeopardise his relationship with her. Already they had both been dealt a blow in the other room.

'Zarri Bano, I get the feeling that you are afraid of me,' he ventured, looking up with a solemn expression in his eyes, 'afraid of my very presence. Please don't be. What is your ultimate fear, Zarri Bano? That I'll demand my rights? For the consummation of our marriage?' He saw her cheeks colour.

'That *is* what you fear most, isn't it? I know you too well for you to deny it, Zarri Bano. You must learn to trust me. I promised you before we got married that everything will be as you wish. The ball will always be in your court. Therefore you have no need to fear me or my presence. The woman I knew five years ago wasn't afraid of me – of anything, for that matter. I ask nothing, my dear, but pure friendship and companionship. What I don't want is you scurrying away from my

slightest touch. Apparently you've done a damned good job on yourself, on becoming totally a *pakeeza* woman, that even the shadow of a man frightens you. Yet I knew and had a glimpse of a very passionate woman once. But enough, I'll not talk about the past.'

'Have you finished with the lecture? The woman you talk about was a wanton one who I am ashamed to remember,' she told him flatly.

'I disagree. She wasn't wanton, just a normal woman, with normal instincts.'

'Therefore, you must know then that the woman you have in front of you is not a normal woman.'

'I will prove to you, one day, just how normal you are, Zarri Bano. But I'll not argue with you tonight. And yes . . .' he ended with a laugh and a mischievous twinkle in his eyes '. . . I have finished my lecture.'

Zarri Bano finally let a smile creep over her face. For the first time he noticed a sparkle in her eyes. His heart swelled with pride and hope. His old Zarri Bano wasn't dead, just lying dormant. She desperately needed time and support to awaken.

'Just learn to trust me,' he appealed, once more coming round the bed and standing near to her. He stared at her face and hair on the pillow, her lips half open. This was the image that had haunted him for so long.

Zarri Bano saw the look in his eyes and tensed. He sat down on the edge of the bed and unable to help himself, reached out and caressed her cheek. Zarri Bano found herself trapped in the fathomless pool of his eyes, which had darkened in shade. Recalling his words, she willed herself to relax, knowing she had to learn to trust him. By now his fingers were on her hair. Heat rushed through her, but she let him carry on.

There was a curious expression on his face. 'You are

the most beautiful woman I have ever met,' he said simply, his voice caressing her like velvet.

'Even more than Ruby?' Zarri Bano shocked herself by her question.

A look of sorrow passed across his face. 'Of course. She was your pale shadow, Zarri Bano. You are still exquisite behind your veil. It is this very face that has tantalised me and haunted me for the past five years.'

Zarri Bano didn't answer. Amazed at the warm glow bursting into life inside her, she revelled in the knowledge that she still held the power of her attraction over him. He still thinks of me as beautiful, she thought gladly.

His fingers finally rested on her lips and traced the shape of them. Then Sikander reluctantly withdrew his hand and he pulled the quilt up over her shoulders, covering her. Then he stood up to leave. One step at a time, I have told myself, and that is how it shall be, he reminded himself silently.

'Goodnight, Zarri Bano. And welcome to my home. You are going to the Far East the day after tomorrow, aren't you?' he said aloud.

'Yes,' she answered, feeling guilty for some reason.

'I'll drop you off at the airport myself. Have all the arrangements been made?'

'Yes.'

'*Allah Hafiz*, Zarri Bano.' He turned to leave.

'Sikander, thank you for everything. Another man would not be so understanding. I appreciate it.'

He turned round to face her. She was now sitting up. The quilt had fallen from her shoulders and her body's contours were outlined against her nightshirt. Feeling his eyes on her shoulders, Zarri Bano made no move to pull the quilt over herself.

Sikander was heartened by this small token of her trust. She didn't see him as a *gheir merd* any more and thus had no need to cover herself.

'It is I who should thank you, Zarri Bano, for going through with the marriage, especially when you were almost blackmailed into it by my son. If, at any time, you feel unhappy about anything, all you have to do is to let me know. We are, after all, husband and wife now. Goodnight!'

Not trusting himself to remain another minute in the room with her, Sikander made haste to leave. Closing the door behind him, he crossed the corridor and entered into his own bedroom.

In bed, Sikander evaluated the events of the day and his relationship with Zarri Bano. He recalled the moment of her entering the lounge hall in her bridal clothes and could still feel the sheer waves of pleasure that had washed over him. She had looked breathtaking, just as he had always imagined it. His heart had swelled with pride as the thought flashed across his mind. *This is the woman I want, have always wanted – and now she is going to be mine.*

His euphoria, however, was shortlived. After he had said his vows during the *nikkah* ceremony, the Imam had turned to Zarri Bano. She had looked straight at Sikander. Then with all the guests as witnesses she called Haris over to her and said clearly, 'Haris, do you want me to marry your daddy? I will only do this if you want me to.'

'Yes, Auntie, yes!' the child said, nodding his head energetically, snuggling to sit beside her.

It was only then that Zarri Bano followed the words of the Imam and finally signed the register. As she held the pen in her hand, poised to sign, she had looked up

at Sikander again. This time her eyes were colder than he had ever seen them before. Sikander's heart sank in dismay. She couldn't have made it clearer. He had been snubbed – spelling to him and all the guests that she was going through with the ceremony for her nephew's sake and only for his. Later when his hand had accidentally touched hers at the dinner table, she had jerked it away with a look of pure panic. Thoroughly disappointed, Sikander realised that stormy times were ahead. He quashed the sudden alarming thought in his head: What if she never changes?

In one day he had achieved a lot, but still needed to be patient. 'I must earn her respect and trust,' he murmured to himself. 'Honour her wishes and desires, even if they are an anathema to me. Even the month-long tour she is going on, in the Far East, after just one day of marriage.'

In her room, Zarri Bano hugged Haris's small body to herself. She was glad that Sikander had come and spoken openly to her. He had alleviated some of her fears. The biggest fear of all that he couldn't assuage, however, was her own fear of her self. Of the loving, sensuous, 'wanton' woman she had buried on the day she had heard of Sikander's engagement to Ruby. 'That woman is dead! I will not die for you ever again, Sikander,' Zarri Bano later cried in her sleep.

Chapter 63

THE NEXT DAY was a hectic one for Zarri Bano as she had to spend time with the wedding guests as well as prepare for her forthcoming tour of Indonesia and

Malaysia. Only the closest family members were aware
that she was leaving her new home for a month, after
only one day of marriage. What they thought of her
plan was anybody's guess. Sikander's mother Bilkis was
very polite about it. His father Raja Din took it in his
stride, when his son discussed it with him during their
midday lunch.

'You know, Father, Zarri Bano has a lot of commit-
ments. She can't just drop everything, now that she
is married to me. One of those commitments is the
women's *Jamaat-i-Muslimeen* tour of Indonesia and
Malaysia. Zarri Bano had made plans for this a long
time ago, well before the wedding came along,'
Sikander explained, hoping they would understand his
wife's action and not hold it against her.

'That is fine, my son.' Raja Din smiled reassuringly
at Zarri Bano as she listened and watched silently. He
looked at his new daughter-in-law in wonder. Fate was
a strange phenomenon. It had brought back the woman
to whom both he and his son had lost their hearts. She
was a different person now, of course, but it was still a
delightful surprise to have her here by his son's side,
where she belonged. 'May Allah fulfill all of my
Sikander's wishes and my own of having another grand-
son,' he prayed. 'A child just like Haris, but with the
eyes of this woman.'

That evening Shahzada, Gulshan and Fatima arrived
to visit Zarri Bano. They were thrilled to see her
dressed in one of the elegant bridal outfits from her
trousseau, instead of the black *burqa* that they had
secretly feared she would still be wearing.

She was looking at her new wardrobe of clothes in
her trousseau suitcase and wondering what to wear for
the journey, when Sikander had come in.

'Wear this outfit for me.' Reaching over her shoulder, he picked out a chenille suit in a dark shade of purple. 'This will look wonderful on you,' he coaxed, holding the suit in front of her and gazing at her with admiration.

'Look at the sequinwork on the bodice. It is much too showy, especially for a journey,' she objected, blushing and hoping that he would move away from her.

'No it isn't. You are a new bride and this is what they traditionally wear. By the way, thank you for not wearing a *burqa* inside this home. That is the rule I am afraid you'll have to obey while you are my wife.'

'A rule! What about any male guests who happen to visit us?' Zarri Bano asked, offended.

'My dear, nobody wears a *burqa* at home. You can wear a large shawl, like everyone else. Surely that should cover you more than adequately? You can drape a whole bedsheet around you, if you like. Although I do remember another time when Zarri Bano was wont to wear nothing but a wispy black chiffon *dupatta*, out in a very public place, amidst strange men, yet she was still modestly dressed. You can be both modest and well dressed. There is no crime in being smart.'

'Thank you for the lecture. But you are speaking of another time! It is unforgivable of you to remind me of it,' Zarri Bano said angrily, flushing at the memory of the *mela*. 'I was an ignorant and a vain woman then.'

'You were never ignorant, Zarri Bano, but I do miss the vain woman, though. I wonder if she'll ever surface again?' Somehow he knew he was pushing his luck too far.

Crouched on her knees over her steel suitcase, Zarri Bano stared up at him for a long time. 'Sikander, it is impossible to turn the clock back,' she said at last.

'Don't say any more, please. You have already ensnared me in your web.'

'I am very sorry, that you feel we have *ensnared* you.' Sikander was offended. 'We thought that this marriage was best for everyone – for myself, for you, and above all, for my son.' He walked over to the window and looked down at their orange orchard in the far distance. Recovering himself he turned to her once more. 'Forgive me, Zarri Bano. You are free to come and go where and whenever you want to. There are no restrictions in this marriage, Zarri Bano. This is a home, a marriage, not a prison or a jail.'

'Don't look at me like that!' Zarri Bano burst out, unable to bear the effect his eyes were having on her.

'Like what?' Sikander queried, genuinely bewildered.

Zarri Bano banged down the lid of her trousseau trunk and glared at him. 'Yesterday, in the car, you crushed my hand in yours. Last night you caressed my face. Now you rape me with your eyes. Will your eyes do next what your hands cannot?'

Speechless and his tanned face pale, a look of sheer hatred flashed across Sikander's eyes. Zarri Bano saw the look and knew she had gone too far this time. Her heart sank. It suddenly dawned on her that she had lost a friend. He stared at her for a long time.

'A beautiful, desirable woman you may be, Zarri Bano, but I am not that desperate to demand my conjugal rights as to resort to raping my own wife!' he snarled from across the room, hurting her as she had hurt him. 'Nor any other woman, for that matter. You don't know the meaning of the word rape! Keep your holy frozen self *to* yourself.' And Sikander stormed out of the room, banging the door shut behind him.

Zarri Bano threw the outfit he had asked her to wear at the door. The large purple embroidered chiffon *dupatta* lay strewn across the marble floor. 'I don't care if somebody treads on it!' she shouted. Then she burst into a flood of tears.

'What on earth is going on here?' Shahzada asked, coming into the room. What is your suit doing on the floor? Are you all right?' She bent down over her daughter. Zarri Bano turned a tearstained face to her mother, not bothering to hide her wretchedness.

'What is the matter, my beloved daughter? Why are you crying?'

'Mother, I cannot cope with all this – with Sikander, with this marriage. Especially with his eyes . . . Mother, I am so afraid of them, of what they do to me. I can't bear them!' she sobbed.

'He looks at you as do all husbands who love their wives very much.'

'That is just it! I don't *want* him to look at me like that! I hate his eyes – I want to run away from them and hide. What have you got me into, Mother? I didn't want to marry!' Zarri Bano cried out to Shahzada, a tortured look still in her eyes.

'I see. I just passed him on the staircase. He didn't look too happy either. In fact, he looked extremely fierce,' Shahzada commented quietly, pulling up a chair to sit near her daughter. She looked down at the pile of outfits in an array of colours and textures strewn on the chair near the steel trunk. 'I hope you know what you are doing, my daughter. He is a decent and a very understanding man, who happens to want you very much. Don't push him too far. You may live to regret it, after it is too late.' Shahzada thought it her duty to advise her daughter. Her own treatment of her husband

during his last five years still plagued her with bouts of guilt.

Her eyes flashing, Zarri Bano turned on her mother. 'It is you people who are pushing *me* too far!' Overcome by a senseless rage, the words jammed in her throat. 'You, Mother, forced me into this marriage and said it could be a marriage in name only. Now after only *one day* you are telling me to be careful of pushing my husband too far. You are all hypocrites! Did you honestly think that once I was married, I could slot neatly into Ruby's place? Well, you were wrong, Mother! I married Sikander to legitimise my stay in his house, not to provide grandchildren for you, or to become his bedmate. This is a marriage in name only. It will always be that until I . . . hear me correctly . . . wish it otherwise. I have had my fill of male tyranny. First my father and now Sikander.'

'Oh, my dear Zarri Bano, I am sorry that you feel that way. Sikander definitely isn't a tyrant, you know that in your heart. Your father was, as we both know. Your grandfather still is, to some extent. They are a totally different breed of men. Another husband, whether it is a marriage in name only (which, as you know very well, is not *Halal* anyway unless it becomes a real marriage), wouldn't have allowed you as a woman, as a wife to go alone to another country. He is a very tolerant husband, but there is always a limit to someone's tolerance, my daughter, and never forget it. Just as today he loves you, tomorrow he could begin to hate you and annul the marriage. The look I glimpsed in his eyes just now didn't bode well. Nothing remains the same for ever, Zarri Bano. Never take anything for granted.'

'He already hates me, Mother. You should have seen

the look in his eyes! Thank you for your advice. Now listen to me clearly. This marriage, apart from how it relates to Haris, means very little to me. What matters is my identity. For the second time in my life I am being robbed of it. I have become a helpless victim once again. From an ordinary girl who loved friends and fashionable clothes, I became a simple devout woman, sacrificing all aspects of my former life. Now that devout woman is being pressurised to fulfil her wifely duties. The essence of my life and my whole being is at stake here. If I cannot be true to myself and my feelings, or respect myself, then I am a lost woman.

'At the moment, I am struggling to make sense of minor details and changes in my lifestyle. For instance, I found myself debating whether I should wear a dull coloured suit, as I have done for the past five years, or to switch over to these pastel shades and bright deep colours. Yet my mind shies away from them. Until now, I have gone everywhere in my *burqa*; now I am requested to discard it at home. I am so used to the *burqa*, feel so totally happy and safe behind it, Mother, that without it I feel naked and disorientated, very conscious of my body and its shape. I have not touched the makeup kit for so long, and yet now I have to make up my face as befitting a new bride and to please my husband. I find all this abhorrent. I have no desire for it any more. Yet I am doing it all. I have compromised, but there is a limit to how much pressure and change I can take, unless you want me to end up in a psychiatric unit.'

'Don't be silly!' Shahzada was really worried now. 'You do what you think is best. All I wish, as a mother, is for you to have what you could have had if Jafar hadn't died. You and Sikander happily married and

settled. There was no better match for you than
Sikander, and you know it. He was the only man to
have aroused that sparkle in your eyes. Never forget
that you have been given a chance to recapture that
happiness. At least let some good come from your
sister's death,' she pleaded softly. 'Don't destroy some-
thing so precious; so beautiful. There aren't many
Sikanders around. He is one in a million!

'And he is not like your father,' she said firmly.
'Habib was a tyrant and yet I loved him. I put up with
his tyranny and he also loved me. I have never told you
this before, but I lived with a terrible fear in the early
years of my married life. As you know, your father was a
very good-looking man and very aware of it. Compared
to him, I was quite plain. His good looks terrified me at
times, Zarri Bano. I was jealous of any woman he came
across, especially if they happened to be better-looking
than me. I was always afraid that he might fall in love
and bring home a second wife. Women in the village,
I'm ashamed to say, were always flocking to his side on
some pretence or another – both single and married
ones. They were shameless – some just couldn't take
their eyes off him. Not surprising as he was very hand-
some, young, rich and the son of the village landlord.
On top of all that, there was a charisma about him
which you have inherited – and it is not just to do with
looks.

'Yet, much to his credit, may he reside in *Jennat*, he
never looked at another woman. The fear of losing him
to someone else only left me in my later years, when I
had a growing family. The pride he felt in his children,
"his beautiful children" as he proudly called you all,
took away that sense of insecurity from me.

'In the end, there was no need to fear another

woman. He focused all his love on me and his children, especially on you, Zarri Bano – you know that, don't you? He adored you because you inherited his looks, including the colour of his eyes. You in turn fed that adoration by worshipping him in return. You were his beautiful firstborn. But I don't know whether you knew or even suspected that your father prevented you from marrying Sikander simply because he was jealous of him. He even threatened to divorce me!'

'Mother!' Zarri Bano looked aghast.

'No, not in the way you think. He was afraid of losing you to him. He glimpsed something in your eyes that he had never seen before for any other suitor and simply couldn't cope with it. If you had agreed to marry Khawar, for instance, he would have happily blessed the union, for Khawar posed no threat to him and the love you bore him. But in Sikander he saw a rival for your affection. You need to know, Zarri Bano, that your father took a personal dislike to Sikander from the very first meeting. As a proud, doting father, he was used to men falling in love with you at first sight, but here was a man, he believed, who had snubbed his daughter. "He didn't even bother to look up at Zarri Bano, but was more concerned with the biscuits" – that is what he said to me after that first meeting.'

'But, Mother, Sikander, had already seen me – at the *mela*.'

'Your father didn't know that. During their second visit, when you returned from a walk alone with Sikander in our fields, again your father was piqued and distressed on your behalf. While Sikander appeared his normal cool, collected self – "arrogant bastard", your father called him – there was a wistful look in your eyes

which spelled to everyone that you were lost to
Sikander. While I as a mother delighted in that look,
knowing that my daughter had at last met her match, a
strong man who would guide, love and respect her, it
frightened your father, my dear. Habib couldn't bear
the thought of his proud, strong-willed daughter being
vulnerable and helplessly in love with this man, who
had the power to break her heart, to hurt her, and more
importantly, replace him in her affections. He was also
afraid that Sikander might even turn you down – and
his pride could never have endured that insult. He
could never have coped with that, my love.'

'Mother, I don't believe this. Please stop.'

'I didn't believe it either, my dear, until I surprised a
look of sheer triumph on his face, directly aimed at
Sikander, after your veiling ceremony. That look
chilled me, Zarri Bano.' She shuddered. 'Any other man
would have let you marry, but somehow he couldn't
permit Sikander to have you. In the end he made sure
that you could *never* marry. Later, as you know, he
regretted his action. He died a troubled man, unable to
forgive himself for making you a *Shahzadi Ibadat*. In the
process he alienated me, I became embittered. If he had
brought home another woman then, I couldn't have
cared less. He could have kept a harem and I wouldn't
have batted an eyelid. Oh yes, he succeeded in keeping
you at home, but he lost me in the process. From then
on, we lived as strangers till the very last moment. And
now I cannot forgive myself for not taking away that
pain from his guilt-ridden soul. I failed my duty as a
wife.

'All I ask of you now, Zarri Bano, is to let something
positive come out of the mess of our lives, since Jafar
died. Don't lose your husband and his love through

your stubbornness! You are the most valued possession in Sikander's life at the moment. Yet loved possessions lose their value, if they are proved unworthy. Don't lose your worth, my daughter. Learn not only to take, but also to give. Human relationships are about giving and taking. Remember that, as an experience of life from your mother. As you should know, having studied your faith, you two are a garment unto each other – complementing one another.'

Shahzada left her daughter staring at the mirror. 'I am not anybody's possession!' she muttered. 'I do not want to be *his* garment!' Alone she mulled over to herself what her mother had told her about Habib. 'I would always have loved you, Father,' she mourned. 'You had no need to fear my loss. Oh Father, how I miss you!'

Zarri Bano bowed her head into her lap and wept for the second time that day.

Shahzada went in search of Sikander, eventually finding him sitting on a bench in the orchard. She sat down beside him, he turned an unsmiling face to her.

'How are you, my son?' she asked in a gentle tone.

'Fine,' Sikander said stiffly, staring ahead at the orange trees.

'Forgive her, my son. She is finding it so hard to cope with the situation she is in,' Shahzada explained.

'Auntie, she said that I . . .' He stopped, his eyes flashing in anger, '. . . that I raped her with my eyes.'

'I know. You see, she is so afraid of you.'

'But why, Auntie? I have noticed it too.'

'Not of you personally, Sikander, but of the emotions, the feelings you arouse in her. You are a threat to her. Remember, she is a Holy Woman now, Sikander,

therefore she is struggling to accept you as a husband. She is not ready to do so yet. Give her time, my son.'

'I am, Auntie I really am. You know she is running away from me and our marriage by going on this tour tomorrow. I phoned Sister Sakina this morning. She informed me that Zarri Bano didn't have to join them in Malaysia until later, but I am letting her go.'

'I know, and I thank you, my son. You are a good man, and a good husband, and one day Zarri Bano will appreciate you, but at the moment, she is like a ship on a journey, and doesn't know which way she is heading. Somebody else has always steered the course for her – you, me and her father. Let her find her own course and destination for once in her life.'

'Like all ships, hers will eventually have to return to its harbour. I will be waiting for her here, or,' a cryptic look flashed in his eyes, 'or I may decide to join her on her journey and discover her course with her.'

Shahzada sighed. 'Whatever you wish, my son. You have my blessing. Be strong but gentle, is all I can advise. She is like a fragile glass ornament, easily shattered, and this time it will not be easy to put the pieces back together. She suffered and bled for you once – went to pieces for you. She won't do it again, my son.'

Still packing in her room, Zarri Bano heard the sound of laughter from the courtyard. Curious she went up to the window and looked out. Shahzada and Sikander were walking back to the house, laughing and talking together.

When Sikander looked up at her window and saw her he smiled and waved, making Zarri Bano's heart skip a beat. Her own face relaxed into a smile. As she lifted her arm to wave back, from nowhere the

menacing words: '*We will always be lovers!*' darted in to her head.

Dropping her arm, she swept away from the window. 'I don't need you! I don't want you, Sikander!' Zarri Bano shouted to the walls of her nephew's room.

Going to her suitcase she pulled out all her bridal outfits and threw them on the bed. She replaced them with her old, simple *madrasah* suits.

Chapter 64

ZARRI BANO'S FACE paled as she walked out of Sister Sakina's room and saw her husband standing in the hotel corridor.

Lounging against the door of her room, Sikander watched her approach with amused interest. She was looking everywhere but at him. '*Assalam-Alaikum*,' he greeted with a mischievous twinkle in his eye.

'What are you doing here, Sikander Sahib?' Zarri Bano asked breathlessly, still unable to look him in the eye.

'I can see I have taken you by surprise. You do not have a monopoly over Malaysia, you know, Zarri Bano. I can come too,' he teased in a voice thick with laughter. 'Here, let me help you,' he offered as he saw her fumble with the room key.

Opening the door wide, he let her pass first and then followed her inside. Looking around at the room with interest, he placed his suitcase on one of the two beds.

Zarri Bano hovered uncertainly in the middle of her room, finding his male presence very threatening. She tried hard to smile, but it came out as a grimace.

'I am sorry I didn't tell you yesterday when I phoned,' he said smoothly. 'I wanted it to be a surprise. I have some business to sort out here. Also I have a lovely new wife here, waiting for me,' he teased.

Zarri Bano silently continued to watch him, her mouth totally dry.

Sikander noticed her unease, and decided to act. 'I am starving, Zarri Bano. Can we get something to eat?'

'Yes, of course,' Zarri Bano found her voice. 'In fact, I was just going downstairs for dinner.'

'Good, let's go.' Sikander held out his hand to her, across the room. Zarri Bano glanced at it, then at his face. The challenging look in his eye compelled her to reluctantly place her hand in his.

His warm grasp was reassuring as he led her out of the room and down into the dining room. He only let go of her hand when she approached the table where her fellow group of *Jamaati* men and women were sitting. She blushed, as she quickly introduced him as her 'husband' and then sat down beside Sakina.

Sikander carried on watching her with a glint in his eye from across the table, as they had the meal.

Later that same evening, Sikander, Zarri Bano and Sakina went on a tour together, to look around Kuala Lumpur city. From the famous Petaling Street market, they bought souvenirs for everyone. Zarri Bano was happy for Sikander to haggle for the goods; strangely, she found herself enjoying his company immensely. It was good for the two women to have a legitimate male companion by their side, especially when the young Malay and Chinese men stared at them in their black *burqas*.

Later as they climbed into a taxi with their bargains

on their laps, Sakina quipped, 'It is nice to have you join us, Brother Sikander. We couldn't have bargained in the way you did.'

'What does my wife think?' Raising one eyebrow, Sikander gave Zarri Bano a look of enquiry.

She dimpled at him, noting the use of the word 'wife'. 'I think we have just become lazy in your presence and let you do all the work – hey, Sister Sakina?'

'Hmm,' Sikander grunted, giving her a gentle pinch on her thigh to show that he was not satisfied with her answer.

They went next to the main indoor market in the centre of Kuala Lumpur and while Sakina and Zarri Bano looked at the crafts, batiks and silk scarves, Sikander disappeared on his own to look around and buy gifts. He returned carrying two parcels.

In the hotel they bade Sakina goodnight outside her room and then went to their own room. Closing the door behind them they placed their parcels on the bed.

Sikander gazed at his wife's reflection in the mirror as he half reclined on one of the two double beds and watched her remove the *burqa* and brush out her hair.

'Do you know what I wanted to do at the dinner table earlier today? But I thought I had better leave it in case I scandalised your holy team.'

Ignoring his question Zarri Bano chuckled, feeling herself relax. All of a sudden, she was happy that he was with her in the room. The trip had taken on a whole new perspective and in a strange way she was looking forward to spending more time with him.

He stood up to open his suitcase. 'It is all right for me to share this room, isn't it? I have brought my cases here.' He saw the smile slip from her face. 'There are two beds here. It doesn't make sense for me to seek

another room. However, if you are really against it, I will go to the reception and ask for another one.'

She fidgeted with her fingers. He could almost feel the tension building up inside her body.

'Yes, of course you may stay,' she said in a low voice, her eyes not quite meeting his. She stood up to pass Sikander to go to the bathroom. He blocked her way, holding her by the arm.

'Zarri Bano, you must learn to trust me. All I will be doing is sleeping in this bed, nothing more. The nearest I have got to you is to touch your hand. All of a sudden, you have clamped up again. You were happy, relaxed and smiling a minute ago. Why are you suddenly turning cold on me? If my presence is upsetting you this much, then I will go now.' Letting her arm drop, he turned towards the door.

'No, Sikander,' she called to him. 'You don't need to go. You can sleep on that bed. I have now got used to your presence. I can put up with you sleeping in that bed. That I can do, but no more.'

He listened with his back to her, his hand still on the door handle. 'We are friends first, Zarri Bano,' he said, turning towards her with a solemn expression on his face. 'Everything else takes second place. All I want is your company, that is all.'

He began to unpack once more. Zarri Bano sat down on her bed and watched him. She saw the parcels he had bought.

'What are those, Sikander?'

'What?'

'Those parcels you bought in the Central Market.'

'Oh those, one is a present for you and one is for my mother. They are clocks set into pictures and I have had them engraved with a special personal message. That is

what I wanted to give you during dinner. Here, would you like to look at yours? I am going to take a shower. Would you mind finding my pyjamas in my suitcase and hanging them outside the bathroom door? I hope you like it – the present I mean, not the pyjamas.' Laughing he handed Zarri Bano one parcel and then went into the bathroom.

Unwrapping the newspaper covering the parcel she looked at the engraved message on the glass face of the clock. *For my beautiful and beloved wife, Zarri Bano from your husband Sikander.* Looking at the message in wonder, Zarri Bano was awed and flattered by it. The word *beloved* leapt at her. Suddenly, from nowhere, came the unwelcome thought: Did he write a similar message for Ruby?

Carefully she replaced the clock into its box, not quite ready to explore her own feelings towards her husband's relationship with her dead sister. Who was his *beloved*? Both of them? One more than the other? She had known him earlier, but Ruby had lived with him for four years. In four years so much could have happened and had happened. They had a beautiful child to prove it and to share.

She remembered his request for his pyjamas and opened his suitcase. Her searching hands came across something black, and soft at the bottom of the case. She drew out the black chiffon garment in surprise. It was the black outfit, the one she had worn the first time she had seen him at the *mela*. What was it doing here? How had Sikander acquired it? The questions rattled away in her head.

Her fingers stroked the material. Closing her eyes, she tried to recapture that day at the fair – and the meeting with Sikander. She felt again his eyes

travelling over her body as they had that day. Why had Sikander brought it? What special significance did these clothes have for him? She was suddenly humbled by his devotion. He must feel something for me, she thought. He must, or why else would he go to so much trouble to find this outfit and keep it?

As she heard the shower being turned off, she quickly replaced the garment in the suitcase and took out his pyjamas. She hung them outside the bathroom door, not daring to go inside.

When he returned she had already changed her clothing and climbed into her bed. He smiled down at her, as he dried his hair with a towel.

'Did you like it?' he asked, knowing that she would understand what he meant.

'Yes, it is very beautiful. Did you bring Ruby gifts like these and inscribe them with such messages?' she asked before she could help herself. The answer was important to her, but so was his honesty.

'I did bring Ruby gifts – many as any husband would, but this is the first time that I have inscribed a message on one.' He stared back at her with a solemn look in his eyes.

Zarri Bano looked down, hiding her own eyes, not happy with his answer. Sikander for his part felt he had revealed too much of his feelings.

'I think it is time we phoned Haris. He has been missing you terribly,' he said, quickly changing the subject. 'He is probably waiting for our call. He said two days ago, "Why did Auntie marry you if she was going abroad".'

He leaned over nearer the bedside to dial the number. Zarri Bano moved back, her eyes on his bare throat, where the button was undone. Intercepting her

look, Sikander looked down at himself. Embarrassed, Zarri Bano turned away, feeling as if she had been caught doing something wrong.

Soon his call was connected and his mother answered the telephone. When Haris was put on, Zarri Bano came closer to listen to the conversation.

'Here is your Auntie Zarri Bano, she would like to speak to you, Haris.' Sikander brought the receiver and the phone line over her head and, in the process, encircled her with his arm.

As Zarri Bano spoke to Haris, she was very aware of Sikander's arm around her. She didn't look at him, but heard his breathing as he listened to the conversation. Bilkis then came on the line to speak to Zarri Bano. As Sikander moved away slightly to make room for her, Haris came on the phone again, wanting to speak to his father. Zarri Bano handed the receiver to Sikander, but instead of moving away she remained where she was.

From whence the insatiable urge came she didn't know, but she wanted to put her hand through his wet crispy dark curls. Before she knew what she was doing, her hand had already crept up to his neck.

Sikander's eyes darted to his wife's in surprise, but Zarri Bano looked down, pretending to listen to Haris. Her wayward fingers, however, continued their exploratory journey upwards until they reached his head, and then mischievously twirled themselves around his thick damp curls. Sikander moved his head to better accommodate her hand.

He then caught hold of her hand and brought it to his lips, gently kissing it, while still listening to Haris. Zarri Bano quickly snatched her hand away, coming to her senses – ashamed. Sikander's teasing eyes laughed into hers as he ended the conversation with his son.

Then he went utterly still, the laughter disappearing
from his eyes as he surprised, saw a look of sheer bewil-
derment mixed with desire in her eyes. *She can't even
make sense of what she is feeling and doing!* he realised,
dismayed.

With a heavy heart he stood up and replaced the
receiver. Too much was at stake. He couldn't afford to
make a wrong move. She was like a fragile silk flower in
his clumsy male hands.

'I think it is time I went to sleep,' he informed her
gently, 'I am still suffering from jet lag. *Allah Hafiz*,
Zarri Bano.'

Zarri Bano sat numbed, her body going hot and cold
in shame. Her arms wrapped themselves protectively
around her chest. *I offered myself to him and he
rejected me,* she thought her mind reeling.

Before her bewildered eyes, she saw him get into his
bed and lie down, with his back to her. 'He doesn't
want me!' she cried inside. Then she too, lay down and
switched off the lamp, feeling so strange inside. It was
the first time in her life that she had slept with a man in
her room. She looked over at the back of his head with
shame. Her fingers had tangled with his hair. 'What
possessed me?' she accused herself, still unable to make
sense of his reaction. 'Has he fallen asleep already?' she
wondered. Turning over, she, too, tried to go to sleep.

Sikander lay still on his side. He couldn't sleep.
Instead he listened to Zarri Bano's shallow breathing.
His head still tingled with the feel of her fingers in his
hair. It was the first spontaneous gesture she had made
this evening and with no encouragement from him. His
heart had sung with joy. He had seen her crushed look
of surprise as he had turned from her and bade her
goodnight and then saw her wrap her arms protectively

around her body. 'I hope she understands my action,' he fretted silently. 'I have done it for her sake.'

How he had longed to take her in his arms and love her like a husband should! But it was too soon. His wife didn't know her own mind yet, or what she felt at the moment. What he had learned today, however, was that his Zarri Bano of the *mela* was alive and well. It was simply a matter of time now – and a lot of patience.

In the darkness, his eyes shone. He would give her all the time she needed. What he would also give her, he resolutely decided, was his hundred per cent presence, so that henceforth she couldn't divorce her new life from him. He would never let her throw him out of her life again.

A couple of hours later, on returning from the bathroom, he felt a compulsion to sit on her bed and watch her sleeping. Then, unable to help himself he had leant forward, and lightly brushed his lips against hers. In her sleep Zarri Bano's arm reached up, almost touching him. Sikander quickly drew back. He wanted to gather her up in his arms, to smother her face with passionate kisses, but with a steel will born out of love and consideration he reluctantly got back into his own bed, and eventually fell asleep.

When Sikander woke the following morning, Zarri Bano was already dressed and wearing her *burqa*. She was concentrating on rolling her rosary beads on her fingers.

'You were so tired. Do you know what time it is, Sikander? It's ten o'clock!' she laughed as she saw him sit up and yawn.

'Yes, I slept well,' he lied. He wouldn't tell her that he had spent at least half an hour watching her while *she*

slept. 'What are your plans for today?' he asked matter-of-factly.

'We are meeting the famous Maulvi Bilal at his home.'

'I have a better suggestion. Now that I am here, wouldn't it be nice if you and I went sightseeing together?'

Zarri Bano looked down at the rosary bead chain in her hand. Then after a pause, she said, 'Sikander, perhaps we can do that tomorrow. I would like to go to this meeting, after all, that is why I am here in Malaysia – not just for sightseeing!'

'I am sure there will be lots of other meetings. Sakina can attend it and let you know what happened,' Sikander pressed, getting out of bed. He hadn't travelled all this way to hang around on his own.

'No. I want to be there. Your sightseeing, Sikander, can surely wait another day,' Zarri Bano answered coldly, looking down at the rosary beads again.

He had his back to her, otherwise she would have seen the answering light of battle in his eye, 'Of course my sightseeing can wait,' he said politely. 'Your meeting is *much* more important. You had better go right now, or else you will be late in joining your party for breakfast.' He left her sitting on the prayer-mat, and went into the bathroom.

Later, as Maulvi Bilal took the party around the National Mosque in the centre of Kuala Lumpur, Zarri Bano couldn't help but think about Sikander. What was he doing now? she wondered.

After their prayers, in the large prayer hall with its rows of mosaic pillars and huge crystal chandeliers dangling down from the ornate ceilings, they sat under

the fans on the fully carpeted floor and rested. The men sat in a separate part of the main hall. Sakina turned to Zarri Bano when their hostess, a fifty-year-old Malay woman dressed in a smart native crepe-de-chine Malay dress, consisting of a long skirt with a matching knee-length tunic and headscarf, went over to speak to another group of visitors.

'What is Sikander Sahib doing this afternoon?' she asked.

'I don't know. He said that he might go out sight-seeing around the city.'

'Why didn't you go with him?' Sakina's surprised tone immediately put Zarri Bano on the defensive.

'Because I wanted to be with you all and attend the meeting at Maulvi Bilal's place.'

'I see,' Sakina uttered, looking down to read a page from the Holy Quran in her hand.

'What do you see, Sister Sakina?' Zarri Bano asked dryly.

'Nothing, Sister Zarri Bano. Only that you are not giving your marriage a chance.' Sakina smiled at her protégée.

'You forget that I went into this marriage unwillingly,' Zarri Bano answered quietly.

'That may be so. Will you let that cloud things for ever? There is more to life, my sister. What have we done this morning that was more important than spending your time with your new husband? You've hardly had any time together. After your wedding, you came abroad with us almost immediatly. I get the feeling that you are trying to escape your husband, Zarri Bano. Yet he followed you here. He too, has other commitments: his son, his home, his family, his business. Yet he came here to be with you, and instead of

spending the time with him and trying to make something of your marriage, you are still trying to cling to your old life.'

'Which old life, Sister?' Zarri Bano asked in a low voice. 'The one five years ago?'

'No, the one before your marriage. It has already become old. You cannot cling to it for ever. You cannot be the same woman, my sister, because there is now another person in your life. Your life has thus taken on a new shape and perspective. Oh it could be so fulfilling. Don't struggle with yourself, Sister. You will always be a Holy Woman like me, but give yourself a chance to be a normal woman too. Let yourself go!'

'I think that I am already doing it,' Zarri Bano whispered, recalling her sudden impulse to touch Sikander last night. Then the anticlimax as he had turned from her and went to bed. Then the shame. She hadn't slept half the night, because the thought kept hammering away: I offered myself to him and he rejected me.

'Why the bitterness, Zarri Bano? I sense a note of it in your voice.'

'Because I am struggling with my feelings, and with my two identities, Sister Sakina; with what is right and with the ghost of my past. At the centre of it all is Sikander. He is always there whether I want it or not. First he was my suitor, the man I so wanted to marry. Then he became my brother-in-law, the husband of my dear sister Ruby, and father of my beloved nephew, Ruby's child. Now he is my husband.

'First it was me who wanted to marry this man. Then my father denied him to me. Then I lost him to my sister – and now finally I have him. How could I switch all my feelings on and off, without it having some

repercussions and me becoming an emotional wreck in the process?'

'Yes, I see, Zarri Bano. You have explained it well. All I am saying is, why not try to compromise? Do you know, when I saw you two at dinner yesterday, I almost envied you. You have a special rapport. Value it! Yet this morning I feel as if nothing has happened. That you are still as pure as the day you were born.'

Zarri Bano blushed, averting her eyes. The conversation was getting out of hand. 'The men are here. Shall we go?' she suggested, relieved that she could change the subject.

From the National Mosque they went on to the City Museum to see the displays of artefacts from many Muslim countries around the world, ranging from Morocco to Malaysia. Contributed and collected together, the artefacts marked the Muslim International Conference and Festival.

It was late when Zarri Bano and her party returned to their hotel and on reaching her room she found it empty. There was no sign of Sikander, but his case was still there. She went down for her evening meal and wondered if she would see him, but he didn't come.

It was about nine o'clock when Zarri Bano returned to her room and prepared for bed. She switched on the television, but was unable to concentrate. Over and over, her eyes kept returning to the clock. "Where is he? What is he doing?" she asked herself.

Suddenly the telephone rang, making her jump. She picked the receiver up to hear the voice of the receptionist. 'Your husband has left a message for you. Do not wait up for him, he is with some business associates.' Zarri Bano thanked her and replaced the receiver with a bang. Piqued, she switched off the television.

So much for waiting up for him, she thought peevishly. Settling herself down in the bed, she eventually fell asleep, not knowing what time he returned to their room.

On waking the following morning, she reached for her *burqa* and went quickly into the bathroom. Sikander was already up and dressed.

'Did you get my message last night?' he called from the bedroom.

'Yes, I did. Did you have a good meeting?' she asked as she heard him moving round the room. She smoothed out the folds of her *burqa* and opened the bathroom door.

'I'm going out – I'll see you later. I hope you enjoy your meetings today!' he called cheeringly as he left the room.

Zarri Bano watched him go, disappointed for some reason. She had had no opportunity to speak to him or to tell him that she would like to go sightseeing with him today. He had gone, not even bothering to have breakfast with her. Almost as if he wanted to abandon her! 'Be reasonable,' she said to herself. 'You've told him that you have your own life. Well, now he has left you to it! But why does it hurt so much?'

She pottered around the room, tidying up the bed and folding the clothes into his suitcase. Again her hand came across the black chiffon suit, and she questioned herself: 'Why did he bring it with him to Malaysia? Does he want me to wear it?' She took it out and held it in her hands.

Closing her eyes she let her mind wander.

Chapter 65

'YOU ARE NOT ready yet, girls? But the *bharat* will be here soon!' Fatima shrieked at her daughters, the cauldron of wedding stress toppling over when she saw that they were still working on Firdaus's face. There seemed to be so many layers of make-up to plaster on.

There were a hundred and one things to do before the groom arrived with his wedding procession. Yet her daughters seemed to think they had all day. She marvelled at Firdaus's calm tone, as she mocked, 'Mother, there is plenty of time,' laughing in the mirror at her. And she was the bride!

Salma was now pinning a small gold and ruby forehead tiara pendant on Firdaus's head. Beaming at her daughter's radiant face, Fatima ushered some young girls, who were peeping and keen to catch a glimpse of the bride, out of the room.

Firdaus quickly read the note in her hand and, crunching it up, threw it in the waste-paper basket. It was from Khawar, sent via Neesa a week ago. In the note, he had commanded: Firdaus I want you to come to my home in a *dholi*. Chuckling to herself, Firdaus had written back: *Of course. Whatever my lord and master commands*!

She personally had no aversion to a *dholi*, a wooden palanquin. In fact, she thought it was one of the best of the quaint village traditions. She'd rather be carried in a palanquin by four men to her new home, like in the old days, than go in Chaudharani Shahzada's car.

The matter did pose something of a problem,

however – for Fatima. For she had to give a special order for a brand new *dholi* to be designed for the ceremony. 'My daughter is not going to sit in a rickety old *dholi* in which scores of other brides have sat,' she had sniffed disdainfully to her family. No way! The villagers would talk about this *dholi* for years to come. The material and its embroidery would match that of her daughter's bridal outfit.

'Why does it take so long to make up a bride nowadays?' Fatima good-humouredly questioned Kulsoom in the courtyard of her home. A beautician had been especially called in from the city's best beauty parlour. 'I don't know, in our day, it was a two-minute job! A dab of cream on the cheeks, a smear of lipstick on the lips and off we went.'

'When we were young, life was much more simple, Fatima Jee. Nobody had ever heard of beauticians or Beauty Parlours then. Nor did we have the money to invite a woman in and pay her thousands of rupees to make up our faces. It would have caused a scandal then. But see, everything is in hand here, Fatima Jee. Let's go and check the wedding marquees.'

Kulsoom led Fatima out of the courtyard, holding firmly onto the chiffon *dupatta* on her head and twitching her long, heavy earrings in place around her ears. The jewellery had been graciously given the previous night, as long promised by Fatima, in gratitude for her part in Firdaus's wedding. Fatima always kept her word. The earrings were lovely to look at and very expensive, so Kulsoom couldn't be so churlish as to complain that they were too heavy for her small ears. She just wished that she had been born with bigger ones. 'Two *tholas* of gold have gone into making them!' she gloated, knowing nevertheless that she was going

to end up with very sore ears by the time the wedding-day celebrations ended.

She was loath to remove them, however, even for a second. 'The pain is a small price to pay,' she said adamantly. She thus schooled herself to sport them on her ears and show them off to other women who were either prospective clients or were about to engage her services in finding suitable matches for their children. After all, if one client was apt to reward her in such a fashion, she could set a precedence for others to do the same. So all in all she was definitely going to ignore her sore ears.

Kulsoom followed Fatima eagerly into the wedding marquee erected in the girls' school playing ground. Chaudharani Shahzada and Fiaz, in his wheelchair, had stationed themselves in that marquee. Both had been bestowed with the honour of receiving Fatima's guests, as well as the groom and his party.

In the other household, Baba Siraj Din had been graciously chosen by Chaudharani Kaniz for the honour of being Khawar's godfather and the elder *buzurg* to lead the wedding procession. The responsibility of overseeing the *nikkah* ceremony was also bestowed upon him. He accepted both roles in a matter-of-fact fashion.

Fatima inspected, with deep satisfaction, the velour upholstered chairs and the beautifully prepared tables, laid with the best china and silver cutlery especially hired from the town's marriage hall. She had long promised herself the luxury of feeding her daughter's wedding guests with style, instead of having them flocking around tables, holding plates in their hands, reaching over people's shoulders to get at the buffet. *Her* guests would be sitting down in style, and waited

upon by scores of waiters. After all it wasn't every day that her headmistress of a daughter was getting married. Moreover, she wasn't going to let Kaniz pinch all the *shan*, all the limelight, from the wedding. It was her daughter's wedding too!

Fatima cast a surreptitious look at the six new large steel trunks, full of clothes and wedding presents which had arrived this morning from Kaniz's *hawaili* for Firdaus and her family. After dinner, the trunks would be ceremoniously opened up before the hawk-like eyes of the female wedding guests, and all the gifts would be laid out on display for everyone to see. Fatima just knew that the presents were sure to dazzle everyone! Word had gone around the village that the *jihaz* Chaudharani Kaniz had prepared for Firdaus was sure to be unrivalled. 'Probably,' it was awesomely rumoured by Kulsoom, 'even Benazir Bhutto has not received a *jihaiz* like this.'

'My Firdaus sure is lucky!' Fatima sighed with happiness. Not to be outdone herself, Fatima had furnished the dowry marquee with many dazzling presents for Firdaus. After all, she didn't send her only son to Dubai for nothing. She didn't work in someone's house for nothing. Her daughter didn't save up her earnings from teaching for nothing if, at the end, they couldn't between them provide a dowry that befitted their station in life and her daughter's profession.

Although Kaniz had said, very kindly, that she wanted nothing from Firdaus's family and that they had everything they needed, Fatima wasn't going to risk letting Kaniz taunt her daughter later by saying: 'You came here empty-handed!' Fatima's pride and vanity were at stake, and nothing would let her compromise. Thus, whether Kaniz wanted a dowry in her

hawaili or not, she was going to get one. There was no doubt about it. What Kaniz could do, so could Fatima!

The imposing marble tiled façade of Chaudharani Kaniz's *hawaili* was becomingly criss-crossed with ropes of small glittering colourful lights. Not a yard of space had been spared. A cavalcade of tall, beautiful brass lamps stood in the street outside, leading the guests ceremoniously into the *hawaili*. The wedding band, later to play a Scottish tune, stood in rows behind the lamps, eagerly waiting for the groom and *bharat* to assemble.

Inside the *hawaili*, the wedding guests roamed freely in and out of all the rooms. For the first time in her life, Chaudharani Kaniz had snubbed no one. On the contrary, she had delighted everyone by inviting all the relatives from both her and her late husband's side. Nor for that matter had she spared any expense. A golden opportunity not to be missed, most of the guests had eagerly taken up the Chaudharani's offer of arriving a week earlier, to enjoy and partake in all the wedding festivities that were sure to take place. After all, it was Kaniz's only son's wedding. There would be no others in the *hawaili*.

Kaniz took both the hustle and bustle of the crowds of people and the consequent stress with good grace, drinking it all in blissfully. She herself supervised the pots full of food being prepared three times each day. Her team of six hired cooks were kept busy for the whole week, almost eighteen hours a day. The preparations for the wedding were mainly carried out and supervised by Sabra, her daughter and Neesa.

Baba Siraj Din sat stiffly in the large drawing room

on a huge comfortable sofa beside Khawar, who was dressed in the ceremonial clothes of a groom. Siraj Din impatiently tapped his ivory stick on the silk carpet, as he waited for Khawar's present-giving and *sehrabandi* ceremony to begin. Dressed in his new, crisply starched suit, a long black coat and a special turban on his head, Siraj Din looked every bit the tribal headman of the village.

'Where is your mother, Khawar?' Siraj Din asked imperiously. 'Everybody is here and waiting! The ceremony should start soon, my son.'

'She'll be around somewhere, Grandfather, in the *hawaili*.'

'Sabra, go and find your sister! I know the *bharat* is only going two streets away, but still we have to get there. The musicians have been standing outside for over an hour. It is quite hot out there. The groom's horse is probably getting restless, especially with all the heavy decorative stuff on his body.'

'Yes, Baba Jee, I'll go and find Kaniz,' Sabra reassured him, leaving the chatting group of women relations she was entertaining on her sister's behalf.

Upstairs in her bedroom, Kaniz drew out a large box with a red and silver painted lid from her wardrobe. Holding it under her arm, she went down to the first floor and headed for Neesa's room. It was located in the far corner of the *hawaili*, in the corridor of the bedding storerooms. Kaniz very rarely visited this corridor. She never had to. Her authoritative voice had done all the work for her. Today the journey to it was like a little pilgrimage.

She knocked on Neesa's door — an action unheard of for Chaudharani Kaniz to perform in her own home.

It was directly born out of sensitivity, in case her housekeeper was getting undressed.

Neesa was, in fact, preparing to put on her own best clothes. When she heard the knock, it prompted her to immediately look up and call, 'Come in.' As the door opened, Neesa paled at the sight of her mistress entering her simply furnished room.

'Did you want me for something, Chaudharani Sahiba?' Neesa stammered, looking up at Kaniz with misgiving. Something must be terribly amiss to have brought her *chaudharani* personally to her quarters.

'Yes, I do,' the *chaudharani* replied, smiling and with a strange look on her face. Neesa stared back nervously, unable to make sense either of the look or her mistress's action in coming to seek her out.

Kaniz held the box out towards her housekeeper.

Blushing with pleasure Neesa looked at it, imagining that her mistress had come to show her a new outfit for the bride. It was an honour indeed that her mistress had thought of her and had come personally to show it.

'I want to give you this,' Kaniz told her softly, watching her housekeeper's face.

Neesa merely stared at the box – speechless.

'Here, take it.' The *chaudharani* gently pushed the box into her servant's numbed hands. 'Open it, Neesa. It is for you. And it is exactly like mine and Sabra's.'

With trembling fingers, Neesa plucked off the lid with her thin workworn fingers. Then she stared down in bemusement at the exquisite blue silk suit, lying on a beautiful bed of delicate white tissue paper. Her mouth fell open, her eyes fixed on the rich intricate embroidery around the neckline of the garment. A suit, just like the one the *chaudharani* was wearing, was an

unimaginable honour indeed. One which she would never have dreamed of in a million years.

'There is a matching chiffon *dupatta* too,' Kaniz elaborated as Neesa touched the soft chiffon scarf, afraid of snagging the delicate material with her chapped fingers, roughened from all the scouring in the kitchen.

A lump was lodged in Neesa's throat, almost suffocating her. Any dunce could see that this suit had been specially prepared and had cost thousands of rupees, she marvelled in her head.

'Now look under the suit,' Kaniz's gentle voice commanded. She was still smiling down at her housekeeper and, with selfish joy, she drank in the look of sheer wonder and shock on Neesa's face as she felt under the suit and drew out a square flat red velvet box. 'Open it,' Kaniz coaxed, a trace of excitement in her own voice.

Once again Neesa's fingers trembled. Clumsily, she flicked open the delicate latch to look, wide-eyed, at the gold choker necklace with matching earrings and a ring, lying on a rich black velvet bed.

Neesa stared aghast at her mistress. 'Is this, for me, Chaudharani Sahiba?' she whispered. She watched amazedly as Kaniz's head magically dipped down and then up again towards her.

It was all too much for poor Neesa! Her small, humble world suddenly lost its bearing on its social axis. Her Chaudharani Sahiba, always cruelly barking orders at her and turning her back on her for half of her life, was now offering her a necklace worth six *tholas* of gold! Leaning back on the chair and putting the box on her bed, which already had a mound of bedding to iron on it, she began to weep into her muslin shawl, her slim shoulders crumpling over.

Bemused, Kaniz stared down at the wiry frame of her

grey-haired housekeeper. A strange love welled up inside her. 'This woman has given her whole life to me and my son, and I have been so hateful to her for all these years!' Kaniz told herself sadly. Then unable to bear seeing Neesa cry, she pulled her housekeeper into her arms and held her tightly against her chest.

Clasped firmly against her Sahiba, the last remnants of her self-control shattered and Neesa wept as she had never wept before. It was as if all those years of sheer loneliness, bereft of human warmth under Kaniz's oppression had been worth it. Even as she cried, she made sure, however, that she kept her humble shawl strategically in front of her face to prevent ruining her mistress's new wedding suit.

'Neesa, why are you crying?' Kaniz asked. 'There's nothing to cry about! You are my sister, just like Sabra. Today I want to show you and the whole world, by this small gesture of a suit and a necklace, how much I hold you dearly and value the time you have devoted to me and my son.

'You have brought up Khawer with your loving tender care as if he was your own. Today it is his wedding day, my dear. I have dispensed presents to strangers, to beggars in the streets, to all the village women and girls. Can't I, therefore, give this to someone who has devoted nearly thirty years of her life to us and who has grey hairs in the process? Take this as a small token of my appreciation, please. I have begun to regard you as a beloved and a dear sister . . .'

Kaniz's voice petered away into an awkward silence. She now did something she never dreamed in her life she would ever do. She held up her hands together at Neesa, her woman servant. 'Neesa, look at my hands. They are held up in *mafi* to you, in supplication.

Forgive me for all of my past cruelty to you. I know I am a difficult woman to work for. I now cannot live without you, Neesa! This home has been your home since you came here as an orphaned teenager. You didn't even marry, in order to stay with us. Today you will stand by my side, dressed like me, *not* in the role of my housekeeper, but as my sister and Khawar's second mother, and you will receive guests by my side. So please, Neesa, don't cry. I want you to change into this suit and wear this necklace.'

'No mistress, I can't do this,' Neesa uttered, physically moving a step back and panicking, before eventually finding her tongue. 'I cannot compete with you.' Her respect for her employer would not allow her to cross the social barriers. Kaniz was the mother of an important landlord of the village, while she was just a servant!

'Neesa, I insist. It is an order – if you like!' Kaniz smilingly cajoled, touched by Nessa's words; her own eyes were now very moist.

'I insist, too.' Sabra's warm voice made them both jump. Leaning against the doorpost she smiled at the two women.

'Sabra! How long have you been there?' Kaniz enquired, embarrassed by the scenario she was caught in.

'Long enough, my dear sister, to make me so proud of you. I love you so much, Kaniz.' Stepping forward Sabra gathered her elder sister in her arms. Over Kaniz's shoulder, she smiled at Neesa, still staring at them with tears in her eyes. Neesa was beginning to wonder how long this weird and wonderful dream would last. Both of the sisters were now in her room!

'Come on, Sister Kaniz, Baba Siraj Din is getting really impatient. I am sure his walking stick has by now

made a nice round hole in your silk carpet, the way he keeps tapping it. The *bharat* is all ready. All the elder men from the village have arrived. You should see them all, Kaniz – all overdressed and their starched clothes seem to have stiffened their manners, too. They are all standing around, proud as peacocks strutting about in your courtyard. Their wives, not to be outdone by their men, are preening themselves in their gaudy colours and cheap suits. It is hardly surprising, as it is not every day that two members from every household and each and every caste in the village are invited to join the *bharat* party. You've auspiciously not deigned to miss anyone. You have been generous indeed, my sister, defying us all and turning the tables on the whole social order of this village community.'

'It is my only son's wedding, Sabra. I want everyone to enjoy it. I shall not see another,' Kaniz replied simply. 'I want it to be the one to be talked about and remembered for decades. Also a Principal, my Firdaus, is coming into this home. She deserves the best reception there could ever be. Now hurry up, Neesa, and get dressed,' Kaniz imperiously summoned over her shoulder as she and her sister left Neesa's quarters.

'Have you got the bundles of five-rupee bills?' Kaniz asked suddenly remembering the village children. They were bound to be present in droves in the street outside, and would eagerly follow the *bharat* procession. Kaniz wasn't going to have her son belittled by showering him with coins, or one-rupee notes. No, it had to be crisp new five-rupee notes; she had ordered them in bundles from the local bank, amounting to thousands of rupees. Kaniz beamed to herself. It was such a pleasurable thought to entertain. The notes floating over her son's head and his party, to be caught and plucked away

by the children's greedy nimble fingers and then eagerly stuffed into their bulging pockets.

'Five-rupee notes! You are definitely getting carried away now, Kaniz,' snorted Sabra dismissively as they walked across the courtyard.

'Sabra, indulge me.' Kaniz shot an appealing look at her sister. 'It is only the wedding of my son that has pulled me away from the precipice of my self-destruction. What is money for, if you cannot buy happiness with it?' she finished rhetorically.

'Yes, yes, my sister, I am sorry, forgive me,' Sabra answered tritely. She didn't want to recall her sister's suffering – not on this day of all days.

'Why is Younas Raees here at my son's wedding? I didn't invite him, Sabra.' The uneasy look was back in Kaniz's face.

'Your son did.'

'I don't want him in my *hawaili*!'

'Don't be silly, Kaniz. Now forget Younas Raees and get a move on! Baba Siraj is waiting.'

In her room, Neesa hugged the suit to her body, her eyes squeezed tight. Then with trembling hands she drew out the necklace set and marvelled at it. She had never owned nor dreamed of ever owning anything so expensive in her life.

Replacing the suit in its box she pulled out the clothes she had originally intended to wear.

In this instant and for the first time in her life, Neesa was going to disobey her mistress. She would wear the suit, but at another time – not today. She could never lower her mistress's standing by being so presumptuous as to dress like her. Her sister Sabra could, but not she.

Chapter 66

'THE *DHOLI* IS coming, Sabra Jee!' Neesa shouted excitedly down into the central courtyard, peering over the *hawaili*'s roof balcony. Her eyes eagerly followed the *bharat*'s journey as it meandered its way through the village lanes.

As she stepped away, Neesa caught one end of the new embroidered chiffon *dupatta* that Chaudharani Kaniz had given her that very morning, on the iron railings. Her eyes widened in horror at the big tear, right across one corner. 'How foolish of me to go peering over the railings like a child in this outfit,' Neesa wailed, wishing she hadn't worn the outfit. Chaudharani Kaniz had, however, insisted that she wear it. She had made her return to her quarters and change.

What a day it had been! Neesa wasn't quite sure what had been more exciting, her beloved young master's wedding or her, a middle-aged servant, all dolled up in a gorgeous wedding outfit, topped with a real gold necklace hanging round her crinkled throat. All afternoon, she had been unable to decide whether to be flattered or embarrassed by all the sly glances she had received from the other village women as she sat at the top dinner table beside Sabra and Kaniz. One thing was certain: there would be plenty of gossip and tittle-tattle in the days to come. Neesa knew from which source it would come too – Kulsoom the matchmaker. Kulsoom in particular seemed to have resented the seating arrangement. She had secretly hoped that Mistress Kaniz would bestow the honour on *her* of sitting at the

top table. After all, wasn't she the crucial link between the two families? It appeared, however, that her rightful place had been supplanted by a mere servant woman!

Four young men especially hired for the wedding carried the *dholi*, the traditional bridal palanquin, with Firdaus in it on their shoulders. They gracefully led the entourage of wedding guests from the reception marquee out through the village lanes, heading back towards Kaniz's *hawaili*.

Kaniz, Chaudharani Shahzada and other women relatives walked beside the palanquin, gaily talking and singing popular folk wedding songs. Khawar, flanked by Baba Siraj Din, his male friends and relations, walked ahead of the *doli*.

Down in the *hawaili* courtyard Neesa shakily handed Sabra the crystal-cut bowl of oil and a large copy of the Holy Quran. Carrying a small basket of traditional sweetmeats, Neesa then followed Sabra and stationed herself strategically at the entrance door to welcome home the groom and his new bride. She thrust wide open the gates for the guests to enter.

Reaching the *hawaili*, the procession came to a stop. The palanquin was lowered and placed on the ground near the gates. Stepping forward, Kaniz lifted the maroon brocade flap and peered inside.

'How was your journey, my dear?' she asked, beaming at her daughter-in-law.

Firdaus, sitting huddled inside the four-foot wide wooden space and still clutching precariously at the two side bars with her hands, glanced up nervously at her mother-in-law.

'As well as one can expect, Auntie,' she managed politely. 'It is not every day that one has the honour of being carried on the shoulders of four men.'

'Come, my daughter, I'll help you out. You were only carried for two streets; I was carried for two miles. I know just how you are really feeling. I kept thinking to myself that I would fall out and break my neck. Of course I didn't,' Shahzada chuckled. 'Welcome to your new home, my dear.'

Letting Chaudharani Shahzada help Firdaus out of the *dholi*, Kaniz joined her sister and stood in the doorway of her home to welcome them all inside.

Firdaus straightened out her bridal skirt, consisting of seven yards of heavily embroidered silk, that had become crushed beneath her legs, before being helped out of the *dholi*.

'Come, my dear. Your mother-in-law awaits you at the entrance to your new home,' Shahzada whispered in Firdaus's ear, leading her through the gates. Khawar walked by her side.

A small china bowl of oil held in the palm of her hand, Kaniz waited with a beating heart, her eyes poised on Firdaus's face as she stood outside the carved walnut wooden doorway leading into the *hawaili*. She stooped down to pour a few drops of oil on the two corners of the doorstep, reminiscent of the centuries-old Hindu tradition of welcoming the new bride into her new home. Still bent on the ground, her large embroidered shawl touching the step, Kaniz caught Firdaus's wary glance.

The world stood still for the two proud women as they both simultaneously remembered the scene in the school office. Firdaus cringed to recall her own flippant words: 'I'd rather die than enter your *hawaili*'. Then, from somewhere, came the frightening thought: Wouldn't it be Kaniz's sweetest revenge if she were now to turn me away from her doorstep?

In Kaniz's head, her own bitter words stabbed. 'I'll never let that washerwoman's daughter step into my *hawaili!'*

Bleakly, Firdaus dropped her eyes before Kaniz, in utter shame. Chaudharani Kaniz now held her *izzat*, her honour in her two hands. She was the one holding the scales of power. It was now all up to her.

Sighing, Kaniz stood tall, rising triumphantly out of the muddy whirlpool of her past life. A smile lit her face, crinkling the corners of her eyes as she took the Holy Quran from Sabra and circled it ceremoniously over her daughter-in-law's head in a traditional gesture of welcome. 'Welcome home, my Firdaus,' she greeted her in a loud, clear voice.

Relieved and grateful, Firdaus stepped into her new home, only to be immediately pulled into the warm embrace of her mother-in-law's arms.

'Sister, you'll ruin her suit,' Sabra scolded Kaniz. Everybody had witnessed Firdaus's reception, including Fatima, who had trailed behind the other women. She brushed away tears of happiness from her eyes. There were no worries now concerning her daughter's future – Kaniz had made it plain to everyone that she was going to be a good mother-in-law. She just hoped and prayed that her own daughter would learn to be a tender and kind woman like Kaniz – and accept everything in life with the same humility and maturity.

Smiling up into the video camera, focused on her by the cameraman brought in from Karachi, Kaniz led her daughter-in-law and son into the drawing room, and seated them on her new special white leather sofa. Following the other relatives into the room, Fatima hesitated for a moment, in the doorway. When Kaniz looked up and saw her, she rose and then, with a

purposeful step, went up to Fatima and gathered her in a bear-like hug. Fatima stood frozen in her enemy's arms, and then hugged her back.

'*Mubarak*, my sister, welcome. Thank you for giving away your daughter to us. We are honoured to have her. You have made me and my son very happy, Sister Fatima.'

Humbled to the very core of her being by Kaniz's generosity, Fatima couldn't help but have a good cry in her big pink cotton handkerchief as she sat down next to her friend and mistress. 'It is my prerogative anyway, as mother of the bride to have a good cry,' she sniffed happily to Chaudharani Shahzada.

The women in this room can never guess the heights to which my heart has soared. They think I cry from sadness, Fatima thought as she sat next to her mistress Shahzada and glanced proudly around the room. All this is now my daughter's. Her heart soared again at the prospect of her daughter becoming the next *chaudharani* and mistress of this *hawaili* and its tracts of land.

Sitting beside Khawar, Siraj Din was observing everything and everyone with philosophical wisdom from under his bushy brown eyebrows. Every day proved to be a revelation – there was always something new to amaze him.

'Well, Khawar, my son, did you ever in your wildest dreams anticipate your mother embracing her lifelong enemy?' Siraj Din asked rhetorically, pointing his stick at Kaniz and Fatima sitting together, both smiling warmly and unreservedly into each other''s face.

'No, but *al-Hamidulillah*, with yours and everyone's prayers, Allah Pak has blessed this household. My mother is a changed woman. She bears no grudge against anyone, even those who have humiliated her.'

Firdaus blushed, knowing the barb was aimed at her.

'I am so glad. I'll leave you two alone and will go and sit with my daughter Shahzada.' Siraj Din stood up and, with the aid of his ivory stick, walked over to the other sofa. As he approached, Fatima quickly vacated her seat to him, deciding to go and sit with her husband Fiaz, out in the courtyard.

'Well, I must say, you do look grand,' Khawar teased, turning to look at his bride. 'I would never have recognised you, Madam Principal, coming out of the *dholi*. Now that was a sight indeed! So was the one of you stepping into my home.'

'Trust you to remind me of that, Khawar. You didn't manage to drown me in the well in our childhood days, but you'll probably kill me with your pointed taunts now!' she tartly said. Khawar's peal of laughter rang around the room. Firdaus fidgeted with her gold-embroidered, jewel-encrusted handbag, feeling all the women's eyes on them.

'They are really happy, Shahzada,' Siraj Din observed, watching the bride and groom from across the room. 'I hope my own granddaughter Zarri Bano is happy too, wherever she is with her husband.'

'*Amin!*' Shahzada voiced fervently, a worried look entering her eyes. 'If only that were so!' she half-whispered to herself.

'*Aba Jan*, last night I had a dream in which I saw a beautiful child in my Zarri Bano's lap – looking just like her. If only my dream could come true! I was thinking that if she is now going to be settled, more or less, in Karachi, there is nothing for me now in the *kothi* in the town. Fatima too, has left us, to return to Chiragpur and look after Fiaz. I was wondering, therefore, whether you would have me come and stay here in the village, in

the *hawaili* with you? I like it here much, much better than in the town. If I am here I can also look after you in the last years of your life. Also Fatima, my friend, is here and I can see her every day . . .'

Shahzada stopped, seeing her father-in-law's green eyes shine with tears. '*Aba Jan?*' she queried in concern.

'Shahzada, my dearest, dearest of daughter-in-laws. You have made me so happy! There is nothing that would give me greater pleasure than to have you back in the *hawaili*. It has never been the same since you left the village and your mother-in-law Zulaikha died. With you here, the place will come alive again. People will flock to my home and keep you company. Zarri Bano will come and *Insha'allah* bring her children with her. She'll have to stay on in the *hawaili*. After all, it will be her children who will inherit it and most of this land, my dear Shahzada.

'To have all this happen in the last days, weeks, months and years of my life would be Allah's true blessing indeed. Thank you my dearest, my Shahzada. You have the place of the daughter I never had in my heart. You know that, don't you?'

'The pleasure will be all mine, *Aba Jan*.' Shahzada was touched to the core of her being, her own eyes swimming in tears. She raised her father-in-law's hand and respectfully kissed it, pressing it to her cheek.

Coming back into the room, Fatima had watched the exchange between Shahzada and Siraj Din. She went over to Shahzada and held out her hand. 'Come, Chaudharani Sahiba, you mustn't cry, not today. It is a day of celebration. Come and have a look at my Firdaus's bedroom.'

'Yes, Chaudharani Sahiba,' Kulsoom said eagerly, overhearing Fatima's words and coming to stand by her

side, 'it is reputed that Chaudharani Kaniz has spent *lakhs* of rupees on furnishing the bride's bedroom for this wedding.'

Wiping her tears away with the corner of her *chador*, Shahzada took hold of Fatima's hand, her lifelong friend, and stood up.

Kulsoom automatically twitched her long dangling earrings in place on her ears, then nearly cried out with the pain. As she led the two up the *hawaili*'s staircase to the first floor she was wondering when exactly Kaniz was going to do her the honour of giving her a gift for her services. She so fervently hoped that it would be a gold pendant. Her poor little ears couldn't cope with any more earrings.

Hoisting her large frame with its bony legs up the marble stairs, Kulsoom just wished to Allah that these important people didn't have so many floors. It would serve them right if, one day, they found her dead on their stairs. Then they would be cursed for life.

Smiling indulgently at Kulsoom's panting face and her rasping breath, Kaniz stood at the top of the staircase and led them gracefully down the corridor. She thrust one door wide open and proudly stood aside, allowing the three women to enter and marvel at length at the contents and the furnishings of the room.

Just for one moment, Kaniz's head tilted proudly to one side, in a gesture reminiscent of the old haughty Chaudharani Kaniz. The expression of wonder and humility on Fatima's face as she gazed reverently around the room, touching and examining everything with awe, was worth each and every *paisa* spent on it.

Chapter 67

'KHAWAR AND HIS *barat* will just have left the *hawaili*, Sikander Sahib,' Zarri Bano informed her husband, looking down at her watch and translating it into Pakistani time.

'Whose?' Sikander asked, offering his hand to support her as they came out of the Batu Caves. They slowly made their way down the steps from the entrance of the caves in the Malaysian countryside.

Lifting her *burqa* with her hand, in case she tripped over the hem, Zarri Bano concentrated on the narrow two hundred-odd steps, carved into the hill, that housed the caves. She watched her feet with trepidation, as two small spider monkeys skipped and danced around her legs.

'Don't worry!' Sikander laughed, holding her hand firmly and moving to her side. The monkeys were everywhere on the steps. At night-time they disappeared into the caves, but during the day-time they hopped and played around the feet of the tourists, especially Hindus, who came to pay homage to the Hindu temple, housing the images of their gods inside the huge cavern of the Batu Caves.

'You remember Khawar, the young landlord from our village?' Zarri Bano told him. 'Today is his wedding day. He is marrying Firdaus, the daughter of our housekeeper. My grandfather and mother will be there at the wedding, of course, as special guests.'

'I see,' Sikander answered, leading her to the taxi

waiting to take them to their next destination, the Malaysian jungle.

Glancing out of the car window, Zarri Bano admired the lush scenery with its tropical foliage elegantly carpeting the rugged mountain terrain, lining the road on either side.

'By the way,' she added, dimpling at him. She had this strange wicked urge to tease him. 'Khawar was one of my old suitors.'

'Was he now?' Sikander returned silkily.

Her cheeks reddening at the look in his eyes, Zarri Bano hastened to explain. 'Oh no, Sikander Sahib, it is not the way you think. Khawar has always had a soft spot for Firdaus. It was his mother, Chaudharani Kaniz who was bent on pursuing my *rishta* for obvious snobbish reasons.'

'And of course, my *snobbish*, arrogant wife turned him down. I suppose I ought to feel honoured that somehow you didn't turn me down like your other string of suitors,' he joked, then turned serious again. 'Yet you still spurned me at the end, Zarri Bano – just like all the others,' he said quietly.

'There was nothing arrogant about it, Sikander,' Zarri Bano said, her face still smarting with colour. 'I have always regarded Khawar like a brother. I played with him in my childhood days in the village. The second reason was that I couldn't stomach the thought of stepping into Chaudharani Kaniz's haughty shoes. It just didn't appeal to me. I was never cut out to be a village *chaudharani* of the mould that my mother or Kaniz are. They are a different breed of women, following a different set of traditions and goals in life. At that time, my heart hankered after the big cities and the international life.

The tranquil village life would have smothered me and my journalistic career.

Zarri Bano thought for a moment. 'Having said that, recently I did enjoy my stay in the village since I have headed the *madrasa* there. I have had two women's colleges built. Firdaus is much better suited to the village life than I am. Allah obviously had another vocation in mind for me – my father just became His tool. Although I never envisaged I would become a scholar of Islam or a Holy Woman, I have now been all over the world as I always wanted to. What about you, Sikander? Do you prefer the city life or the country-side?' Zarri Bano ventured to ask, just as the taxi came to a stop, hoping he would look at her again. He didn't.

They climbed out and stretched their legs. Then they followed the driver up the gentle slope of a hill leading into a rubber plantation. Looking around, they were amazed at the wonderful milky green haze that seemed to cloak and surround the trees. Climbing further up they eventually came to a small hut built on a raised platform on the hillside. In front of a small wooden table, an old Malay gentleman was sitting on a chair, smoking. As he saw them approach, he stood up to welcome them with a warm smile.

'*Assalam-Alaikum*!' the rubber-tapper greeted. He could tell by Zarri Bano's black veil that they were Muslims, like himself. Smiling broadly, he took them to a nearby tree and, with a special knife, demonstrated how rubber was extracted. Zarri Bano and Sikander watched fascinated, as the jelly-like orange-brown gum oozed out on to the surrounding bark.

After thanking and tipping the old man for his dem-onstration, Sikander and Zarri Bano followed the Tamil driver further up the hill.

'This forest will gradually become a jungle,' the driver stated, waving his hands up at the dense forest ahead, disappearing beyond the horizon. 'Would you like to go and explore by yourselves for an hour or two? I'll wait for you down below.'

'That would be nice,' Sikander replied, nodding in agreement.

'Don't go too far, in case you get lost,' the man warned. 'Just stay in the clearing and follow the paths.'

Thanking the driver and holding Zarri Bano's hand firmly, Sikander led her up the slope and into the jungle proper. Soon lush green foliage and tall mature trees, reaching high into the sky to form a dense canopy above, surrounded them. The atmosphere was magical, full of the strange sounds of distant animals. Everywhere, there were butterflies and moths, some so big that they could hardly fly, flitting between the trees.

'I like to be where you are, Zarri Bano.' Sikander whispered caressingly.

Zarri Bano stopped in her tracks. 'What?' she asked, not understanding him at first. Sikander stared back at her, his eyes expressive with a meaning. A curious light flickered down from the green canopy above, making Zarri Bano look incongruous in her black *burqa*.

At last understanding him, heat rushed into her face and, as usual, she immediately tried to escape. Carefully stepping through the undergrowth, she held the hem of her *burqa* up, in case it got caught by the shoots of the plants and shrubs.

'Don't go cold on me now, Zarri Bano, please!' Sikander urged from behind, pushing aside a small branch, and reaching her side again. 'We had a very natural conversation back in the car. You were relaxed then and actually talked fully. Now I can actually feel

you drawing back into yourself – into your inner world. Please don't do that.'

'Look, Sikander,' she said desperately, 'I am trying my very best, you know, but I am finding it all so hard. During the past month or so, everybody has been pounding on my doors. Little by little they have managed to sneak in. In your case, you have not only pounded but barged right in. Now there are not many locked doors left, Sikander, before you reach the old Zarri Bano.' Zarri Bano felt suddenly worried in case she had revealed too much.

Sikander didn't answer immediately. Instead he looked around. They had entered a large clearing. Zarri Bano, too, looked up with pleasure at the clear blue sky peeping through the green rooftop of the trees. Both marvelled at the flashes of brilliant colour as tropical birds and parakeets flew from one branch to another.

'It is like paradise here, so peaceful. Almost as if we are the only people in the world,' Zarri Bano said, wiping her damp forehead.

'Why don't you take off your *burqa?*' Sikander softly suggested. 'There's nobody here, Zarri Bano. Nobody can see you – except me. Here, let me help you.'

Feeling the solitude of the place and with no prying male eyes, Zarri Bano thought it safe to remove her cloak. As Sikander helped her to pull the *burqa* off, her hair tumbled out of the hood and down to her shoulders, falling heavily in a tousled riot of waves. In the sunshine streaming down from the cracks between the trees, it became ablaze with a deep earthy fire.

Sikander gasped at the beauty of it, fighting the urge to put his hand through it. Then he went utterly still as he saw what she was wearing underneath – the black chiffon outfit from the *mela*, that he had so loved and

the image of which was so clearly etched on his mind. Zarri Bano knew instantly that her clothing had a symbolic meaning for him. She remembered the *mela* so well – and that passionate look in his eyes . . . All of a sudden she felt self-conscious, needing to escape from him again.

She walked on until she came to a spot with a large gnarled tree trunk, its roots jutting out and spread across on the ground. Sikander watched her sit down on one of the roots. She looked stunning against the backdrop of the jungle, an elegant figure in an outfit which defined and flattered the feminine shape of her body.

He followed her and stood by her side. Unable to help himself, his hand reached down to her hair, marvelling at the silkiness of the strands as they flowed sensuously through his fingers.

Zarri Bano froze as she felt his fingers creep up her neckline from behind and into her scalp. Strangely she recalled her own similar action the other night. 'This is what I did to him! How could I?' she cried to herself, shuddering in shame and pleasure.

'You have such beautiful hair, Zarri Bano. Please let it grow down to your waist,' he whispered, leaning down near her head.

'How it used to be, you mean? When you first saw me in this outfit five years ago, Sikander?' Her voice was weary. 'My hair can grow, but to expect other things to revert to the same is impossible.'

'Is it?' he said, straightening up. 'But I am looking at, and I think and hope I have found the woman I lost.'

'Then I am sorry to have to disillusion you, Sikander Sahib. You are definitely chasing rainbows! What you see in front of you is very deceptive. I may appear the same, but take a look inside my soul and you'll find I

am not the woman you think that you are seeking. I have changed too much, Sikander. It is impossible to make some dreams become a reality.'

'I disagree with you, Zarri Bano!' Without realising it, his fingers were tugging painfully at her hair, forcing her to look up at him again. 'Dreams can often, with effort, be realised. It is personal barriers that prevent us from realising them. In this case, you yourself have become the biggest barrier. Once it was your father.' He stopped abruptly. 'I can never forgive him for what he did to you and to us.'

'I forgave him very soon. Did you know, Sikander, that my father was jealous of you – obsessively jealous, in fact. My mother recently told me how he felt threatened by you and saw you as a rival for my affection.'

'You don't have to tell me that. I suspected it all along. He hated me, Zarri Bano. Why else do you think he stopped us from marrying and made you into a Holy Woman? What I don't understand is, what did he think I was going to do to you? After all, you were still his daughter and would always remain so.'

'He loved me too much, Sikander. He was afraid of you eventually replacing him in my affections – that was his ultimate fear. He also thought that you had the power to hurt me emotionally.'

'Well, he succeeded in keeping you for himself, didn't he? He kept you at home in his ivory tower, so that no man could ever get near you. I'll never forgive him, Zarri Bano, no matter what you say. He altered the whole courses of our lives.' She could feel the anger vibrating in him, through his fingers. They were still tugging painfully at her hair.

'You must remember, Sikander, if Jafar hadn't died, my father couldn't have prevented us from marrying.

It was fated to happen. It was in our stars, Sikander. You must believe this if nothing else,' she appealed earnestly.

'Whatever you say, Zarri Bano. The fact remains, however, that I cannot forgive him. As my wife, I want to have nothing to do with your inheritance, your land. It is *haram* for me, I tell you.' His eyes shot angry darts at her.

'It is neither mine nor yours, Sikander. It belongs to Haris. I don't like it either. I have in fact already sold some of the land to build the *madrasas* and provide for their running costs.' She was feeling upset now.

'My son is having nothing to do with your inheritance, Zarri Bano!' he hissed, withdrawing his hand from her hair and stepping away.

Zarri Bano felt a physical shock when he took his hand away. She wanted it back in her hair, wanted him to re-establish that warm physical and mental rapport that they had just been sharing.

'Very well! If you won't let "your" Haris inherit it, you cannot stop "my" son from doing so!' she threw at him, before realising what she was saying. 'The land is very important to my family. I have to keep it in my father's memory.'

A strange silence settled in the jungle.

'What son?' Sikander softly queried at last.

Zarri Bano could feel his breath on the nape of her neck as her hair fell like a heavy curtain around her face. She bent her head lower, hiding her face from him with her hair and hugging her legs up to her chin.

'The son that I may have in the future, Sikander,' she mumbled, so quietly that he had to bend down close to hear her.

Sikander stood up, his face relaxing into a smile and

his eyes shining in the sun. He looked around at the scene anew and saw that orchids were growing out of the trunk of the tree where Zarri Bano was sitting. They were just above her head and looked like a crown of gems. His body uplifted with joy, the world had suddenly become a glorious place for Sikander.

With a beating heart, Zarri Bano peeped up, waiting for his response. She met his tender eyes, feeling very vulnerable under their scrutiny. She had unlocked for him – almost – the last door to her inner self.

'If that is the case, then I cannot prevent *your* son, I mean *our* son, from inheriting the land.' His husky whisper was rich with warmth and laughter.

'I am glad, Sikander Sahib,' she answered shyly, glorying in his look of love.

Sikander plucked one of the brilliant orchids from the tree and placed it tenderly in her hair.

'I love you very much, Zarri Bano,' he murmured.

Chapter 68

ZARRI BANO'S EYES focused on a large Raja Brook butterfly as it fluttered and landed on a small bush in front of her. She didn't know what to say nor what to feel. Afraid to speak. Afraid to feel.

Gazing down at her bent head, Sikander waited. Then: 'Zarri Bano, did you ever love *me?*' he asked, breaking the poignant silence enveloping them. 'I have laid bare my soul to you, but I don't know if I ever captured the heart of the woman who bewitched me with one glance at the *mela*. You agreed to marry me then – but I have no idea for what reason. Tell me!

Look at me, Zarri Bano!' he demanded in a voice roughened with pain and longing.

Eventually, she turned away from the huge black and green butterfly and stared up at Sikander, letting him see her wrestling with the painful forces within her.

'You ask if I ever loved you, Sikander?' she said in a quivering voice. 'I have died for you, Sikander, a thousand times. You slew me! The day I found out that you were to marry my sister, I begged and prayed to my Allah Pak to help me! To rid me of both you and the ache I harboured for you. You were the deadly serpent, who had eaten away my innocence. While I sat on the prayer-mat I begged Allah Pak to smother and bury the woman who was, though heavily cloaked in a mantle of devoutness, still passionately in love with you. *Still longing for you!* I had to kill that woman who bled for you. Otherwise I was doomed. My Allah Pak, who is so generous, heard my prayers – those of a sinner. On the day you were married, I promised myself that Zarri Bano would never die or cry for another man ever again. It was at that moment I became a true Holy Woman. Allah Pak doused out my fire for you, as if my whole self was rinsed with the holy *zam zam*, the water from Mecca – and I became totally pure.'

With the gateways of her soul now thrown wide asunder and with nothing left to hide, there was nowhere for her to shelter from him.

'Before Jafar died,' she continued. 'I simply adored you. You were the man of my dreams, the handsome stranger of the *mela* who strode ruthlessly into my world and, with one piercing look, stole away my heart. The man who robbed me of my innocence, drowning me in a torrent of longing for you. Like Sikander, the ancient King of Greece, your namesake, you conquered

and I helplessly became the spoils of your conquest, and would have followed you to the ends of the earth. You turned me into a passionate woman, someone who was frighteningly beyond my comprehension and control.

'Then, as you know, fate conspired against us. Circumstances forced me to turn you away.' Zarri Bano's voice dipped with sadness. 'You thought I was cruel, but you will never know how hard it was to sacrifice you! Nor will you ever know the sheer agony I suffered in turning my back on you and letting you walk out of my life. I bartered you, my love, and womanhood for duty to my parents. I ached and wept for you for months, Sikander.

'In your bitterness, that day in the courtyard, you promised me revenge. Well you had it – when you married Ruby!' She stopped, tears sprang into her eyes. She would never forget that night. 'Why did you marry her, Sikander? Was it to punish me? For if it was, you couldn't have chosen a better weapon. It was a fatal blow. I died for you then, Sikander. I'll never do it again!' Zarri Bano wept in agony.

Sitting down beside her on the tree trunk, Sikander gently turned her face towards him with his fingertips.

'I never meant to punish you,' he whispered. 'You must believe me, Zarri Bano. As Allah is my witness, I could never do that to you. You see, it was the same for me. No one had ever set me on fire like you did, and when you said that you would not marry me, I felt like dying – I felt so betrayed. I had thought you loved me and I couldn't understand how you could suddenly turn away from me. I was very bitter and revenge *was* often on my mind. The marriage between Ruby and me, however, was not done to punish you. Although it was my mother's idea originally, if I am honest with myself,

at the back of my mind I wanted to be near to you. If I couldn't have you, at least I could be a part of your world. But, Zarri Bano, it all backfired on me.

'While you truly became a Holy Woman, I, on the other hand, was left to burn in the flames of hell. I still desired and wanted you, while married to your sister. Can you imagine this sort of hell, Zarri Bano – married to one while still lusting after the other?' Zarri Bano saw his eyes change colour with the intensity of his feeling, that his words tried to express.

'While truly loving my wife, your sister, I never forgot you either, Zarri Bano. You were always there. I tried my very best to be a good husband to Ruby, but at times it was as if she knew that a part of me was forever locked away with you. Many a night, in my bed, I agonised over it.'

Sikander stopped and stood up. His hands in his trouser pockets, he looked around at the beauty of the jungle. Everything seemed strangely silent. It was as though all the wild animals and birds had stopped to listen to them and pay homage to their story.

'My punishment, Zarri Bano,' he continued, turning to her with a pain-creased face, 'was loving two women – two sisters. Seeing you with that bearded Egyptian in Minah made it all crushingly obvious that the past was *not* buried, as you so wanted us to believe. My explosive feelings for you were always simmering beneath the surface. I couldn't endure the sight of that man standing so close to you, no matter that you regarded him as a brother. My jealousy led me to make an utter fool of myself.

'Zarri Bano, I need to know. I am still plagued by the thought: did that man ever mean anything to you? I can still see you both, standing talking so intimately

together. He had no right to look at you like that, Zarri Bano! No man has that right – except me,' he ended passionately.

'You did us all an injustice, Sikander,' Zarri Bano replied sadly. 'He is married now. He married Selima as soon as he returned to Egypt. Perhaps we can visit them some time?'

'Perhaps,' Sikander shrugged, knowing it was the last thing he would want. He would never be able to endure the thought of any man wanting his Zarri Bano in the same way as he did.

'No man meant anything to me then, neither him nor you, Sikander,' Zarri Bano explained.

'And now?' he prompted, after a long pause and with a catch in his voice. He was terrified of her answer.

Zarri Bano's eyes drifted away from his again. 'I am sorry, Sikander. I am so afraid! Afraid of you – of what you arouse in me. Afraid of myself, of the woman buried deep within me. Don't ask me to fall in love with you again, Sikander. I couldn't cope with it. I have suffered so much . . .' she looked up at him '. . . that I truly believe I am now emotionally bankrupt. I don't know if I am capable of taking that big leap you are asking of me.' Her eyes shone like emeralds, magnified once more with tears.

Sikander's heart leapt in response to his wife's pain and plea for understanding. Taking her hand in his own he held it against his cheek. 'My beautiful bride. My Holy Woman.' His earnest voice reached out to her. 'You are not emotionally bankrupt. There is nothing to be afraid of, my beloved. You'll not have to suffer on my behalf, nor die for me ever again. No one should have to. With Allah's grace, I will be by your side, always.

'I am not asking you to take a big leap, Zarri Bano.

All I request is that you let me step back into your heart
once again. Make space for me there, please – even a
tiny one will do, my darling. Don't fight me or your
feelings. Let down your barriers! We have always had
something special between us – you know that. You can
sit on a prayer-mat all your life, but you will know in
your heart it will never be over between us. Never!

'Let the passionate woman come to life again. There
is nothing to be afraid of, nor to be ashamed of,
Zarri Bano. We are not committing a sin or a crime. I
promise you, you will always be a Holy Woman. You
can still carry on leading your life the way you have
chosen to do. You can run your *madrasas*, go to conven-
tions, hold seminars – whatever you want. I am not
going to stop you or be the *Shahzadi Ibadat*'s rival. I
will not strip you of your religious identity, if that is
what you are afraid of. I respect and accept you as you
are. In fact, it is a great honour for me to have a *pakeeza*
woman and a scholar for a wife. Do not see me as a
threat to yourself, but as a friend.

'Zarri Bano, there is a unique relationship between a
husband and a wife, between a man and a woman. All
I ask is that you include me in your life, and allow
yourself to discover the joys of womanhood, and of
motherhood.'

His eyes searched her face, assessing her feelings,
thoughts and expression. 'Zarri Bano, don't let your
mind say no when your heart and body are saying yes.
Please don't turn your back on what we have always had
between us. You cannot! I will not let you! Don't fight
what neither of us can help. Last time you let your
father decide for you. This time, *you* have to decide,
Zarri Bano.'

He stopped, his face growing pale as he came to a

sudden turning-point in his mind and in his life. His heart sank, for he knew distinctly what he had to do. He had no choice – the stakes were high, but he had to gamble. For he would have it no other way. 'You have to decide,' he continued, 'whether we go forward in this marriage or . . .'

'Or?' Zarri Bano prompted, holding her breath.

He stared at her for a long time. Her heart beating, she waited.

'Or . . .' She would never know what it was costing him to say these words. 'Or I am letting you go! You threatened to walk out of this marriage after a year. Well – I free you to walk out of this marriage *now*. You married me under compulsion for Haris's sake. You must only stay in it now of your own free will. If you wish it, you may return to your total life of *Ibadat*, if that means more to you than our marriage or me. For you see, I will have it no other way, Zarri Bano.'

Zarri Bano stared up at his strained face, unable to believe what she had heard. He was letting her go free! Leaning forward, she put her head on her bent knees. Then crossing her arms she held them in front of her, shielding her eyes and face from him.

I am swamping her! Sikander chided himself, gazing down at her bowed head. Resolutely he walked away.

At the sound of Sikander's feet moving through the low undergrowth of the clearing, Zarri Bano's head jerked up. A wave of longing washed over her. She couldn't do it. She wouldn't let him walk out of her life a second time.

'Don't you dare walk away from me, Sikander!' she shouted, springing to her feet.

'I am giving you the physical space you obviously

need and want!' he threw back at her, over his shoulder, but continued to walk.

With a light tread, she reached his side.

She touched his arm, then hesitantly slipped her hand into his. Holding her gaze steady, she let him read her face. There was no smile, but a gentle, poignant openness about her. The bereft look was still in his eyes. She couldn't bear it.

'You have won, Sikander,' she offered simply. She let her eyes say it all. They whispered to him: *I need you! I want you! I love you!*

'No, Zarri Bano, *we* have won. There are no losers,' he teased her gently.

They stood side by side at the edge of the clearing, staring down at the green blanket of treetops as the jungle suddenly fell and spread itself into a lush green valley below them. It was as though the blanket was covered with jewels from the shining colour of the flowers, birds and butterflies. Both were silent with awe, overcome by the true greatness of Allah's world.

'What do you want to do next?' Sikander asked, after a few poignant seconds. 'The taxi is waiting. Shall we go on with our tour as planned, or shall we return to the hotel?'

'Whatever you say,' Zarri Bano uttered softly, looking up at him with her heart in her eyes.

'No, Zarri Bano! *You* decide. The ball is in your court, as it has always been,' he told her, his face solemn.

'Then,' she said simply, her eyes shining with open honesty, at peace with herself at last. 'I prefer the hotel.'

There was no hiding his triumph as his eyes gleamed with joy at her reply. He looked at her tousled hair, where his fingers had roamed and tugged. 'I'll get your

burqa, otherwise that old Malay rubber tapper will be wondering what has been going on up here in the jungle,' he joked.

Zarri Bano laughed. A rich, natural sound that sang in the air around them.

Sikander returned to the tree to collect her *burqa*. 'After all,' he continued naughtily, 'we wouldn't want to shock him, would we?'

In a companionable silence the couple retraced their steps through the jungle and the rubber plantation, down the gentle slope to their waiting taxi.

On the journey home, Zarri Bano stared out again at the majestic scenery, blessed with natural beauty. She moved close to Sikander's side and placed her hand over his. His fingers crushed it tightly, his face unfolding into a smile meant only for her. She smiled unreservedly back at him. There was nothing to hide. Nothing to hold back. He had unlocked all her doors and also held the key – to everything.

'After tomorrow, we are heading down south to Singapore for the honeymoon I promised you five years ago, Zarri Bano,' he whispered in her ear.

The old Malay rubber tapper on the hill, scraping away at the tree to let the rubber gum ooze out for the benefit of some new tourists, watched out of the corner of his eye as he saw the taxi, with the woman in the black veil in it, drive away.